The White Fence

JACQUELINE WHITE

iUniverse, Inc.
Bloomington

The White Fence

Copyright © 2013 Jacqueline White

Certain characters in this work are historical figures, and certain events portrayed did take place. However, this is a work of fiction. All of the other characters, names, and events as well as all places, incidents, organizations, and dialogue in this novel are either the products of the author's imagination or are used fictitiously.If there are only a few historical figures or actual events in the novel, the disclaimer could name them.

iUniverse books may be ordered through booksellers or by contacting:

iUniverse
1663 Liberty Drive
Bloomington, IN 47403
www.iuniverse.com
1-800-Authors (1-800-288-4677)

Because of the dynamic nature of the Internet, any Web addresses or links contained in this book may have changed since publication and may no longer be valid. The views expressed in this work are solely those of the author and do not necessarily reflect the views of the publisher, and the publisher hereby disclaims any responsibility for them.

Any people depicted in stock imagery provided by Thinkstock are models, and such images are being used for illustrative purposes only.

Certain stock imagery © Thinkstock.

ISBN: 978-1-4759-8799-7 (sc)
ISBN: 978-1-4759-8801-7 (hc)
ISBN: 978-1-4759-8800-0 (e)

Library of Congress Control Number: 2013938383

Printed in the United States of America

iUniverse rev. date: 5/2/2013

He moves in darkness as it seems to me~
Not of woods only and the shade of trees.
He will not go behind his father's saying,
And he likes having thought of it so well
He says again, "Good fences make good neighbors."
~~Mending Wall, Robert Frost.

This book is dedicated to first loves, whoever they may be.

Contents

— 1 —
"City Limits"

On I-565, just past mile marker 340, in place of where a prominent cotton field once stood, construction of a tourist welcome center had begun. The center's job, once it is completed, is to share with the world-or at least those who pass through this part of it on their way to somewhere else-the tale of how Bakersfield was pulled from obscurity, and turned into a space exploration Mecca, in just a couple dozen years. This nearly impossible feat had happened with nothing more than a little ingenuity, luck, determination…and several hundred million in government dollars. For now, though, beside the rocket that stood as a nod toward Bakersfield's new nickname, The Space Base, sat a highway-green sign that read: *WELCOME TO BAKERSFIELD, ALABAMA! A FINE PLACE TO CALL HOME.*

It was this very same sign that had stood guard, on this very same stretch of road, when my mom and I had first made this drive years before. Then, for reasons known only to her at the time, she had packed up everything we'd owned, and moved us from our home in Wilmington, Illinois, to head south. It was on this road, too, that I'd gotten my first taste of true southern hospitality. Having never seen a 'Whites Only' sign before, I'd mistakenly used the wrong restroom. For my ignorance, I'd been boxed on the ears by the shop owner's screeching wife, and shouted back to our Ford. My mom, instead of consoling me, had simply remarked, "Things are different down here." That said, she started our car, turning it in the direction of our new house in Bakersfield, a place I knew I'd never call home.

That was the summer of 1960. Five years later, Bakersfield was tentatively taste-testing this thing called integration. The 'Whites Only' signs had since been taken down, and legislation had been passed to remind the South that yes, the Constitution *did* apply to Blacks as well, yet little else had changed along this road, or in the mindsets of the people, since that day that I discovered that I was not quite good enough to squat in the same facilities that a white woman could.

I was the first to see the smoke.

It appeared unexpectedly on our left, a few miles past the "Welcome to Bakersfield" sign. In the fading light, the smoke looked blood-red as it rose, ominously from the northeast, like a thin, snaking, serpent. I tensed at the sight of the smoke, the hairs rising on the back of my arms before my mind had even comprehended that something was altogether wrong. My best friend's brother, Marcus, who had-in between his crooning to the Four Tops' *I can't help myself*-been keeping a careful eye on the time, his speed, and the sun lest we get caught on the highway at night-fell silent as he, too, noticed the smoke.

I watched his eyes track to the spot that had drawn mine. "What do you think that is?" I whispered.

"Nothing good," he assured me.

Patrice, who was still mentally in Atlanta, was too occupied with her recently purchased clothes to have noticed anything. She looked up at his pronouncement, clueless. "What's not good?" she questioned, absently. Marcus pointed at the spot in the distance.

"That's tha Trick, ain't it?" Patrice was the first to figure out. The Trick was what everyone–black and white-called the Bakersfield Black District-the area where the majority of the black schools, a few of the homes, and most of the business were located.

"You don't think that *it's* on fire, do you?"

Neither Patrice nor Marcus answered me, afraid that to speak the words would make them true. Tensely, Marcus took the next exit off of the highway, as if this was just the normal end to a long trip, and we hadn't seen the smoke. "No!" Patrice screeched. "Don' go home, Mark. Take us to Cherry Street!"

"Mama said to come straight home," he protested. "She'd skin me alive if we get caught up in-,"

"We won'! Just drive by!" she urged." Don' you at least wanna know?"

Marcus hesitated, indecisive, but after a block his curiosity must have gotten the better of him. He turned the Gordon's car down College Drive, the street that ran past the newly designated Alabama University-Bakersfield campus, heading away from our neighborhood, and towards the Trick. It seemed almost as soon as he'd made the decision, a bitter scent invaded the car, confirming that something was burning.

The roads heading toward the Trick were oddly empty for it to be the last Saturday night before school started back. That wasn't a good sign. Life was lived out on the streets. Few homes had air conditioning, so it was often just as hot inside as it was out, and you couldn't hear any good gossip locked behind the walls of your house. Missing, too, was the steady foot traffic of those that were coming home from their jobs, and the children who were trying to get in the last minutes of play before they were called inside.

The closer we got to Cherry Street, though, the more crowded the streets became. Marcus seemed to realize that we'd have to get rid of the car if we wanted to get any closer, and it was easy to see just how much he didn't want to do that. After a long moment's thought, he pulled the car to a stop on Hitch Row. "Stay here," he instructed. But Patrice had already swung the door open, and was out of the car, dragging me along with her. "Pat!" She paid her brother no mind, and I gave him a shrug before I got pulled into the crowd. Marcus had no choice but to follow after us as we made our way towards Cherry on foot.

The Trick *was* on fire.

We were overwhelmed from the smell of it as soon as we got out into the open air, and the roaring rush filled our ears even over the excitement of the crowd. The worst of it, though, was the intense heat from the flames. That, coupled with the leftover heat from the nearly 100 degree day, had beads of sweat making an appearance after only a few minutes. Holding hands, and coughing from the smoke, Patrice and I weeded our way through the crowd until we were close enough to see the cause: Winton Tolliver's car had been driven into the front of the Tolliver's barbershop. From the shell that was their brand new black and silver Comet, it looked like the car had been set on fire first.

With little to slow down the flames, the mostly wooden barbershop was steadily in the process of burning to the ground. Beside the shop, Nell's

Flowers showed signs of smoke damage, blackened from the fire coming from Tolliver's. The flowers that Nell had planted at the beginning of the spring and normally brightened her window, sat wilting in their boxes, unable to stand up against the intense heat. The shop wasn't on fire, yet, but it was easy to see that it was only a matter of time before the fire spread.

In front of the buildings, a brigade of workers had formed intent of keeping that very thing from happening. Without cessation, water-filled buckets were carried from the pool (and apparently even from the sinks of the other stores), and passed down the line to the Barbershop, but it looked as if they were fighting a losing battle. They worked tirelessly to smother, drown, and beat back the flames that licked mercilessly at what was left of the Tolliver's building, but it didn't seem as if they were gaining any headway.

The sight of the burning building was so engrossing that it took a moment to realize that beneath the sound of the flames, there was an almost steady stream of shouts. The calls weren't from the ones who were working to keep the fire from spreading, but from the crowd that had formed around them. On one side of the street, our neighbors were busy yelling at the parked fire trucks that stood off to the side, impassive. The trucks' owners were out of their engines, leaning against them, fully dressed in their gear, but doing nothing to fight the flames.

"Y'all devils just gonna watch it burn?" an angry voice demanded. The shout was met by a chorus of agreeing bystanders, but only landed on the deaf ears of the firemen.

On the other side of the street, and looking alien in the Trick, was an equally angry mob of Whites, determined not to be outdone in insults or indignation. They yelled back at our neighbors, swearing and throwing racial slurs like they were stones. From the looks of things, those had recently been thrown, too. Trash littered the usually pristine streets of the Trick, waste cans had been overturned, and several store windows had been shattered.

It was no small wonder that all that was going on at the moment were the shouts, since both sides were so incensed, but I was sure that was mostly due to the barrier that separated them. In between these two angry groups, police stood on scene, dressed in full riot gear, but they, like the firefighters, watched the people, and the flames, and did nothing. The only movement from their lines was the dogs that struggled against their leashes, anxious to sink their jaws into yielding flesh.

And all alone, off to the side and seemingly incongruous to the whole thing, but the apparent cause of it all, was a very roughed-up looking 14-year old kid named Pollie Tolliver. From the way he sat in the police car, his hands must have been handcuffed behind his back. He paid no attention whatsoever to the scene around him-not to the crowds or the fire, not to his older brother and father fighting to save what was left of their business, and not to his mother who was in the arms of a neighbor, crying hysterically, tears running down her face-staring almost meditatively in his lap, refusing to look up as the flames, and the anger, laid claim to the scene around him.

Patrice turned towards the closest neighbor, seeking some answers. "What's goin' on, Bullet?"

"Pol," he nodded at the police cruiser, "took his ole man's car out ridin' earliuh, and sideswiped Miz Tillie's car." Matilda "Tillie" Mitrand, was the 80-year-old, half-blind, half-deaf wife of the former police chief. If Pollie had sounded a horn, or shouted a warning, she was unlikely to have heard it, and just as unlikely to have seen him driving by. "Ran 'er off inta uh ditch. Don' look as if it be good for 'er." It didn't look so good for Pollie. "He run off home, and They," his mouth curled as he jabbed an angry finger toward the Whites lined up across the street. "Come marchin' 'round heah fo' Pollie when she took uh bad turn."

Bullet went on to say that when Winton refused to surrender up his son, one of the Whites had started the car, set it on fire, and pushed it into the shop. The crowd had gotten ahold of Pollie when he came running out to escape the flames. The police had arrived on the scene sometime after Pollie had been beaten. A quick glance at the snarls on the faces of those across the street said that their arrival had probably saved his life.

There was a loud pop! followed by the sound of shattering glass, causing the crowd to respond as one. People screamed, ducked for cover, and covered their heads a little too late to protect themselves from spraying glass. Illogically, there was a sudden swell, and the crowd surged forward. I got pushed forward with it, caught up in the wave. Patrice did too, pulled in an opposite direction. Marcus was nowhere to be found.

I had a moment of panic, worried that I was going to get swept away in the crush of my neighbors who seemed determined to make it to the other side of the street. Before I could get caught up in the thick of it, a steady hand grabbed for my arm roughly, pulling me determinedly from the fray. "Stay here," Marcus ordered. He went back for his sister and, taking both of us by the arm, dragged us all the way back to the car. "I don't want to hear it," Marcus snapped, cutting off the protest Patrice seemed about to make.

Angrily, he wiped the sweat from his face, and somehow he even managed to look threatening. "I'm not 'bout to allow something to happen to you just cause you want to be nosy. We're going home," he said firmly.

He not so gently pushed his sister towards the back seat, giving me a hard stare, too, as if I might protest. I wasn't. Once we were all in the car, he carefully backed it up around the people who were rushing to go where we'd just been. Nothing was said between the three of us as we drove towards Willow Street and home.

Mrs. Gordon rushed from the house as soon as the car pulled to a stop. Although her look was frightened, she still had the presence to be angry once she took in our appearances. "Where in thuh hell y'all been?" she demanded. Our appearance was answer enough. In the surprisingly little amount of time that we'd been in the crowd, we'd managed to get dirty from the heat and smoke. We all had ash on us and, I noticed with disdain, my shirt had gotten torn. "What time it be?"

"We just got back," Marcus tried to explain, the same time Patrice blurted, "Mama, they set fire ta Tolliver's!"

Marcus scowled at his sister.

"Hush, chile," Mrs. Gordon hissed, her gaze darting nervously over her shoulder. "Get in heah, I knows that!" She tugged on my and Patrice's arm, pulling us into the house. She moved her thick frame as if the hounds of hell were nipping at our heels, slamming the door and locking it, as if the bolt would be enough to stave off the danger if a mob *were* actually behind us. "What I cants figure is whys y'all down at thuh Trick."

"We saw the smoke from the highway-,"Marcus began, but cautiously fell silent when his mama raised her hand in the air, but she only jabbed a finger at him.

"I on't care if'n you saw thuh face uh God, you wuz supposed to go'n come back. I's here thinkin' y'all still on they road, when y'all busy puttin' yo bizness where it ain't belong. I didn'say go to 'Lanta, go 'round findin' trouble, then come on home, if'n it please you!"

Marcus looked helplessly at his mother, and said the only thing he *could* say. "Yes, ma'am."

The lines creased her face. Now that the anger was gone, the worry returned. "What be happ'in?" she whispered.

In the same tone she used, we told her what we knew. She returned the favor, filling in the details of what had happened earlier today while we were gone. She reminded me to call my mom, which I did. She wasn't home, but even if she was, I don't think Mrs. Gordon would have opened the door again for anyone less than Jesus, Sean, or Mr. Gordon. While Mrs. Gordon stayed at the window, we each took a seat on their faded floral second-hand couch. Mrs. Gordon refused to turn on the light, so we sat there in the near-dark while she paced nervously in front of the closed curtain, wearing a run in their already strained carpet.

"How's y'all trip?" she remembered to ask after a while. Her voice hadn't rose from a whisper, and she didn't turn from the window, her mind clearly on what was going on outside. "How be Lewis?" she inquired about her oldest child.

Patrice started to answer her mom, but Marcus beat her to it. "Mama, why don't you call him Abdul, like he asked?"

Mrs. Gordon did turn, then. "Just cause he ep'n decide he wanna take up wit dem race baitin' Moslem's don' mean I's gotta go callin' him some fool name he done made 'ep," she snapped. "If they Good Lord, in his infinite wisdom, told yo daddy'n me ta name him Lewis, than that be what his name goinna stay. How it be if Eb come home one day and tole you he don' wanna be called daddy no more, wanna be called uncle? Don' make no kinda sense, do it?"

"He's fine, mama," Patrice said over whatever her brother was going to say to that. "So's Marline. You gotta see Rosa, though, she gettin' ta be so big. She talk so good now. They all give they love."

Something, a sound we missed, or an instinct, made Mrs. Gordon turn back toward the window. Patrice stood up at the gesture, motioning for me to do the same. Marcus got up, too, but he joined his mother at the window instead of following us out of the room. We saw him put an arm around her as we were leaving. "What you think's goinna happen?" Patrice whispered as we climbed up the narrow stairs to her room.

"I don't know," I returned.

Mr. Gordon showed up a few hours later, and even from upstairs we could hear Mrs. Gordon alternating between beating up on her husband for being late coming home, and voicing her pleasure that he'd made it home safe. Marcus poked his head in the doorway of Patrice's room while we were in the middle of listening to their reunion.

"Daddy go down there?" Patrice questioned. He nodded. "And?" she demanded, impatiently.

"Miz Nell's shop went up, and they're fighting the grocery right now." He turned towards me. "Say, Trace, how 'bout I walk you home? Daddy said your mama's there now."

I said good-by, and followed Marcus down the stairs. "Sean?" I wondered on our way out the door, not missing what hadn't been said.

"He down there," he confirmed. I could hear the tension ringing in his voice while we both tried not to imagine what Marcus' hotheaded older brother might get into. I wondered, too, if Marcus was going to make another trip back to the Trick once he walked me to my house. I wondered what I could say to him so that he wouldn't go. I didn't want him down in that crowd.

My mom was there to meet us at the door. She thanked Marcus for walking me before turning her gaze to me. Wordlessly she gave me a long stare before giving a slight nod, which I took to mean that she was glad to see me safe, sound, and unharmed. She looked like she was going to say something, but in the end said nothing at all. She turned off the light in the living room before heading up to her room, the floorboards creaking in her wake. I said a quick good-bye to Marcus, before I followed her upstairs.

In my room, you could still see the bright orange glow of the flames, even from behind the curtain. It provide me little consolation to know that the fires burned several streets from our own. What if the fire burned all the way through the Trick and made its way this way until our neighborhood burned, too? I stared at the glow behind the curtain until my eyes grew heavy. When I couldn't keep them open any longer, I finally turned my back on the sight and fell asleep.

I dreamed of fire.

— 2 —
"The Novel Reader"

My grandma and your grandma, sittin' by the fire, my grandma says to your grandma, 'I'm gonna set your flag on fire'."

"Talkin' bout 'hey now'."

"Hey, now-,"

"Hey, now-,"

"Buh-bruh you bet git inside fo' mama-"

"I can't help muh-self-, I-"

"I like coffee...and I like tea...I like a pretty boy...and he likes me-,"

The slapping of feet hitting the sidewalk, was chorused by kids imitating their favorite singing groups, joined by the sounds of bats against balls, and was chased by the footsteps of those that were running, dashing after each other, and hoping to get caught up in the endless games of summer time. The voices crept up to the front door, the back door, and the windows, the same way the heat crept up and clung to the body, cloying, jockeying for attention in the stiff heat of the afternoon.

There was a war going on in a land that few of us had ever heard of before, a kid our age sat alone and scared in a prison cell, there were still scorch marks and debris in the heart of our community, and more questions than answers hovered about the future, but you wouldn't be able to tell it by looking around, because it was the last day of summer, and no one wanted to see it go to waste.

Tomorrow, Patrice and I would start our first day of high school at Mason High, where an old slave master with a wooden cane named 'Dixie', hung over the entrance of the front hall of a school whose inhabitants were proudly nicknamed 'the Rebels'. When Marcus had started school there, there had been mothers and ministers, doctors and church goers alike, lined up across the street, loaded down with rocks, eggs, trash, picket signs, and hate. He had been one of only a few, handpicked by the community to be one of the first black students to attend school at Mason High. Like James Hood a 150 miles south of here at the University of Alabama, he'd walked silently past signs that likened him to an ape, called him a jigga boo, a bush monkey, and worse. Tomorrow, Patrice and I might have to face the same degradation, but that was tomorrow.

Today, all the hate that was going on with the world, the country, the state, didn't penetrate into our private little sphere of living. The singing, jump ropes, cans, bats, and balls, had been vocal all day, and I'd mostly succeeded in tuning them out until I realized that one of the calls was personalized.

"Tracy! 'Ey, Tracy!" I stuffed my pencil in my notebook, going to the window. "Tracy! Can you hear me?"

I opened my window. "The whole neighborhood can hear you! I'll be right down!"

"Hurry up!" she yelled back at me.

I located my shoes from beneath my desk-really just an old table with a milk crate for storage-before I chased down my coin purse, and my school class schedule. I was halfway out the door before I remembered to grab my bathing suit, turned, and went hunting down that, a towel, and the latest book my Grandpa had sent me, before stepping out into the late afternoon heat.

"What'choo doin' in tha house?" Patrice demanded once I'd made it outside, indicating that such behavior was sacrilege. "You tha on'y one that's inside."

"I was writing," I said in answer.

Her hands went to her hips, her usual reaction to my strangeness. "What you writin'?" she demanded. "School ain't even start yet!"

"Just writing," I mumbled, *my* usual response to her when my motivations were questioned.

She shook her head, as if she couldn't comprehend the action. "Wastin' away tha end uh tha summah," she informed me. "I on't know whats to do wit you sometimes."

We dropped my clothes off at her house before we turned towards the

Trick. After church on Sunday, all the local black congregations had come out to help repair the damages that had been done by the rioters the night before. The Trick wasn't just where we shopped: it was our pride and joy. Just like a rising tide, Bakersfield's growth and prosperity had meant a certain elevation for the Blacks in our community as well. Banned from the white stores, the shopping district had grown to become a place where we could shop, congregate, and exist, without being made to feel as if we were any less. A place where we could buy groceries without having to wait for the shop owner to get done with his white customers first, or where we could look at and try on clothes, without being carefully watched by the clerk. On Sunday, by the time the last person had gone home, the Trick might not have looked the way it was supposed to, but at least it didn't look as defeated as it had the day before.

"You got your schedule?" Patrice demanded bossily. I pulled out the folded piece of paper from my jumper pocket, showing it to her. She gave it a brief glance before she frowned in disgust, tossing the paper back to me. "All yo classes are egghead classes." She grunted. "So much for gettin' a class togethuh."

I glanced over her shoulder at her schedule. "We both have science fourth," I noted. "You could transfer into Biology with me."

We each pulled a nickel from our coin purses, and passed them over to Roger Clemmons, who, in this heat, looked more hopeless than elegant in his pressed white shirt and tie-the standard uniform for all of the workers in the Trick. He unlocked the gate, holding it open for us to pass through. "Why would I do a thing like that?" Patrice wondered of my statement. "There ain't nevuh any solid guys in nerd classes."

"Because *that* should be your sole motivation for taking an accelerated class," I responded, sarcastically. "What do you have fifth?"

"Ain't tha same's you," she said defensively.

"What is it?"

She put her hands on her hips. "Home Dynamics," she declared, daring me to say something about it. "I needed an elective."

I tried to stop the look that was forming. "Okay..., but Home Dynamics?"

"Sean said it's a real easy A, and I could use one uh those."

I loved Sean, but I didn't really think that Patrice should be taking academic advice from the brother that had dropped out before he'd finished high school. "Has anyone ever told you that nothing in life comes easy?" I questioned.

"Yea, says tha egghead, but everyone ain't as smart as you, chicky, and I ain't tha one tryin' to get inta some fancy college like you is. I'll take tha easy grades when I can get 'em."

"I'm not saying that you have to be aiming for Harvard," I said, reminding her of the name of the school, "but don't you think you should have a little challenge in your schedule?" I wondered practically. "What about college?"

She laughed loudly. "Who round here thinkin' on college? What 'em I goinna go ta college for? Become uh teacha?" she rolled her eyes. "Yea right!"

"You don't have to be a teacher," I responded.

"What else be out there but for us to teach?"

She had a point, and I knew it, but I refused to accept that. "Now, maybe," I allowed, "but as long as you take that viewpoint, that's all there's ever going to be. The world's changing, Pat!"

She looked around significantly. "Not from where I see."

I refused to let her pessimism dampen my optimism. "That's because you haven't opened your eyes big enough!" I declared, grandly. "This Civil Rights Act that President Johnson just passed is going to change the world. You'll see. No more begging for anything! If you want something, you have to take it. Ché and Kwame didn't just sit around waiting!"

She gave me a dumbfounded look. "Who they?"

"Argentine/Cuban and Ghanaian leaders. Kwame-," she yawned theatrically, so I cut myself short. "My point is that until it's demanded, it won't be available. We've got to be prepared."

She shrugged off-handedly, her usual reaction whenever I talked about things that were deemed revolutionary. It didn't matter that she had begged her parents-to a resounding 'no'-to let her march with her cousin in Selma this past spring, and she-like just about every other member of her congregation, mine, and every black church in Bakersfield-had donned on blue jeans instead of new dress clothes on Easter Sunday three years ago to protest the segregated lunch counters downtown-whenever *I* started talking about change, she acted blasé. "I'll membuh that," she stated with her customary eye roll.

We zigzagged through the crowd, trying to find a spot to sit. To everyone's surprise, Mr. Clemmons had announced that the regular back to school pool party would still take place, so the pool was pretty crowded. All of the lounges anywhere close to a cover were already taken, but we found two spots near the five foot marker, and unrolled our towels. Patrice kicked off her thongs, and sat them side by side before stretching out, while I neatly stacked my Mary Jane's underneath the inside of the chair and pulled out my book.

"You serious, Trace?" Patrice muttered, before she lay down across the lounge, crossing her legs pristinely before her. She pulled her hat down, obscuring most of her face, donned her pair of oversized B&L sunglasses, and pulled out a magazine that she pretended to read, instead of paying attention to the chaos surrounding us, even though the chaos was the sole reason we were down at the Trick. Patrice craved an audience, and she'd come to be seen.

"Can you believe that, startin' tomorra, we'll be goin' ta school wit practically men?" Patrice questioned lazily. "Men wit cars? Daddy wants ta be like Ward Cleaver and say I can' date 'til I'm 16, but we'll see. It must be nice not havin' your dad 'round ta always boss you. When's your mama say you can date?"

I shrugged from behind my book. Men were the last thing that I was thinking about. "We haven't talked about it, but I don't think she'd give me a restriction. She trusts me. Besides, she knows that I don't want to date anyway."

Patrice gave me a disgusted look. "How can you not want to?" she demanded. When I shrugged, she shook her head. "Girl, if folks goinna see you wit me, you goinna have ta be more groovy. By tha end uh tha year-," Patrice looked me over and reconsidered, "by tha end uh our senior year, girl, you goinna be it. Well, aftuh me," she amended.

"I wait in anticipation," I remarked, dryly.

She clicked her teeth together. "Unh unh, girl, none uh that," she added. "We goinna have ta work on yo English, too."

Patrice went back to surveying, and I went back to reading. Someone sat down on the end of my lounge, and I looked up in irritation, thinking it was one of Patrice's admirers. "Brought you an ice cream sandwich," the intruder remarked sweetly.

I gave a smile. "Hey, Frankie," I said, brightly, accepting the sandwich.

"Hi, Frankie," Patrice mirrored. She stared pointedly at him. "You bring me one?"

Frankie looked down at the ice cream sandwich that he held, and after a long moment of thinking about it, he grudgingly handed it over. He didn't even have to glance at me before I halved the one he gave me, and passed it to him. He smiled as he removed the wax paper.

"Y'all hear Mr. Paul Wakefield's dead," he questioned in between licks of his sandwich. This was news. Mr. Wakefield was a member of the Forest Lake Adventist church, and just as old as Mrs. Tillie. "Got smoke in his lungs," he said in a matter-of-fact tone. "Miss Tillie, it look like she'll recover, but ain't no one coming for justice for Mr. Wakefield. Hell, if the fire ain't turn toward their side, wouldn't be surprised if they just let the place go on and burn."

We stayed at the Trick until shortly before the streetlights started to come on, and most of the businesses were closing their doors for the day. As we headed for home, Patrice griped about missing out on barbecue, and not getting to see the playing of *Psycho*. She dragged her feet, but not enough to prevent us from making it back home before dark.

Our neighborhood, Burbank, was less than a mile from the Trick, and was considered to be one of the 'good' black neighborhoods. It'd originally been built in the late 30s to house the scientists that'd first come to work on the missile project, but had since moved on to better neighborhoods. Our house may have been small, and cramped, but the neighborhood was safe, kept clean, and each house had its own little yard, and enough space to insure a little privacy. Burbank wasn't considered as classy as the homes of the families that lived and owned business in the Trick, but it was considered a huge step up from the shotgun houses that you'd find in the Hole, and far better than the converted slave quarters that you'd find on the bigger farms out in Hazel Green and Meridianville. I may have had to walk through the kitchen to get to the bathroom, but at least we had indoor plumbing.

When we got to Patrice's, we made sandwiches and watched an episode of *Ben Casey*, before we trudged upstairs to her room. "What you wearin' ta school tomorra?" Patrice questioned as her door swung closed. She went straight to her closet. "You should see how I look in that green outfit we picked out in 'Lanta. I kill!"

I kind of looked at the outfit she held now, enviously. Patrice had gotten a brand new wardrobe for the first week of school, while mostly everything I had was left over from last year. Even living in the good neighborhood, money was still tight for us. My mom had been able to afford one outfit, but I'd gotten no new shoes.

"Is your dad going to let you walk out of the house wearing pants?" I questioned.

"Probably not," Patrice answered, letting the outfit fall to her side, disappointed. "Man, he's so square! I've gotta find somethin' really groovy for tomorra, though; I want every eye in tha place on me. It's a shame we ain't goin' to Groovy cause that's where ever'thin's really happenin'. You should borrow somethin' uh mine cause I seen what you got picked out, and that just ain't goinna jive. It's time you stepped up yo game. We in high school now; practically adults, mature…sophisticated."

My eyebrows rose. "Sophisticated?" I questioned.

"Hey, *I* am," Patrice responded, her nose going up in the air. "Tha New Cosmopolitan says so." She picked up her magazine and plopped down on the bed beside me, showing the spot where she marked. "See look!" I spared the magazine a quick glance, picking up my own book again. "What's that anyway?" she demanded.

"The Other America," I informed her over the pages.

She scrunched up her face. "What it about?" she wanted to know.

I put my finger in the book to mark the page, accepting that I wasn't going to get to read it right at the moment. "The other side of the American dream," I explained.

"Sound borin'," she decided.

"It's not," I assured her. "It's about what's going on in this country, with women, and minorities-,"

"Borin'," she dismissed, taking the book from my hand. "I know how it

— 16 —

be, why I wanna read about it? 'Sides, you on't bring books ta sleepovers," she instructed. She casually tossed my book aside. "Take this quiz wit me…then you can go back ta Tha Otha Side uh tha American Dream…," she rolled her eyes. "Whatevuh that means."

"Come on, 'Triece!" I protested.

She had no ears for that. "Hush!" she commanded, throwing a finger up. She flipped to the proper page. "Question 1…your boss wants you ta stay aftuh work ta finish a project…"

She went through the entire questionnaire, and despite me rolling my eyes at just about every question, we got through it. A smile spread across her face as she read over the results.

I feigned interest. "Let me see," I directed, taking the magazine from her after she'd stopped reading. I looked at the outside cover, surprised that some of the articles contained within actually seemed intelligible. I found it terribly ironic, though, that an article about Betty Friedan was featured in the same magazine that this quiz was, especially since I was sure that most of the predictions had something to do with intimate affairs with good looking guys, maybe a little wealth thrown in for variety. "That's ridiculous," I decided.

"Argue wit it if you must, but it won' change nothin'. This's fact," she said with certainty. "It says that you, or your love, is goinna die young."

"And there's another fallacy,"

"What's-,"

"A flaw in your theory; your thought process," I explained.

"Whyn't you just say that?"

"I did," I remarked, confused. "But that's your other flaw because when will there ever be a man in the picture?"

She gave me an once-over. "True," she said, smirking. I hit her with my pillow. She gave me an affronted look. "You're goinna regret that!"

She jumped up on the bed, grabbing her pillow as she did. She swung it at me. I ducked, as I scrambled up to join her, but got hit solidly on the side of my head before I had the chance to plant my feet. Our little impromptu pillow fight was interrupted a few minutes later by Mr. Gordon appearing like smoke in the doorway. Our smiles froze on our faces.

Mr. Gordon was a tall and heavy-set man, with thick lidded eyes, and a weathered look that made him seem permanently tired. He had a few teeth missing due to fights in his youth, and he'd lost a finger working one of the machines at the mill. Hard work and years of smoking, were the cause of the rings that gathered around his eyes and the wrinkles that pooled at his neck and cheeks, making him look older than he was. The stern look he fixed us with was enough to stop us instantly. Patrice sat down suddenly.

"C'mere," Mr. Gordon grumbled in a low, gravelly voice. Patrice stalked over to him. "Why's y'all still up?" he demanded. "It's near ta midnight, and y'all here wastin' my monie. Y'all got school in thuh mornin'."

"Sorry, daddy."

"Sorry, Mr. Gordon."

"Now, y'all bet get ta bed."

"We was," Patrice explained. "We was just finishin' gettin' ready fo' school."

"Uh huh. Lemme see yo hands." She brandished them, palms up. "And yo teef." She stuck out her tongue. He grabbed her nose playfully. "Bedtime is...?" he questioned, moving her nose so that she shook her head.

"10:00," she responded nasally.

"Right. So I don' wants ta catch y'all ep at midnight no mo." He swatted her bottom playfully. "Get ta bed! You got an early day tomorra."

We got into bed, and Patrice's dad tucked her in. "Thuh next time I want ta heah yo voice is tomorra mornin'." He kissed her on the forehead. "So nighty night. I love y'all."

"Night, daddy," Patrice responded.

"Night, Mr. Gordon," I chorused.

Mr. Gordon came over and kissed me on the forehead, too.

"Goodnight ladies. If I 'on't gets uh chance ta see you 'fore I go, have uh good day."

He turned off the light and closed the door. Patrice waited until his footsteps had retreated down the hall. "He's so square," she remarked, rolling over. I made no comment. "Have sweet dreams uh your prince tonight," she added before she fell asleep.

— 3 —
"Room # 2"

Patrice was up way too early the next morning. Since she took longer to get dressed, I gave her the first shower, but even with that head start, I was dressed before she was. While she stood in front of her closet, trying to figure out what to wear, I brushed the stray strands of my hair back into the French braid my mom had done the day before, and was dressed in a matter of minutes. "What's wrong with the outfit you picked out last night?" I questioned.

"Didn' fit right," she said dismissively. "I'll on'y be a minute." Patrice's minutes could turn into hours. I headed downstairs to wait for her.

In the kitchen, Marcus was up, too, and busy cooking. As he treaded back and forth over the orange linoleum of their kitchen floor, tossing pots around as if he did this often, I stood there a moment to watch. To me, Marcus was the best looking of the three Gordon boys. With skin the color of chestnuts, he was the darkest of the three, and the tallest after Abdul. His broad nose, thick lips, and really rich, cocoa brown eyes, rested almost symmetrically in the middle of his thin, angular face. Though he was slim in the waist, because his shoulders were so broad it made him seem like he was larger than he really was. At the moment, he was still in his pajamas and robe, his hair kind of bunched up on one side in that 'just up woke up' look. Marcus' hair was in the process of recovering from his attempt at an Otis Williams hair style... which he thankfully given up a few weeks ago.

He nodded at the space across the counter. "Mornin'," he declared.

"Morning." I sat down in front of him. "When did you start cooking?"

"Gotta be up for work anyway, might as well let mama sleep in." He looked at me over the counter, a smile teasing his lips. "You excited?" he wondered.

"About?"

"Your first day of high school! Big day today!"

Mostly I was nervous. All night long I'd kept seeing those indistinct faces from the crowd, their eyes filled with hate as they yelled at us, eager to see part of our lives destroyed. Them, or some of their kids, friends, neighbors, would possibly be in the same classes that I was. *Not everyone is like that*, I kept reminding myself, but I couldn't imagine going through what Marcus had gone through. I fidgeted a little just thinking about it. The only thing that had stopped me from begging my mom to let me go to Groverton High instead of Mason was the knowledge that I'd get a better education at Mason. And since I wanted to go to Harvard after I graduated, I needed the best education I could get. (Forest Lake Academy, the Adventist private school that was attached to Forest Lake College, would have been the best place to go, but we couldn't afford the tuition).

"I'd be more excited if I were you," I decided.

"Oh, and why is that?" he wondered.

"You start college in a few weeks!" I reminded him. For me, the only thing that was significant about the start of high school was that it meant that I only had four more years to go before I would be saying goodbye to Bakersfield forever.

"Yea, but I still have to take the trash out when the parents want me to, I still have a curfew, and I still have to do chores. It's hard to get excited 'bout that."

"But in a few years you'll have a degree! Think about what you'll be able to do once you graduate!"

"For now, how bout I just think about what I can do while I'm doing it? Listen, young'n, if you spend your life looking for what happens afterwards, you're going to miss out on the transition."

"Maybe," I allowed, "but if you have no foresight, you spend a lot of time looking back through hindsight."

Marcus laughed, mussing my hair. Unlike Patrice, I didn't care. "You're an old soul, Tracy. Just try'n have a little fun. Tell me that you at least have *small* butterflies."

Reluctantly I grinned. "All right, I'm a little excited," I admitted.

The front door opened, and the middle of the Gordon boys, Sean, strutted in. I think the only way he knew how to walk was a strut. Sean was a pretty boy, who couldn't seem to keep himself out of trouble. He was the shortest of the Gordon boys, the thickest, and according to most, the most attractive. He, like Patrice, was a light brown color, with reddish undertones, had brown eyes, the same broad shoulders that Marcus had, and a derriere that filled out a pair of Wranglers nicely. He drove around in a caramel '55 'Vette that his uncle helped him buy and fix up, and no matter the time of year, he liked to wear his leather bomber jacket. Like Mr. Gordon, he'd dropped out of school his junior year to go work at the Mill, and that's where he still was. The Mill was considered one of the better laborer jobs around, and I'm willing to bet that the only part of it that Sean didn't like was the rules, and the navy blue coveralls that the Mill workers wore.

He lit a cigarette as he sat down at the counter. A round knot featured prominently on his forehead, a souvenir from the weekend.

"'Choo got fryin', baybra?" Sean demanded in a very relaxed drawl. Like his daddy, Sean couldn't be rushed about anything.

"Nothing for you," Marcus remarked, slinging a plate of pancakes in front of me, diner style.

Sean looked at my food hungrily. He licked his full lips. "Come on, Mark, I'm starvin'!"

"Well, then, you should've eaten 'fore you left your own pad." He fixed himself a plate at the words, leaning against the counter to eat.

"Boy…" Sean threatened.

Marcus slid the plate over to his brother. "Here, baby, take it."

Sean pointed his fork at his brother's back as Marcus started fixing another plate. "You bet watch yo'self, fo' I have ta hand out an ass whuppin'."

"Like you still could, old man," Marcus jeered.

The two of them glared at each other, before laughing it off. "Where daddy?" Sean wondered between bites of food.

"Close yo mouth when you eating!" Marcus hissed. "Can't you see they's a lady present?" Seamlessly, Marcus' voice had adopted a more casual talk around his brother, and that shift was something I'd never learned how to perfect. Most people I knew had two ways of talking: the way they talked around the neighborhood, and their 'white folk tawk', as Mrs. Gordon called it. Because I spent more time in my books than with my peers, and my parents and Grandpa always corrected every mispronunciation I made, I never really learned how to code switch, a fact that caused my neighbors to think I was always putting on airs.

Sean locked his eyes on me. "Shoot, aine like she aine seen food 'fore. What's got choo ovuh so early, T-girl?"

"I spent the night. School starts today."

"Fo' real?" he scratched his head. "Man, I fo'got. What grade y'all be in now?"

"9th."

"Fuckin' A. Y'all startin' yo first day of hy'school! Y'all gettin' all big on me, aine choo? You goinna be up at Groovy?"

"Mason," I corrected.

"Mason?" His face clouded over. "Wit 'em White folks?" He sat his fork down. "Y'all bet watch yo'selves 'cause I know somethin'. Listen: any uh 'em pecker's even looks at you wrong, you come tell me. Where Beanie at? I wanna talk at her."

"She's still upstairs, looking for something to wear."

His humor returned as he chuckled. "Guess we aine seein' her for a while, den." He looked down at his watch. "Man, if daddy done git on down heah, we goin' be late fo work, and Dixon's ole cr-," he looked over at me and reconsidered saying the word, "would loves him any excuse to fire 'im some Negroes. Speakin' of, though, what I gots to say to Beanie, go fo you, too, T-girl. Mind yo business, don' look at 'em, don' talk to 'em, neithuh. I done wanna have ta come up there'n bust some heads."

"You don't have to worry about that," I assured him.

His hand came down on the counter. "Bet," he responded.

Patrice finally came down the stairs, looking around at all of us sitting at the counter. Although there was a small, four-seated table that took up the space between the lone wall and the back door, the only time I'd actually seen anyone eat at it was when the counter was full, or during Thanksgiving when the kids ate there. All the other times they ate on barstools, or by leaning against the open counter that separated the kitchen from the living room. The Gordon kitchen wasn't very large, but it was easily the centerpiece of their family, and it never seemed quite complete unless it was filled.

Since our houses were made around the same time, the features of theirs weren't that different from ours. At one point we'd probably had the same wall paper on the walls, but theirs had since yellowed and withered away, while ours was a dull white with tiny pink flowers. And though our floors were two different colors, we both had the same geometric pattern on the floor, the same amount of counter space, even the same green Frigidaire that didn't seem to go with either house. But since my mom and I were the only ones who occupied our kitchen, and rarely at the same time, our kitchen always seemed bigger.

"Where's my plate?" Patrice questioned. As predicted, she was dressed to kill.

Sean took one look at what she was wearing and decided that he didn't like it. "Who you lookin' all womanish for?" he demanded. "Aine choo lookin' a lil too good to be goin' ta school?"

She paraded in front of him, giving a twirl. "Ain't yo business move outta mine when you moved outta this house?" she said smartly.

Mr. Gordon appeared suddenly. He popped Patrice on the back of the head. "You watch yo mouf," Mr. Gordon warned. "That's yo olda brotha."

Patrice looked more annoyed than repentant. "Yessir," she mumbled.

Mr. Gordon was always less playful in the mornings. "You bet keep that smart mouf to yo'self, and mind yo teacha's, heah? Y'all goinna school wit dem White folks. Don' get caught lookin like you ain't been raised right."

"Yessir," she repeated.

Mr. Gordon cut his eyes to look at me. "You heah me?" he wondered.

"Yes, sir," I responded, meekly, while his three children snickered at me behind his back.

We left shortly after Sean and Mr. Gordon. Even though it was still early to be leaving for school, there were plenty of people already out: moms heading off to jobs at the department stores downtown, or to the homes of the wealthy where they worked as domestics, dads and older brothers off to the mill, the yard, or in search of work for the day. Even some of the younger kids were up and dressed, playing pick-up games in the street, but carefully, lest they mess up their clothes before school started: even the poorest families dressed in their best for the first day of school.

At the end of the street, Frankie's lanky figure stood waiting for us. He looked sharp in the Forest Lake Adventist Academy's yellow and gray uniform. "Hey, Frankie!"

He didn't need any other invitation. "I can't believe school's starting back. It feels like we just got back from Barbados when all this happened. I didn't even get a chance to get some new clothes." Since Forest Lake Academy dressed in uniforms, I wondered why he'd need them. "Summer passed by too quickly, didn't it?" Frankie had a kind of orator's voice, and he talked in a way that seemed stiff, and very deliberate, even when he fell into a more relaxed speech. "It's a shame y'all going to Mason stead of the Academy," he went on. "Ain't it goinna be weird going to school with 'em White folks?"

Until this weekend, I hadn't really been worried about it. In Wilmington, my family had been one of only a few black families in town, so I was used to going to school with mostly white children. On my first day of school here, I remember walking through the doors of the elementary school and being taken away by how many black people there were. Everywhere I looked there were students of every shade of black, brown, tan and red, walking up and down the corridors, talking to each other, laughing and acting as if this were a normal scene, in a normal school, and not some divine creation handed down by God. I got the biggest surprise of all, though, when I walked into my fourth grade classroom and was greeted by the smiling face of Mrs. Greene, a black woman. Until then, I'd never had a black teacher before.

"It's not like they're two headed monsters, Frankie, they're like us. It's probably as weird for them as it is for us. We just have to figure out how to get along."

"Yea, they just like us, but I ain't hear one of *them* telling those firemen to turn on them hoses to help. You think that if'n you wanna, but I bet you won't be thinking that same thing after school. That's why Forest Lake is better: ain't no mixing going on."

We went our separate ways when we hit River Lane. Frankie turned north to continue on towards Forest Lake's campus, and we turned south. As we continued through the neighborhoods and towards Mason, we picked up a couple of other students on the way. Nick, an old boyfriend of Patrice's who was a sophomore this year, started chatting up Patrice, and I idly listened to the conversations that were surrounding me, my thoughts on other things.

We paused in unison when we crested the hill, and Mason came into sight. It was hard to ignore the scrubbed over "Go Back to Afreeca, Nig-." The rest of the letters painted over when I guess the janitor realized the words wouldn't scrub out. Outside of the school's reach, on the side of a house that overlooked Mason's campus, someone else had painted: "If God intended us to mix, he wouldn't made us separate."

There was otherwise nothing else, though, and I thought: not so bad. I'd come across worse than bad spelling and bad grammar before. This was nothing in comparison. A head shake was the only acknowledgment that anyone in our group had read the words that'd been written, and we kept walking toward the school. We didn't slow down again until we reached the outer parking lot where there was a group of students, all white, lounging against the cars. They looked up as we walked by. "Parking lot's theirs," Nick informed us.

We continued on into the building. For it to be early, the school was surprisingly crowded, and noise and confusion seemed to be the dominant feature of the hallway. There were parents and students everywhere, the parents demanding that their kids schedules be changed, or wanting to know where classes were, or at what time, and of course the "I know the school board said otherwise…but isn't there something that could be done? Anything at all?"

But by now their complaints had mostly turned to grumbles, and there were no more picket signs. Instead, in replacement of them, or in acceptance of how it was, everywhere you looked there were kids catching up with each other, or stopping dead in the middle of the hallway to talk when they saw a friend they hadn't seen since before the start of summer. The handful of police officers that stalked the hall were merely a footnote, a minor reference to the slight tension in the air, an explanation for the reason that Whites and Blacks were walking through and around each other, seemingly oblivious, though still clearly aware.

Three years ago, Mason became the second school in Bakersfield to integrate when a handful of black students had been granted admission. While the hoses were being turned on schoolchildren, and marches were taken place 90 miles south of us in Birmingham, the doors had been unceremoniously opened, first at McDonnell Middle School, and then at Mason High. It'd happened in advance of the legislation that would have made it mandatory to do so for a very simplistic reason: the schools couldn't afford to remain segregated any longer.

Bakersfield was somewhat of an enigma for Alabama, and the South. Despite what happened this weekend, Bakersfield could boast of having a pretty clean track record as far as racial violence went. It wasn't Selma, or Birmingham, or Montgomery; there weren't sit-ins, protests, and violent upheavals. That was due in large part to the existence of the Blackrock Arsenal. Before the Arsenal, Bakersfield had been little more than an insignificant dot on the map. During the late 30s and 40s, the government brought over a group of German scientists, and with the 50s came the Arsenal, which dramatically changed the landscape. Early on, Arsenal officials let it be known that if there was any racial upset towards the black soldiers, they would move the Arsenal, (and consequently the millions of dollars, jobs, and benefits) elsewhere.

So, hesitantly, Mason became integrated, but it hadn't happened without its problems. Marcus had had rocks, sticks, even manure thrown at him. He'd had his clothes torn, his books ripped, went to classes amid his teachers' and his classmates' scorn. But he had suffered through it, and by now things were settling down. There was a slight charge to the air, but maybe that was just excitement about the new year. One could hope, anyway.

When the bell rang, the common area erupted in a concussion of noise as everyone reluctantly got up to go to their classes. On our way out to the stairs, I was bumped roughly from behind. Patrice was the only thing that kept me on my feet. I bent to pick up the notebook that'd been knocked from my hand, while Patrice set her sights on the guy who'd run into me.

"'Scuse you," she called out, loudly. The guy turned. He was no taller than either of us, had brown hair badly in need of a haircut, brown eyes that looked near black, and skin that was so tanned it seemed leathery. His unfriendly face was splattered in brown freckles that looked like little dots of cinnamon on his skin. Like me, his clothes weren't new, but with his clothes it was more noticeable. He didn't look as well put together. He'd worn jeans, that were almost threadbare, and even though his red button-down shirt was tucked in, it was done sloppily, one side hanging out. It was too big, too, buttoned hastily, and obviously hadn't been ironed. "S'okay ta just run into someone where you come from?" she demanded of him. "You ain't got no home trainin'?"

The guy gave the both of us a look-over, and grinned menacingly. "My fault," he said, insincerely, his voice as oily as his presence. "Didn't see ya in this heah dim light." He turned back toward his friends, and they laughed as they walked away.

"Idiots," Patrice mumbled, shaking her head. "You okay?"

"Fine," I remarked.

She handed me a stray pen. "I'll see you aftuh class, then. Good luck!" she added excitedly, crossing her fingers.

It was hard not to share in her excitement, even if it was for different reasons. I've always loved the first day of school, and it seemed that the only thing that could temper my first day of school excitement…was, well, the first day of school. I think they do it on purpose. Teachers, principals, the school board. It's like they have to make the first day as boring as possible to kill off any leftover energy that you managed to carry over from the summer. I thought since we were in high school it'd be different, but it turns out that the first day of school is always the same, no matter what grade, state, race of the students, or its place in history.

My second to last class of the day, French I with Roberta Diece, was located on the first floor, in room 2. Mrs. Diece was a short, bouncy, older woman, who was a welcome change from the string of dry teachers that I'd faced so far that day. Instead of sitting behind her desk, waiting for her students to come in, she stood at the door to meet them as they walked into the room. "Bonjour!" she greeted, exuberantly. "Have a seat, any seat!"

I chose one in the middle of the room, right in front of the center of the chalkboard. I was just getting settled when I felt a tap on my shoulder. I glanced up, startled by the casual contact.

"Hey," the tapper said. He gave me an engaging smile. "I don' mean to be uh pain," which meant that he was about to be one, "but…me and my buddies were kinda hopin' to get seats togethuh. I's wonderin' if maybe my friend could have yours?" I studied the guy speaking, going past him to the two other guys he was with. I recognized one as the guy who'd run into me earlier. The tapper was cleaner, more put together than the other one, and had blue eyes and near black hair, to his friend's all browns. He wasn't much taller, either, but the third member of their trio was tall to the point of being intimidating. None of them seemed like the kind to want to sit so close to the front of the room, but a quick look around revealed that no one had chosen to sit in the desks on either side of me. These were the only three empty ones together.

He waited patiently, despite his friend's obvious irritation. I didn't really care about the seat one way or the other-except that it had the best view of the board-but something about his attitude made me hesitate.

"No, take it," I said after a moment.

"Thanks," he responded. "You're uh sweetheart."

I abandoned the desk. Before I took my seat in one of the remaining empty ones, the guy gave me a backward glance, smiled, and waved. The three of them laughed. I set my shoulders, pulled out a composition book, and waited for class to start.

At the bell, Mrs. Diece closed the door, clapping her hands for attention. "All right, settle in ladies and gentlemen! I know y'all have the first day jitters, but if I could have a moment of your time?" Instantly the class quieted down. She smiled at the effect. "Thank you!" Her voice was infectiously sweet, and went perfectly with her elementary school demeanor. "Bonjour et bienvenue au Français I," she greeted in a voice that seemed at odds with her own southern accent. "Je suis votre le professeur Madame Diece! Hello and welcome to the first installment of French!" Her enthusiasm this late in the day was nothing short of commendable. "I'm Mrs. Diece," she said as she wrote her name on the board, "pronounced 'Dey Ce,' and I will be your teacher for this course! But before we start on this wonderful academic journey, I would like each of you to stand up beside your desk!"

She waited until she was looking into the faces of the nineteen students standing obediently by their desks. "When you first walked into the room, I gave each of you a card with a number spelled out on it in French." She demonstrated by holding up a similar-looking card. "I want all of you to sit according to the number on your card. If you need help figuring out your number, you may look at the very first page of your French books, which are sitting on my desk, but in order to get the book, you have to be able to tell me at least one French word. Commencez!"

We all sort of looked around at each other, until one brave soul moved in the general direction of another seat, staring cryptically at the card in his hand. "Mine says 'Dix'," he declared helpfully, and I looked down at the number on my own card, which I had no trouble translating. My Grandpa's family was from Martinique, so I knew a handful of French words and phrases. I moved to the seat in the center, and a row back, from where I'd originally sat down.

It took a little while, but eventually everyone found their correct seat. Mrs. Diece surveyed us once we were all sitting back down. "Now that we got the blood pumping, and the seat situation worked out, I just want to go over some quick rules: first off, this is a French class, so the majority of what I say to you will be in French. When y'all get to French II, the entire class will be conducted en Français, so it's imperative that you're able to first understand, and then speak, French. Secondly, I've taught French for nearly fifteen years now, and I can assure you, you're not as funny as you might think you are. The rest of my rules are standard: respect me and each other; be civil towards each other. I will not tolerate disrespect towards me, or any of the other students in this class. If you've got a problem, you can work it out with Mr. Lamont in detention.

"With that being said," she wiggled her fingers at us. "Now that you know a little about me, I would like to find out a little about you." She sat a stack of worksheets on the first desk in the row, and the student, a slender girl with brown hair and a red-checkered smock dress, got up to start passing them out. "So I'm going to pass around a questionnaire for you to fill out to turn in to me by the end of the class. Meanwhile we're going to go around the room, and when I point to you, you will stand up, tell me your name, grade, and something interesting about yourself."

I listened with one ear open to the introductions. When she got to the tapper, he made a big show out of standing up, waiting until everyone was looking at him before he spoke.

"J'ai m'appelle Elvis, parce que je suis Le Roi."

Mrs. Diece glanced at the roster, before looking back at him. "Parlez-vous Français, Monsieur Leroi?" she questioned.

He gave her a half smile. "I just know that much."

"Derek," Mrs. Diece explained to the rest of the class, "loosely translated means 'the king', and in French 'le roi' means 'the king'. Derek said that his name is Elvis, because he is the king, which, coincidentally, is his last name as well. So, Monsieur Leroi, what grade are you in?"

"I'mma junior," he said with all the cockiness of an upperclassman.

"Vous êtes la première? Bon. And what is it that is interesting about you?" she posed.

He glanced toward his friends full of bravado. "Everythin'," he responded, laughing at his own wit. His two friends, and the brown-headed girl, laughed along with him. He gave a wink in her direction when she looked at him.

"Bon, Derek," Mrs. Diece exclaimed. "But next time, be a little more specific," she directed.

"Bone," Derek said. My eyes narrowed before I got up to do my own introduction. You always had to have at least one clown.

— 4 —
"The Great Glass Roof"

The guidance counselors' office was like a miniature version of the main office upstairs. There was a small reception desk in the center of the room, with four doors branching off, one for each of the counselors. Although it was spacious, it, like a lot of the other rooms in the building, had a claustrophobic feel that made the space seemed cramped. It was rumored that Mason was originally built during the Second War to be a bomb shelter, and it felt like it. There were no windows anywhere around the office, no windows anywhere on the first floor, actually, since the main level of the building was built underground. You could feel that fact as you walked down the hallways. If you had all of your classes on the first floor, the whole world could implode outside the windows and you wouldn't know about it until the final bell rang at 3:00.

I signed in and took a seat. The office looked like you'd expect a high school guidance office to look: it was filled with information about different types of equivalency tests, colleges, financial aid packages, scholarships, grants, and competitions. Smiling blondes, confident red heads, and energetic brunettes, gazed at me, inviting me to join one of the many clubs and organizations that you could find on campus. My name was called just as I was contemplating picking up a pamphlet.

My counselor, Mrs. Rupert, was a short, heavy, blonde-haired woman with constantly appraising brown eyes. I gave her a nervous smile, and she gave me an encouraging one in return. "You may come in," she said warmly. I followed her into her office, and sat in the seat opposite her. Once I was seated, her smile changed from encouraging, to a mother-with-cookies smile. Mrs. Rupert was younger than my own mother, not fresh from college, but not quite old enough to have children high school age. Her demeanor suggested that she wanted me to regard her as a friend. "Thank you for stopping by," she remarked. I smiled, demurely; it wasn't like I'd been given a choice.

"I called you in so that we could sit down and have a chat about your course selection," she began. In front of her she had an office folder already filled with several papers, despite the earliness of the semester. I leaned a little towards her, trying to surreptitiously give a glance at the file's contents. "Yes, let's see," she said aloud, fingering the papers. "It says here that you're in the college tract." It wasn't posed as a question. I waited for her to continue, but she seemed to be expecting something.

"Yes, ma'am," I responded.

"*And* you're taking all advanced courses your first year, too," she went on.

I nodded patient, waiting. "Yes, ma'am."

Mrs. Rupert put a hand on my file, making eye contact. "Tracy, I called you in because I like to touch base with all my students. As you know, I'll be your counselor while you're here, and during that time it's my job to see to it that *every* student does the best to *their* abilities. We-," she gestured in a way that indicated all of the counselors, the teachers, the principal, and maybe the outside world in its entirety, "want all-," the way she said 'all' was diminishing somehow, "our students to be successful. To graduate and become productive...*hard working*...members of society. Do you understand?"

"Yes, ma'am," I responded, nodding. I understood.

"I know that the first time a student gets the opportunity, *chance*, to pick out their own schedule, it can be a little daunting...er...*hard*. Can you tell me what your goals are? What do you expect from your time at Mason?"

I considered her words briefly. "To get a good educational foundation so that I'll be well prepared for college after I graduate," I responded. I'd already had a strong indication that I knew where this conversation was headed, but I still wanted to assert myself as someone with intelligence. Maybe I could convince her of it.

She nodded encouragingly, though I knew she didn't like my answer. "Great! We encourage...*get*... our students to plot their own schedules because we want them to get into the mindset of figuring out what's the best route...

the best *course...* for them. Your freshman year marks a matriculation...*an entry*...into young adulthood, a time when you should learn to begin to make decisions, *choices*...about life.

"This is why we allow our students to choose their own classes. We only try to step in when we believe that the student is unable to truly gauge... *to figure out*...what they can handle. I invited you in today because I think maybe you were unaware of the nature of the classes you chose to enroll in. It is our belief-," someone other than she had seen my school file?-"that perhaps you have taken on too heavy of a work load." She fingered through my file, looking for the evidence to back her up. "You've got a lot of difficult classes on your schedule...there's business law: Mrs. Stanley's class is a very difficult one; juniors, and seniors, even, have expressed how difficult they find her class. Home Dynamics would be far easier, and you'd probably enjoy that more...

"And let's see, you're enrolled in Advanced Biology...*and* Geometry-,"

"Yes, ma'am," I agreed.

She looked over the file at me. "Tell me...why'd you sign up for Advanced Biology when there are other science courses that aren't as strenuous...as *hard*?"

"I'm on the college tract," I reminded her. "You have to sign up for a math and science every year."

"That is correct, however the Mechanical College doesn't require you to take any advanced courses," she informed me.

"No, ma'am," I agreed, respectfully, "but in the event that I consider colleges outside of the area, they might."

There was a slight pinch around her eyes at those words. "And where else *might* you be considering?" she inquired. Her tone was still friendly, still encouraging, and I realized that she truly felt like she was helping me. That made it 10 times worse.

"I haven't fully decided, yet," I remarked, even though the only school that I ever really wanted to go to was Harvard. Somehow I knew, though, that my telling her that I wanted to go to one of the nation's most prestigious universities wouldn't go over too well. "I just aim to be prepared," I said evasively. There was a slight chance that I *had* gone a little overboard with my schedule, but I knew I'd never make it to Harvard if I came from a school that wasn't competitive, and took classes that weren't challenging while I was there.

Her gaze fell back to my folder. "I don't believe the courses that you've chosen will do that. Your freshman year of school is quintessential...is *very important*...in mapping out the rest of your high school experience. Too heavy of a work load-,"

She paused at this, and I just gazed up at her. I'd finally realized why she kept pausing. She was waiting for me to be the one to decide that maybe I *had* taken on too much. She didn't want to be the one to crush my dreams, to tell me that they weren't a possibility. That way she didn't have to feel bad about handing me the knowledge of where I stood in life. She wanted *me* to reassure *her* that I knew where things stood: namely that I shouldn't forget that I was a black girl, in over my head. And gee, wasn't it so nice, too, that I got to go to school with real people, even though I wasn't qualified, sorry, able, for that? "-Could cripple you for the rest of your time here," she finished when I didn't say what she desired. "We want all of you to do *your best*."

"I managed to maintain all A's at Chancel," I remarked defiantly.

"And I'm sure you realize how different Chancel is from Mason," she declared, her voice condescending. "Middle school is a far different environment...*setting*...and Chancel," she gave me a knowing look, followed by a slightly encouraging smile, which translated into: 'We both know what kind of education you got there, as opposed to a 'real', meaning white, middle school.'

"Yes, ma'am, Mrs. Rupert, I do," I remarked, forcing my voice to sound humble. My palms itched as my pride ping-ponged with the knowledge that this woman could undue my future with a stroke of her pen. Pride, Harvard, pride, Harvard. Pride. Harvard won. "I understand that going from middle school, to high school, is a big transformation, and maybe I did take on a few too many difficult classes," I allowed. "I'll just have to try my best, and use every resource I have to make sure that I don't fall behind in my classes."

Her smile expanded, and she was back to offering me cookies. "Well, you're in luck because it's still early enough in the semester to correct this error. It would be no problem to change over your schedule." She slapped her hand on the desk. "Why, we can even put you in the same classes as your friends;

teachers realize that children make mistakes all the time, that's why I called you into my office to discuss this."

I nodded as if I were considering her words. "And I thank you for bringing this to my attention," I said, overly gratuitous. "I'm very fortunate to have people to look out for me," I added, humbly. "I thank you for your consideration, but I think that it's best that I stick to my decision. How else will I learn from my mistakes?"

The smile dropped from her face for the first time. "I cannot be held responsible for your progression if you refuse my advice," she said, sternly.

"Yes, ma'am, I understand," was all I could think to say. She gave me a long, hard stare, before she finally dismissed me. I got up from my chair, my legs shaking despite my calm. Did she have the power to change my schedule without my permission?

Once I was outside of her office, the unfairness and condescension finally got to me, and my emotions came spilling out, unwelcome. When I realized that I might start crying, I forgot where I was, and made for the closest bathroom, locking myself in the stall.

While I sat there, oddly it was the words of the devil-not the biblical one, but Shaw's serpent in Back to Methuselah-that came to me in that moment: "You see things; you say, "Why?" But I dream things that never were; and I say, "Why not?"

Slowly, I started to feel better. That glass roof that seemed to hover over my future seemed a little farther away. I just had to remind myself that just because this woman couldn't dream along with me, didn't mean that I couldn't still dream. She might not think that some little colored girl could handle the classes I'd chosen, but I knew better.

By the time I emerged from the bathroom, lunch was almost over. I knew Mrs. Diece had her planning period right now, so instead of going back to eat with my classmates, once I fixed myself up, I made my way down the hall to her classroom.

The room was blissfully empty so I pulled out my notebook to start writing. I'd barely made a dent on the page, when someone walked into the room. I looked up, surprised to see Derek. Usually he walked in, seconds before the bell, laughing with his buddies, Roy and Quinn, about some horrible joke, or some exploit that he'd done. Derek had taken Mrs. Diece's first day announcement as a sort of challenge. He was the sort of guy who loved to make the stupid jokes, to have all eyes on him, to do whatever it took to disrupt the class. I kept waiting for Mrs. Diece to throw him out, but most of the time I guess she thought he was more enduring than obnoxious, so he got to stay.

He looked odd without his buddies flanking him, but he strode into the classroom with purpose. He smiled when he saw me looking at him, and strutted over to my desk in a way that made me think of a peacock.

"Bonjour," he said, silkily.

I glanced up at him briefly. "Hi," I said, just as shortly.

"You're Tracy, right?" He put emphasis on the way he said my name, making sure that I noticed that he knew it. I was surprised-to almost everyone in the class I was invisible-but I wasn't impressed.

"Yes, Leroi? Or was that Elvis, I forgot?"

"That was jesta joke." He chuckled throatily, taking a seat on the desk. "I'm Derek." He picked up my hand and shook it. "Nice to meet ya, Tracy."

I gave him a grimace, but he ignored it, smiling and reeking of arrogance. He tilted his head ever-so-slightly so that a strand of his longish black hair fell into his eyes. He combed the stray hair back into place. "You likin' tha penguin's class so much you come even when no one's here?" he questioned, smiling brilliantly.

"Penguin?" I wondered.

He pointed to the desk he was sitting on. "Mrs. Diece," he stated. My eyebrows raised in question. "Come on." He smiled. "I know that you noticed how she sorta waddles when she walks-," he lead.

"Like a penguin," I supplied.

He laughed. "Yea, you get it!" His hair fell into his eyes, again, and he wiped it away. Again. "How you likin' tha class?"

"It's nice," I responded in a less than conversational tone. I wished that he would just cut to the chase so I could go back to what I'd been doing. I'd been looking forward to having a few minutes alone.

Derek noticed the small note of annoyance in my voice, but pretended that he didn't. He nodded. "Yeah, I kinda like this class too," he said breezily.

"She's pretty funny." Not as funny as you, though, right? "I wasn' tryin' to disturb you or nothin'. I saw you and thought I'd say 'hi'," he said next, still trying to engage me in conversation. He glanced at the notebook on my desk. "What ya writin'?"

I placed a hand on top of it. "Nothing," I responded, promptly.

He gave me a leading smile. "You had to've been writin' somethin'...your pencil was movin'. You workin' on homework?"

I looked at the paper in front of me. "Yes," I lied.

"For this class?"

"No."

He became a little more casual. "Did you do tha homework we had to do last night? I had uh lotta trouble wit' it."

I met the eyes that shone beneath his dark hair, and I wondered if this routine ever actually worked for him. It had to work at least sometimes, because he had his approach down to a science. I guess I was supposed to be disarmed by his cuteness and just roll over. "I bet you had no trouble wit' tha work at all," he continued, flatteringly. "You seem to get this stuff pretty well. I notice you always seem to get good marks." He let the words settle with me for a moment before he questioned, "D'you think that you could maybe help me uh little wit' last night's assignment?"

The bitter part of me noted that this guy didn't seem to doubt that I could handle the course load. "Yes, sure," I responded, which I knew was what he wanted to hear. He got out his book and listened to me as I explained what he was supposed to do. After I had gone through the first problem, he glanced at the clock as if noticing the time for the first time.

"Gee, we won' be able to get through all this 'fore class starts." He suddenly got bashful. "Do ya think that mebbe I can see yours, just this once, and you can explain this to me latuh?"

I looked him over, from the top of his head, down to his shoes. "No," I said, flatly.

Derek was clearly surprised by my refusal. He quickly tried to regain his composure. His lips adopted a slight pout. "Please, Trace, just this once?"

"Sorry," I replied, going back to what I was working on before his interruption. "I don't cheat, and I don't aide others in cheating."

"I ain't askin' ya ta help me cheat," he said, feigning mild outrage. "Don' be so square; I just needa lil help to get this assignment done on time."

"No," I said again, not even looking at him this time. I was aware that Derek gave me a long, probing look before he noisily got up from the desk, and went to his own seat. He shook his head angrily, got out his book, and started flipping through the text. I tried not to smile as I went back to my writing.

— 5 —
"The Vagabond"

Is that Frankie?" My mom questioned as we pulled to a stop in front of our house. I checked the figure that was standing by the fence, waiting. "Looks like it," I remarked. "Doesn't he look sharp, mama?" I questioned. She shot me a sideways glance, a smile teasing her lips. I contemplated her look. "I didn't mean like that," I let her know. "I just meant he looks sharp." Although Frankie'd always looked well put together, he'd recently started copying the boys from Morehouse so he was starting to look distinguished, too. My mom's smile deepened, despite my words. She'd always liked Frankie, and I knew she wouldn't be too upset if I did have feelings for him.

I got out of the car. Frankie smiled, nodding in my mom's direction. "How do, Miz Burrows?" he called to her. She nodded his way amicably as she got out of the car. "How are you, Frankie?" she returned, barely pausing to hear if he answered.

Frankie paid her about as much attention as she gave him. "What took y'all so long to get home?" he wondered. "Pastor Pride keep y'all long?"

"No, mom just likes to talk after church," I responded. For mom, church was like her second home. Despite never showing much of an affinity for church while my parents were married, almost as soon as we'd crossed the Mason-Dixon Line, it seemed that she'd discovered religion.

We trailed in behind her, going into the den. Frankie sprawled out comfortably on the couch without invitation. "So how has it been at Mason?" Frankie questioned. "Y'all lucky y'all can wear what you like. Forest Lake we gotta wear these bogus uniforms, and a tie, just like we at church all the time," he complained.

Frankie talked with his hands like his minister, Pastor Otis Johnson, and spoke with the same conviction. I thought that he'd make a good lawyer someday, but his ambitions were bigger than that. The thing I liked best about him was that he wanted to get away from Bakersfield as much as I did. "Mason's okay," I remarked. "Unimpressive actually." I could tell from the first day that it was far different than the education I would have gotten if I'd gone to Groovy, but even though it was more difficult than middle school, I didn't have any classes that seemed as if they'd be too much of a challenge. "You'll probably get a better education at Forest Lake."

He 'pshed' my words, letting me know with his actions that that was the last thing he was concerned with. "So, what's it like going to school with all them White folks?" he demanded.

I took a moment to think about it, leaning towards him as if I were conspiring with him. "It's like going to school with all black folks…only they're white," I answered.

"Only a Yankee'd say that," Frankie decided. "Most folks don't have no call to be 'round them 'cept when they working or when they come down to the Trick, and even then they keep to they selves. Course daddy has to talk to them every now and then," he made certain I knew, "but that ain't the same, you know?" Frankie's dad was the colored doctor.

"Guess not," I remarked, not really wanting to imagine Frankie's dad having to kowtow to anyone, especially white folks. I'd only met the man once because I'd only been invited over to Frankie's home a handful of times, but he was intimidating in the same way that Mr. Gordon was warm and inviting, despite his gruff appearance. "I don't see the big deal. People are just people, far as I'm concerned."

Frankie shook his head. "You sound like a hippie when you say things like that. They just different. You got Coke?"

"We have RC," I offered.

"I guess that'd be alright," he remarked. I got up and got the drink for him, glad that this time, at least, we had some in the house. Usually we didn't. Mom was a no-frills shopper when it came to food. Snacks were rare. "Got any fancy grahams or shortbread?" he wondered, while I was getting the drink. We didn't. I brought out some carrot sticks and peanut butter, which he looked at like he'd never seen before. "No thanks," he grumbled.

I shrugged in an aloof way, turned on the TV for his benefit, and sat down beside him. We watched mostly in silence, until the door opened and Patrice stepped in.

"Frankie's here," I informed her. Patrice had shed her church clothes, and was wearing a blue polka-dotted short set with a ruffled shirt, and a matching vest that came down past her knees. "Is he?" she questioned without pause. "You wanna go down to tha Trick?" Frankie looked at her, and she spared him a nod.

"Why?" I wondered.

"Just to be seen," she answered.

"Not really," I said honestly.

She huffed. "Well, what're you goinna do wit tha rest uh yo day?" she demanded. "Just sit around? It's not like you've got homework; you do that on Fridays."

"I'll walk with you," Frankie piped up. "Daddy asked me to pick something up for him, anyway."

Patrice spared him a glance. "That uh sorta defeats tha purpose, slim," she remarked, biting down hard on her gum bubble. "So, that's really a no?" she wondered of me.

"Yes."

"You're no fun, Trace, you know that? What's on tha TV, then?"

I shrugged. I hadn't really been paying attention. Frankie told her the name of the program. Patrice dismissed the show. "Hey, mama got me this McCall pattern, says it's straight off tha racks in New York. Why on't we go ovuh ta my place? 'Membuh my honey yellow bell bottoms? I got 'nuff fabric left ova from that ta make tha outfit for you, too. You'd just gotta cut it. You'd look really smart in it, and I know how to make it look like you got somthin' back there!"

Frankie looked like he was sizing me up, and he smirked. He tried to shoot a furtive look at Patrice as well. "Boy, don' you even cut yo eyes at me!" she snapped. "What you say, Trace? I can' just sit 'round and do 'nothin.'"

"Well, what'm I supposed to do," Frankie moped. "Tracy and I were hanging out."

"Didn' you say that yo daddy told you to pick somethin' up for him?"

— 41 —

she demanded. I wondered at the exchange. Their relationship didn't usually seem quite so antagonistic.

I decided to try to make peace with the both of them. "I can walk down to the Trick with you," I remarked to the air. "And then we can come back and work on the patterns?"

"That'd be alright, I guess," Patrice remarked. "Give us a chance to look at some more fabric."

I told my mom of my plans, and headed to the Trick with my friends on either side of me. Frankie walked with his hands stuffed into his pockets, looking put out. Patrice ignored him, talking animatedly the whole time, and I listened to her, and made small talk with my other friend, wondering what the deal between the two of them was. Frankie said good-bye as soon as we reached Henderson Street, heading off in the direction of the Pharmacy.

"Are you going to tell me what that was about?" I questioned once he was gone.

"Frankie's been talkin' wit Cecilia Johnson aftuh church," she stated, bracingly.

"And why is that a problem?" I wondered in confusion.

"Cause ain't he wit you?"

"Does it look like he's with me?" I remarked. "It's just Frankie."

"And everyone knows that y'all is business."

"No, we aren't," I remarked.

She sucked her teeth. "I on't like him no way," Patrice decided. "You know how all those light-skinned folks thinks they high and mighty? Well he tha high and mightiest uh them all, always braggin' to his friends that his daddy done bought him a forty dollar pair uh shoes, or that soons he turn sixteen, his daddy's goinna buy him a 'Stang. Shoot he think his daddy's tha greatest thing in tha world, and we all know that he's just as low down as tha folk he thinkin' he better'n, always chasin' aftuh young cat. His mama ain't no bettuh, pretendin' she all better'n everyone, too, like her husband ain't Tom'n around!"

"This has nothing to do with you maybe liking him, does it?"

"Girl, please! And you kno I ain' mean that 'bout you, just folks like him. Always talkin' 'bout Barbados, too, like we supposed to be impressed that his granddad's from some raggedy little island. He was alright back in middle school, but they somethin' 'bout this summah that changed him," her voice fell off at the sentence, and she shrugged, changing the subject. "If it's alright, I'mma need some help wit my homework aftuh we're done workin' on tha patterns, and aftuh that we can run some drills... 'membuh you promised."

I groaned, because I had. After much pestering on my part to get her to change her science class, she'd finally told me that if I would come to softball tryouts with her, she would transfer into Biology with me. I hadn't expected her to actually go through with the promise, but when Patrice found out what Mrs. Rupert had said, and even more, what was implied, her decision became cemented.

So on Monday, I found myself among the other 20 or so girls that showed up on the day of tryouts. Mason High's softball team was implemented when Mason became integrated, but since it was still considered a club activity, its booster club was small, and most girls had little desire to be involved. When the coach saw the turnout he seemed disappointed, but not too surprised. He gave a brief speech, before turning the tryouts over to the upper classmen to run...and that's pretty much all we did. We did something called a homerun derby (there's no bat or ball involved, so it's not nearly as fun as it seems), we ran around the school, we ran wind sprints, we ran suicides, we played cat and mouse (again, not nearly as fun as it sounds), and then we did it all again. Pride wouldn't allow me to quit in the middle of the tryout, but I knew before the day was over that I wasn't going to come back on Tuesday.

After we were done for the day, it just seemed like pure torture to have to climb up the hill after practice, and Patrice stood back, watching me struggle. "Dang, you goinna make it, girl?" she joked.

"Trying," I said back.

Miraculously, like the angel he was, Marcus appeared at the top of the hill, and walked down to where we were. He shouldered my bag. "Looks like they killed ya today, T. How's it?"

"Groovy," Patrice said. She looked like she could go run a couple more miles and still be unfazed. "I can' believe coach let us off so easy." *That'd been easy?* "What'd you think?" she questioned of me.

"It's pretty bad when you can't make it on to a no-cut team."

"Don' tell me you quittin'," Patrice said, laughing.

"No, I'm not quitting," I remarked, "I'm gracefully accepting my limitations."

Marcus looked amused. "Hey, don't sweat it, Trace, we're all good at what we're good at."

"And you can' be perfect," Patrice chimed in helpfully. "I mean, you gotta be bad at somethin', right?"

I went to try-outs again on Tuesday, but while Patrice went down to the field and started warming up apart from the other girls, I found a shady spot on the bleachers and sat down. I pulled out my notebook to write, but didn't get much further than that because I kept getting distracted by calls and shouts on the field.

They were actually doing drills today, and if we had done that the day before I might have stuck around. The girls were all lined up in the position that they hoped to play, and the assistant coach rotated hitting balls to each position. Patrice was in the line for shortstop, and every time the ball was hit her way, she made sure it didn't get past her. If they were cutting people, she wouldn't be the one to be cut.

I'd just picked up my pencil again, when a shadow fell over my notebook. "Lemme guess," Derek began as a salutation. "You're doin' homework."

I looked up in annoyance. "We both know you're not," I shot back.

Derek's stance became somewhat defensive. "You could've helped me," he stated.

"You could've done it at home. It was *home*work."

He flipped his hair back. "You're uh real geek, you know that?"

I ground my teeth. "What's your point?" I questioned.

"You should lighten up some," he suggested.

"And you should study harder," I responded curtly. "That way you don't have to spend all of your time trying to scheme up ways to disrupt the class."

"I'll get right on that," he condescended, smiling down at me. I waited for him to clear out, but he didn't. Instead, he sat down, indecently close. I moved over a little to remind him of his oversight. "Thought I seen you out there yesterday," he said, conversationally. "Not tryin' out today?"

It took me a second to adjust to the change in the conversation. "I was supporting a friend," I responded.

His eyes scanned the field. "Who's your friend?" he questioned, though I thought it should be obvious; Patrice was the only girl of color on the field.

I toyed with my notebook. "You wouldn't know her." I was purposely being unfriendly, hoping he'd get the hint.

He didn't.

"Try me'n I might," he suggested. Reluctantly, I pointed Patrice out. At the moment she was in the middle of a play. She charged the ball, scooped it up, and tagged third, before throwing to first in time to get the runner out.

"Pretty good," he commented, "and see, you're wrong. I do know her. Her name's..." he paused, trying to draw it out. "Patrice, right?" Derek smiled in satisfaction at my surprised look.

"How do *you* know her?" I demanded. Apparently Patrice wasn't just popular with our black classmates. For some reason it irritated me that he knew who she was. He shrugged, casually, leaning back against the bleachers. "She baby-sits for my buddy's mama sometimes," he explained.

"Who's your buddy?" I questioned. I didn't know any white people that Patrice baby-sat for, and I was certain that if she did baby-sit for any, her parents didn't know about it either.

"Orion Taylor," he said with a certain flair.

I was surprised by the name. "*You're* friends with Orion?" I questioned, skeptically. Orion, who Patrice said was 'bad' with reverence, didn't seem like the type of guy who would have Derek as a friend, and vice versa. Derek was a clown; Orion was untouchable. And from the few times I'd been around him, he definitely didn't seem like the kind of guy to hang with someone who said the word 'buddy'.

"O's my best friend in tha whole wide world," Derek said, and I was sure he was mocking me. "Small world, huh?" He waited for me to say something. When I didn't, he questioned, "You know who I'm here supportin'?"

Actually I was wondering why he was still here talking. Friendly boys made me cautious, friendly white boys made me nervous. "Your sister?" I questioned, sarcastically.

He pointed across the field. "My girlfriend; she's tha blonde at first."

— 45 —

I looked over at the blonde at first. She was tall, and slender, and noticeably athletic. Her hair was shock blonde, as if it was helped a little by peroxide, and glinted in the sunlight. I wondered if her eyes were blue, too. It figured; she looked like the kind of girl he'd be in to, though I was a bit surprise he was interested in someone who was obviously not a powder puff. Derek waited for me to say something, and when I didn't, he shifted uncomfortably on the seat.

"Guess I'll leave you to your homework since you ain' bein' so friendly," he decided, a hint of mirth in his voice. He climbed the bleachers to find somewhere else to sit, and someone else to bother.

Marcus showed up early, and instead of waiting for us to slog our way up the hill, he came down to the field to watch the last part of the day's tryout.

"How's Pat doing?" Marcus questioned as he took the seat behind me. I leaned against him, comfortably, tilting my head up to look at him.

"She'll be first string, no problem."

He tapped me on the nose. "What're you working on?" he wondered. "Homework?"

I shrugged. "Just writing," I replied.

"The 'Great American Novel'?" he teased good-naturedly. Marcus was the only one who didn't think I was strange for writing all the time. I smiled at him, but said nothing.

As the first of the girls were coming back to the softball field, a male figure took his time walking over. He was tall, darker-skinned, and walked with a gait similar to a sailor who'd just come off of a ship. Patrice, who was near the front of the line, saw him and gave a wave in his direction.

Marcus didn't miss the exchange. "Who's that?" he demanded in full big brother mode.

"I think his name's Omar," I replied, pulling the name from some remembered conversation between me and Patrice. The only other thing I could remember her saying about him was that he was a junior in her freshman history class.

My answer didn't satisfy his curiosity. "What's he doing here?"

"Don't know," I responded. As soon as all the girls made it back to the mound, they were dismissed for the day. Patrice walked over to the guy, giving him a very flirtatious look.

"What're you doin' here?" she questioned of him.

"Gurl, please," he remarked. "You beg me ta come and now you wunderin' why I's here? Why'ont I just leave if'n you on't know?"

She grinned. "Don'," she said. "Thank-you for comin', O-mar," she added.

He shrugged, slouching. "You lucky, cause I on't do this fo' evvyone. You must be som'in kinda special." Marcus rolled his eyes as he stood to make his presence known. Omar gave the classic look that a guy gives when he's faced with the relative of the girl he may not have pure intentions for.

He took a step back from Patrice. "This yo bro?" he questioned, looking Marcus over.

"Yeah, kid, I'm her *bro*," Marcus asserted. "Who're you?" I'd never known Marcus to sound so intimidating before.

"Omar," the junior taking a freshman class responded. "Yo sis's told me uh lot 'bout you," he said, trying to lighten the conversation.

"Huh. She ain't said nothing 'bout you," Marcus returned. "Pat, let's go. I have to get to work."

Patrice frowned at her brother, smiled at Omar, and informed him that she would call him later. "Right on," he said, before he sauntered off with the three of us watching. Although Patrice had pointed him out to me before, this was the first time I'd actually heard him speak. I was disappointed. Not that I had high expectations from a junior in a freshman class, but the guy was nothing more than a cute face. Patrice could do a lot better. Maybe they had wonderful conversations, I thought dryly.

"So who's that punk," Marcus questioned, irritated that he even had to ask. Patrice looked back at me and mouthed the word 'punk'.

"Ah, leave me alone," she said to her brother. "He's pretty gone."

"How old is he?"

She sucked her teeth. "None uh your business."

"Don't play that with me," Marcus asserted, "I'm the nice one. Keep it up and I'll call Abdul."

"He's a junior," she answered with a smack of the lips.

— 47 —

"There's only one thing that a junior wants with a freshman, so you better watch yourself."

"Probably tha same thin' you wanted at his age, stop bein' a hypocrite."

"I ain't being a hypocrite, I'm being a brother. You're my kid sister and don't forget that."

He took her bag from her, and walked ahead of us. She rolled her eyes at his back, letting him get a safe distance ahead of us. "There's some white boy lookin' at you a few minutes ago," she said in an accusatory tone. I glanced back at the crowd.

"Y'all's talkin' earliah," she added.

"Derek," I said, dismissively. "I have a class with him."

Patrice looked thoughtfully back his way. "I know him from somewhere?" she wondered.

I bit down on my lip. "He says that he's friends with Orion. Nicole's brother?"

"Oh, yeah, well, he wuz definitely lookin'," she decided. "What's that 'bout?"

How would I know that if I hadn't even known he was looking? "It's probably because I wasn't too friendly, earlier," I decided. "He knows I don't like him too much. He tried to copy off my work, and got upset when I wouldn't let him. And you remember that guy that ran into me on the first day? That's Roy, one of his friends, and Roy could give Bull Connor a run for his money."

"That guy?" Patrice demanded. "I've seen him 'round; he just plain mean. I watched him tip a freshman's plate in tha garbage, just cause." She nodded behind us. "He like that?"

"You know what they say about birds of a feather," I replied, "and the two of them are always together." Patrice gave me a mysterious smile before we continued our trudge up the hill.

— 6 —

"The Prevalence of Ritual"

Impatiently, I sat in the pew while the choir warmed up, wishing that there was a clock somewhere in the sanctuary. Even though I knew that Pastor Pride ran his service like clock-work, I was inexplicably worried about not getting out of church on time. While a few stragglers came in, the voices in the choir worked themselves to be heard, and Sister Johnson wondered, *"Can we find a friend so faithful, who will all, all our sorrows share?"* I hummed along tunelessly as they started in on 'What a friend we have in Jesus'.

"Yes, Lord!" Sister Ritter shouted at the last words of the song. She was early today: she usually got hit with the Holy Spirit around the middle of the second song, and wasn't scared to let the whole church know it. This usually happened right before Pastor Pride made it to the pulpit, alerting us of his coming, and while she could get worked up while the choir sang, she'd sit, quiet as a dormouse once Pastor Pride was in the pulpit. (Sister Hale was usually the screamer during the sermons, because, of course, he was always speaking to her).

When the song ended, David Johnson stepped forward, and silence fell. Even my nerves seemed to disappear once he opened his mouth. *"I was boooorn by the River,"* he crooned passionately, giving Sam Cooke a run for his money. *"In a little tent. And just like that riiiiver, I've been running every since."* It seemed that not a person stirred while he belted out his lyrics. When David sang, the church ladies listened with glazed eyes, the kids stopped fidgeting, and the men took note. We were all lulled by the spell that was Mr. Johnson, because on top of having the best voice around, he was also very good looking with a charisma that made him liked by all.

David was 25, hugely popular among the church family, and often went around to other churches to share his strong, deep, melodic voice with the other congregations. Despite his popularity, however, the fact that he was so eligible, and was still single, caused for the occasional gossip. David sang, though, like he didn't know what was said about him behind his back, like he was singing for the Lord only, and for four minutes I didn't worry about the time.

When David finished, the choir sang two more songs before Pastor Pride took his place. I kind of liked the pastor. He had a style that didn't stray too much from the script. He wasn't a 'shuck 'n jive' minister, he didn't go into theatrics. He simply spoke passionately, warned of hell fire, and then sat back down. It was impossible to zone out during his sermons because they were responsive, and if you didn't pay attention you were likely to miss a "let the church say amen", but he was *quick*. He would preach for fifty minutes, work in two five minute prayers, and then invite the choir back to sing while he caught his breath, content to be one of the saved among the sinners.

It was great that Pastor Pride's sermons were so compact, but whatever time advantage they gave us was lost because my mom was what I called a miller: she would spend hours at the church even after services were over. In Wilmington, I'd grown used to my mom's constant company during the day, but here she didn't invite people back to the house-I think she was too embarrassed to-so instead she spent her free time at the church, treating it as if it were her second home.

Even though mom was more on the quiet side, she'd always been social, and didn't seem quite as at odds with Bakersfield as I was. My mom had grown up in Connecticut, and she still talked like it. She refused to develop any sort of drawl or twang to her voice, and without ever saying a word to me on the matter, impressed upon me to do the same. She never walked with her head bowed, or her arms cocked, she made eye contact with whoever she was talking to, and her laugh, like her speech, was reserved. Every part of who she was stood out. The children gawked at her when she walked by, and the church ladies referred to her as that 'high talkin' Sibby', but that didn't keep them from loving her all the same. I think they viewed her as their Prodigal Daughter: she'd been raised in that evil north, but had gathered her senses, and through Grace had been brought back home to raise her daughter among the sainted, so they welcomed her.

She knew that I wasn't quite so social, and she didn't require me to linger or to mill around with the rest of the church. So while my mom rehashed the sermon with the church ladies (and agreed that Pastor Pride 'sho preached it today') I went to our car, retrieved the book I kept in my purse for after church reading, and sat half in, half out of our Ford Falcon, anxiously waiting for my mom to come back.

I heard footsteps, before I heard the voice that said my name softly, and I looked up from my book to see who'd addressed me. I recognized the guy only slightly, knowing him to be one of Omar's friends, and the nephew of the Pastor. He was plain looking in a nice neighborhood boy way. Wholesome, certainly one you would take home to mama. Like Marcus, only not as cute.

"Hi," I said, politely, courteously returning his greeting. I put my book aside. "You're Omar's friend, right?"

There was a note of appreciation at the recognition. "Yeah, that's me. I'm Ricky, but ever'body calls me Preacher, cause've being kin ta Uncle."

I tried to think if I had run into him enough times that an introduction would seem embarrassing, but then I remembered that he had called me by name, so there was really no point in telling him it.

"What'd you think of the service?" Ricky questioned, searching for something to say. I tried to recollect what it'd been about. Perseverance I think. Job, then. Job seemed to be every pastor's favorite preaching subject when it came to perseverance. Or maybe that was steadfastness. I'd think, though, that colored people would have had enough of Job to last a century. "Preachy," I remarked, honestly.

"Uncle's just 'mindin' us of tha road 'head," the young man responded. "He thinks if he don't say it, we won't 'member to stick to the straight and narrow when we gets tested. I see you 'round all tha time, but I never said nothin' 'fore cause folks say you was sweet on Frankie."

I wondered who these folks were, and why they were all of the wrong impression. "Frankie Banks?" Preacher nodded. "We're just friends," I said in answer.

— 51 —

The slightest smile crossed his face. "Well, okay. I just saw you sittin' by yoself, just thought I'd say hi."

"Hi," I responded back. I wasn't sure what else I was supposed to say. This was probably why everyone thought I was stuck up, but honestly I didn't know how to respond. I wasn't good with social situations. I was good with books. I fidgeted with the one I brought, wishing I could get back to it. Ricky, or Preacher, scratched the back of one of his legs with the other.

"Well I sees you readin' so I guess I'll leave you to it," he said gracefully. "I'm supposed ta be watchin' tha kids, anyhow. Nice runnin' into you."

"Nice seeing you, too."

"Maybe we can see each other at school sometime," he added.

"Maybe," I replied neutrally. As soon as his back was turned, I went back to my book. Thankfully, my mom didn't keep me waiting long today, and she returned to the car far sooner than she would have on any other day. She gave me a look, saying without words that she knew how anxious I was.

My best friend and her brother were waiting for us when our car pulled to a stop in the driveway. "Happy Birthday!" Patrice called excitedly as soon as I got out the car. I didn't get the chance to change before I got shuttled into the Gordon's car, and we drove to the Trick for lunch and a movie. Marcus waited until his sister was distracted with getting snacks from the snack bar to give me his gift. "I'm supposed to wait for 'Riece, but what can I say, I'm impatient."

He brandished a book-shaped package nicely wrapped in gold wrapping paper. "Hope I don't ruin the surprise by telling you that it's a book." I neatly removed the paper surrounding his gift. The book had no title, and was filled with empty pages. "For whatever you write," Marcus remarked. "Happy Birthday."

Because we were both seated, our hug was a little awkward, but I smiled at him. "Thank you, Marcus!" I said with nothing but sincerity in my voice; his gift was perfect. He returned the smile because he knew that it was. When Patrice returned, she passed over her gift: an outfit she stitched, and a brand new copy of one of her latest fashion magazines. I held in my grimace, and thanked her heartily.

They dropped me back off at my house late in the afternoon, and while

I waited for 6:00, I went to my room and got out homework that I'd already done, pretending that I was working instead of merely watching the clock. At six, right on cue, the phone rang, and I was down the stairs with the phone in my hand, before it could ring again. "Hello, Burrows," I said breathlessly into the mouth piece.

My heart skipped a few beats at the sound of my name. "Hi, dad!" I exclaimed, and winced at how excited I always sounded whenever he called.

"Happy Birthday, kiddo," he declared. I thrilled at the sound of his voice. "I can't believe you turn 14 this year! You know, I was just saying to myself the other day: 'Ben, you're getting old'. Before I know it my little girl's going to be in college, living on her own," he continued. "You started high school this year, didn't you?"

"Yes, I did!" I said more proud of that in this moment than I had thought to be on my first day. "School started on August 11th!"

"Well how does it feel to be in high school?" he questioned. "Tell me about it." I filled him in on my first month, told him what classes I liked, which ones I didn't, told him about the organizations I was involved with, and conversation went on for a while. He listened as I talked about what was new in my life, but the things that I really wanted to talk to him about, the things that went beyond the surface, went unsaid, as they always did. My dad called only for a progress report, and I knew my role.

On the same clockwork that made my dad call, my mom came back home five minutes before seven. "Is that your father?" she questioned. I nodded. "Tell him that I said 'hello'." I relayed the words back to my dad. Five minutes later, at exactly 7:00, dad clocked out, telling me how much he loved and missed me, and how great it was to hear from me again, but he hung up none the less.

It was a sort of birthday tradition: every year I received my birthday card on the day before my birthday, and every year on my birthday my dad would call at six o'clock. Dad always had to go at seven, and my mom always came home at the end of the conversation and asked if I was speaking to my dad. When I said yes, she would tell me to tell him hello. Then the two of us would go out to eat at some moderately priced restaurant in the Trick, but after, never before, my dad called.

Today was no variation from any of the other birthday's I've had since my parents divorced, but today I glanced at my mom over dinner, and wondered if she anticipated my dad's calls every year. I wondered if she came in at the end of the call, too, so she wouldn't have to be the one to pick up the phone to say hello to him, but wasn't completely able to miss the call, or for the moment that I reassured her that dad said "hi" back. I wondered if she waited all year for that one word.

The first French Club meeting of the year was on Monday, the week after my birthday. French was easily turning into my favorite class. It was challenging without being too difficult, and you could tell that Mrs. Diece loved what she did. Her enthusiasm made you want to do well in the class, and even though it didn't entirely sound the way my Grandpa's French did (we were learning Meridional French and my Grandpa spoke Antillean Creole-with a little drink to it, he liked to say), taking the class still made me feel closer to him.

When I got to the classroom, it was still early, so there was only one other person in the room, a thin, short, jet black, curly-haired guy, who was busy pushing the desks into a circle. It felt weird to just watch him work, so tentatively I questioned, "Do you want some help?"

He turned at the sound of my voice, startling. He gave me an appraising look, and I could see the hesitation in his eyes, as if I had suggested something inappropriate. "Sure," he said, slowly, in a low, nasally voice. "I'm just pushing the desks together," he added unnecessarily. I wondered if he doubted my mental capabilities that much. I pushed the thought aside, though, and started helping him on the opposite side of the circle.

More people began to trickle in, and the guy stopped what he was doing to talk to one of the guys who'd just walked in, leaving me to finish his task without even a word to me. Someone sat down in the last desk that I was moving, while I was busy trying to move it, and I looked down in irritation. He beat me to talking, though. "How's it that you're always everywhere I go?" Derek questioned. "Keep it up, Trace, and I'mma think you're followin' me."

I glowered at him. "How do you presume that when I was here first?" I questioned.

He laughed at my frown, and easily slid out of the seat, moving the desk where it was supposed to go. "You don' take jokes easily, do you?" he wondered as he sat the desk down.

"Oh, was that a joke?" I questioned.

He pretended to be hurt, rubbing his side. "Ouch. Way ta bruise my ego there. Y'know, you should try laughin' more. Frownin' just ain't becomin'."

"Neither is being narcissistic."

"Well look'it you, Miz Webster, showin' off your vocabulary." He fluttered his eyebrows. "But you don' have to try'n impress me wit' your big words, Trace."

I scowled. "For the record, my name is Tracy," I remarked stiffly. "T-R-A-*C-Y*," I spelled out. "Not Trace."

He mouthed the words, mocking. "I'll try'n membuh that," Derek remarked, sarcastically.

"Doesn't Carol have something going on?" I wondered irritably, wondering why he was here, and more importantly, why he felt the need to talk to me.

"Ah, so you do know her," he beamed, happily. "Thought so…she said she knew you. She's doing something with her girlfriends right now. "

"So you decided to just come here and waste time?" I questioned. "Not enough time in class to get through all of your jokes; you needed some more time after school to finish?"

He looked intensely proud of himself. "Nope, today I actually managed to run through my entire set durin' class."

It figures he wouldn't be dissuaded by my lack of friendliness. "It's nice to see that you can finish some things," I noted, "but that doesn't explain what brings you in today? Extracurriculars seem like they're beneath you. I mean why put forth extra work when you don't have to?"

He stretched out in the seat as much as it would allow, folding his arms behind his head. "See, that's my philosophy for life: sit back'n let it all come to you! I knew you understood me!" Derek said mockingly. "And normally they are beneath me, but I happen to know that tha French Club is goinna be takin' uh field trip up to tha University of Virginia tha same weekend that they're showcasin' some of Ethan McMillan's work. I've always wanted to see them up close, so…" I wondered if he was being serious. The meeting was called to order before I could figure it out.

Frankie was walking down our street when I got home from school. I grinned at the sight of him. "Hey Frankie," I called. Frankie had already changed out of his school clothes, and was wearing an outfit I'd never seen on him. It seemed like he'd grown another inch since the last time that I saw him. He grinned toothily at me. "What?" I wondered.

"Nothing," he remarked, still grinning. We went inside, and I got a glass of water, and gave a Coke to Frankie. Frankie worked off his shoes, making himself at home. "Patrice 'bout to come over?" he wondered, idly.

"Probably not; I think she's meeting up with Omar at the Trick."

"Omar who?" he demanded. "Not Reynolds."

"Yeah."

"He's an idiot," Frankie assessed. "What she see in him?"

I'd wondered the same thing. "He's good looking, I guess," I remarked. I wasn't sure why I'd said I guess because Omar *was* nice looking. He was better looking than Frankie, who was currently too skinny, and all arms and legs. My mom said that he would round out as he got older, but so far I didn't have any evidence of that.

"Uh huh. Your friend always seemed kind of airy to me, but still: Omar?"

I didn't like him attacking Patrice's judgment; that was my job. "I'd heard that *you* had taken a fancy to Cecilia," I stated.

His back straightened as soon as I said her name. "Who told you that?" he demanded indignantly.

"Don't worry about it," I remarked.

"Nah, I want to know who had my name in they mouth," he said, hotly.

"Why, you going to go scrapping against them," I wondered, teasing. I couldn't really picture Frankie getting into a fight with anyone; he'd mess up his clothes. "If that's true, you don't have any room to talk because that girl isn't too smart, herself."

He seemed personally insulted by my assessment. "Don't be jealous."

His words stopped me up short. "Did you say jealous? Franklin Banks, you can absolutely date whoever you want to and I wouldn't care."

He gave me a sideways look. "You wouldn't," he wondered in surprise.

I wondered at his surprise. "Why would I?" I questioned.

"Well...cause...," his jaw snapped shut, and in that gesture it occurred to me that maybe Frankie thought I took a fancy to him. "Don't you and her have history together?" he questioned.

I had to think about it. "Yeah, why?"

"You want to ask her out to the Founder's Day picnic for me?"

"Why don't you ask her out?" I asked.

"How'd I look coming up to Mason, just to hear her say no?"

"Ask her at church, then."

"So folks can be gossiping about me, and I can get laughed out by God's people. Nah."

I thought about it. "Sure," I decided.

He started. "Really?"

"Yeah, really. I'll pass along a note for you."

"Well...gee...thanks," he said in surprise. "You ain't mad that I ain't taking you?"

"Why would I care?" I questioned.

"We've always gone in the past," he stated.

"Okay...?"

"It's just...I could really impress some folks if I went with Cecilia."

"I told you, I don't care," I remarked, ending the conversation before Frankie put his foot in his mouth. "Want me to get you some paper?"

He looked over at me. "Yea...yeah," he declared.

— 7 —

"A Necessary Angle"

Derek's girlfriend, the blonde at first, Carol Torcette, and I, had second period history together with Coach John Dewitt. Carol, who had barely spared me a glance before softball tryouts, suddenly started talking to me after she saw me talking to Derek at tryouts. And since he and I started working together on Bridges–the French Club's big service project for the year where we went and taught elementary school children French–she'd started sitting next to me, initiating conversations, probably hoping to glean some more information from me about her boyfriend. I guess she missed the grimaces and lukewarm reception that Derek and I gave whenever we saw each other.

Carol gave a friendly sort of wave when she saw me, and I half-heartedly returned it before heading to the back of the classroom to face Cecilia, the new object of Frankie's desire. Although I truly didn't care who Frankie went around with, I couldn't honestly say I was very fond of Cecilia, or her best friend, Vivian Rogers, either, for that matter. Everyone knew that the two of them were only friends with each other because they both thought they were better than everyone else.

Since I'd known them, they'd always been the wealthiest girls in our grade. Cecilia's father, Pastor Johnson, was the minister at First Missionary Baptist, the first and largest black church in the area. Back when the state was hesitant to appropriate funds to their Negro schools, First Missionary and Forest Lake were the ones that took up that cross, so to speak, and First Missionary still held that importance in the community. It was where the 'old' families attended church, and as the pastor, her dad had a lot of pull in the community.

Vie's father was the undertaker, and owned a few other businesses around town, too. Vie wasn't pretty at all, but she liked to think that she was better than everyone else-and wasn't afraid to let you know it, either-because of how white-looking she was with her fair skin, blue-gray eyes, and red-brown hair. She didn't like to think of herself as 'colored', and you had to pass the paper bag test for her to even talk to you on friendly terms. I was slightly darker than she was, but light enough, and for this reason, Vie had tried to be friends with me when I'd first moved to Bakersfield. When she found out that my parents were divorced and we had no money, though, she stopped talking to me. Even before our falling out, I hadn't been really impressed with either of them, and Cecilia, though not actually stupid, was about as shallow as a crack in the concrete.

When I marched to the back of the room to deliver Frankie's note, she gave me a disdainful glance, sizing up my homemade clothes, white patent leather shoes, and French-braid ponytail, before her eyes made it up to my face. "What's good, Tracy?" she questioned haughtily. Cecilia hadn't liked me from the moment we met, I guess because she thought I might steal her best friend from her. Any chance of us ever being friends, though, ended in 7th grade when she and Patrice got into a fight, and my friend sent her home with a split lip. For months afterwards, her daddy tried to find out who'd given it to her, but Cecilia wouldn't tell, and no one else had spoken up because they were either scared of Patrice, or hated Cecilia as much as we did. Back then, Frankie had been one of the ones who had been fueling the fight; he'd once been really sweet on Patrice.

"Frankie wanted me to give you this," I remarked without preamble, holding out the folded sheet of paper.

Cecilia looked at Vie, and smirked. "Frankie?" she repeated stupidly, as if she didn't know who I was talking about, as if they and their mother's hadn't seen each other in Jack and Jill meetings since they were 2, or they hadn't gone to the same church, and didn't live more than a couple of blocks from each other, in the best neighborhood on our side of town.

"Frankie Banks," I said in irritation.

I could tell by the way her eyes unfocused that she was tallying up his stats. Apparently they were decent enough. "Oh, that Frankie!" she remarked, and I was suddenly irritated at Frankie for asking me to talk to Cecilia; it was like talking to a wall.

"Yeah, that Frankie," I reiterated. I dropped the note on her desk, and went back to my own, already second-guessing my decision to act as mediator between them; Frankie deserved better. On second thought, if she was what he wanted...then he deserved exactly what he got.

The bell rang, and Carol said good-bye to Derek. He sauntered off, late as usual to his 2nd period class. When he was gone, Carol looked over in my direction, with a look like she wanted to talk to me about the boyfriend she'd just said good-bye to, but thankfully Coach Dewitt didn't give her any chance to open her mouth. As soon as the bell rang, he started right in with his daily butchering of history.

I loved history. My Grandpa was passionate about the subject, and I never tired of hearing him craftily weave stories about those who had come and gone before us. I'd listen eagerly as he spouted facts, figures, and dates without having to pause to look them up. My Grandpa'd learned his version of American history from a displaced Frenchman as his tutor, so most of the history he got was from the viewpoint of trappers, the church, native accounts, political scientists, or from other outsiders looking in. It gave him a completely different perspective than the history we learned in schools, and was a far cry from the history that Dewitt taught.

History in the South, like church, was just one of those things that I'd just had to get used to when we moved to Bakersfield. In Bakersfield, Plymouth Rock, the American Revolution, the Industrial Revolution, and just about everything else prior to about the 1850s, was all covered in the first month of school. The rest of the year was spent discussing the miraculous growth of the South and making a case for the 'War of Northern Aggression', proving how the federal government had encroached upon the southern spirit, finally bullying them to the point where they'd had to secede if their way of life was to be protected. States Rights' was the only reason for the Civil War, and slavery was conveniently forgotten.

Our history books, written by southerners, referred to the antebellum period as 'a happy time for Whites and Darkies alike', and spoke of the colored in child-like declarations. Like with Civil Rights, the Civil War had been instigated by outsiders who just didn't understand the loving relationships between Whites and their Negroes.

Dewitt, and a lot of people around here, held on to the Civil War the same way Atlas held on to the world, as if it were some sort of punishment they couldn't shake. Southern Whites were proud of that legacy, of the 'good ole times' when God was in charge, men were courageous and honorable, and [white] women were chaste and noble. But 'The Old South' that both northerners and southerners venerated in media such as *Birth of a Nation* and *Gone with the Wind* was nothing of what the South had really been like. The South had led the nation in infant mortality rates and death from curable diseases during this time, and public education had only made its way here after the Civil War. Yet, they called this the good times; the Camelot of the southern world. To argue was base treason. Rather than spend an hour grinding my teeth, I usually just tuned him out completely.

I cast a sideways glance at Carol, who was busy doodling Derek's name, coupled with her own. I know that Dewitt's lectures were preferable only to getting your teeth pulled, but spending time thinking about that guy, in my opinion, was a complete waste of time. Although she may have been crazy about him, working with Derek was quickly turning him into one of my least favorite people.

Since Bridges was voluntary, I for the life of me couldn't figure out why Derek had gotten involved with the project. He didn't really seem too interested in it, and when we got together to discuss strategies, he'd had nothing to offer. Yet when we went over to Evans for the first time, while I was still trying to work up the nerve to get started, he just jumped right in. And of course they loved him immediately. Why not, he was their *buddy*. Derek's maturity level was about the same as the kids we were supposed to be teaching, so he connected with them.

All of the initial excitement I'd had for the project waned after only a few days of working with him. Having him for a partner was frustrating, to say the least. He never had any opinion on anything, never gave me any feedback on any idea that I brought to the table, yet he was always all energy whenever we got to Evans. I was left as the person who had to calm everyone down, which made me the witch, and Derek the guy that everyone liked. He cracked the stupid jokes that he couldn't get away with in Mrs. Diece's class, got the kids laughing when we were supposed to be serious, and generally was just a pain.

I shook my head at the stupidity of high school love, opened my own notebook to an empty page, and began writing, pretending to copy down Mr. Dewitt's dribble.

After classes were over for the day, Patrice came tearing across the asphalt, rushing in her excitement. She waved a piece of paper at me even though we were still a few yards apart. "You should read what Omar just wrote me!" she said when I was within feet of her. "He's tha sweetest! We met at tha Trick to see a movie, and he paid for it, and he said that I could get anythin' I wanted from tha snack bar! Isn' that *so* sweet? I wish that mama and daddy didn' say I couldn' date 'til I'm sixteen 'cause I want them ta meet him. Don' laugh, but I think me and Omar might have somethin' serious."

I gave her an appraising look. "Isn't it a bit early to have something serious?" I asked.

"You wouldn' understand," Patrice said dismissively. "Oh, hey, listen: Preacha's bin askin' bout you," she informed me with a smile. "Wouldn' it be so neat if you and him were ta get togethuh? Then we could double!"

I tried to picture how that would happen. "You know I'm not looking to get with anyone," I reminded her.

"But Preacha's not exactly like…I mean he's like a kid, he's so innocent. He like hangs out wit old ladies and looks aftuh all those kids."

"I don't doubt that he's sweet-,"

"He's like you, actually," she decided. "I think you should at least think on talkin' ta him. I mean he might not be tha best lookin' man out there, but he's your speed."

"Droll, Pat."

"Nah, I mean it. You on't want ta end up wit someone who's gotta lot uh game when you're just startin' out, you know. Then you'd get taken advantage uh like that." She snapped her fingers. "And Preacha's a real sweetie."

"I wonder what you really think of me sometimes," I told her.

"You knows I love you," she responded. "Hum. Preacha wanted me ta give you this." She handed me a folded piece of paper. Curiosity made me open the letter. "Innit that Derek?"

"What?" I wondered. Slowly I looked up from the note she'd given me, looking toward the direction that she was looking. The subject in question was leaning against the bleachers casually, his gaze in this general direction. "Yes, it is," I responded, wondering what he was doing here. He waved, indicating for me to come over. I looked over my shoulder as if I expected to see Carol or Roy behind us.

Patrice did too, but she looked back sooner. "I think he wants ta talk to *you*," Patrice said, surprised.

"Why?" I mumbled.

She gave me a little push. "Well, go find out," she instructed. "And catch me up," she added in a whisper, veering off to catch up with the rest of the students heading into the building.

I looked Derek over. "What're you doing here?" I asked. "Shouldn't you be in class?"

"Well, hello to you, too," he remarked with a smile. "Don' worry, Miss Burrows: I have uh pass. I'm not in tha hall without permission."

I said nothing in response to his statement. Most of our class had already made it back into the P.E. building. "Did you want something?" I wondered. "I'm in the middle of class."

"There's like ten minutes left," he noted. "No one's goinna check to make sure you shower." I scowled at him. He grinned in return. "Relax," he directed. "I come in peace." He held his hands out in front of him as if to show me that he carried no weapons with him. "They let us outta class early today, so I just thought I'd come back here and offuh you uh ride to Evans so you wouldn' have to walk."

Derek's seventh period was at the trade school across town. My eyes narrowed in suspicion. "You came all the way back here to ask me if I wanted a ride?" I questioned, distrusting. He'd made the offer at the beginning of Bridges, but I'd turned him down because I didn't want to have to depend on him for anything, and because getting a ride from Derek would require me to be in an enclosed space with him, possibly make small talk, not to mention that being seen in a car with a boy, especially one that was white, would cause all sorts of rumors. The thought made me uncomfortable, and I knew that my mom definitely wouldn't like it.

"You don' have to ovuh think it, Trace. I had to get somethin' out of my locker and I thought I'd be nice. So nod, say yes, and I'll meet you in tha carport aftuh tha bell. Does that work for you?"

I nodded. "Er…yes."

He shook his head. "Now's that so hard?"

When the final bell rang, I walked to the carport, half-way expecting Derek's car to not be where he said he would be, but it was.

"I see you didn' get detention for skippin' out on tha last few minutes of gym," he greeted as I got in the car. "Did you miss out on learnin' any new exercises?"

"I suppose that's supposed to be funny?" I demanded.

The tops of Derek's ears turned red. "Othuh people would've thought so," he mumbled. He toyed with the radio. "You don' mind do you? What station do you like to listen to?"

"I don't listen to the radio all that often," I responded. In my mom's car she was the only one allowed to touch it, and it stayed on AAMU's-the Alabama Agricultural and Mechanical University-student run station, 90.9, which played mostly only gospel.

He gave me a sidelong look. "You're kiddin', right?"

"No. I find the background noise distracting."

Derek was momentarily lost at my response. "God, you sound like my parents. Come on, you gotta listen ta somethin'? Who don' like Rock & Roll? Soul? Tha Beatles, tha Byrds?"

"I like classical music," I said with a shrug. "Occasionally I listen to the Bell Musical Hour, nothing really current."

Derek shook his head. Fishing for something else to say, he questioned, "Are you goin' to tha game Friday night?"

To be honest, I didn't even know that there was one. "What game?" I questioned.

"Tha football game," he said incredibly.

"Oh…no, I'm not."

This seemed to irritate him for some reason. "Why not?"

"It's not my kind of thing."

"What *is* your kind of thing?" he questioned. "I mean othuh than sittin' at home and studyin'. You do realize that you're like, what…fifteen?"

"I'm fourteen," I responded, my back stiffening, "and I was actually well aware of that fact, but thank you for bringing that to my attention." I turned in the seat, staring out the window.

"I just…I was tryin' uh make conversation," Derek spluttered to my back. I turned back around reluctantly, but my posture didn't relax, my arms didn't uncross.

"Are you and Carol going to the game tomorrow?" I questioned, just to be conversational.

"Of course! We've got spirit, yes we do," he pretended to shake some Pom-Poms. "We got spirit, how 'bout you?"

"I do well academically," I replied. "Best show of spirit there is."

He lowered his hands with a sigh. "One of these days, kid, you're goinna realize there's more to tha world than facts and figures."

"I could say the same about clothes and music," I snipped.

"Hey, there's nothin' in this world greatuh than music," he declared, loftily. He turned up the volume on the radio, and as too fast, drum-heavy music filled the car, I remembered Ricky's note and opened it. It was a lot longer than I was expecting it to be, but like the notes that Patrice and I passed back and forth throughout the course of the day, it said a lot without saying much of anything.

"What's that?" Derek questioned, actually taking his eyes off the road in an attempt to make out some of the words.

I didn't look up, or over at him, but I did raise my shoulder a little self-consciously. I hated people reading over my shoulder. "Note from Preacher," I responded, absently.

"Your pastor writes you notes?" he said in wonder. "Like some Psalms to ponder ovuh your sandwich?"

"No. It's from a guy," I responded. "Preacher's a nickname."

"Oh," he remarked, followed by a moment of silence. "What's it say?"

"Note things," I responded. "Apparently Preacher wants to know the same thing that you do; if I'm going to the game."

"So're you goin' now?"

I wondered why he was asking me that question again when I'd already answered it. "No, I told you, it wasn't my thing."

"Is this 'Preacher' someone you like?"

"He's a nice enough guy," I responded. I looked over at Derek. "Oh, like that…no. I don't date."

"Then what do you do?" he wondered in exasperation. I didn't really feel like answering, so I didn't. The silence stretched. "You don' like me very much do you," Derek questioned suddenly, baldly. It startled me enough to get me to look back at him.

"W-what makes you ask that?" I returned, not answering.

"Well you don', do you?"

"I never said I didn't."

"But you don'," Derek insisted.

"I didn't know that I was supposed to," I replied.

"Everyone likes me," he stated.

I couldn't see that as really being true. I mean I knew that people liked him well enough, but I was nearly certain that 'everyone' didn't. "I'm not everyone," I responded, and added, "I don't really know you well enough to make a flat judgment, but no, I suppose from what I know, I don't."

He made a choking sound. "Wow, honest to tha point of bein' flawed. You could've lied uh little, you know." I probably should've lied a little, I thought a moment after he said the words. It was probably a bad idea to insult the person that was giving you a ride.

"You asked," I remarked a little defiantly, "so I answered. I imagine that you don't like me very much either, so it balances out perfectly."

A smile teased the corners of his lips. "Who says I don' like you, Trace?" he questioned. "For all you know, I could be very fond of you."

"That's unlikely," I decided. He laughed to himself.

I finished reading Preacher's note before tucking the paper in the back of the book I was reading. Three pages went by before Derek spoke again. I realized that we were in the Evans parking lot. "So there was somethin' I wanted to ask you about Bridges."

"You're dropping off the project?"

"Why do you sound so excited about that?"

I thought about my recent reaction. "I didn't," I determined.

"No, Trace, you're still stuck wit' me." I couldn't understand the sudden anxiousness in his voice. "Actually, I had this idea. I's thinkin' that since Halloween's comin' up we could do somethin' really special wit' tha kids, like make monsters or somethin', and then let them describe their creations to tha class, in French. What d'ya think?"

It sounded like a lot of work that I'd most likely end up doing. "That… sounds like an idea," I responded, diplomatically.

"I thought maybe we could do it at tha end of tha week, or tha beginnin' of next week."

"I don't think that I'd be able to put something together that quickly," I stated.

"I wasn' askin' you to," Derek said defensively. "I'm halfway competent, yanno?" he gestured. "Just tha other day, I tied my shoes for myself."

"I didn't mean it like that," I said quickly, realizing how it must have sounded to him. "If you want to do it, I don't see a problem with that. If you wait until next week you'd have more time to put it together, and we can make sure that the kids know what to expect…"

"Glad ta have your permission," Derek grumbled.

I waited a moment to see if he would say anything else, but when no other words seemed forthcoming, I reached for the door handle. Derek immediately jumped out of the car in an attempt to open the door for me, but I beat him to it. "Want me to carry your books?" he wondered. He bit down on his lip right after the words were spoken, as if he hadn't meant them.

I pulled my items to my body, as if he might take them from me. "No, I've got it," I replied. He lagged when I started for the doors to the school. "You can go on," he directed, "I need to check somethin' out on tha car. I'll be in, in uh minute."

As I headed toward Mrs. Gunter's third grade classroom, I wondered if he was going to cut out on me. I didn't put it past him. He'd think it was a great joke. The kids started coming in, and Derek still hadn't made his way to the classroom. I was about to get started without him when he finally sauntered in. My eyes narrowed at his appearance. "What were you doing?" I wondered in a voice low enough that the kids wouldn't hear.

Derek gave me a sideways glance before sitting a paper bag on the table. Without answering, he took a step out into the hallway and brought in a yellow and purple dollhouse, placing it on the table next to his grocery bag. He instantly had everyone's attention. With wide eyes, and expectant grins, all the kids stopped to watch to see what their buddy was about to do this time. Deliberately slow, and well aware of his audience, he pulled out a creature made from Elmer's glue, Popsicle sticks, Q-tips, cotton balls, and construction paper. He held him up for everyone to see. "Bonjour, c'est John Luc," he began with gusto. "Tout le monde," he gestured to the kids, "dit à 'Bonjour, Jean-Luc'!"

They laughed even as they chorused in response to his command, "Bonjour, Jean-Luc!"

Derek looked at me deliberately, casting a stern look my way as his hands went to his hips. "Tout le monde means *everyone*, Tracy, can you say 'Bonjour' to Jean-Luc?"

With a practiced effort not to tighten my lips, or to let my irritation show at his antics, I said, "Bonjour".

Derek accurately read my expression. He grinned triumphantly to himself. "Jean-Luc ees ze monster," he declared. "He's ah terre-fying, scarrree monster." Derek made the stick creature wave his arms. A couple of the kids giggled. "Jean-Luc likes to hide sous le lit, alors que vous dormez. Who knows where Jean-Luc likes to hide?"

A timid hand went in the air. "Under the bed?"

"When?"

"When I'm sleeping," the timid girl responded.

"Exactement! Anyone know ze monster like Jean Luc?"

Hands shot up eagerly. Derek smiled, carefully not looking at me. "Aujourd'hui Jean-Luc has invited his friends overre to play," he went on. "So, what you arre goin' to do ees you're each goin' to create your own scarree monsters with zeese," he dumped the contents of his bag out on the table, filling it with art supplies similar to what Derek's 'monster' had been made from.

"An' zen you ahre going to pick zay room in ze house zat your monster likes to live in, an action zat zay're doing, what zey do to try to scare you, and zen you will share your monster avec ze class and tell us about him, en Français! If you get stuck on how to say uh word, look first in tha workbook, and if you still don' know, Miss Tracy and I will help you."

Once he gave the go-ahead, the kids attacked the supplies. I didn't move immediately, mildly in shock. I was used to Derek interrupting lessons, but this was a new one for me. One of the kids, Tyler, tugged on my arm. "Are you going to make a monster, Miz Tracy?" he questioned. Derek looked over, hiding a smile. "You can use some of my paper, and I can help," he directed, ushering me into the seat beside him.

I took the proffered sheet of paper. "What kind of monster should I make," I questioned, offhandedly.

"A giant, purple one," he answered enthusiastically, "with big teeth, and big hands to grab people with, like this!" He demonstrated for me.

"What're you making?" I questioned.

"Lumpkin," was his response. "He lives in the closet and attacks you if you don't put away your shoes. He likes shoes," Tyler finished solemnly. I hid my own smile at his words, caught Derek's eye, and we both snickered.

We were so occupied with the project, that we lost track of time, and were still working when the parents came in to collect their children. One of the girls, Mary, jumped up immediately to show her mom what they were working on, and I listened to her eagerly rattle off in French about her monster. I didn't realize until then that Derek had combined two lessons into the one project.

When all the kids were gone, and Derek and I were left alone to pack up all the supplies and materials, Derek looked at me expectantly. "Well? Go 'head. Let me hear it."

"Hear what?" I asked, reaching for a stray crayon.

"I know you're dyin' ta tell me off," he declared.

I was confused by his reaction. "No, I'm not. Actually...I was going to say that I thought your monster idea was a good one-"

"Don' sound so surprised," Derek instructed.

"-I just wish you had told me about it before you did it, though."

"I did tell ya," Derek replied.

"You know what I mean."

"I didn' know I had to clear my plans wit' you."

I sighed. "You don't have to clear your plans with me," I corrected, "I'd just like it if we were on the same page. I'm your partner, you know. You don't have to fight me all the time."

"I wasn' fightin' you, Trace," he responded, hotly, "but I knew that if I'da brought it up to ya, you'd put it down, tha way you did in tha car earlier. This was tha only way I could do it; prove to you that I could so that you could see that I could. Otherwise you woulda thought it was stupid. I didn' miss your reaction in tha car."

"You just kind of sprang it on me."

"But you see it was uh really good idea."

"Yes, it was," I agreed, "but do you honestly blame me for being skeptical about you? All you ever do in class is disrupt it, and well…you don't exactly seem like you're interested in any of this, you know? Every time I try to get your opinion, you don't ever offer anything."

"Because you don' trust my opinions when I offuh 'em," Derek returned.

"That's because all you ever do is joke around."

"Maybe you should try it 'stead uh bein' so serious all tha time," he returned.

"I'm not serious all the time," I declared. "I'm serious when it's appropriate, and I have fun in the proper medium."

"In 'the proper medium'," he said, imitating me. "Geez, d'you evuh get uh listen at yourself, Trace? When do you have fun? If I left things solely to you, this would be like some French language boot camp: 'Learn French or Die!' These are 7 and 8 year olds here!"

"And the remedy for that is not to act just like they do. Children need structure. There's playtime, and there's time to work. All you ever want to do is play…"

"And all you evuh want to do is work!" he returned. "You act like there's somethin' wrong wit' havin' fun. Those kids'd like you uh lil more if you learned ta lighten up."

Since Derek was so busy always being their buddy, if I did we'd never get anything done. "Because of you, I can't!" I asserted. "You make it all about having fun. One of us has to be serious at some point, and you made sure it had to be me!"

"Don' try'n blame me for that! You were serious before you evuh met me! I bet you sit at home on Friday nights and do homework!"

I wondered what one had to do with the other. "And I'm sure you don't!"

"How much time d'you actually spend wit' people your own age?" he demanded.

"Who I spend my time with is none of your business, and different people have different concepts of fun."

"I bet anytime you find yourself enjoyin' anythin' too much you stop doin' it."

"I don't appreciate how you presume to know me so well. I actually enjoy studying! I like to read books, and I like learning new things. That is what I *enjoy* doing, and I enjoy the company of the people around me. Just because I don't find you as funny as you find yourself, doesn't mean that I don't have fun! I don't have to make a fool of myself to have fun."

His face was red at that statement, and I could see his anger growing. "No, you just get your pleasure in pretendin' that you're better'n everyone else, right?"

His words stopped me up short. "What're you talking about?"

"Oh come on: you treat that desk of yours like it's some type of throne, and you wait for tha rest of us to make idiots of ourselves before you give tha answuh you knew ten minutes ago, just to prove how much smarter you are!"

My jaw dropped, indignant with the falseness of that statement. "If I said the answer every time I knew it, I'd be accused of being a know-it-all, and if someone else knows the answer, I don't see anything wrong with allowing them to answer the question first. Do you know how boring the class would be if no one participated? As you can see, it's hard for a teacher to stand in front of a room at all, even harder when the students aren't interested in learning."

I pointed my hand at him, which was still filled with spare crayons and

Q-tips, the cleanup temporarily forgotten. "And don't act as if you don't think that you're better than your classmates, or at least Mrs. Diece, because you do!"

"How d'you figure?"

"Penguin?" I reminded him.

"Tha's uh joke!"

"That you made at her expense," I remarked.

"Well 'scuse me for not bein' as perfect as you," Derek said, snidely.

"I don't pretend to be perfect," I stated, "but I do try to treat the people around me the way that I would like to be treated, and I'm sure Mrs. Diece is well aware of the way she walks. She doesn't need someone to tell her about it. So, yes, you do act like you're better than your classmates because you do whatever it takes to interrupt her class, so you must think that what you have to say is more important than whatever she does. I'm not the only one in the class who wants to learn. Why do you have to tear someone down because of it?"

"D'ya really think that knowin' how to say 'ball' in French is goinna change your life?" he jeered.

"Maybe not," I reasoned, "but knowing how to be open to new things will. And my Grandpa speaks French, so that's something that we'd have to share, not to mention that if I work outside of this country, I'm going to need to know how to correspond with those that speak languages other than my own. When you learn another language, you also learn culture, and word origins, which will help me when I take my college boards.

"And Mrs. Diece is a very nice woman. At the least she deserves your respect because of what she does. So it does not matter if that class will or will not change my life, I have every right to get as much out of it as possible!"

"You're such uh goody-goody, you know that," he said, hotly.

"And you're an ass!"

Derek blinked in surprise, his eyes twinkling as he tried to hide it. "My, I didn' know you used such language," he mocked.

"You bring it out in me," I responded, frostily. "I can't even give you a *compliment* without you being a jerk about it!"

"That's on'y 'cause I know how much it pained you to say it." He hesitated. "You know somethin', Trace? If you evuh decide to become human, no one'll hate you too much for it."

— 8 —
"Racing Thoughts"

D o you think I act like I'm better than everyone else?" I questioned.

Patrice seemed thrown off by the question. "No," she answered immediately, but then really considered the question. "But that's only cause I know you. Someone who don' know you so well probably'd say yes."

I was a bit thrown by her honesty. "Why?" I wondered earnestly.

She actually took a minute to think about it. "Well, you can come off kinda…superior, sometimes," she said, honestly, "but that's because you're confident. Like in Biology, you're good at it, so you're confident that when Colben asks a question, you'll know tha answwuh. So, when he calls on you, you don' mumble tha answwuh like most uh us do, and you sound confident in your response. That might make it seem that you think you're better'n everyone else, when really it's just confidence. You get what I mean?" I could understand what she was saying, even though I didn't like the thought of people thinking that I thought I was better than them; especially since I spent so much time wondering if I was as good as they were. "You different girl," she declared, digging her elbow into my side, trying to change the look of concentration on my face. "You still sound like a Yank," she smiled, "and you on't dress like everyone else-,"

"Only because my mom can't afford the latest fashions, and what not," I interjected.

"-and you carry yourself differently, too."

"So do you."

"And you *know* people think I'm fulla myself. But it's different for me cause I relate ta folks. I tawk like dem," she said, emphasizing her southern accent in contrast to my lack of one. "I hang 'round them. I'm one uh them, and always will be. You, it's like you know you're different, and you don' even have tha decency ta feel 'shamed 'bout it. You have that whole temporary air about ya, too; like you're only here for a while. And you're pretty, so people get weird about you, and then they turn it 'gainst you, like you're stand-offish 'gainst them, cause folks don' know what ta do wit you." She paused in her evaluation. "What brings this up?"

"Derek." A familiar grin grew across her face at those words, and I was beginning to think she had something for him. "What's the grin for?" I wondered. She shook her head, still smiling.

Frankie was waiting outside my house when I left Patrice's. "So what'd she say," he questioned eagerly. I'd forgotten all about Cecilia until I saw him standing there. He was actually bouncing on his feet, waiting for my answer. "Did you give it to her, yet?"

I opened the door, and he followed me inside. "I gave it to her," I responded.

We went into the kitchen. "Well, what'd she say?" he prompted.

"Nothing."

He frowned. "What do you mean nothing?" he wondered, staring at me, looking for any clue. I didn't have any to offer.

"She didn't say anything," I reiterated. "She just took the note."

He frowned, his eyes traveling. "That's it?"

"Yes."

He seemed to be searching for something redeeming in our conversation. "Well…w-what'd she say when you told her it was from me?" he questioned. "What'd you say, and what'd she say back to you. I mean everything?"

I tried to recall the exact words. "I said that Frankie wanted me to give this to you, and she was like 'Frankie?' and I said 'Frankie Banks'."

"That's it?" he demanded, deflating.

"That's it," I assured him, certain I'd gotten everything.

"Hum." He collapsed onto the kitchen chair, looking miserable. "Should I write her another note?" he wondered aloud.

I didn't see what good that would do. "Why waste your time?"

"It wouldn't be a waste of time. The Founder's celebration is in a month."

"Why don't you just talk to her?" I questioned.

"I wouldn't know what to say," he said, resting his head in his hands.

"Why not just tell her what you tell me?"

"S'not that simple," he said, morosely. "I suppose if she doesn't go with me, I could always take you, but I really want Cecilia to go with me."

"I have feelings you know," I reminded him.

Frankie's head rolled over to look at me. "What do you mean? You know what I mean, Tracy. We're friends. I'm talking about a sweetheart. Would ya talk to her again for me?" he wondered. "I mean just remind her about my note?"

"I guess so," I responded. I wondered why he wasn't asking Patrice to do all this for him since she was better at the whole match maker thing anyway.

At school on Monday, I got to History early, hopefully so I could catch Cecilia for a moment before the bell. Derek was, as usual, hanging out around the doorway. He nodded at me as I walked into the classroom, and in an attempt to be friendlier, I gave a nod back at him as I walked past. Cecilia and Vie came into the room dressed in the same dress, Cecilia's yellow, Vie's pink. They wore matching hair ribbons, and matching shoes, too. How nice it must be, to be them and have no worries past coordinating the perfect outfit.

I put on as fake a smile as I could muster. "You guys look very nice today," I remarked, cordially. Cecilia glanced down her nose at my white blouse and plain A-line gray skirt.

"You...too," she remarked, prissily. *This is for Frankie*, I reminded myself.

"Frankie wanted me to ask you if you read his note," I said. "I think he really wants to go to the Founder's Day celebration with you."

Vie and Cecilia turned to each other and giggled little tinkling giggles. "Does he?" Cecilia wondered.

"Yes."

She whispered something to Vie, before speaking to me. "Well, then, why hasn't *he* asked me to go with him himself, then," she questioned, and beside her Vie nodded.

I rolled my eyes at the stupidity of it, and closed them, trying to refocus myself. "Because he doesn't go to Mason," I remarked simplistically.

Vie and Cecilia bowed their heads together, had a quick whispered conversation, and giggled some more.

"Well you can tell Frankie that if he would like me to go anywhere with him, he'd best to ask me out himself. Tell him he can call me tonight, if he'd like."

"I'll pass that along to him," I remarked. "Frankie's a real good guy," I added, feeling the need to put in a good word for my friend. "You should give him a chance."

Cecilia gave me a dismissive look. "Thanks," she remarked.

I headed back to my seat just as the bell was ringing. Dewitt seized on me. "Tracy," he said, shortly. "Take this to Mr. Wilks." He wrote out a hall pass, tore it off, and kind of threw it at me. "Go on now, and you wait for him to write you back a response."

Despite his insulting tone, I willingly left the classroom, glad for any excuse to miss his lecture. Dewitt wasn't just a butcher of history; he was completely self-absorbed, too. He'd often go off on ten or fifteen minute tangents about himself and his family. If you could believe what he said, Coach Dewitt was distantly related to both Jefferson Davis and George Washington. He'd once met President Johnson in the men's room of a gentleman's club in D.C., and when asked what he thought of America, he had replied he thought it was a 'great society'. Coach Dewitt had also once single-handedly won the county football title for Mason High, and has hit a hole-in-one on every single hole on the green at the Bakersfield Country Club. His wife was once Miss Bakersfield, his father was once a principal, too, since great educators ran in his family... and on and on.

"Now, what's this? Tracy Burrows actually in tha halls aftuh tha bell?" I slowed at the sound of Derek's voice.

"Don't you ever get in trouble for always being late for class?" I wondered. I hadn't sounded too friendly when I said the words, so I forced a smile, hoping that made up for it.

Even from the corner of my eye, I could tell he smiled. "Do it bothuh you?"

"I'm not as big a stickler for the rules as you think I am." I responded.

"Yea, right."

"It's not the rules that I care about," I insisted. "I'm college bound. I don't want anything to ruin that."

"Isn' gettin' uh detention goinna mess that up?"

I realized he was talking about being in the hall after the bell. "I've got a pass," I remarked. "Dewitt wanted me to pass along a note to Wilks."

This seemed to get his interest. "What's it say?" he questioned, eagerly.

"I didn't read it," I declared.

Derek started reaching for it. "Give it here'n I will!"

I held the note closer to me. "No!"

"You're such uh teacher's pet, you know that?" he teased.

"No, I'm just not that interested in Dewitt's personal thoughts," I responded.

"Personal?" he blew out a breath in doubt. "It's probably 'bout baseball. Coach Dewitt and Wilks are as bad as girls 'bout passin' notes."

I stopped where I was, crossing my arms. "As bad as whom?" I demanded.

He took a moment to seem sheepish. "Ah, you know what I mean."

"If I'm not mistaken, you pass just as many notes yourself. Carol's always got a new one, anyway."

Derek turned red, though he smiled. "S'not tha same thing at all," he remarked. He suddenly seemed worried. "She don' let you read them, do she?"

"We're not that close," I assured him.

He seemed satisfied with my answer. "Well, good. I'd waguh you and that Preacher pass just as many notes, so no sense in you makin' fun of me."

"Preacher and I don't pass notes," I clarified. "Not a lot anyway."

"Passin' notes beneath you?" he teased. "Wouldn' want to interrupt Dewitt's lecture?"

My mouth worked before I realized what it was saying. "If I thought Dewitt had anything worth writing down, perhaps."

I snapped my mouth closed, but not before Derek's face took on a look of surprised delight. "Are *you* bein' critical of uh teacha, Tracy?" he questioned, mockingly. "You?"

"Teachers who only have jobs because of their cousins don't count." It was widely known that the only reason that Dewitt worked at Mason was because he and Principal Vaughn were related.

"Isn' Dewitt somethin'," Derek said in wonder.

"Who God?" I questioned. Dewitt reminded me of Jody from *Their Eyes* with all of his 'I, god's'. Dewitt postured around as if he was one of God's greater creations, and in fact, sometimes I wasn't quite sure if he *was* one of God's creations, or if he, Coach Dewitt, had created God, to hear him tell of it. Even though his God given blonde hair was steadily in the process of turning gray, and he was old enough to be our parent's age, he still skipped around the classroom as if he were reliving his glory days.

After I said the words, I worried that Derek would take them as being sacrilegious so I added, "Dewitt just seems to posture around as if he were greater than God."

I caught Derek's sideways glance. "He does, doesn' he? Did he tell you 'bout tha time that he won tha state title? How he ran tha football in from 80 yards out in tha last few seconds of tha game, wit' uh broken leg?"

"A broken arm, too, wasn't it?"

"Next thing you know he's goinna say that he snapped, caught, and threw tha ball to himself." Derek laughed, and I smiled, quickly covering it up when I realized that we had shared a moment. "Tha only thing worse than Dewitt, is Dewitt tha second." Derek went on, not noticing my response.

To me the whole family wasn't worth much. Although Dewitt acted like his children were preparing for the sainthood, it was rumored that it barely took the cost of the movie to get his daughter, Shelly, to park, and although Dewy looked like the perfect angel, he was the kind of guy who'd pick a fight, then turn around and tell his dad so that person would get in trouble. "I don't think anyone's going to be upset when Dewy graduates," I remarked. "Him or Shelly. God the way she flutters around this school as if she smells like roses..."

The grin that formed was almost too big for his face. "Why, Tracy, I declare: that's tha first time I heard you insult anyone," Derek teased in a proper southern accent.

I hadn't meant to speak the words out loud. "I…just don't like her too much," I explained.

"We dated freshman year," Derek admitted, and I thought, *Hmm… another blonde.* "I go to church wit' tha Dewitt's. Can' get rid of them, actually. Roy and Dewy have been hangin' round togethuh, lately, so I get to see uh lot more of him than I'd like." He shook his head. "It's sad because Dewy's just usin' Roy, and Roy don' see that."

I stopped suddenly to face him. "Why're you friends with Roy?" I demanded. Derek could be a clown, but Roy was downright mean. He was gangly, awkward, poor and ornery, and angry at just about everyone, especially non-whites. He called women nasty names, and spoke derogatorily toward Blacks and Mexicans. He had the air of trying to command his presence, but no one took him seriously, which made him angrier. By themselves they were no picnic, but Dewy and Roy together were a holy terror.

Derek shrugged. "Our moms were friends," he remarked. "And I mean Roy can be alright…sometimes. Don' you have any friends that…don' make sense?"

His words made me think about my relationship with my best friend. At times it seemed that we had absolutely nothing in common, and it still surprised me, every now and then, that despite our differences, we were still friends. "I have Patrice," I replied, thinking about how oddly matched we seemed, "but she's not mean," I asserted, "and Roy, he can be a devil sometimes."

Derek kind of kicked at the ground. "I know…but he gets it hard, and I might not like all of tha things he says and does, but everyone needs uh friend."

That was true. I couldn't imagine being friends with someone like Roy, but maybe I should be able to. Maybe all guys like him needed was a good friend. I admired Derek, (slightly, imperceptibly even), for trying.

"So, why don't you ever get in trouble for being late to class?" I wondered, mostly to change the subject.

Derek smiled. "I have Warner," he chirped. Warner was one of the football coaches and the junior history teacher. "He don' give uh lick 'bout nothin," he remarked.

"Oh," I responded. We reached the end of the history corridor. We'd actually reached it some time ago, but we had lingered.

"I guess, I'll be gettin' to class," Derek remarked. "See you latuh, Trace. Pick you up, okay?"

"Okay," I responded. Derek backtracked to get to his class, and I went on to deliver Dewitt's note to Wilks.

— 9 —
"Night Watch"

Mrs. Taylor answered the door in a hurry, looking distinctly disheveled. "Come in," she said, breathlessly. "I should be back in they mornin' 'round six; no later than eight. Nicole's already eaten, and Orion may or may not come over while I'm gone. If he does show up, he won' stay, so I'm goin' still need you. I left a plate warmin' for y'all in they cooler," she looked at me. "And y'all welcome to cook. You know her bedtime and everythan; don't let her stay up too late, and don't let her trick y'all into eatin' junk, neither."

"Yes, ma'am," we both chorused in unison.

"And you know they house rules?"

"No boys."

"And?" she prodded, giving the best stern look she could muster, though she still had nothing on Mrs. Gordon.

"Definitely, no boys."

Mrs. Taylor seemed in momentary contemplation of us, as she was every time we were over. "Well, I know y'all be good girls, so I don't have to worry," she decided. "The number for they hospital's on they fridge. Goodnight, girls. Night Nicky, mama loves you."

"Night, mummy," Nicole responded. Mrs. Taylor hastily walked out the door to her car, backing out the drive so quickly she scraped the bottom of the car as she did. Patrice, who was currently wearing a wholesome blue jumper, went into the bathroom to change, and a few minutes later, Omar's dad's beat up Bentley rolled into Mrs. Taylor's space. He honked twice, and Patrice squealed. "Oh, that's him!" she fluttered in her skirt. "How I look? Did I tell you that you're tha best for doin' this for me?"

"You might have mentioned it," I remarked.

"Well, you're tha best girl," she remarked, giving me a big hug and a kiss. "I should be back no later'n midnight, so just leave tha door open will ya?"

"Yep."

Patrice spun where she was, before she remembered the youngest person in the room. "You're pretty groovy, too, Nicole," Patrice remarked, giving her a Hershey bar, as per agreement. She bent down and kissed the little girl as well. Omar honked again. "See you latuh," she said, before heading out the door. Omar stepped out of the car, and she ran into his arms. He caught her up, and gave her a kiss before he packed her into the car, and the two of them drove off.

I looked down at Nicole as she looked up at me. We both shrugged.

We went into the living room (the Taylor's didn't have a den), and Nicole sat down to eat her candy bar. "I should've held out for some bottle caps and Mary Jane's, too," she mused.

"How about I bring you some the next time I come over?" I offered.

"Really?" she questioned excitedly. "Hey, didja bring your records with you?"

I went reaching for my bag. "I brought Mozart's 5th and some Tchaikovsky."

"Ode to Joy would have been perfect playing in the background when Tricey ran down the drive, don't you think," Nicole reflected. I couldn't help but laugh at the statement and image it created.

Nicole was the kind of kid that it was rewarding to baby-sit for. She was six years old, but didn't act like it at all. Her school work might not have earned the highest marks, she may have been passing at spelling and her math was on par, but she was the most theatric little person I'd ever come across. Any and everything that had to do with theatre, or the stage, fascinated her. We shared a mutual appreciation for classical music because it went along with theatre. On one other occasion when I was babysitting, she had begun what seemed like a promising sketch to Vivaldi's *Cello Concerto in A Minor*. She thought it sounded like squirrels fighting over acorns, and the resulting dance that she came up with had me and Patrice laughing until we cried.

After Nicole got dressed in her nightgown, we put on my Tchaikovsky .45, and I read to her from *King Lear*. We both played around with reciting the lines in different accents, some horribly horrible, some so amusing that we couldn't stop laughing. We were settling down, falling into somewhat of a stupor, when someone knocked on the door. I figured it was Orion, but still went to check cautiously.

"Hello?" I questioned.

I couldn't see who the knocker was. "'S me. Open up!" I opened the door only slightly, and noticed Derek at the same moment he noticed me. "What're you doing here?" we both wondered. His familiar smile crept up on his features, and as soon as I realized I was wearing a similar one, I attempted to hide it. Until that moment, I'd forgotten that Derek had said that he'd known Orion.

"You goinna lemme in?" Derek wondered.

"Depends…are you allowed in the house?"

"Uh ha ha," Derek said. I hadn't been joking, but I didn't want to let him know that. I stepped back to allow him to cross over the threshold.

There was a rush of movement as soon as Derek stepped inside. "Derek!" Nicole called familiarly. To my surprise, she ran over to him, and jumped into his arms, planting a kiss on his forehead. It took me a second to realize that she was acting in imitation of Patrice and Omar from earlier.

"Hey little bit, how's it goin'?" Derek asked. He hugged her, mussed her hair, and sat her back on the ground. The whole thing was so familiar that it caught me off guard.

She bounced in place. "Great now that *you're* here!" she enthused.

"I only came ovuh for uh sec-," he warned her.

As soon as the words were started, Nicole's lip came poking out. "Oh," she said, softly. "Okay." She turned towards her bedroom as if she were willingly going to bed on her own.

"I guess I can stay uh few minutes," Derek relented, and she turned around quickly, smile back on her face.

"Really?" she wondered, hamming it up. "You're the greatest, Dare! I've been working on this new piece," she remarked. "Wanna see it?"

Derek gave me a look that was a mix between embarrassment, and some other strong emotion. "Sure, what'cha got?"

She went running into her bedroom and emerged fully dressed. She planted her feet, gave a brief look around the living room making sure that both of us were watching her, closed her eyes, and took a deep breath. "Friends," she began dramatically; well not so much dramatic as all inclusive, "Romans…countrymen," her voice lowered imperceptibly, so we leaned in closer towards her to hear her words. "Lend me your ears." She surveyed us, judging our temperaments. "I have come not to praise Caesar," she scoffed, curling her fingers into a fist, "But to bury him!" she slapped her fist into her palm at those words.

She continued with her soliloquy, speaking with more understanding and emphasis than you'd expect from a child her age. She strutted around her little space, commanding it, serious as a heart attack. I was familiar with Nicole's theatrics from babysitting her before, but I'm sure she gave a little more because Derek was there watching her with all the attentiveness of a boy watching his favorite little sister. She knew that she had Derek wrapped around her finger, and she milked it. When she ended, I wanted to start chanting "Caesar!" and was ready to march against those who had dared to betray the greatest member of the triumvirate.

Derek pretended to throw flowers. "Bravo," he cheered, clapping enthusiastically at her conclusion.

"It's *brava*!" Nicole corrected him. She gave a low curtsy. "I'm a lady."

Derek paused, mid-clap. "Well I thought that since I's listenin' to Mark Anthony that 'bravo' would be more appropriate."

"It's always brava," Nicole asserted.

"Well, then, bra…*va*… Madame."

"Thank ya kindly, sir," she remarked, lapsing into a *Gone With the Wind*-esqe southern belle accent, "I appreciate yo-or concession." It was hard to imagine that Nicole was only six years old. It was often easy to forget that after spending more than a few minutes with her.

Derek laughed heartily, his eyes twinkling with the effort. I was more than a bit surprised by the intimacy the two of them shared. They were so comfortable with each other that I wondered how often they spent time around the other. Nicole clearly loved Derek, and Derek adored her. She curtsied to Derek again, giggling as she did so.

"All right, now," I remarked, feeling as if I should assert some sort of authority. "Back in your nightgown.

She corner turned towards me, saluted, and went back into her bedroom departing with a "And Nicole departs."

Derek's laughter followed her out of the room. "Wow," I remarked. Not knowing what else to say, I said it again. "Wow."

"She's somethin', ain't she?" Derek said in wonder.

"She quotes Shakespeare," I stated.

"Orion's doing," Derek explained. "He'd read it to her at bed time. She loves plays. Anythin' wit' stage directions and she's captivated."

"And I get all the best parts in the plays we put on in church and school," she remarked, coming into the room, dressed again in her pajamas. *"And* I never forget any of my lines, unlike my other classmates."

"Of course you don', lil bit," Derek agreed. "Because you're tha best," he assured her. She beamed. "And 'course you wouldn' be tryin' to sneak up past your bedtime would ya? You're not givin' Miss Tracy here uh hard time, is you?"

I came to her defense. "No, she's not," I remarked. "We were actually drifting off to sleep before you knocked."

Derek looked at his wrist watch. "Isn't it uh little early for you?" he wondered.

"It's contagious," I remarked, yawning and giving my own little bit of theatrics. "Are you ready to go to bed?" I questioned of Nicole.

"Can't we at least finish Lear?" she wondered. "Please, Tracy? Just the rest of the act?"

Derek puffed out his lips, and batted his eyes. "Puh-lease, Trace," he imitated. "Pretty please?" I couldn't help but laugh along with Nicole.

Nicole got *Lear* and curled up on the couch, beneath her blanket, stretching out between the two of us. She insisted that Derek and I take turns reading while she listened. I stopped reading in the fake accents, but when Derek read, he hammed it up for Nicole's benefit. Near the end of the scene, he stopped reading suddenly and tapped my shoulder. Nicole had fallen asleep curled against him. Very carefully he stood up, lifting her as he did. I followed him as he put her in her bed, and tucked her in. Derek looked up when he was finished, as if he had momentarily forgotten that I was here.

We quietly walked back into the living room, and I started to clean up the little mess we'd made. Derek moved to help, folding up the afghan and draping it back over the back of couch. "So, you never answered my question," I said.

Derek turned to look at me. "What question's that?"

"What're you doing here?"

"You didn' eithuh," he noted.

"I asked you first."

"I think we ast each othuh at tha same time," Derek declared with a sideways grin. "I came ovuh to see Orion. I told ya that I live right across tha street. I needed to get somethin' from him. And you?"

"I'm babysitting for Patrice so that she could go to the dance."

"You didn' want to go? Didn' Preacher ask you?" I didn't comment. Derek looked contrite as soon as he said that. "I'm sorry; that ain't really my business."

"I didn't say that he did or didn't," I remarked. "I wasn't going to the dance so I said I'd baby-sit. Nicole's just as entertaining."

"That she is," Derek remarked fondly, sitting down on the couch as he said the words.

"Weren't you going to the dance?" I wondered.

"What? Umm, yeah, I was…am. Any chance Orion said when he'd be back?"

"I haven't even seen him," I remarked. "So, no."

"Okay."

"I'll tell him that you came by."

"So what're you goinna do now that Nicole's in bed?" he wondered, not picking up on my subtleties.

"Probably read," I remarked. "Wait for Patrice to come back."

"Oh, so she didn' completely ditch you?"

"She didn't ditch me at all."

"Well, she's not here," Derek stated, looking around as if to prove that point.

— 86 —

I rolled my eyes. "Her dad won't let her date alone, so she told him she was baby-sitting so that she could go to the dance."

He wagged his finger at me in a mocking manner. "You women are sneaky."

"Oh, don't tell me you're a saint when it comes to Carol," I returned without hesitation.

Derek smiled to himself. "Course, I am," he remarked.

"I thought you said that you were going to the dance," I reminded him.

He jumped up suddenly, looking at his watch. "I am," he remarked. "Man, it's late," he added. "I'll see you 'round, I guess," he said on his way out the door. I watched him dash across the street before I shut the door behind him.

— 10 —
"The Shore Line"

Patrice and I paused to watch some kids blowing smoke rings into the air as if they were smoking cigarettes. We paused long enough to laugh at them, even though we had done the same thing when we were their ages. As we walked, I kept looking up at the sky, hoping that it showed some signs that this year there was actually going to be snow. Beside me, Patrice shivered in her heavy winter coat. "Does it hafta be *this* cold?" she muttered, increasing her pace.

"Do you think it's going to snow?" I mused.

"It feel like it's cold 'nough ta, don' it?"

I thought about the winters we'd had to endure in Illinois. "This isn't cold," I dismissed. I pointed to a shack in the distance. "Is that her house?" I questioned, uncertainly. The structure looked like something straight out of a history book; a slave quarters in the middle of our progressive city.

"Yea, that's it," Patrice mumbled.

The grayed wooden steps creaked as we climbed them, and it might've been my imagination, but I think that the house swayed a little when I knocked. "Come in," a small voice called from within. Patrice waved me forward. "Go on. She talkin' to you."

I opened the door to Miz Hattie's home and walked in. As soon as we were inside, Patrice gratefully went to the stone fireplace in the middle of the room, building up the fire that had almost gone out. Gradually, the room warmed a little. Miz Hattie's house was without electricity and running water, modern conveniences that, so far in my life, I'd never had to live without. It was made of wood, and seemed older than Miz Hattie herself, which said a lot. "Good afternoon, Miz Hattie," I remarked. "I'm Sybil's daughter, Tracy, and this is my friend, Patrice."

Miz Hattie, who, during the week cooked the deserts for the Sunset Diner and a couple of other places around town, and every Sunday sat perched in the front pew with flawless posture like a bird ready to swoop on the sinners, lay hunched under her blankets, looking pale and small despite her obvious size. She smiled warmly through her cough, though, as if us being there was the best gift she could have gotten. "Well lookit who dun come ta see me," she remarked, mostly to herself. "Go on'n sit. Sorry I ain't the best right this moment; the devil's got muh health, but they Lord woke me up this mornin', sho nuff, so I's blessed. Amen!"

"Amen, ma'am, I reckon you is," Patrice responded. "We just came by ta keep you company and fix you somethin' ta eat."

Miz Hattie nodded. "Well, I's sho 'preciate you, and I kno' ya soon's I look atcha. You's Ebbert's baby ain't choo?"

"Yes, ma'am, I is."

"Y'all can stay s'long's you like," she said, decidedly.

I dragged Patrice into the part of the room used as the kitchen. Miz Hattie'd recently fallen sick, and as one of the mothers of the church, she had people coming in just about every day to visit with her, cook for her, and clean up. Today just happened to be my turn to do it, and I brought Patrice along to help pass the time.

When we finally worked out how to get Miz Hattie's cast iron stove hot, Patrice fried some pork chops and potatoes, and after I remarked that she'd probably need something healthier to eat, put some greens on to cook. While she was cooking, I cleaned up what I could, swept out her wooden floors, changed her pot, and opened the windows to let some sunlight in. Her cabin was shabby, but certainly well taken care of, and cared for. She didn't have much, just a hodgepodge of furniture that was in varying degrees of decline, a few creature comforts, and two books: a much used bible, and a surprisingly well-read copy of *Carry on, Mr. Bowditch*.

There was no tray for us to put Miz Hattie's food on, so we put it on one of her tin plates, and brought it to her. Watching her eat was like watching a little baby. She only had a few teeth left, and she sort of gum-chewed her food. She fell asleep soon after, and Patrice and I finished cleaning, set some clothes out on the line, and went home.

For the next couple of weeks, I went over to Miz Hattie's place regularly, without being asked. Miz Hattie fascinated me to no end. I wanted to know every detail of the life that had brought her to the cabin that she was living in. She didn't have the same head for dates and figures as my Grandpa did, so I couldn't be as sure of her accuracy, but she was fun to listen to in any respect. It tickled her when I brought a notebook to record what she'd said down in, and told me that if I wanted to waste paper on her life, I could, but she didn't have anything interesting to tell me. I disagreed.

Miz Hattie had been born in Bakersfield in 1879, in that very same cabin that she was living in now. She had seen Bakersfield grow and flourish, and watched other places shrivel and die. She'd seen every one of her ten brothers and sisters killed or dead before she was forty, during her 'sinful years' had been a brazen young woman who "drank and smoked lak tha best uh dem, chile", had lost a child in the first War and two more to Polio, and had, in her youth, made her way from Bakersfield, Alabama, to Bakersfield, California, mostly on foot. Miz Hattie was the kind of woman who populated towns all across the south, who sat beside you in the church pew, who strengthened the heartbeat of the community, and were largely overlooked when the story of America was told. I'd done my own overlooking, and wanted to rectify my inadvertent neglect.

So, I started talking and interviewing her and some of the other elders of my church, and in the neighborhood, in order to get their stories. There was one couple I came across who "not even Gawd" (fingers crossed) "could separate." They had known each other all of their lives, had been married since they were sixteen, and were still married 64 years later. I think it was their intention to die at the same time, and were just waiting for the right day to go. Their lives seemed like strand after strand of sadness weaved together, but they still had each other.

My newly developed zeal led me to also interview some poorer Whites, Mexicans, and even a Chinese person who had lived in Bakersfield for years, widely ignored. Although it shouldn't have been, what was the most surprising was how similar the stories were to each other, and how eager people were to tell them; they just had to be asked. I wasn't sure what I was collecting, but I thought about putting a book together, *Voices of the Voiceless*, or something hokie like that. And even if I didn't put it all together in a book, I still wanted to have it. I didn't think that these people should pass on without a little part of their histories being known.

It also got me thinking a lot about the decisions that we made in life, the paths that we walked down. Miz Hattie was from a period I couldn't even fathom. She was only a generation removed from slavery, lived during a time when there had been even fewer options available for colored women; few chances for a bright future. Then, survival meant accepting your role in life, and not moving from where you were. But Miz Hattie had broken with the character of the times by taking her cross country trip, had operated outside of what was expected of her. Had she not, she would have lived, worked, and died, all within the confines of one very small paradigm.

I added this new project on top of the ones I was already doing, and time passed without regard to the things that made it up. In the way that high school relationships did, life-long loves ended abruptly, and new ones began. The blonde at first changed into the brown-headed girl who had laughed with Derek on the first day of class, and while Frankie became Cecilia's steady, Patrice and Omar broke up, and new guys quickly stepped in to fill the void.

Midterms showed on the horizon, and study hall became the most popular class around school. Bridges ended in December, and though Derek and I didn't suddenly become friends after our little argument, working with him did become easier. Derek stopped trying to be their buddy all the time, and I stopped acting like their school teacher. In December, when the kids took the evaluation test Larry and Mrs. Diece created, ours were the highest scorers. I breezed through my own midterms, and considered the possibility of graduating from high school early. As soon as I told my mom that idea, she gave me a flat 'no', and that was the end of that thought.

Once Bridges was over, the time that we'd spent doing the project became dedicated to preparing for the French Club convention in April. I faced the event with a certain amount of trepidation, not because of the competition, but because of the locale. Although Virginia was farther north than our own state's capstone of higher learning down in Tuscaloosa, I wasn't entirely sure that Mr. Wallace's sentiments of 'segregation now, segregation tomorrow, segregation forever' wouldn't be echoed in the sacred halls of Jefferson's University. The only thing I really knew about the University of Virginia was that a few years ago Dr. King had given a speech there about higher education being more accessible to minorities, but who knew if it left any resounding mark on the place? It took a good deal of work trying to convince my mom to allow me to go to the convention, since she didn't know the answer to that either.

On a Thursday, the second weekend of April, before prom and the final events of the year transpired, we got up at four in the morning, loaded down with more than a weekend's worth of stuff in order to survive those few precious days outside of our comfort zone. My teammates jockeyed for the best spots at the front and back of the bus, and I chose a spot dead in the middle.

While the bus seemed to fall into a stupor, I stayed up, self-conscious about falling asleep around my classmates. I located the notebook that I'd tucked away for this very occasion, and began writing. As Bakersfield slowly morphed into the highways of Tennessee, the sun dramatically rose in front of us, giving light to the world and illuminating one of the prettiest landscapes God had stopped to create. I wondered if Miz Hattie had taken the time to appreciate every sunrise as she moved cross country, or had that just been like a footnote, another breath of incredible that went by unnoticed in the process of the everyday. She hadn't gone through Tennessee anyway.

"It figures that you'd be tha one doin' homework on uh class trip." I recognized Derek's voice, sneer and all, before I even raised my eyes from my paper to see his head poking over the seat in front of me. From this angle, his hair fell helplessly in his eyes, and I wondered how he was ever able to see out of them. "Don' you evuh take uh break?"

Even though he'd interrupted a train of thought, for once he didn't sound antagonistic when he asked that, so I questioned, "Did you want something?" as cordially as possible, making a concentrated effort.

Derek gave just the slightest smirk, as if he knew exactly what I was doing.

"Still don' like me, huh?" he questioned. I didn't dignify that with a response. "So what class couldn' take uh break?"

"I'm not doing homework," I said honestly.

The bus halted to a stop, suddenly, and I looked out the window for the first time since we left I-65. "Lunch break. Forty-five minute stop. Please look out for each other."

Derek turned towards the front. "Yea, everyone grab uh buddy," he joked.

"That's not a bad idea," Mrs. Diece declared. "Mr. King, you can be mine."

If the back of his neck was any indication of what his face looked like, it didn't take much imagination to see the blush that had probably infused it. "You aren't the only one who can joke, Monsieur King. Be back here by 11:00."

While my classmates pushed for the doors in somewhat of a semblance of a line, I didn't rush, taking my time. I glanced out the window, trying to size up the place where we'd stopped. I got off the bus only to use the bathroom, and didn't waste any time getting back to it. I ate the lunch that I'd packed specifically for the occasion, instead of eating in the diner with my peers. I couldn't imagine Miz Hattie's journey.

Derek ended up coming back on the bus well ahead of the rest of our classmates. He unceremoniously sat down in the empty space across from me. "I brought you uh Coke and some chips," he declared in an offhand way, shrugging at the same time that he handed them to me. "Figure you might get thirsty."

I was surprised, and distrustful, of this sudden generosity. He gave a timid smile. "Promise I didn' poison it," he said, assuring. "I told you, Orion's my best friend...I just know-," and he shrugged. It went without saying why I'd eaten on the bus.

"Thank you, Derek," I said to him with genuine appreciation. He smiled at me, and after a brief moment, I returned the smile.

We arrived in Charlottesville promptly at 4:00; in time to check into our hotel and have dinner before the welcome ceremony of the convention. Before we retired for the evening we were reminded not to leave our hotel rooms during the night, got a long spiel about how we were expected to conduct ourselves as young men and women, and were told the itinerary for the weekend. Everyone who went was expected to participate in at least two of the events offered. My two individual events were original poetry, and translation, and I did the dance and had a very minor role in the play. When we'd been practicing our dance, I'd felt mildly stupid thinking that we were going to get laughed out of school, but after seeing the other school's performances, I still felt mildly stupid, but in good company.

When we weren't personally competing, we either went around to each other's events to watch our classmates compete, or we attended one of the many seminars on things like French folk art, the history of France, the history of French speaking colonies, or what being a global world was about. And there was, of course, the obligatory tour of the University of Virginia's campus, because the convention was nothing if they couldn't get at least one convert to the University.

The tour ended back on the steps of the Rotunda where it started, and instead of heading back inside for the rest of the competition, I stayed out on the Lawn, finding a spot beneath a shady tree to keep to myself. So far I'd mostly stayed with the group because it was impossible to miss how few black faces there were milling around the campus (unless they were cleaning, cooking, or some other menial task). Obviously King's plea had yet to take shape, though I had to admit that there was a sight deal more black students here than a reasonable person would expect to see on, say, the University of Alabama's campus. That said something, at least.

For a while I watched the students that populated the campus, until I grew tired of that, and my attentions fell to my lap where my notebook was waiting. For me, writing was just something that I did. Even before I could even really write, I had been creating my own stories, trying to transform the world around me. What I lacked in communication skills, I made up for in the written; it was a way to make the world make more sense to me.

Time must have gotten away from me because when I looked up again, it was darker and heading steadily towards sundown. Just as I was getting up, I saw Derek making his way towards where I was sitting. "I need you to be my buddy, Trace," he remarked with a slight smirk. I wondered if he did that solely because he knew how much it irritated me.

"I was heading back now," I stated. "I'm sorry."

He gave me his best puppy dog look. "I'm just goin' to tha museum," he remarked. "Mrs. Diece told us that if we was goin' to head off, we should have someone go wit' us," he reminded me. For good measure, he managed to make his voice hold a note of disapproval, as if I had done something wrong by being off by myself. "Promise it won' take long," he added.

A part of me wanted to tell him that his interests had nothing to do with me, but it was late, and I didn't exactly want to have to walk back to the convention center by myself, not that I'd ever tell him that. "Where are we going?" I questioned.

He gave a smile in relief, naming the hall. "You're tha best," he thought to add.

We walked across the length of the campus to the other side, away from the other convention goings on. Derek, with his church best and his frat hair actually combed neatly back, looked as if he could easily fit in among the other students. Guys nodded at him as he passed, girls made meaningful eye contact. As I walked alongside him, I couldn't help but notice how I seemed to stick out like a sore thumb. When I wasn't invisible, I was a curiosity, something out of place on their pristine campus. Almost certainly it'd be the same when I went to school at Harvard. I wondered if I was just destined to always stick out, no matter where I went. The thought made me pause, until I was reminded that I'd never really fit in anywhere, so even if I didn't fit in at Harvard, it wouldn't be anything new; some people were just never meant to mix-in with the crowd.

I must have physically paused, too, because Derek gave me a sidelong look, his eyes probative. Did he always look that intense? I thought about trying to explain my thoughts to him, but he didn't ask anything, instead continuing purposely toward the Art Museum.

Compared to the darkening outside, the museum was brightly lit, welcoming. The antechamber was large, and almost drafty. We had only taken a few steps inside, when I startled where I stood. At the entrance, right inside the antechamber, there was a grizzly bear in full attack mode, its claws extended, legs braced, mouth opened, eyes as dead as a teddy bear, and body just as stuffed. Before I could read the placard that could explain such an aberration, Derek had crossed over to the other side of the room. I hurried to catch up.

We passed through several different rooms with various items on display to be examined. We strode past waxworks and steel creations, a motif of bones, leaves, and fauna, colors of every hue of the color spectrum, and even a set of average tennis shoes...without pausing to figure out why they were displayed.

Finally, we seemed to have found the room he'd been looking for, because his pace slowed to a leisurely stroll. This room was filled with paintings: eyes that could have been alive, mouths that were opened as if to share their last secrets, buildings that were occupied or stood vacant, and skies that were filled with stars. Derek loitered, gazing with mild interest at each picture that he passed. Occasionally there was one that drew his attention for more than a few seconds, and then he'd pause.

I'd begun to notice a pattern with the paintings, and I stopped at one that reminded me a lot of *Starry Nights*. I read the artist description of the painting and saw that this was an art student's interpretation of the morning after such a night.

I sat contemplating the picture for so long that when I looked up, Derek was gone. There was a brief moment when I felt a small flair of anger: had he left me here by myself to have to walk across this campus alone? But then I found him at the back of the exhibit, in a small corner off to himself. I paused for a moment, disarmed by the illusion of his solitude. He seemed so utterly alone in that space, and was standing so still, that at first I didn't even see him. I wondered what had captured his attention so completely, and stepped forward to take a look. My heels clicked noisily on the floor, and I winced at the sound, stopping where I was. Derek didn't act as if he heard me, though; he didn't as much as shift. I let out a breath.

Walking on my tiptoes to minimize the sound, I moved towards him to see the cluster of pictures that he was looking at, stopping before I made it to his line of sight. The first picture in the series was named *The Height of Man*, and showed the sun shining down brilliantly on a stone altar. The second one was a picture of a very colorful, ornate, cathedral in the middle of a dingy, European street. The last painting was that of a boat, landlocked, left on its side, empty, on top of a cliff. There were no names to the second and third pictures.

The paintings were simplistic, not overly ostentatious. I wondered what it was that held Derek's attention so raptly when none of the other's seemed to have that power. To me, there was nothing particularly spectacular about the paintings...until you went back and really looked at them. The altar had been laboriously treated, and had the unnerving look that it had actually been chiseled onto the paper, instead of painted. Despite the chips and cracks in the base, and its careworn and weathered look and lack of embellishments, it was a handsome thing that hinted at a former life of grandeur.

My eyes only shifted to the second picture when they felt that they had seen what it wanted from the first. The second picture didn't have the same kind of feel that the first one had, nor had the same technique been used. In this picture, not as prominent as the cathedral, was the faintest outline of a man's face gazing up towards the sky as if to derive meaning from the clouds that halfway obscured the sun. The direction of his gaze, too, was towards where the cathedral sat in its terrible opulence, but the man was unable to see the church, or feel the sun, because of the buildings that were in his way.

The third painting reminded me a lot of the painting *Christina's World*, by Andrew Wyeth; it had that same feeling of longing, of separateness. In this one, the boat was the first thing you noticed, but when you looked back at the picture, you saw the land that it sat on top of was mostly barren, with only the smallest spots of grass dotting the plain. In the distance was a great expanse of ocean, one lone wave crashing onto the shore. This one was so unlike the first, in brush, stroke, and style, and not much like the second, that they didn't seem to be connected in any way. If you were just looking at the first and last one, you wouldn't have known they were by the same artist.

"Have you evuh simply been in awe of somethin'?" he questioned into the silence, breaking my silent evaluation of the paintings. He didn't wait for my response. "I mean have you evuh seen somethin' *so* overwhelmin', so... astoundin', that you can' find tha words to describe how it makes you feel?

Ever see somethin' so beautiful that it makes you want to laugh and cry at tha same time?"

I was too surprised by his words to come up with an answer. I'd forgotten he was there, and since he hadn't turned around, I didn't think that he'd known I was. "Tha first time I saw these," he said in a quiet whisper, "I thought to myself, 'I could nevuh do anythin' this great', but then aftuh I heard tha story behind them, it changed to 'I hope I nevuh get tha chance'."

His words held my interest. "What's the story?" I whispered, my voice automatically lowering to match his. There was something about this space that necessitated intimacy.

Derek hesitated for a moment before he pointed to the first of the three. "Tha first picture was painted when McMillan's first and only son, William, was born. Notice how light tha picture is? There is no question about his joy, his exhilaration. You can almost imagine him kneelin' there, offerin' uh prayuh in thanks."

His gaze and his finger moved on to the second picture. "Then you have tha picture of tha cathedral. Notice tha change in his use of colors, in his use of paints? He went from watercolors to oils. This one was done aftuh he found out that his wife and son were both ill. Can you see how he's beginnin' to test his religion? Tha church is still there, like in tha back of his mind, but he's havin' trouble seein' it, findin' his faith." Derek paused, letting his words strike a chord before he moved on to the third picture, which I could pretty much guess about by now.

Derek's tone was subdued when he spoke. "This was actually tha last picture McMillan ever painted. When you look at it you can tell that he was sayin' good-bye. Look at his brush strokes, tha sharp edges, tha dark colors. Even when he found out that his wife and son were sick, there was still uh sort of lightness to tha picture, uh latent hope. This one tha storm hit.

"This last picture was painted aftuh his wife and son died," he paused, turning back to the last painting, studying it. "Even tha way he painted changed. I can' imagine what it would feel like to be in that boat: so lost, so far from sea, tryin', desperately, to make it back, and still failin'. Notice how, in this one, there's no sort of religious symbol here? He lost. Six weeks aftuh tha paintin' was done, he died of heart failure." Derek's gaze turned back to the one that showed the altar, as if he could turn back the years. "He's already so low, if only he had managed to get to his knees..." his voice trailed off as he stood in contemplation of the man's life.

Before I had a chance to reexamine the paintings to compare to his words, Derek turned and looked at me for the first time since we'd come into this small room. I felt like he was waiting for me to say something, so I said: "I didn't know that you were so into art." His look didn't change at my statement. Instead his eyes pierced mine, and he was so serious that I almost wished that he would make a joke. When he looked at me just then, his eyes dark and intense, there seemed to be something different in his gaze, exposed maybe, and it was unnerving. It was like..., but that wasn't...inexplicably, I felt a blush start to color my cheeks.

"Yea, well there's uh lot you don' know about me," Derek remarked, still holding my gaze.

Disarmed, I gave a nervous laugh. "I see that you weren't lying about your reasons for joining the French Club," I said, trying to lighten things between us.

It took him a second to figure out what I was talking about, but then he smiled, softly. "Oh...? Yea," he said. Something changed in his expression, and he finally broke the gaze. "I guess we should get back 'fore we're missed," he remarked after a heartbeat had passed. He gave one last look at the center painting before he flashed me an unreadable smile.

The awards ceremony for the convention took place early Saturday morning. As soon as we collected our awards for the events that we were the best in, we loaded the bus and headed back home. I sat alone for the ride back, utilizing the time to write. Every so often I would glance away from my notebook to see Derek looking back at me. Not really knowing how to process his attention, I purposely kept my head down as much as possible.

We got back to the school an hour before we were supposed to, and people reluctantly woke up to gather their possessions together. I glanced at the front of the bus, and once again made eye contact with Derek. He let everyone else go ahead of him. When I passed by, he looked like he wanted to say something to me before I got off, but he let me pass without a word. Outside, I found my luggage quickly, and disentangled myself from the crowd, trying to put space between me and everyone else.

I joined the queue to use the payphone, before parking myself in the carport to wait out the hour before my mom could make it to pick me up. I'd only been sitting down for a few minutes when a maroon car pulled up beside me. The window rolled down. "Need uh ride, Trace?" Derek questioned.

"You're probably not going the way I'm going."

Derek leaned over to open the door. "I'm headin' whichevuh way you're goin', Trace, get in." I considered, and after a long minute I tossed my stuff in the back, before I slid into the seat beside him. "Where do you live?" he questioned.

Reluctantly, I gave him directions to my house. I was suddenly nervous sitting beside him, suddenly very aware of his presence. For a while, neither of us said anything to each other. Derek, who usually talked non-stop, was uncharacteristically not saying anything. Every now and then he would give me the briefest of glances, before he returned his gaze back to the road.

"What's on your mind?" he finally questioned. "You look like somethin's botherin' you."

There was, but I couldn't put my finger on what. I wondered what was on *his* mind. "Just thinking," I replied.

"About?" he prodded.

"Nothing much," I responded. "Just thinking."

"Oh," he said in response to that. The silence lasted only a few seconds. "Did you know that Mrs. Diece has been all ovuh tha world?" he questioned, suddenly. "She speaks Spanish too, and was uh missionary in Argentina before she became uh teacher here. She also taught ovuh in Cameroon. I wanna do somethin' like that. I mean not teach, but travel tha world, see all there is to see." He turned towards me, suddenly, placing a hand on top of mine. "Let's travel tha world togethuh, Trace," he exclaimed with a sudden sense of recklessness. "We can view tha Palace at Versailles, see tha Eiffel Towuh, take uh trip to Buenos Aries, peruse Florence, pose beside Victoria Falls. I can be tha travelin' artist; you can be my press writer and translator."

I tried to think of some quick response, something just as clever, but nothing was forthcoming. All I could think about was the geography of

Derek's hand, the closeness of him beside me, the images that his words conjured. "Bank's closed by now," I replied, unable to think of anything else.

Derek's eyes held mine for what seemed like an eternity before he gave a sad smile that was what, accepting? Disappointed? Jeering? "Some othuh time, then," he declared.

The car pulled to a stop in front of my house. It was dark in that way that said no one was home. Derek noticed. "You home by yourself?" he wondered. I nodded. "If you don' have nothin' planned, why don' we catch uh movie or somethin' so you don' have to be stuck in tha house alone on uh Saturday night? We can go to tha drive-in. It always has somethin' playin'."

I shook my head. "I have school work that I need to get done," I said.

"On uh Saturday?" he questioned, but he dropped it, shrugged. "Some othuh time then." I nodded and, thanking him, I got out of the car. "If you evuh need uh ride, I'll be happy to give you one," he offered as I was shutting the door. I nodded, thanking him again.

Derek watched me to my door, and only once it was open did he start back down the drive. I watched his car until he had turned out of the neighborhood. Once inside, I got some books out with the intention of studying, but sat thinking instead. Not about the trip-I wasn't ready to think about that yet-just about Derek in general. I really had no reason to say no to seeing a movie with him. It wasn't like he'd been asking me on a date; I doubt he was even trying to be a friend. He'd just seen that I was alone and asked me to see a movie.

So what prevented me from saying yes?

— 11 —
"Inner Space"

After the convention, French Club was basically done for the year, and most of the club and sport activities were similarly winding down. The hierarchy of life shifted. Formerly on top of the world seniors looked toward graduation and life after, and maybe wished that it was the end of August, and not May. Juniors walked with a new swagger, as did Freshmen, anxious for the new school year when they would come to class to find that they were no longer at the bottom of the heap.

At the begging of June, just as the weather was beginning to heat up and settle into its summer temperament, my mom's church announced that they were going to help sponsor a home build in connection with another church, and asked for its members to help volunteer. It was something new, different, a variation from the summer that I was already seeing settle into a routine of boredom. For a fleeting moment my mom talked about it as if it were something that she would like to do, too, but when the date for the build came around, all she did was sign the waiver, and drop me off at the site.

I walked alone to the sign-in table, got my name tag, and was told to go across the street to find Bill Massey to get set up on a project. Bill was a sturdily built, older man, with a full head of gray hair, who was trying to do about twenty things at once. When I introduced myself, he shook my hand hurriedly, while feeding directions to someone else. "If you'll see my junior assistant, he'll be more than happy to get you started," he said brusquely, before turning to someone else who demanded his attention.

"Who's the junior assistant?" I questioned to the air.

"That'd be me," a remarkably familiar voice announced. If Derek was surprised to see me, he concealed it better than I. He gave a smile, pulling his hammer off his tool belt, spinning it around in his hand, gun-slinger style. "Tracy," he said, pronouncing my name slowly. "Out of all tha construction sites, in all tha towns, in all tha world, she walks onto mine," he quoted with a certain flare. "You're one of tha last people I'd expected to see on my terrain."

That made for the two of us. I looked at him spinning his hammer and was tempted to say 'Draw'. "Junior assistant to the director?" I questioned instead.

He stopped looking sinister and smiled. He had such a nice smile, I noticed. I wonder why I hadn't noticed it before. "Yea, I run tha show here." He hitched his blue jeans up at the waist, hooking his fingers in the loops in a way that made him look very rugged. He posed, before laughing it all off. "Really it just means I'm uh glorified helper. I work wit' tha first time volunteers, keep them outta tha way, see that they got somethin' to do. I make sure all tha house leads have all tha things they need, make sure everythin' is gettin' done, and if there's need for more workers on uh project, I get them to where they need ta be." That all sounded very...responsible. I was a little thrown off.

He holstered his hammer. "Is this tha first house that you've worked on?" I nodded. "Evuh do anythin' like this before?"

"Me and my friend once tried to build a tree house," I offered helpfully. He smiled, and for some reason his smile made me smile. "We never finished it though," I admitted.

He tilted his head to the side, giving me an appraising look. "Well, this here might be uh lil bit harduh than buildin' uh tree house, and if'n you come to build, you might be uh lil disappointed. Tha old guys don' like to relinquish their hammers to tha younguns, especially tha females. And if'n you ain't on uh crew, you don' do any of tha frame buildin' or settin' up."

There didn't seem as if there was much left to do after that. "So what *will* I be doing?" I wondered, trying to combat my sudden disappointment.

"We nevuh have enough gophers," he suggested with a shrug. "You don' get to build, but we always need people to run water to tha crews, bring nails, shovels, spades, and tha like off tha truck, hold tha end uh tha wood when it's bein' cut, that sorta thing. I can get you set up on insulation when tha frames are in place, but I'll be honest: it itches like crazy and ain't much fun."

"Do I get a hammer to do it?" I questioned, trying to be optimistic.

"You get uh staple gun," he responded with a smile. "When we're ready for that, I'll come find you," he said. "Let's see what we can get you started on for now…"

I got set up doing a different sort of insulation for the roof of the house. Derek left to go work on something else, but he would work his way back around to me every now and then. When he saw that I was nearing being done, he drew me away for another small project. By the time 5:00 came around, I was tired, sweaty, sore, my hands had blisters from working with a shovel, and I had more than one splinter.

On Sunday I was back after church, and I helped work during the week when I was not working at the church's day camp, or at summer school. I saw Derek on site often, but we didn't get a chance to say much to each other. Derek had a lot to deal with, and I was amazed at how dedicated he was to the job, not used to seeing him so motivated. He didn't just supervise, he actually threw his weight in. When it was determined that the walls of one room were off by three inches, he took out his hammer, pulled out the nails, and made the adjustment himself. When a project was short a person, he was the first to volunteer. When I got on site at 7:30, he had already been there for an hour and a half, and he was there until 6:00 at night.

The following Saturday, I spent most of the day doing stucco work. Around noon, his growingly familiar shadow fell across my work, and I looked up in expectation. "Workin' hard?" Derek questioned, a familiar hint of teasing in his voice.

"Hi," I said in response. "Yes."

"Well…it's lunch time," he announced. "Time to take uh break."

"I just want to finish this," I said, wiping a bead of sweat from my forehead.

He shook his head. "Nevuh quit on uh project do you? Well, you have to take uh break. Food's here and we're 'bout to bless it."

"I-I'll be right there."

Derek gently lifted me up by my forearm. "You don' have to eat lunch

— 104 —

right now," he said, leadingly, taking the tool out of my hand, "all you have to do is come across tha street while we say Grace, and then you can come right on back. You can eat latuh if'n you want."

"Just-,"

"Come on," he coaxed, taking my hand. He shook his head. "You're too cute."

What? He seemed as surprised by the words as I was, but he said nothing of it.

Across the street, there was a big ceremony before the build coordinator blessed the food, and everybody began crowding the line. I went back to working on what I'd been working on before I got pulled away. I wasn't the only one who was putting off lunch. At every house there still came the sound of guys shouting instructions to one another, of nails being driven in, shouts coming back. Derek came trotting back across the road, just as I was finishing up, two plates in his hand. "I brought you food," he said, grandly. "Tha line was long."

"Thank you," I replied. "Let me just finish cleaning up." He nodded, and waited for me to clean off my tools and wash my hands. When I finished, Derek, still holding on to the two plates, climbed up the diagonal to one of the roof beams without spilling anything. "Comin'?" he called down to me.

I studied the piece of wood he'd just effortlessly climbed up. "I like the ground, thank you," I decided.

"Best view on tha site. You'll nevuh appreciate what you're doin' 'til you look at it from up 'ere."

I followed Derek's example, and climbed the diagonal, not entirely convinced I wouldn't fall. Derek sat the plates down, and when I neared the top, he helped me the rest of the way. Once I was safely on my feet, he gracefully sat down on the beam. I sat down beside him.

"Thank you," I remarked.

He nodded, awkwardly it seemed. "My pleasure," he said, slowly. "I take it you're enjoyin' tha build since you keep comin' back. What d'ya think?"

I paused to consider while I tried out the food. "This is what community is supposed to be about," I said in appreciation. Black and white churches, alike, had sent workers and helped sponsor the build, and there'd been no animosity as far as I could see, just a sense of shared determination. "People mutually helping each other, no matter what race, religion, creed. Could you imagine what the world would be like if we were all willing to work together to help each other?"

"So people really talk like that," he observed with a chuckle, and even though he laughed, it didn't feel as if he was laughing at me. "Nah, I know what you mean. You're sayin' it'd be nice if people could just see people as people, instead of all these other concepts we try to make them. You know, like if brainy, know-it-alls, could see handsome, construction guys, as people worth gettin' to know."

I nodded, vigorously. "Exactly! Or if show-off, cocky, class clowns could see driven, intelligent, women as people worth listening to," I returned.

Derek held out his hand for me to shake. "I'm Derek," he said.

"Tracy," I responded. We shook hands jokingly, equally amused.

"Nice to meet you," he declared. We smiled at each other, and after a moment's thought, I took my hand from his.

I turned away slightly. "I can't believe that these houses are almost finished," I remarked. "It's amazing how quickly all this has come together."

Derek gave a hearty laugh, though it sounded slightly off. "This?" he wondered. "This's nothin'. Three houses in two weeks? Ha! This is uh rush!"

"Is it safe to build a house this quickly?"

He shrugged. "Of course. Tha houses still have to follow all tha regulations and codes uh regular house has to, and we take as much care, more even, than uh paid crew; I mean for them, it's just 'bout money. Here, it's uh learnin' cycle; tha olduh folks teach tha younguh folks, and everyone's here cause they wanna be. We're uh community."

He sat his fork down on his plate, a bite of spaghetti still wrapped around the tines. His whole body took on a more relaxed posture. He kicked his feet idly. "Man, I love this," he said, casually, staring off into the distance. "Greatest portrait evuh created, if you ask me. I can' get ovuh how beautiful it is…how can anyone not love this? Nothin' compares."

I might not have been in love with Bakersfield, but I couldn't deny that it was beautiful. It looked like one giant park. Everywhere you looked you saw dense foliage; something that was green or in bloom. Bakersfield was fed by the Tennessee River, rested in the heart of the Tennessee Valley, and was bordered by the mountains. When the cotton was in bloom, or when the trees were busy changing colors, it was truly something to see.

"I don't know about nothing," I spoke up, feeling the need to reclaim my hometown a little. "You don't beat beautiful until you wake up to the world completely covered in snow: everywhere you look flawlessly white, the sun glinting off of it like there's a sea of diamonds as far as the eye can see."

"Warmth nowhere to be found," he added. "Snow, hunh?" he shook his head, shivering at the thought. "Figures you were uh Yankee. Where bout you from?"

"Wilmington, Illinois."

"Is that close to Chicago?"

"No, it's southern Illinois; outside of East St. Louis. Wilmington's pretty small, smaller than Decatur, maybe even Athens, but it was so much... *different*...there than it is here." The words were strengthened by the longing in my voice. I couldn't really think of Wilmington without missing it, without missing the life that we'd had there. Me and my friends had moved in and out of each other's lives, and homes, as if there were no walls to divide us. I didn't know if this was a northern-southern thing, or if it had merely been because we were kids back then and didn't know better. Whatever the reason, I missed it all, especially the innocence. It wasn't really until we moved here that I started to feel race.

"How so?" Derek questioned.

The fact that he even had to ask showed how different our worlds were. In mine, race was like this constant background noise, like the sound of an insect buzzing in your ear; impossible to miss. I gave him a glance, saying without words that he knew what I was talking about. There had been no segregated bathrooms, swimming pools, or restaurants in Wilmington. No strange looks or places that were off limits just because of my skin color.

"The attitudes of the people," I responded, tactfully. I wondered if Derek even realized how much he didn't have to think about the kind of things I thought about every day. For me it was rare to even go a day without being reminded, in some way or another, about the color of my skin. "And the landscape. Just a lot of things, really; I miss it."

"You sound like it," he noted. "So, how'd y'all end up here, anyhow?" he wondered. My lips pulled in, and I guess Derek noticed. "Wasn' tryin' to be nosy."

I stared down at my hands. "No, it's not that. We moved because my parents split."

"Oh," Derek remarked. "Sorry for bringin' it up."

"Not like you knew," I responded. "I'm here because I have to be, but as soon as I'm old enough to leave, I'm not looking back," I said confidently.

"Goin' back ta Illinois?"

Oddly, it had never really occurred to me to try and go back. "The only way I'd end up back there is if I went to the University of Chicago for undergrad, but that's unlikely."

"Why's that?" Surprisingly his interest seemed genuine.

"Because it's so far down on the list of schools I want to go to," I responded. "I've never been to Chicago, so even though it's in Illinois, it doesn't really have the same appeal to me."

He looked for something in my expression when I said that. "Where do you *wanna* go?" he wondered.

The answer was ready before the question had even been asked. "Harvard," I said without hesitation.

He blinked. "Can' say I'm surprised," he said to my surprise. I got many reactions when I voiced that goal, none of them the one he gave.

"Why's that?" I wondered.

"You just seem Ivy League to me," he said off-handedly. "Only tha best for you, right?"

Even though I don't think he meant it that way, his words made me feel like I was overreaching. "Well, I want to make sure that I get the best, or as close to the best education that I can," I explained. "Which is why I want to go to Harvard. They don't currently let women in, but that's bound to change soon, and even if I can't go to Harvard for undergrad, they do let women into their law school."

"You wanna be uh lawyer?" he picked out. He didn't seem any more surprised by this ambition than he had of my college choice.

I nodded. "That's the goal."

"What makes you wanna do that?" He didn't ask in the same disparaging way that most people did. No matter who was doing the asking, white or black, male or female, adult or child, that statement always seemed to be met with the same sort of incredulity. "I mean…well…it's not like tha most common career choice," he explained.

"For a black woman?" I stipulated. No, it wasn't, and there weren't many others to set the example for me, but that didn't make it impossible. Derek didn't comment on my statement. "I guess not," I replied, more than willing to acknowledge that it wasn't the norm. "I don't really know why, I've kind of just always wanted to be a lawyer." Lawyers were educated, and could make a good living, and I wanted to be able to have a nice lifestyle without having to depend on someone to give it to me. That was its biggest appeal, but there were also some laws on the books that were just morally corrupt, and needed to be changed. "I want to be able to say that I actually did something to help the world, instead of just taking from it. I would like to be able to say that I had a part in changing the legal dialogue, like Thurgood Marshall has done."

I knew I wasn't the type of person who could sit impassively at a lunch counter while people poured drinks or spilled food on me, or be the type to lead a crowd of people towards a common goal. I didn't have that Fannie Lou Hamer or Malcolm X kind of verve, but I could see myself like Vivian Malone, quietly marching past an angry mob to enroll at a school I'd earned the right to be at, letting my accomplishments speak for themselves. I knew what I *was* good at, and what I wasn't. "Being a lawyer is my own way to help change the world," I concluded.

Derek nodded, and I could tell he had removed himself from the north and my plans of grandeur in that small gesture. He looked back out across the view. "Me? I'd be happy doin' this for tha rest of my life. Buildin' houses for uh livin', maybe someday buildin' my own. I don' need nothin' grand or flashy, just uh small place on uh decent piece of land. Uh place where I can sit back and watch tha grass grow, raise uh family," he declared with a lazy smile, and upon seeing it, I wondered if it was as hard for him to imagine my plans for the future, as it was for me to envision his; I'd just never been attracted to the idea of a house with a white picket fence. Sure it was a nice thought, but it just cost too much to get it.

"I love everythin' 'bout this," he went on. "Drivin' nails, puttin' up walls, even tha taste of sawdust in your food don' bothuh me none. If'n I could do this for tha rest of my life, I could die uh happy man."

Eventually his eyes fell on my empty plate. "I didn' mean to talk your ear off. Guess I'll be gettin' back to work now," he said, stretching out. He got to his feet. "Madame," he said, extending his hand to me. Our eyes met. I can't say that my eyes widened in surprise, but I had a moment of pause where I just stared, not really sure what I was seeing.

Derek pulled me up beside him. "Merci," I replied, confused.

"No problem," he said, grinning.

He's so adorable, I thought, and immediately wondered where the thought came from. I looked at Derek as if he could mysteriously read my mind. He only smiled.

— 12 —
"Still Life"

At the very end of the build there was a brief ceremony where the home owners were given the keys to their newly finished homes. One of the men, a grizzled, middle aged man who was raising his four kids with the help of his mom, simply broke down and cried. It was a teary, emotional thing, and I felt a sense of pride in being able to help this family in this small way.

After the build, I tried to fill up the rest of the summer with more books, more assignments, and more scholarship hunting. I sent away for the University of Penn and the University of Chicago's brochures. I researched both of their undergraduate programs and law schools. I wrote letters to my dad and my cousins, doubting that they would even respond, but I did it because it gave me something to do, because in the moments where I wasn't doing anything, where I allowed myself too much time to think, my thoughts were annoyingly occupied by thoughts of Derek.

They would creep up out of nowhere like uninvited guests to a party. I'd close my eyes, and suddenly see his blue ones looking at me, see his smile. I kept hearing voices that reminded me of him, kept thinking that I saw him around town. The more I tried not to think about him, the more he seemed to creep into my thoughts. I even considered the possibility of voluntarily babysitting Nicole just so I could be in that same area, and maybe run into him again. I never thought of Bakersfield as being so large before, but during the summer it suddenly seemed massive.

The rest of the summer trickled by, inhumanely slow. No matter what project I tried to come up with to pass the time, it felt like I was merely counting down every day in increments of minutes and seconds. The first day of school could have been Equality and Christmas, wrapped into one elusive package, considering how long it took to come. The night before the new school year started, I spent the night over at Patrice's, and typically I couldn't sleep.

"Do you think he'll be there?" Patrice whispered into the air once the lights had been off for some time. I'd assumed that she'd fallen asleep, but apparently she couldn't sleep either. "He said he'd be waitin' in tha commons... so that means he'll be there, right..."

I could hear her trying to reassure herself. She was talking about her latest fling, Darnell Fuller. "I'm sure he will," I responded. Even though it was too dark to see each other clearly, I turned towards her anyway, wanting to ask her a question, unsure of how to go about it. "Did you like what I picked out?" she wondered nervously, while I lay there in contemplation.

"It looks fine," I said, automatically. As usual, she had a new set of clothes that accentuated all of her nicest features.

Her mattress groaned in unison with her. "Fine? He's not goinna notice fine," she whimpered. "Oh, no."

It felt as if I had only just closed my eyes when the sun came peeking in through Patrice's window. Patrice was out of her bed, and had rushed off to freshen up before my eyes were even opened properly. Predictably, she'd switched the outfit that she had sitting out, and offered the 'fine' one to me. Patrice and I were around the same height, and weighed about the same, so I could wear her clothes, but she was far more endowed than I was, so it didn't look quite the same on me, but still, I took the outfit.

Patrice convinced me that I should forego my French braid, and she broke out the hot irons to tackle my hair since it hadn't been rolled the night before. While we waited for the irons to heat up, her fingers idly combed through my hair, loosening any tangles. When it was down it fell right to my shoulder blades, and refused to grow any longer. "I wish I had hair like yours," she remarked, wistfully. Patrice's own hair was a short, thick, crown that looked nearly jet black. Normally she slathered lye on her hair to get it to lie flatter, but today she was wearing a Diana Ross style wig. "If I had that good hair, I'd wear it out *all* tha time. I can' figure why you always keep it in that braid."

I shrugged. Usually I couldn't figure out what to do with it, so I liked to keep it hidden, not liking it when people made a deal out of my hair. Patrice may have liked it, but I liked hers just as much. "Because it's easy, and I know how to do it," I responded. "'Sides, my hair won't hold a shape like yours."

"Girl, you act like that's a bonus," Patrice remarked.

Because I'd slept in the braid, my hair was already wavy, so Patrice just curled it to accentuate its natural pattern. I spent only a few minutes looking at myself in the mirror, but I liked what I saw.

"Mm," Patrice remarked at her work. "Just like Lena."

We rode to school with Patrice's brother. I sat up front with Marcus while Patrice and her friend, Marla, rode in the back, catching the other up on the latest gossip. At 7:25, Marcus stopped unceremoniously in front of Mason High.

"Just think," Patrice said grandly, as she was getting out of the Gordon's car. "This time next year we'll be tha ones drivin' ta school!" She threw her hands up in open supplication of the thought, but paused in her dreams of grandeur. "Well, when daddy lets me borrow tha car," she amended. "But 'magine tha possibilities!"

"Remind me not to get on the road," Marcus chided.

"Oh, ha ha, Mark," Patrice declared, giving him a sound punch in the arm before getting out in a huff. She slammed the door closed for good measure.

I looked over at Marcus and shared his laugh. "I'm a bit scared of the idea myself," I declared.

He shook his head. "It's amazing to think that y'all little one's are going to be allowed on the road," he teased. He gave me a one armed hug. "Have a great day at school, *sis*."

"I'll try," I remarked, doing my best to sound grave.

"Hey?" he called as I was getting out the car.

I looked back at him. "Yes?"

"Try'n play nice. Don't make your classmates look *too* bad."

"I'll do my best," I promised. Patrice rolled her eyes at the exchange between me and her brother.

With an air of steeling herself against the worst, she squared her shoulders and marched inside. As usual, it wasn't long before we ran into someone she knew, and if she was tortured by the idea of her classmates, I missed it. Even though Darnell was all she could talk about last night, (and as we were getting ready for school, and in code while we were in the car with her brother), she paused in her stride long enough to talk, to catch up, to trade gossip and talk about summers with just about everyone we passed. With an attempt to be sociable, I slowed my stride and pretended to know the people, too. I said "Hello," and chimed in whenever either of them remembered that I was there, matching their gait as they slowly meandered toward the common area.

By the time we made it down the stairs and into the cafeteria, we had gained two other of Patrice's friends. They treated me with a casual indifference. One of the girls, Sylvie-Ann, went to my mom's church, and the other, Mildred, I'd gone to school with since we'd moved here, but it would have been a stretch to say we were familiar. Conversation must have drifted toward current flames because, "There he is," was followed by a couple of squeals, and I looked up as the four of them tried to look utterly nonchalant.

Darnell had taken up a post in the middle of a crowd of friends that were sitting or leaning against the stairs heading into the abandoned lunch line. He was the picture of cockiness, even down to the casual way he was dressed. He looked up, perhaps in response to the squeals, and his eyes settled on Patrice with a smile that suggested that she were a particularly satisfying piece of meat. Patrice's stroll changed as she sashayed her way to him. He watched her movements, and lazily got to his feet to meet her, a smile playing behind his soft, light-brown eyes.

Darnell, like Omar, was tall and athletic, but that was the end of their similarities. While Omar had been a 2nd string bench warmer, Darnell was one of only a handful of black starters on the football team, and, as he loved to tell you, a central player on the team. He had spent his first two years of high school at Groovy, but supposedly Mason's coach had coaxed him into transferring to the better school (and better team). That, in itself, had his head pretty big, but then he was pretty good looking, too, and just about everyone in the school seemed to know him, or at least know who he was. So he thought that gave him the license to be an ass, which he was unsurprisingly very good at, as well. In the brief instances that I'd spent time with him this summer, he was such a sleaze that I actually missed Omar.

Darnell looked me over and winked once, before draping an arm around

Patrice. "Missed you, baby," he declared. He reached for her hand, which she supplied eagerly. During their reunion, I let my eyes glance over the crowd, pretending that I wasn't looking for anyone specific. The noise in the cafeteria rose unexpectedly, loud even for the first day of school. "What's that about?" Sylvie-Ann questioned.

Darnell, looking easily over Patrice's head, only rolled his eyes. "Bunch uh idiot White boys doin' what they do best," he declared, looking toward the small stage at the other end of the area. Our eyes followed. On the stage there was a group of upperclassmen horse-playing. We were too far away to hear what was being said, but the people closest to it were laughing hard, so it must have been funny.

The actors were hardly distinguishable, but one of the figures was recognizable solely because it was the one that I most wanted to see. My best friend noticed him, too. "Hey, speak uh tha devil," she said, cheerfully. "Isn' that Derek?" I nodded in what I hoped was a casual manner, but inexplicably, my heart started racing.

"You should go talk to him, she prodded, trying, and failing, to be discrete about it.

At the exchange, Darnell looked at me, and he started laughing. "Aw, don' tell me that Tracy actually likes somebody," he guffawed, looking down on me. "And here I thought hell'd have ta freeze ovah first. Figures you'd like cream pie stead uh beef cake, though."

I turned away from them when he said that, pulling away, but Patrice held on to my arm. "T, he's only joshin' you," she said. "Be cool, Darnell."

Darnell ran a hand along the back of his neck. "Ah, geez, babe, I'm just messin' wit her; your girlfriend shouldn' be so sensitive."

Patrice refused to let go of my arm, so we loitered where we were for a while, me bored and waiting for classes to start. I wanted to leave, but didn't want to draw attention to myself, lest Darnell, or someone else, notice I was still there, and say something else about me. I was forgotten for the moment and I wanted to keep it that way. Darnell talked about something he'd done to fix the motor of his car with his guy friends, and the girls talked about clothing. Despite wearing Patrice's clothes, I felt like a fraud. Tomorrow I would be back in my regular, plain clothes, the kind that no one paid attention to. I wished that I had better clothes, better shoes, more money for things outside of rent and food. I sullenly looked away from the crowd, only to have my eyes fall back to the stage.

"Tell you somethin' I know," I heard Darnell say in the background, "if they try'n draft me, I'mma tell it to them like Ali: *I ain't got no quarrel with no Viet Kong, ain' no Viet Cong evuh called me no nigra-,*"

"Shoot, I'd go," another boy interjected over the rest of their laughs. "They give me a gun, I might forget who I'm supposed ta be shootin'!"

Patrice nudged me, seeing where I was looking. "*Go* talk to him," she urged in a whispered voice.

"Why'd I want to do that," I questioned.

"Oh come on, girl, you really goinna try'n pretend that you don' like him? How many times did I hear his name ovuh tha summuh?"

"I don't," I responded. "I mean, like as nothing more than a friend." Characterizing him as even that much was a bit generous. We'd only talked to each other a few times. That didn't exactly add up to friendship.

"Well go be friendly, then," she directed.

"He looks busy," I mumbled.

The bell rang, the skit broke up, and people started to move, to contemplate heading to their first classes for the day. "He on't look so busy now," Patrice whispered in my ear.

"I don't want to be late for class," I remarked.

She rolled her eyes. "You're hopeless," she declared. She turned, and I turned with her. "Hey, Derek!" she shouted, suddenly. She waved when he looked up, and Derek smiled, waving back at us.

"Patrice!" I hissed as he started to walk over. She disappeared into the crowd right before he drew even.

"Hey, Trace!" he greeted with a smile. It easily covered ear to ear, transforming his face as it grew, finally making its way to his eyes. Had they always been that particular shade of blue? "How's it goin'?"

I don't know if I was grimacing or smiling in return. "Uh...it's...um... going good," I managed.

"How was tha rest of your summuh," he continued, cordial.

"Err...good," I got out. What was wrong with me? This was Derek for crying out loud! A moment passed in which I imagined that I had come up with something unwittingly enduring that would make him fall in love with how witty and clever I was, or something that would ease us into the type of conversations that we had when we were working on the build together, or...

"How's yours?"

He clapped his hands together. "Great...adventurous...exhausting; glad to be back: ready to catch up on some zzzz's!" He laughed in that way he had, and suddenly it didn't seem so cocky to me, less boisterous. I pretended that we were back on the roof of the house we were building, sitting inches apart... why hadn't I realized we were so close then...close enough to feel each other, close enough...I lowered my eyes in embarrassment.

"Yeah," I said, feeling like the biggest dork in the world. Since when did I have trouble talking to Derek?

A pair of hands appeared from nowhere, covering his eyes. "Guess who?" a tinkling female voice directed.

"Josh," Derek teased.

"No, silly, it's me!" the girl said unnecessarily. She stepped around him, into my line of sight, tossing her reddish-brown hair as she moved. "What're you doing?"

"Talkin'." Derek nodded at me. "Am, Tracy, Tracy, my girlfriend, Amelia."

Amelia's eyes rolled to take me in, and she gave a kind of forced smile, looking uncomfortable by my presence. Suddenly Derek did too.

"Hey, well," he gestured over his shoulder, "tha bell's 'bout to ring, so I'll see you in class?"

I nodded, slowly. He had a girlfriend. "See you latuh," I remarked, but he and Amelia were already gone.

— 13 —

"La Couleur de Mon Amour"

So what's goin' on wit you and this White boy?" Patrice demanded.

I paused in the middle of pouring myself a glass of milk. "What're you talking about?" I wondered.

"I ain't blind, girl," she declared. "You shoulda seen your face when you saw him, and I ain't missed how he was *lookin' at you*. What's *that* about?"

I finished pouring the milk so I didn't have to look at her. "Nothing," I remarked.

"Do you *like* this White boy?" she probed.

"His name's Derek," I corrected as I shrugged. "He has a girlfriend."

"That ain't what I asked," she reminded me.

"I don't know," I responded. "It's, I...don't know," I finished lamely.

"I can' imagine it," Patrice remarked.

"I bet not catch you 'maginin' it neithuh," Sean declared suddenly, coming into the room. I flushed at the sound of his voice. "What's this bout choo likin' uh White boy?" Patrice's brother questioned, looking down at me. I shot Patrice a look, and she quickly looked away. "You hear me talkin' at ya?" Sean questioned. He got close up in my face, making it impossible to ignore him.

"I didn't say I liked him," I mumbled.

"You shouldn' even be nowhere near 'em," he cautioned. "I warned you two last year bout dem damn peckerwoods, and Tracy: you supposed ta have bettuh sense than that." He shook his head. "I guess yo daddy ain't here ta put some good sense in ya, so I see I'mma hafta do it. You don' go likin' you no White boys. They don' respect Black women, especially tha kind that call theyselves being friendly. All uh them, they got this idea that sleepin' wit uh Black woman's some sorta sport, somethin' to do 'fore they die. They'd cut uh Negro for lookin' at they girls, but they don' mind sleepin' wit ours. You ain't bin round them yo whole life lak tha rest uh us have, so you on't have tha same good sense ta stay 'way from 'em, but ask anyone, and they'll tell you how it be. You on't need ta be nowhere near 'em."

"He's just a friend, Sean," I mumbled. "He's an okay guy."

"Ain't no such thang as an okay one. They all smile up in yo face, and stab you in yo back soon's they get tha chance. Ain't nothin' good goinna come from no type uh relationship wit one uh them, and you can take that ta church," he asserted. "Don' listen ta me if'n you don' wanna, see what happens, but I'm tellin' you that you askin' ta be hurt, you wanna fool 'round wit 'em. Go'n ask yo friend Priscilla if you don' believe me."

Priscilla Hill was two years older than us, and after developing a reputation of liking to be around white boys, ended up having a baby fathered by one. Everyone had seen him coming in and out of the neighborhood, but when she'd told him she was pregnant, he had very publically low-rated her, saying that he'd never so much as looked at her before. He went on to say that just because she went whoring around, didn't make him the father of the child, so she better stop telling people that he was. Anyone who had known of them, knew that he was the only one Priscilla had been with, but that changed nothing.

"Them White boys they think that if they can get uh Colored girl to date 'em, they can get 'em to do anythin' they want."

I understood where Sean was coming from, and what he was saying because when we moved here, I inherited those horror stories that worked their way around our community; the kind that made it hard to ever truly feel comfortable around each other. It seemed that just about everyone in their family had the story about the female relative who was raped, or humiliated, by white men, or of a male relative who had been cut down by them. I wasn't ignorant to that. It was a part of my own family's history, so I wasn't oblivious to it.

I wasn't naïve about the horror of the real world; I just tried to circumvent it as often as possible. It wasn't that I simply became color blind when it came to Derek, either. I knew it was there, but when I looked at him, I forgot that he was white. I forgot because when I looked into his eyes, I got that fluttery

— 119 —

feeling in my stomach. I imagined depth, not because of the color, but because I wanted the illusion that there was something more when I looked at him. When I looked at his hair, it was mostly in disgust because he kept it in that frat boy cut that was just long enough so he could wipe it out of his eyes, which made me look at his eyes, and then I'd get lost. When I listened to his voice, it was to hear that barking laugh, which annoyed me, or his full laugh, which didn't, and when I looked at his lips, I saw his smile, which I loved.

I couldn't say that I was an artist, but I read a lot of books, so the way things appeared in my head was the way I saw the world. In my mind d'Artagnan had been black, while Athos had been Latino. Louis Carol may have made Alice white with blonde hair, but I saw someone like Nicole when I read the books. I saw the world through the ignorance of literature, through pretty words, good deeds, grand gestures, and absolution by the last page.

Maybe it was *because* I read so much that I saw people more as individuals: every book was different, no matter what the cover looked like. I couldn't look at Derek and think Roy, or look at Mr. Gordon and see my father, and have that be good enough for me. I couldn't even look at Sean and see Marcus. They just weren't the same.

"I gotta get to post," Sean declared, "but we ain't done wit this talk, heah?"

Sean left the room as silently as he had entered it. Patrice and I contemplated the silence for a moment. "Don' let him rile your feathers," my friend remarked to my surprise after a quick moment had passed. "You know how protective he be. If you wanna like your White boy, be careful, but go 'head and like him."

School trickled past with its usual slowness for the first couple of days, but it didn't take long for the year to settle into its routine. To make up for the lack of challenge in Mason's curriculum, I found things outside of school to help fill in the gaps. Mr. Colben, my Biology teacher from last year, brought a fellowship to my attention that he wanted me to apply for. The 1st place prize was a $1,500 scholarship, and even if I didn't get to claim 1st place, I was determined to do my best on the project: 2nd and 3rd place weren't so shabby either. Also one of my service groups, Helping Hands, had a big service project that we were working on this year, and of course there was still Bridges.

My new partner was a sophomore, too, and a lot more dedicated, and easier to get along with than Derek had been. We listened to, and respected each other, didn't argue with each other, and I didn't have to worry about her making stupid jokes, or being senselessly interrupted whenever I tried to talk. But…I missed working with Derek. I missed being interrupted with a lame joke and hearing his laugh, which I missed more than I would have liked to admit to myself.

"It's not even like he's *that* cute!" I declared out of the blue, slamming my pen down in frustration. Instead of trying to figure out chemical yields, my mind had fallen back to the French Club trip. *The French Club trip that had meant absolutely nothing*, I kept trying to tell myself. The fact that he was dating Amelia now meant that, didn't it?

Patrice looked up from her homework. "Who isn'?" she wondered. But then a smile crossed her features as she caught up with my thoughts. "Well, I guess he kind uh is," she replied, unhelpfully. "For a White boy," she thought to add.

"I mean, I understand that most people get crushes during this time," I said mostly to myself. Even though I would have liked to bypass the whole crush stage of adolescence, I could understand having feelings for someone if this *were* the beginnings of a crush, but we were talking about Derek. *Derek*!

He was an inch, *if* he was taller, and of no particularly special build. His blue eyes were usually obscured by that stupid haircut, and in stature he wasn't skinny, or buff, or athletic. He was solid. Not solid like 'right on', just solid. If we were younger, he'd be described as chubby. He kind of had this lumbering gait, too. He may not have been tripping over his own feet when he walked, but his posture was only one step up from terrible (well maybe two or three up); hardly the embodiment of charm or grace. No one would look at him and mistake him as their Prince Charming; he wasn't handsome, or pretty, or beautiful, he was cute. But when he smiled…it didn't transform his face, it completed it, and then he could have been Michelangelo's *David*.

"He's a little funny, too," she replied. A *little* was right. He imitated comedians from the TV, told jokes that everyone already knew the punch line to, entered into conversations that he wasn't a part of, and ignored half of the people around him, yet always seemed to be in the center of something. He was probably one of the hardest people to have a serious conversation with, not counting the times where our conversations had drifted toward the serious.

My lips drew together into a full on pout. "You know, tha only reason you even think 'bout him so much is cause you don' have no one," Patrice observed. "That'd go away if you'd just date."

"I don't want to date anyone," I asserted.

"Yet, you still thinkin' bout that boy," she noted. "I'm tellin' you, I could set you up wit someone if you won' go talk ta him."

In answer, I picked up my pencil again. For some time we worked quietly, but after I finished my chemistry homework, I had nothing to do but think about how *not* cute, and *not* funny Derek was. It just didn't make sense.

I shot a glance at Patrice stretched out on her bed, gnawing on her eraser as she contemplated the math problem in front of her.

"Need some help?" I questioned. She gave no indication that she'd heard me. "Are you *almost* done at least?" I prodded. I wasn't trying to be snappy, I just didn't need any more downtime; I didn't like what ended up running through my mind when I had it. "Maybe?"

She looked up a few minutes later. "Okay, done. What'd you get?" Even though Patrice and I weren't in the same class, I'd taken the time to work through her homework problems. I told her my answer. She looked down at the paper in frustration. "I didn' get that," she declared. "I got -3. How'd your answer end up positive?"

I sat up on my knees. "Let me see how you worked the problem," I directed. I checked her work, circling the step that she got wrong. "You had everything right up to this point," I informed her encouragingly, handing the notebook back to her.

She squinted over it. "Why's it wrong?" she demanded in frustration. "I did tha same thing that you said to do! It's tha same kind uh problem, so it should be worked out tha same way!"

"It did work out the same way," I assured her, "It has different variables, though, so that changes the way you go about trying to solve it. Be sure to watch your signs as you work through your problems, too, or else you'll end up doing all the right work and still have the wrong answer."

She looked back at her own paper in irritation, then looked at the way I'd worked out the problem. Slowly her features softened. "Oh," she muttered. She reworked the problem and ended up with the right answer this time. "Can we do anothuh?" she questioned.

I had nothing else to do. "Sure," I said, agreeably.

"Good," she said, stabbing her pencil towards her homework, "cause I really wanna do well on this test. I made a high C on tha last one, and I wanna do bettuh on this next one cause I wanna least make a B in tha class. Lawler's tha type uh guy who enjoys failin' people."

"Then why not make an A?"

"I can' make an A." The way she said that statement made it sound irrefutable, but Patrice was a lot smarter than she gave herself credit for.

"Why not?" I demanded.

She held her hands up and let them drop. "I ain't you, T, I can' make an A. This is math."

"You can be good at anything with practice," I directed.

"No *you* can. Can we please just work through some more problems? I'm supposed to be callin' Darnell at 8:00, and I wanna be done wit this 'fore he gets home."

"Where's he anyway?" I wondered.

"Coach got mad at tha team tha othuh day so he scheduled a late practice. They bettuh win as much as they've been practicin'. You goinna come ta tha game on Friday?"

"I didn't intend to," I responded.

"Come on, Trace," she pleaded, "keep me company?"

"Since when has being kept company ever been a problem for you," I questioned. "Within a few minutes of going anywhere, you always have a swarm of people around you."

"Alright, I *want* you ta come, then. We hardly spend time togethuh no more, and at least you don' ask me constantly if tha rumors are true 'bout Darnell, and if we're...you know? You're like tha only one that don' want to be bothered enough ta care."

I looked over at my friend, contemplating her words. "What are you and Darnell supposed to be doing?"

Something about the way I asked made Patrice laugh, even though she quickly grew serious. "You know…," she responded hesitantly. "It."

I was surprised because the thought had never crossed my mind. "Are you?" I questioned, at the same time wondering if I should sound disapproving.

She ducked her head in embarrassment, and didn't answer immediately. "Not yet," she finally responded, speaking from around her hands.

"So you would?" I wondered curiously.

She shrugged. "Maybe."

"And I do care," I asserted. "I just figure that your relationship with Darnell is none of my business."

"Since when've you cared 'bout what is and ain't yo business?" she questioned good-naturedly. "If you can' tell me tha truth who's goin' to?"

"True," I agreed. With only a little hesitation I wondered, "So when's maybe?"

"I on't know! I on't even know if I want to, but Darnell keeps bringin' it up, and I mean I like him and everythin'. Maybe aftuh homecomin'."

"Isn't that only a few weeks away?" I questioned, surprising myself that I knew that information. "Are you ready for that?"

She shrugged. "Dunno," she remarked, biting down on her lip.

"Do you love him?"

It took her some time to answer. "I guess, maybe, I on't know."

I thought about that, and the next question I blurted out without really thinking about it. "Did you love Omar?" I questioned, trying to sound nonchalant. She looked at me in surprise, shrugging in an off-hand way. "I dunno."

"You two spent a lot of time together," I pointed out.

"He's easy ta spend time wit," she returned.

"So is that why you were with him, to spend time?"

She gave a coded smile. "It wasn' tha only reason," she declared.

"But you two broke up," I responded in confusion.

"It happens," she said, dismissively. "No one expects a relationship ta last forevuh. Omar and me just kinda decided that…tha relationship got a 'lil too real for Omar. He just wanted someone ta spend time wit."

"Is Darnell the same way?"

"I on't know! You can' really compare Darnell ta Omar; two completely different guys and situations. I don' think that he's that way, though. Darnell is more confident in himself."

"I noticed-," I muttered.

Patrice ignored it. "And I feel...I dunno, more connected ta Darnell."

"Connected," I repeated. Patrice probably thought I was teasing her because she shrugged. "What do you expect from him, from your relationship?"

That question seemed to irritate her for some reason. I wasn't trying to pry, I really wasn't, I just was trying to figure out why she dated the guys she did; the motivation behind it. "I on't expect nothin'! We like each othuh, and maybe it turns out that we spend a lot uh time togethuh, but maybe we don'."

Considering how many ways there were to get in trouble, that didn't make sense to me. "Then why date?" I questioned.

"Why not? We're in high school, we're supposed to! Find out what we like in a guy, I guess. How do you know what you like unless you test tha waters? You don' want ta marry without figurin' that out. Just so's I know, this's bout Derek again, right?"

I wondered how we were back on him. "No!" I said, quickly. "It's just, I...I don't get him," I faltered lamely. "I don't know what I feel about him, but I barely know him." I tried to put to words exactly what I felt. "I'm... *confused*."

I thought it was the perfect word for the situation. He had me confused to no end. I realized that I'd never told her about the French Club trip, so I told her about it, the ride home, and the community build, leaving out the part about what I thought I saw when he looked at me. With her interrupting every few seconds it only took about fifteen minutes to get the whole story out.

"Why're you *just* now tellin' me this?" she demanded, actually sounding angry.

"I feel foolish even bringing it up," I admitted. "But I just can't stop thinking about that moment, and him since, even though I know he's not sitting there thinking about me."

"How you know that?" she questioned, instead of telling me how stupid I was for spending so much time thinking about a boy who probably saw me as a joke. I mean Derek's track record practically screamed it: he was a clown.

"I think I read way more into it than I should have," I decided. "I mean if we had something, we'd at least acknowledge each other, right? We barely even talk to each other, 'Triece."

Judging by the look she was giving me, I imagined that if she wasn't sitting on the bed, her hands would have been on her hips. Instead they just flared around. "So what?" she demanded. "*Start* talkin' ta him!"

"Easy for you to say: you don't ever seem to have any trouble talking to anyone, and I don't know how. Besides, he's white-,"

"You say that like it actually mattuhs ta you," Patrice remarked.

"It matters to people like Sean."

"You think *I* listen ta everythin' my big brothuhs say ta me?" Patrice said dismissively.

"He's not the only one who feels that way."

"Does it mattuh ta *you*?" she posed.

"No. Yes. Imagine how embarrassing it is to get turned down. Now imagine that he's white, too. And according to you, isn't he supposed to notice me first, otherwise I'm fast?"

"Oh, he's *definitely* noticed you," Patrice declared with certainty. "That's obvious. Why don' you just try'n talk ta him? See where it goes from there?" Considering the subject matter, I was a bit surprised by her advice. Everyone else would tell me I was a fool for entertaining the thought of Derek liking me.

"Why, so I can make an idiot of myself?" I felt a sudden appreciation for Frankie when he wanted to take Cecilia out. "He has a girlfriend-," I interjected.

She didn't let me get away with that one. "Would you talk to him if he didn'," she posed before I'd even finished.

"And anyway," I responded, not replying to that, "he doesn't like me."

"He ast you out, didn' he?" she reasoned.

"He asked me if I wanted to see a movie with him because he felt bad that I was going home to an empty house. That's the only reason, if it'd even been that. He might have been just joking on me, or maybe he's one of those guys who thinks that black girls are an easy lay."

"Didn' sound like it," she returned. "How do you know what his feelings are? Why don' you talk to him and find out what he feels instead of just thinkin' you know everythin'?"

"If he liked me, he's had plenty of moments when he could've said something."

"Guys're idiots," Patrice asserted. "If you're goinna wait for them ta come around, you'll be waitin' a long time."

"What if he doesn't feel the same way?" I wondered.

Patrice gave me an understanding look, chewing on her pencil. "Then it's tha pits, and you eventually get ovuh it, but you'll nevuh know unless you try. You should give yo'self more credit. Guys *want* ta talk ta you, but I swear you make yourself so unapproachable sometimes. They have feelings, too, and they don' want ta try ta talk ta someone who they know's goinna hurt they feelings."

"Whose feelings am I hurting?" I wondered. "I don't talk to anybody. I stick to myself."

She tossed her pillow at me. "That's my point! People expect you ta be more open. So are you goinna come to tha game wit me or not?" she questioned abruptly, throwing me off.

"I don't like football," I reminded her for like the millionth time.

"See that's where you mess up," she informed me. "It don' really *mattuh* if you *like* football," she said in irritation. "It's not about *likin'* tha thing, I don' *like* football. I don' go ta tha games cause I *like* ta watch a bunch uh silly boys jump on top uh each othuh. That's not what it's *about*. It's about havin' school spirit, and bein' seen. Meetin' yo classmates; spendin' time wit folks outside class."

"I do that..."

"Hangin' out wit Colben aftuh school and seein' folks at church on Sunday don' count, Trace."

"Maybe not, but that's free, and I've got the right clothes for it."

"You're free to borrow anythin' uh mine," Patrice offered generously. "And you wouldn' need more'n a dollar." I thought about the groceries that a dollar could buy. I didn't like asking my mom for money because I knew how little of it we had. The money my dad sent was just enough to cover the rent, occasionally a little extra, and I knew my mom didn't make a lot. "We're in the best years uh our lives!" she said with gusto, no thought to my conflict. "Don' waste your best years sittin' at home."

"Did anyone ever tell you you'd make a good cheerleader?"

"I'm serious, Trace. You *might* actually have fun."

"That's doubtful," I remarked, grumpily.

— 14 —
"Gossip in the Sanctuary"

I let Patrice convince me to go to the game and predictably she had at least six other people around her in no time at all. It seemed like every time she went somewhere, someone was stopping to say hi to her. I went unnoticed for most of the evening while I read the book I'd brought with me, and Mason High took home another win. I think they were on a streak or something.

After the game, Patrice and her friends all went to the Trick to celebrate, and when I went along with them, I got a few surprised looks from some of Patrice's other friends. But Patrice was nothing, if not loyal. She took my book from me, though, before we all crowded into two booths. There were so many of us in so little space, that I was touching arm to arm, or toe to foot, with half a dozen different people. I found myself sitting across from Patrice and Darnell, and beside Shelton Pierce, another one of the players on the team. The arrangement, I was sure, was the reason why Patrice's friend, Lina, who I didn't have the best of relationships with on a good day, and was sitting on my other side, kept giving me funny looks. *Middle school all over again.*

"So, hey, uh, Tracy," Shelton said stiltedly after a look from Patrice that I wasn't supposed to notice. "Hi."

Patrice gave *me* a pointed look this time, and I searched for something to say. "Good game," seemed appropriate, but I couldn't really think of anything to follow that up with. I couldn't pretend I'd watched the game; I didn't even know what position he played. That didn't seem to bother him, though; he seemed as if he were used to people not knowing what to say around him.

Shelton was the teenaged dream; he was the kind of guy that you were *supposed* to have a crush on. I was certain that half the school did, and being this close to him, it wasn't hard to imagine why. He was adorably cute, like a tall, well-muscled baby, and one of the major players on the team. He had a Jackie Robinson-like possession to him, too, an ease and toughness of skin that had allowed him to win over all of those people who didn't want 'some Negro kid' darkening the football team.

Because of the lack of room, his arm was flung casually over the top of the booth, and I was sitting less than an inch away from him, practically pushed into his side. He still had the slightest sheen to his hair, and even in the plain white t-shirt that the players wore underneath their jerseys, he looked good. I couldn't deny that.

A 'gentle' nudge from Patrice had me searching for something else to say, but I hugely doubted that he wanted to know what experiments Mr. Colben and I were working on, and I didn't know what else might be interesting to him. I was inept at making small talk, but I tried. I listened to the rest of the conversations that went on around us, and mimicked them the best I could, but I felt seriously out of my element.

Lina must have agreed because she kept talking over me, making me feel even more out of sorts. It was a tremendous testament to Patrice that Shelton kept talking to me, kept directing conversations at me, making eye-contact with me. Even though it was overwhelming when Shelton gave you his full attention, it still didn't feel quite the same way it did when I was looking at Derek.

I breathed easier when it got close to Patrice's curfew, and I had an excuse to excuse myself from the crowd. Shelton looked after me when I got up, pausing in the middle of a conversation he was having with one of his teammates. "You leaving, Tracy?" he questioned. He actually managed to sound as if he cared.

"Yes," I said, feigning a nonchalance that I didn't actually have. "Curfew."

Lina snickered, already scooting closer to him. "I ain't got no curfew," she declared. "I ain't still some baby."

I gave Lina a look. *If you want him, have him*, I thought at her. I smiled. "Thanks for letting me come out with you guys." Patrice looked up at my words, and pulled away from Darnell, his arms, and his lips.

She paused to give him one more quick kiss before she followed after me. "Peace, y'all. See you at school tomorrow," she called over her shoulder.

I was glad to be away from the noise, and I was so into my own thoughts that it was awhile before I realized that Patrice was even talking. "Tracy!" she said again sharply.

I looked at her. "Yes?"

"I ast what you thought 'bout Shelton. He was sure friendly, wasn' he?"

"Did you bribe him to talk to me?" I wondered.

She scowled at me. "Uh course not! He asked 'bout you all on his own. So what'd you think?"

"I barely know anything about him."

"You on't have ta know his life story ta check out tha guy, Trace! Geez, girl!"

"Well," I considered, "then I think he's all right."

"Alright? *Shelton?*" she wondered in disbelief. "Shelton is a senior and a real solid fox, and all you can say is he's okay?"

"We both know that he's gorgeous," I responded. "Otherwise, he seems like a nice boy," I declared.

"You're hopeless," Patrice responded. "I give up!"

Mrs. Dressler snapped the door shut with a firm finality at the bell. "Please pass last night's homework assignment to the front," she commanded. "I've finished grading last week's tests, and I have to say, I wasn't impressed." As the homework papers made their way to the front, she started to pass back the test papers. "I hope to see better on next week's test." I remembered feeling very confident when I turned in my paper, so even though the first two recipients didn't seem happy with their grades, I wasn't too worried about mine. Mrs. Dressler sat my test paper in front of me. "See me after class, Miss Burrows," she directed. My paper had no grade on it. From one seat over, Sam Williams smirked at me.

The class dragged as I worried about what Mrs. Dressler had to say. While she worked examples out on the board, I reworked the test problems. I'd only gotten part of one question wrong, so why hadn't she graded my test? I tried to tell myself not to worry over nothing, but that didn't work too well. Finally, the class ended, and I stayed seated while the rest of my classmates left the room, a few glancing back at me. "Close the door behind you, Mr. Williams," she directed Sam on his way out.

When the room was completely emptied, and the door was closed, Mrs. Dressler focused her attention on me. She was in no way one of my favorite teacher's, but as of yet I hadn't had much reason to dislike her.

"I want to talk to you about your test," she said bracingly. "Are you familiar with Mason's Academic Integrity Policy?"

I nodded; it was one of the many forms they made you sign at the beginning of the year, but I was confused by her choice of openings. "Yes, ma'am."

She looked down at me over her very petite nose. "Mason has a very strict policy concerning cheating," she went on. "It is a suspendable offence, expellable even. A student has brought it to my attention that someone-," from the way she was looking at me, I was sure that someone was supposed to be me-"has been less than honest in the work that they have turned in, and for that I cannot be more disappointed."

I felt a sinking feeling in the pit of my stomach as I waited for the axe to fall. "If I can be candid, I wasn't thrilled to have you placed in my class for this very reason, but Mrs. Rupert says that you refused to change your schedule. It is one thing to not be able to do the work-y'alls brains just aren't made the same-but for you to cheat just to make people think that you possess an intelligence that we know you don't have, that's something completely different. I won't allow cheating. If I catch you in the act, I will be sure to do everything I can to make sure that you are aptly punished for it."

Her words were like a slap in the face. My eyes fell to my paper, because if I kept looking at her, it would be impossible to maintain my composure. The work that I'd turned in to her so far had been all mine, and nothing sort of exemplary; I was never even late to her class. But apparently that reeked of some falseness to *her* truths, and somehow that made *me* dishonest. The only way, then, to remedy the situation would be *to* cheat, but it would be to cheat myself by making poorer grades. I'd make it through the rest of high school easier, but I'd certainly never make it to Harvard.

I took two very long breaths. "Mrs. Dressler, I haven't cheated on anything in your class-" I tried to assert, making my voice sound respectful.

She didn't let me finish though. "You mean you haven't been *caught*," she barked, angrily. My mouth opened in protest, but then I thought better of it. It wasn't like I hadn't come across this type of behavior before. It was one thing, though, to be treated as if I was a dumb beast, and another for the words to actually be laid out in front of me, over an ungraded test that I knew I'd aced. Her disbelief in my ability was even more startling because she was a female math teacher, the only one in the school, and no doubt she knew exactly what it felt like to constantly have to prove yourself. It was baffling how she could experience that herself, and still think so little of me.

"Ma'am, what about my test?" I questioned, once I'd found my voice. She looked down at me coldly, hate almost pouring out of her features. She wrote a 'C' at the top of my paper.

"A C?" I protested. "I didn't get anything wrong!"

"You're lucky it's not a 0," she said, harshly. "You can take a make-up test in Saturday detention, otherwise you're stuck with that grade. I'd advise you, too, to keep in mind that cheating will get you nowhere in life."

I stared hard at the desk in front of me, concentrating on my breathing until it returned to normal. When I felt like I was calm enough, I got up out of my seat, and left the classroom behind. I stopped the thought of tears; they were useless. So was being overwhelmed by how unfair it was. I didn't live in a world that was fair. If I was going to let myself get caught up by that then I wasn't going to get very far in life. Besides, I knew the information covered on the test. That wouldn't change even if I had to take it again.

I was so preoccupied by Mrs. Dressler, that I almost missed Shelton waiting outside my classroom, nearly walking past him without registering his presence. Well, okay, so I noticed him standing there, he's 6'1 and 200 lbs., so of course I noticed him, but it didn't register that he was waiting for *me* until after he called my name. Even after I heard it, though, I was still having trouble believing that he was talking to me. Guys didn't usually talk to me. Girls didn't usually talk to me. Usually I was invisible.

"Err...hi," I said to his greeting. In our little high school world, Shelton was like Sidney Poitier, and I was the kid on the set who fetched the coffee.

There was no logical reason that he was waiting outside of *my* classroom for *me*. I wondered if I had fallen asleep in class, and was still sleeping; or maybe it was Patrice that'd fallen asleep, and I was just living in her dream.

Shelton shifted his stance, seemingly as confused. "I…um…have first period on this hall, too," he explained, "and I saw that you did, so I thought maybe we could walk to our next class together?"

"Sure," I remarked, off-handedly. He'd waited all this time just to walk with me to class? The absurdity of it was enough to get my mind off of Mrs. Dressler's cheating allegation. He matched my footsteps, and if walking with Patrice made me feel invisible, walking beside Shelton was ten times worse. He couldn't walk a few feet down the hallway without someone congratulating him, or shaking his hand. Whites and Blacks, alike, stopped to speak to him, and sarcastically I thought that if Willie Mays or Joe Louis had led the Civil Rights Movement, we would have gotten all the schools truly integrated, and one of our own in the White House, faster than it took to blink.

Shelton deposited me safely at the door of my next classroom, and hesitated before going off to find his own class. I watched after him, even once he was gone, thoroughly confused by the entire exchange.

*

I'd read, once, that the nearest star to Earth is Alpha Centauri, and to get to it would take 4.22 light years. Scientists say there's nothing faster than the speed of light, but that's only because they've failed to realize how fast gossip can travel in a high school. It seemed that in no time at all, everyone seemed to know that Shelton Pierce had been seen in the hallway with Stacy Carrows or Tricia Murrows (and other variations), and who in the world was I anyway?

Tracy? That smart girl? The kiss up? The one that's always hanging around with Darnell's girl…Patrice?

That siddity, yellow, white-talkin', know-it-all?

She's high on herself, ain't she?

What does Shelton see in her?

I always thought she was pretty.

Not pretty enough to be with Shelton.

Ain't it tha truth!

And have you seen her clothes?

My God, on my mother!

You think Shelton and Tracy are going to go to the dance together?

If he's going to go with her, I bet I could get him to go with me.

Light-skinned girls all think that they somethin' special.

She's so square!

I bet she puts out.

You think? I don't.

Teacher's pets and preacher girls are always the ones who end up 'in the way'.

If she don' put out, I bet she will if she's with Shelton.

And on and on and on. I became instantly known overnight…except that mostly no one actually knew who I was so I could walk right past these conversations, and people didn't realize they were talking about me. But the odd thing, or what was funny about it, I guess, was that there was absolutely nothing going on between us. Shelton and I had 1st, 4th, and 6th period classes on the same hallway, at the same time, and we had the same lunch period, so occasionally we would have lunch together; or rather I would have lunch with him, and his friends, who overlapped with Darnell's friends, and their teammates. I ended up going to the next two football games, too, because Patrice dragged me along with her, and I hung out with them afterwards at her insistence.

That didn't mean I'd suddenly become popular, either; I was pretty much a nonentity, except to Shelton, who almost made it a point to talk to me. He would sit on the outside of the group, turned in his seat towards me as if to include me, and if I didn't say anything to him, he would try to draw out responses from me.

If I wasn't being truthful, I would say that all the sudden attention was more annoying than flattering, and totally unappreciated, but that was only if I wasn't being honest. Shelton was attractive in a way that made you feel shy to be around him, while at the same time somehow made you feel prettier that someone that good looking was interested in you. I couldn't say that I didn't enjoy the attention he was suddenly giving me, either. I understood the feeling that Patrice got whenever she could point out her boyfriend on the field and say, "He's mine," even if Shelton wasn't mine. I could understand the theory behind high school relationships…but there was just too much at stake to want to be a part of it.

Young love, high school love, was confusing to understand, but an interesting thing to witness and watch grow. We got our first lessons in love in middle school when girls suddenly stopped thinking that boys were the grossest thing in the world, and were now calling them 'boyfriends'. Of course in eighth grade that word meant nothing more than that you now had someone to write notes to and sit by at lunch, or someone to give up their deserts to you because that was an infallible requirement: it wasn't true love if he didn't surrender his Twinkie. Relationships were merely school-yard companionship. You didn't go anywhere out in public with your 'boyfriend', and you only dated for a few weeks.

Break ups were public affairs, and usually required one group of girls, declaring to one group of boys, or vice versa, that one member of their group didn't want to date the person in the other group anymore, for one of those predetermined reasons that ended middle school relationships; sometimes it could be as simple a reason as one not folding their note the right way.

The high school version of the dating game was a little more sophisticated, but went along by the same basic rules: guys always asked girls out because a girl that asked a guy out was just plain fast, or womanish. Conversation was initiated by lone boys who were sent to ask a giggling group of girls whether it was all right if he dated a member of their number, and the girl always said no publically, while privately arbitration was secretly carried out in notes until arrangements were eventually made. Relationships were experiments, and break-ups were plentiful and happened sometimes for as arbitrary a reason as the reasons in middle school.

But while middle school relationships had no more physical contact than the occasional and rare hand holding, high school relationships ran the spectrum in physical experimentation. For the most part, the amount of action in a relationship depended on how old you were, where you lived, and how many parents were in the house. Most parents allowed their children to at least group date by sixteen, but some of the more relaxed parents let their children go on singles as soon as they reached high school (though a girl of any age, spending too much alone time with her beau, was fodder for gossip).

Sex was something that everyone seemed to think about, some did, and many paid for, but no one really talked about. Tommy Whittle even got kicked out of school for bringing up contraception in Health. Parents treated sex as if it were something despicably horrible, yet we all knew that we had gotten to this Earth somehow, and basic math could tell us that our parents weren't as chaste as they claimed to be when they were our age. Parents didn't want to talk about sex with their children so children got their mostly wrong information from ads in *Ebony* and other magazines, or from whispered conversations with older children, or they stumbled about in ignorance, easy prey for enterprising men.

High school love came to one of three possible ends: break up, marriage, or pregnancy. Break up was the most common; pregnancy the most devastating. People spent too much time in everyone else's business for everyone to not know which boy had knocked up which girl, but if there wasn't a daddy with a shotgun to go after the boy to convince him to do right, the boy got a free pass, and everyone looked at the girl like they could smell hell's fire on her. The boy was free to continue his schooling, while the girl disappeared for a couple of months. Sometimes she didn't come back at all.

I thought that with odds like that, it was much too risky to attempt, and I'd made up my mind before I'd even started high school that I had no intention of doing it.

But I continued to allow Shelton to walk with me to class.

— 15 —
"Light and Shadow"

There was a newspaper lying out on the table, and I picked it up, waiting for my mom to come out. I scanned the headlines casually before I went back and really read the article that made front page news. I was steaming before I read more than a few sentences, and livid by the time I reached the bottom. "Journalistic integrity," I grunted. This was why I rarely read the local newspapers. My mom rounded the corner while I was re-reading the article. One of her church friends, Mrs. Parker, was with her, and they were gossiping about a deacon. I tried to rearrange my facial features before she noticed.

"You ready to go?" she questioned although I was the one waiting for her. Her question caught Mrs. Parker's attention and she looked me over as if she didn't see me weekly.

"Good lawd, Tracy, you gettin' ta be so grown! How old is you now?"

"I'm fifteen, Mrs. Parker," I responded, patiently. "How are you doing, ma'am?"

"I's alright, chile. Cant's complain cuz I know I's blessed. Your mama's tellin' me how you mades thuh honor roll 'gain. Congratulations!"

"Thank you, ma'am."

"You know Sibby's always talkin' 'bout you. She couldn' be more proud. I've gotta be gettin' home," she said in the same breath, "Mr. Parker'll be lookin' fer me and his dinnah. See you Sunday, Sibby. Nice seeing you 'gain, Shugah."

"Yes ma'am," I replied. I waved good-bye, and we made our way out to the car. Once the door was closed my mom questioned, "What's got you so upset?"

So she noticed after all.

"Did you see what they put in the newspaper, mother?" I questioned.

"No, but I'm guessing that the Tolliver trial is finally over?"

I nodded. Winton had done everything he could think of, including getting the NAACP's lawyers involved, and attempting to take out a second loan on their house, in order to assure his son had a fair trial, but it was all for naught. There was no such thing as a fair trial for a colored man in Alabama. "It's a bit of a stretch to call it a trial, mom," I said. "Try a massacre of justice. Attempted murder? They said that he was deranged, crazed. That it was just his nature, when it was nothing more than an accident; a case of involuntary manslaughter, at best, *if* she had died, but she didn't!"

She frowned with regret. "He got life?"

"What else would he get in Alabama? Either they give you life, or they take it from you. Do you remember when Lacy Walker burned her dad's house to the ground with him inside? She got off with a warning, and only had to pay a fine! Or when that white girl got raped and they blamed it on Bigsy McKnight, and when they found out that it was really her brother-in-law they didn't even issue a retraction? Didn't apologize to the man they claimed it was, either, no matter that he got beat up, killed almost!"

"No one said the world was fair," my mom retorted, and it was there, in her voice, how easily we accepted that fact about life. Hadn't I, myself, got a huge dose of that? I could accept that life was unfair, but I couldn't just accept that there was nothing that could be done about it. Pollie was a kid who should be looking forward to school dances and ball games, not preparing to spend his life in jail. If he were white, he wouldn't have even been on trial. It would have just been an unfortunate accident. None of the people who had set fire to the barbershop that night had even been arrested. I doubted they even got a talking to, even though *their* actions had resulted in the actual death of another human being. Just because this was the way that it *was* didn't mean that we should just accept a second class existence.

"I know that, mother," I said, trying to keep the irritation out of my voice. I wasn't irritated with her, just the world. "That doesn't mean that we should just accept the injustice just because that's the way it's been done. Things *have got* to change."

"You remember that when you have your expensive, big city education."

— 139 —

"Ah, mom, not you too," I mumbled. "Come on, you're from the city."

"I only mean that you be sure to remember this type of outrage after you have your Harvard law degree; don't just pretend that it doesn't exist because it becomes convenient."

"Never," I responded. Once I was in a position to evoke change, I planned on doing it. Period.

That was pretty much the end of the conversation for most of the ride to the grocery store. My mom and I had never really managed small talk, so when we lapsed into silence, neither of us tried to break it. Normally we did our shopping at Winn Dixie, where the clerks were friendliest, and they gave you the most green stamps for your purchase, but since they closed early on Wednesday nights, and we were coming from my mom's church, we went to the Kroger's instead. To try to make the trip as short as possible, my mom split the list in half, and handed part of it to me. I looked at the paper, tried to strategize, and when that didn't work, I picked an aisle and started down it.

I was contemplating the choices in the canned foods section, when I became aware of someone behind me. A few seconds later I heard Derek's voice saying, "If we keep runnin' into each othuh like this, I'm goinna think you're tryin' ta catch me, Trace."

I was smiling before I even realized that his presence should not elicit that type of reaction from me. I took a few seconds to make sure that I didn't still have the smile on my face when I turned around. "Hello, Derek," I said, hoping I sounded very casual. Inwardly, I was trying to figure out how it was that, once again, our paths crossed, because it seemed that we were always running into each other.

Once I'd realized that there was a (very slight) possibility that I could (*maybe*) have feelings for Derek, I attempted to avoid him as often as possible. In French it was easiest because I knew where he sat, and if I came in early and found work to be absorbed in when he came in, I could avoid his eye, his gaze. Out in the hallway, and around the school, it wasn't so easy. Derek had a similar schedule to mine this year, so there was the potential to run into him often. I changed the way I went to my classes when I knew he'd be on the same hallway, just so that I wouldn't pass him in the hall. I avoided the places that I'd seen him at the most, so that I wouldn't run into him between classes. I stayed later than I usually did, I lingered more, or left earlier, but no matter what I did, it still seemed like I ran into him way too much; the more I attempted to avoid him, the more I ended up running into him.

And when our paths did inexplicably cross, and there was a point where I had to greet him, or speak to him, my mind always went blank. I couldn't look at him, I sputtered over words…I was completely helpless. So to make up for it, I was pretty short with him, and not very nice at all. It was utter madness. If Colben and I weren't already well committed to a project, I would have recommended that we do a study on high school relationships and the effects that crushes have on the teenage psyche because, I swear, it was a phenomenon.

I wasn't sure if Derek bought my nonchalance, but he gave his usual smile. "So, what brings you here?" he questioned.

I looked at the space above his ears, which seemed to help in talking to him. "Shopping with my mom," I explained. "You?"

He nodded down at the shopping cart he was leaning against. "Tha same, but don' tell nobody. I have my image to protect." I was aware, a second too late, that he was waiting for me to respond to that. When I didn't, Derek's eyes fell to examining our wares, and I was glad that there wasn't anything embarrassing in there; the Kotex were on my mom's half of the list. After a moment, he looked back at me. "How're classes?" he questioned with a smirk whose meaning I couldn't even begin to guess.

"They're going well."

"Yea? Someone told me that your French II was really hard, but well worth it 'cause there's this really charmin', *really* good lookin' guy makin' sure that everyone's properly entertained." The laugh I gave came out a little squeaky, and my tongue caught as I tried to figure out something to say. Derek seemed suddenly put out when I didn't respond. "Hey, so where's your new shadow?" he asked awkwardly, like he was going for casual but wasn't exactly able to make it.

My confusion made my voice sound normal when I questioned, "What shadow?"

"Tha guy from tha football team," Derek remarked. "Tha corner?" To my blank look he explained, "Tha tall, bronzed-skinned guy? Every time I see you now, seems like y'all togethuh."

"Oh, Shelton!" I realized. "He's not my shadow, he's just being friendly."

Skepticism was written all over his face. "He don' look very friendly," Derek asserted. "I didn' know you went for tha big, stupid jock type."

"He's not a stupid jock!" I remarked, defensively. "He's plenty smart. And it's not like Amelia," I stutter-stepped over her name "is the sharpest tool in the box."

I felt bad as soon as I said that because I really had no reason to dislike his girlfriend, and-except for a classmate of mine named Jane who had a crush on Derek-I didn't know anyone who did. Amelia was just the kind of person everyone seemed to like. She was a junior class officer, was in every play that the school put on since she started going to Mason, sang in her church's choir, and wanted to be an actress when she grew up.

And if that wasn't enough, she wasn't just high school good-looking, either. She could have been Samantha Eggar's little sister for how she looked, right down to the freckles, feathered hair, and probing eyes. Even though I wanted to, I couldn't deny how nice the two of them looked together. Somehow he looked better, taller, stood straighter, seemed more distinguished when he was around her, and she seemed more approachable. He looked at her as if she was the sun, and similarly she orbited around him. She wasn't slow either. In smarts, she and Patrice were probably on par (though I'm certain Patrice was a little smarter).

Derek bit down on his lip at my words, but didn't respond to what I said. "So, are y'all goin' to tha dance, togethuh?" he wondered.

For a second I had to remember that there was a dance coming up. "I think he might be," I responded. I only caught the 'y'all' after I finished talking. "Are you and Amelia planning on going?"

"Of course," he said without hesitation.

Someone who was passing by, glanced back at us, as if we shouldn't be talking to each other. I sub-consciously took a step away from him. Before either of us could restart the conversation, my mom rounded the corner, and she took in the scene. "Hi, mom," I said more eagerly than I normally would have.

The look she returned was very stern, and not at all inviting as she quietly assessed the situation. "Who's your friend?" she questioned in a clipped voice.

"This is Derek," I remarked. "We have a class together."

Derek extended a hand. "Nice to meet you Mrs. Burrows," he remarked, a hundred percent parental charm. I must have looked surprised because Derek looked a little put out by my reaction, but that could have been due to the expression that my mom was giving him, or the fact that she hadn't shaken his hand.

"Well, *Derek*, we have some things to attend to right now. It was nice meeting you." She sounded like the opposite was true. Although we didn't talk often, Derek's name had still managed to crop up during a conversation or two between us. I could tell that my mom was certainly not pleased.

Derek's hand fell to his side, and he looked away. I whispered a soft good-bye, and followed silently behind my mom as she steered us towards the next aisle. She held in what she had to say until we were alone. "Is that *the* Derek you're always talking about?" she wondered once we'd rounded the corner.

"I wouldn't say *always*," I mumbled. She glanced briefly over her shoulder, and I automatically turned to look, too, even though I knew he wasn't there.

"You get outraged about the Tolliver case, but that's who you're always going on about? That's dangerous, Tracy," she remarked.

I felt the need to defend him. "He had nothing to do with what happened at the Trick, and mom, you know I don't go around with boys."

"Good, because like I said, that's dangerous. You shouldn't even be as friendly as you are with him. I don't want to see you caught like that."

"Since when have you had a problem with me being friends with someone?" I wondered. "When we were in Illinois-,"

She cut me off. "We're not in Illinois," she said, sharply. "And you weren't of dating age then."

"I don't want to-,"

"I hear what you're saying, but your face says otherwise."

"Mom, I'm not looking to put down anything more permanent than necessary here," I replied. "Once I graduate, I'm gone."

"You make sure you remember that," she remarked. "I thought you had better judgment than that," she added for good measure.

The next day at school, Shelton's increasingly familiar form was waiting for me in the hallway. "Hey," he greeted, matching my stride.

"Did you hear about Pollie?" I wondered angrily.

He frowned, the case obviously one of the last things he'd been thinking about. "Yea, my mom can't stop talking 'bout it. Not surprised."

"No one's surprised," I replied. "That doesn't mean we shouldn't be angry about it."

"Yea. He's a solid guy." Shelton shook his head. "Life's rough," he summarized. "What you goinna do?" A beat passed. "Hey, so are you goinna stop by practice this afternoon?"

"What practice?" I wondered, realizing a second too late that he probably meant football. He said as much. "Why? What's happening at practice?"

"Well nothin', really, but I'm goinna be there."

"Aren't you always," I replied.

Shelton's look was unreadable. "Yea, but I wanted *you* to come by."

"I have tutoring," I responded, still trying to figure out what his look meant.

"Oh," Shelton commented. "Well what you doin' aftuh you're done with tutorin'?"

The answer was automatic. "Homework and research."

"And aftuh that?"

"Sleeping, hopefully."

Shelton shook his head. "When will you *not* be busy, Tracy?" he wondered, pointedly.

I missed the point. "I'm usually always busy," I remarked. "School and projects mostly take up all of my time."

"So, there's no time 'tween aftuh school, and 'fore you go to bed, to do nothin' else?"

I felt like I was missing something. "Was there something that you wanted?" I questioned, unsure.

"Yes, I *wanted* to talk to you," he stressed, "and I was wonderin' if you would be available to talk sometime tonight? I mean only if yo momma don' have a problem with boys callin'."

"Oh," I responded, and then as it suddenly dawned on me, "Oh! Umm... hm. I guess you could call me later. What did you want to talk about?"

"Just wanted to talk," he replied, vaguely. "We don' get to talk much durin' school. Tryin' to get to know you bettuh, since, well I thought maybe you'd like to go to the dance-"

I didn't let him finish his statement. "Did Patrice put you up to asking me that?" I questioned, humor in my voice.

Shelton didn't share my amusement. "No. She didn' put me up to nothin'. If you don' want-,"

"It's not that," I responded, quickly. "It's...I don't dance," I attempted to explain. "I'm horribly inept when it comes to those sorts of things."

"Oh," Shelton remarked, surprised. I don't think that he got turned down all that often. I almost told him that I was sure that Lina would love it if he asked her to the dance, but I didn't think that would be too helpful.

I tried to salvage things a little bit. "But if you want to still call me or something, I don't mind," I decided.

"Oh," he responded shortly. He didn't say much else.

— 16 —
"Diary of a Genius"

Tracy, you didn'!" Patrice moaned.

"How do you manage to sound surprised?" I questioned.

"You didn' really turn down *Shelton Pierce* did you? What's wrong wit you?"

I frowned, taking her words a little too seriously. "You didn't have to talk him into going to the dance with me," I remarked. "I didn't want to go anyway."

"I *didn'*, Trace. Did you turn him down 'cause you thought I set you up? Well if that's tha case, call 'im up! I've nothin' ta do wit his actions. Girl, it's Shelton! Who in tha school *wouldn'* want ta go out wit him? It's not like one dance is goinna kill your prude streak."

"I'm not prude!" I said indignantly. "I...don't dance."

"Shel-ton," she reiterated.

"Which is another reason for me not to want to make a fool of myself," I responded. "Besides, I have research that still needs to be done, and I can't waste a Saturday. I don't want to turn in a project that's less than perfect, and there's still too much that's left to do before the end of the year." And, not that she asked, but I didn't have the money to buy a dress, or the shoes that I'd need to go with it, either, for that matter.

"*Tracy*," she moaned. "You can' be serious! It's Homecomin' and you was ast ta tha dance by one uh tha foxiest guys in school!"

"It's not like he'll have any trouble finding someone else to go to the dance," I reasoned.

She looked like she wanted to shake me. "But he *wanted* ta go wit you! What's tha deal? I thought y'all been hangin' out. I thought you *liked* him."

"I do like him," I agreed. "We're friends."

It was no wonder her eyes didn't bug out of her head. "You're not supposed ta be *friends*," Patrice said, shrilly. "Does this have somethin' ta do wit Derek?"

How had this suddenly turned into something involving him? "This has nothing to do with Derek," I insisted. "Why do you have to bring his name into this?"

"Because you're not goin' ta tha dance wit Shelton, so it has to be somethin'."

"It's…I never feel comfortable in those situations; I always feel awkward, and silly, and out of place. It's not my *scene,* not to mention that I don't have a dress, or money to spend. Is that really that hard to understand?"

"*Yes!*" she hissed, truthfully, and I realized how, for her, it could be. Her parents might not have had much more money than we did, but Patrice was still used to getting what she wanted. If her parents wouldn't, or couldn't, give it to her, one of her brothers was sure to. It wasn't like that for me. Maybe if my parents hadn't divorced, I'd be different. Maybe I'd be just like her, or like Vivian, or Cecilia. When my parents were still together, we'd had clothes from catalogues, we did our shopping at the 'good' grocery store; there'd been plenty of money for extras. Maybe if I'd grown up that way, I'd be more social, but it wasn't just about showing up: you had to look a certain way while you were there. You had to speak a certain way, too, and my books hadn't supplied me with that language.

"It's very hard ta understand why you turned down tha most eligible guy in school," she went on. "I mean, if it was because you were waitin' for Derek, that would be sorta understandable, maybe, except that you don' wait for a guy, evuh, and you certainly don' wait single."

"I know this may sound hard to believe, Triece, but I don't want to date Derek either." Which was true. Besides that I didn't want to date anyone, Derek was the epitome of everything that I disliked about high school and high school guys in general. He didn't take much in life seriously, school was an afterthought, and I was sure he never paused to contemplate the future. I may have felt something that might have been jealously when I saw him and Amelia together, but she wasn't what I wanted to be. I could see exactly what she would become, what she would do with her life, and I wanted nothing of that sort.

And the fact that he was dating Amelia just seemed to cement more how asinine any feelings that I thought I possessed for Derek were. If you could look at everything in an empirical vacuum, any guy who was attracted to her and what she stood for-the ideal, the convention, the dream-couldn't be attracted to me, and the reverse was true as well. I wanted the exact opposite of what Amelia represented, so how could I even possess feelings for someone who was attracted to that?

So, I didn't really know what I wanted, what the feelings meant, but I was sure it wasn't that I wanted to be with him. I honestly didn't want to date anyone. To me, most high schoolers dated because it was something to do. I had enough to do, so I didn't bother. So what did I want then? "I, I want to be there for him," I stuttered, as I tried to put my feelings to words, "you know, if he needs me, be a shoulder for him to cry on, or lean against, or silly little things like that, but I don't want to date him; I just want to be there for him."

Why? I wondered. Because I thought I saw the disconsolation in his smile? Because I thought I sensed his loneliness, and understood it because I felt it way too often? Because I felt like, in one instant, I'd gone from knowing Derek, to truly seeing everything that he tried to hide, and if I had seen that him, then what had he seen when he looked at me? Or had he seen nothing, and I was the only one with the responsibility of what I thought I saw?

Eyes weren't wells for the soul, I rationalized. It wasn't honestly possible to see what I think that I saw when I looked in his eyes. Logically the only thing I'd actually be able to see when I looked in anyone's eyes, not just Derek's, was a reflection of what that person was looking at, at the moment. So why was I imagining that I'd seen something similar to an empty stage after a play's over, when it's just the actor standing there, alone, with no make-up on?

"I care about him," I summed up. "I...just don't know why. I mean, there's no reason for me to, there's nothing about him that's different than anyone else."

I don't mean that he wasn't worth being around...just that he wasn't... he wasn't *who* I could imagine falling for. Not that this was my type of guy, either, but he wasn't the star of the team, or the top of his class, or the guy that *everyone* had a crush on, so you were expected to like them, like Shelton. If he was that, then it'd be easier to understand, but Derek was just an average guy, a class clown, a smooth geek who was beautiful when he smiled, and appreciated art, and worked on building homes for people in his spare time.

"But he's different to you, and that's all that mattuhs," Patrice said. It was never all that mattered. "Why don' you just go'n talk to tha boy?" she suggested rationally.

She already knew most of my objections, so I decided to add some more. "Because every time I try to, I come out sounding like an idiot, and I know he doesn't feel the same way about me." I was sure of it. I mean, he always seemed friendly, well not always, which meant that he didn't like me, but he was sometimes, which meant what? Why was I attempting to divine the slightest meaning from the littlest gestures? Why was I acting like a crush was life or death? It was just emotions.

"High school relationships are pointless," I declared. "So, say I talked to Derek," I thought aloud, "and by some miracle he happened to feel the same way for me. It's not like we could even date each other. He's a senior. So, even if he did like me back, that means we'd have, what, a semester together, and then we say good-bye? What's the point?"

"Maybe havin' some fun 'long tha way!" she asserted. "Tha fact that he's graduatin' this year should make you *want* ta talk ta him. What if he's like your soul mate or somethin'? Do you really want to regret nevuh talkin' ta him?"

I tried to apply her words to the situation. "My *soul* mate, 'Triece? I don't even *like* him." Well… "I mean I like him, but I don't like him. Sometimes he can be sweet and nice and all, but other times he's a serious jerk." Though the times when he was a jerk had reduced greatly, but I chopped that up to not being around him as much. Last year we'd spent a *lot* of time around each other. "There's no future with me and Derek, anyway." Even if he weren't white, or a senior, there still wouldn't be. "When *I* graduate, I'm moving. Preferably 1,100 miles away from here."

She shook her head. "I nevuh understood what you like so much 'bout that school."

I didn't understand why she couldn't. "It's a great school," I said simplistically. "The best. President Kennedy went to Harvard."

"Yea, but he was tha President."

"Exactly!" I agreed. "*Presidents* go to Harvard, senators go to Harvard. The future leaders and policy makers of this country, *go* to Harvard."

"Kennedy's a White man though."

"Du Bois went there, and he's black."

"He's a man, too, girl, and last time I checked, you ain't."

"That doesn't matter," I insisted. "Once, they didn't allow Blacks to go there, either, but that didn't stop Du Bois. Time changes all things."

Patrice steered the conversation back to where we'd been. "So what's wrong wit havin' a boyfriend, *just* ta have a boyfriend?"

"Because that's when you get into trouble," I reasoned. "All a boyfriend would do is consume time, and right now I have too much to worry about; too much to do without adding that kind of worry."

"You need ta stop livin' in tha future so much, T," Patrice declared, "or else you're goinna wake up one day and realize that you missed livin' your life. So what if Derek don' fit in wit your equations? Life ain't some math problem. Are you really not wantin' ta talk ta him because he don' fit wit your plans?"

It wasn't just that he didn't fit; it was that I couldn't see how he could. I couldn't make him make sense to me. "I just don't want to end up going nowhere, or doing nothing with my life because of a couple of bad decisions," I said. "The deck is heavily stacked against us as it is, why make things even harder?"

"I don' care how hard you try, you're goinna end up makin' a couple uh bad decisions," Patrice declared in her talking-to-idiots voice. "It's life! If God wanted it ta be easy he would have given us tha ansuh key. Life don' always work out cordin' ta plans. What's that they say, 'tha good, thought-out schemes go wrong'-?"

"The best laid plans of mice and men often go astray?" I supplied.

"There you go! Life doesn' always work out tha way that you plan it. Life isn' just made up uh clear-cut puzzle pieces that fit togethuh nicely. People get hurt, people lose their way; it happens."

And I was trying to prepare myself for those incidentals; the things that happened that I couldn't control. That's why I wasn't just satisfied with knowing class material enough to take a test; I wanted it completely committed to memory. It was why I planned, and plotted, and planned some more. "That's why you strive for the best, and prepare for the worst," I replied. "You become what you set your mind to become."

"You can plan all you want, but things still don' always work out right," Patrice said, firmly. "And if you refuse ta make relationships just 'cause it might mess up your goals, you're goinna find that tha only thing you do have is regret. That's tha truth uh it."

"But we'll still be friends, so it doesn't matter much, does it," I responded, lightly. Patrice rolled her eyes, but she smiled.

I wasn't discounting what my best friend was saying, but I thought it was all about the opportunity cost: what you were willing to give up now in order to get what you wanted later. I didn't really think that a few missed dances, trips out, or awkward conversations, was too much to give up so that I could go to Harvard. But that wasn't really all of it, though, because my reason for not doing things wasn't *just* because I wanted to get away from Bakersfield. I simply wasn't *good* at being around people.

In Wilmington, I was better adjusted, but here I just didn't *think* the way that was normal. For the most part, people accepted the hand they were dealt, which is fine I guess, if you were at least given a hand that you could play. I couldn't say what life would have been like if we'd stayed in Wilmington since I was still young and hadn't yet become aware of how things were there before we'd left, but I knew that there wasn't much opportunity for me *here*. No, I wasn't still being told to get off the sidewalk, but I was still barred from education, from getting a decent job, with decent wages, from maintaining a dignity that should be afforded to all peoples, and I wasn't willing to just play that hand. I wanted more than that.

I didn't want to be mediocre, to be average. I didn't want the best that I could hope for out of life to be to accept only what people were willing to give me. I didn't want substandard and second best. I wanted to have a hand in changing what was unjust and changeable. Present my children-if I did ever actually get married and have them-with actual possibilities for the future, and if I didn't have kids, I wanted to leave a brighter future for those who came after me; even the playing field a little. I wanted to make sure that boys like Pollie Tolliver didn't get life in jail just because of their skin color, and minority and poor juveniles didn't fall through the cracks.

And sure, I wanted a nice house, with nice things, and maybe a nice car, too, but more than that, I wanted the space to just be who I was. I didn't want to just read about life. I wanted the dream. I wanted to explore as much as possible, meet new cultures, see new ideas. I wanted to be able to visit all of those landmarks and historical places that we talked about in history and art classes, do the things that I read in books, see the world.

At that thought, another conversation worked its way into my head, and for one very brief second…I imagined traveling the world with Derek. Unless I learned another language, we'd be restricted to places that only spoke French or English. We'd have to find odd jobs everywhere we went, we would never be able to spend more than a little while in any one place, and the living conditions wouldn't be all that great, either. But…I could see us watching the sun set over water in a dozen different cities, and Derek knowing just as much, or more, about the architecture and the artwork that we'd go see. I could imagine the sound of his laughter as he told me some quirky thing about something we'd seen. He had such a beautiful laugh, and his smile… it would never be in short supply.

The image was so real that I knew instantly that it would never happen. But in the whole realm of 'what-ifs' and 'could be', it didn't seem like such a bad future…

Shelton ended up taking Lina to the Homecoming dance, but he continued to walk with me to my classes, and I briefly entertained the notion of dating. As unlikely as it was, Shelton certainly seemed interested, and I liked him. It wouldn't have been difficult to say yes. But when I thought about relationships, about what people did in relationships, it halted the thoughts.

Besides, Shelton wasn't my pace. Next to him I felt shabby in comparison. He could pretty much have any girl he wanted to, and they practically threw themselves at him. I didn't want to have to worry about the kind of hassle that Patrice had to deal with. Darnell said constantly that Patrice was his steady, that there was no one else in the picture, yet he was unfaithful and everyone knew it. I know that Shelton wasn't Darnell, but when you're faced with lots of temptation, you have more opportunities to fall prey to it. I didn't want to have Patrice's kind of worries.

Eventually, Shelton realized that I wasn't about to return his affections, or he got bored with me, and we continued to talk or have the occasional lunch together, but he stopped giving me as much attention, and things went back to the way they were. In English class we started a unit on Elizabethan era poetry, and after reading Elizabeth Barrett Browning question 'How much do I love thee, let me count the ways', in her "Sonnet 43", I discovered a newfound love for poetry. It helped me to reexamine the world around me. When I had too much time to think about people that shouldn't be on my mind, I found myself trying to divine my feelings through verse. The poetry that I penned was mostly the confused, jumbled up words of someone who was trying to figure out life, and it reflected that.

The only real consolation I got from my horrible attempts at poetry was that some of them were so ridiculous that they made me smile. Poetry helped me come to the conclusion that there was no logicality in me being in love. I couldn't figure out how it could conceivably exist between Derek and I, but when our eyes had connected...

I saw.
It was a glimpse into a soul. A sneak into a love that
Transcends the most complicated of emotion
Disrupts the orderliness of thought
Both verbose in its meaning, and laconic in its message
A look into a person that I never knew existed.
When I looked into his eyes,
I was able to see into the core of the earth,
Where the Titans lie.
Where the mystical creatures of ancient lore rest.
I saw into the kingdoms of a child's fantasy.
I saw all the gallant knights, and lost adventures
And forgotten dreams,
And the world changed.
Something new, never perceived before

Maybe never to be again.
Was it him I saw in me or me I saw in him?
I saw through the papier-mâché, and gaudy circus paint.
I saw the disconsolation in his smile
The condescendence, the façade of bravado
Broken to stone. The end of the play.
When it was just he and I,
I saw the one no one sees.

— 17 —
"The Rejected Lover"

Patrice didn't waste any time in shedding her sweater once we were outside the church yard. Even though it was early November, it wasn't yet cold, but that didn't stop Mrs. Gordon from demanding that her daughter still carry a sweater with her. Patrice gave the discarded sweater to Marcus to hold. "Umm...I'm telling," he chided.

"You do and you're dead," she returned with a smile.

"Now...uh...children..." Marcus began, imitating Pastor Johnson. "Tha lawd...I said...Tha lawd commandeth you to be-uh in obedience to your parents...and when...I said when-uh they command you to wear-uh sweatuh...you best keep it on your-uh body."

The four of us broke out in a fit of laughter, fueled by Marcus' friend, Lamont's, play-by-play of this morning's sermon. Pastor Johnson was just so over the top that he was easy to imitate and Lamont did it to perfection.

When we reached Hatter Street, Marcus and Lamont went one way, heading back to their houses, and Patrice and I continued on towards the Trick without them. My shoes kept pinching the sides of my feet, and I contemplated where I'd get money for new shoes. I wondered if my mom would pose too big of a resistance about me getting a job. Most of the places that you could work around the Trick went to the kids of the shop owners, but maybe I could get a job at the book shop, or at one of the department stores downtown.

Even though it took them nearly 45 minutes to change and come back, the courts were still pretty empty when Marcus and Lamont met back up with us. Patrice's church started early, and was one of the first to get out for the day, so the rest of the Sunday crowd hadn't made it out, yet. While they waited for more players to join them, the two of them started passing the ball back and forth between each other. When a third person showed up, that turned into a game of H-O-R-S-E, which morphed into a game of two on two, before slowly transforming into a full five-on-five game.

The courts slowly began to fill, and Patrice became more interested in who occupied them, than in her brother's game. "I'll be right back," she declared.

"Pat-,"

But she was gone, off to talk to one of the guys that was hanging around on the benches in between courts. I tried to figure out if I knew the guy from somewhere; if I'd seen him around, but he didn't seem familiar despite Patrice seeming as if she knew him pretty well, or was getting to know him pretty well, at least. Although she was hurting from her recent break up with Darnell, it didn't seem as if it was going to slow her down. That was all well and good for her, but I'd come along to help cheer her up, and now she was gone and I didn't even have a book to keep me occupied during her absence.

I was reconsidering our friendship when a guy walked into my field of vision, leaning against the far end of the bench I was sitting on. "What's tha score?" he questioned conversationally.

I gave a look over at the speaker. I didn't recognize him, but he smiled at me as if we were acquaintances, showing off the slight gap between his two front teeth. I gave him an embarrassed smile. "I couldn't tell you," I admitted. I'd given up attempting to keep track of the score a long time ago.

My visitor gave a chuckle. "How about we say it's close. I'm Coley," he said casually.

I told him my name, and since he hadn't held out his hand, I extended mine. He gave a glance at it before he shook it, smiling slightly. "You ain' from here, is you?" he questioned. "I'd uh rememba if I'd seen you before."

"I don't come to the courts often," I replied. "Just came to watch my brother play."

Coley's eyes flickered at those words. "Which one is your brotha?" he questioned.

I described Marcus as I pointed him out, and after giving a look that way, Coley seemed something, relieved maybe, when he saw him. I guess

Marcus wasn't the kind of guy people were intimidated by. We passed a little conversation for a while before he got up to get some sodas. Patrice returned to take up his vacated spot, a smile on her face.

"What?" I wondered.

"Who's yo friend?" she questioned.

I glanced about, looking in the direction that he'd gone off. "Coley, he said."

She gave her head a shake. "You've no idea, do you?" she remarked with amusement. My face showed my confusion, which only made her laugh harder. "You're so lucky you have me as your best friend," she decided.

"What're you talking about?" I questioned. I looked back in the direction that he had gone off to, and glanced at the next court over, startling at the unexpected sight of Derek, who stood out glaringly from the crowd. Whites occasionally frequented the Trick, to shop, to sight-see, or for business, but they usually came in groups, and they never made it to this part of the area, which was a little too close to the neighborhoods for comfort. I searched for some sort of answer to this phenomenon, and found it in the tall, curly-haired, medium brown-skinned guy in a gray t-shirt and gym pants that stood next to him. This was Orion, and I knew that the red-headed, lighter skinned boy with him was his cousin, Simpson. I didn't know who the fourth guy in their group was, but their fifth was Quinn. He was as tall as Orion, and the same color as Derek, yet for some reason he stood out more than anyone else did.

Derek glanced over our way quicker than I could look away. I turned back towards Patrice...only to once again find her gone. I wondered what would look stupider, staying turned towards someone who obviously wasn't there, or turning back to look at Derek. I chose to pretend that I'd turned away because something else had caught my attention.

"Alright, now, this has got to stop," Derek remarked as he made his way over. "I know that I'm handsome, and charmin', and just all around perfect, but you can' keep followin' me 'round like this, Trace. People're goin' start talkin'."

I couldn't really tell from his tone or expression whether or not he was serious, so I took him for being serious, which made me angry. "No one's following you," I snapped.

"No, then what brings you 'round, cause I'm here every weekend, and this is tha first time I've evuh seen you here?"

I bit down on my lip, choosing not to reply to what he'd said. Coley returned with two Cokes in his hands, and I was relieved, grateful even, to see him. Even though he had to pass in front of Derek to sit down, he made no notice of him. "Thought you might be thirsty," he remarked, handing me the can. I thanked him, knowing that I only accepted the drink because Derek was there. I didn't glance back Derek's way immediately, and by the time I did, Derek had already slinked back in the direction he'd come.

In between watching Marcus' game, and talking to Coley, my eyes kept glancing over at the second court, looking away quickly lest Derek catch me at it. But Derek seemed thoroughly engrossed with his game, playing with a determination that was impressive. He was one of the shorter ones on the court, but that didn't seem that much of a hindrance for him as he raced around the other players in pursuit of the ball.

As the day lengthened, more pick-up games, and people, crowded onto the courts. I finally began to understand what Patrice had laughed at earlier: Coley was flirting. Once I realized that, I wasn't as friendly, and Coley decided to spread his attention to a skirt that was more talkative. Marcus' game ended, and he came dripping off the courts, breathing hard. "Did you guys win?" I questioned.

"You know this," Lamont remarked, slapping Marcus on the back. "Good game," was uttered by one of them.

When Marcus straightened up, he gave a glance around, seeing Patrice talking to one of the players on the other team. Wearily, he went over to where she was, to make his presence known. Lamont started talking me up, and I talked back more willingly than usual. Lamont seemed a bit too pleased that he was able to keep my attention, and I could tell he was working a little too hard to engage me in conversation.

In a pause in Lamont's sentence, I gave a quick sideways glance at the other court, and found Derek looking over this way. A hand clamped down, suddenly, on the back of my neck, startling me. "What choo doin down *here*, lil sista?" Sean questioned at the same time that I recognized his hand.

The friendly smile on his face let me know he hadn't seen where I was looking, so I gave him a smile in return. "Hi, Sean!" I greeted. He gave me a hug with his free hand. The other was wrapped around the hand of a pretty, green-eyed, light-skinned girl, who seemed to think that there was nothing better than holding onto Sean's hand. I wondered what it had taken her to get him, and if she realized he was far easier to get, than he was to keep. I'd never really made the correlation before, but he and Darnell had that in common.

Sean gave a nod at Lamont, and a significant look at me. I shook my head in answer. "Where Beanie?" he wondered.

I pointed out his sister, who, despite Marcus, was still chatting with the other guy. Clark, I remembered suddenly. His name was Clark. His friends, too, I recognized: Alex and Gabriel Layton. Alex seemed to have eyes only for Patrice, while Patrice only seemed interested in Clark. Gabriel seemed like me, disjointed and out of place. He hadn't played basketball with the other guys, was still dressed in his church clothes, in fact.

The game on the other court must have ended because the bench area got even more crowded as the other teams walked over. Off the court, Quinn seemed even more out of his element, staying close to Derek. His head swiveled from side to side as if in search of possible threats. Derek, on the other hand, seemed perfectly at ease. Orion greeted a few of the guys, slapped hands with them, and made small talk. A few guys acted familiar with Derek, too, and mostly ignored Quinn, who seemed to be doing his best to seem invisible. Derek acted as if I didn't exist, which was fine with me because I was pretending that he didn't exist either.

"Y'all good for 'nother game?" Orion questioned, directing the words at Marcus. Marcus eyed Derek with a look that even I recognized as hostile.

"Nah, I've got to book," Marcus remarked. He gave a glance over at his sister-who didn't seem as if she were going anywhere any time soon-before heading off the court. I took the opportunity, and decided to follow after him.

I fell into step beside him. "Who's Sean's girl?" I wondered, realizing that he had never told me her name. It occurred to me, now, that just about every girl I'd ever seen Sean with had been light-skinned, and very much so, which seemed unfair to me because why could he date near-white looking girls, prefer them even, but got on to me for possibly liking a white boy? It wasn't like I went looking for them, or was only seen in their company, like Sean and his girls. We were talking about one guy, and so far, the only guy I'd been interested in.

"Her name's Doreen," Marcus informed me. "But I doubt she'll last. They never do."

I threaded my arm in his. "When are *you* going to have some girl hanging on your arm again, Marcus?" I teased.

He looked down at me with an easy smile. "I already do, don't I?" he returned. I gave his arm a comfortable squeeze.

*

"So the podiums should go here, the tables here, and if we put the judges on the ground…," Mr. Fulcher paused in his stride, thinking, "or we can have them sit out in the audience because the debaters need to be able to see the judges. So, we have a podium here for the host, a podium here and here, for the debaters, two tables behind them for the rest of the team to sit, and the judges are going to be on the row in front of the stage." I nodded as he spoke, easy enough.

Mr. Fulcher was paged over the intercom. "Great," he mumbled. "You can handle that, right, Tracy?"

"Yes, sir."

"Perfect, thank you."

I got to work moving the furniture. Maybe five minutes passed when I heard the door open. I looked up automatically. Expecting Mr. Fulcher's return, I was thrown off guard when two figures trailed into the room. The auditorium was off limits to students unless there was an event, which made it the perfect place to come to when you wanted some privacy on school grounds. There was that awkward moment when I saw them, but they hadn't seen me, and I had a choice of either making my presence known, or pretending to be invisible. The former was preferable to them making out in front of me, until I recognized that the couple was Derek and Amelia. I hesitated long enough to hear the first words of their conversation, and when it dawned on me that they were in the middle of an argument, I ducked behind the curtain; I'd rather sit through another year's worth of DeWitt's class lectures, than be discovered by Derek in that moment.

As I contemplated the semi-darkness, I tried to figure out what it was about me and this guy, and how our paths always seemed to cross. Even though I'd been here first, somehow Derek would probably think that I'd followed them into the room. God, his ego. It was no small wonder that he could even get it to fit inside a classroom. I paused in my mental bashing of Derek…Amelia was really letting him have it. All attempts to tune out their voices proved futile; Amelia's voice was penetrating.

"-Doris was all excited about seeing you, and my mother-!"

"Yea, Doris seemed real eager-"

"-if you had come to brunch! She was worried about getting back home."

"I told you I was goin' to tha Trick. I go just 'bout every Sunday-"

"Which means you could have spared one for us-,"

"You didn' ask-,"

"-and for the life of me I can't figure out why you spend so much time with *them*, anyway. That you'd rather play with those…,"

"Those, what?" Derek demanded, cutting off the words she was about to say.

"You see! You defend *them* over me! Do you even want to be with me, Derek?"

"You didn' finish that sentence," Derek reminded her.

"Are you going to answer my question?"

"What were you about to say about my best friend?"

"I don't even know why you hang with him!"

"Why wouldn' I? Orion's uh stand-up guy."

"If you could only *hear* the things they say about him-"

"Yea, 'cause they know him better'n I do."

"Yes, they do," Amelia asserted. "You just don't want to see it. You mark my words, Derek, if you keep hanging 'round them Coloreds, you're going to get tainted. So what if you guys were friends when you were little? Things're different then; you aren't little boys anymore. When're you going to realize that they're just not *like* us? They don't have the same values or morals as we do. They're always causing fights, they cheat, they lie, they steal. I know you like to see the good in everyone, but it's going to be your undoing. Do you know how Daddy thinks of you? He calls you my 'Colored boyfriend', did you know that?"

Derek was silent for long enough that I peeked from behind the curtain to see if they were still there. His hands were jammed firmly in his pockets, his eyes on the ground. He lifted them to look at her. "And how do you think of me?" Derek questioned in a low voice. Even from a distance I could tell he was speaking through clenched teeth.

She didn't directly answer. "How do you think that makes *me* feel, having daddy think that about you? I *like* you Derek; I want my family to like you, too. I want to be with you, but sometimes, I don't rightly know about you. It's like you'd rather be with *them* than your own kind."

"Orion *is* my kind, Am. He's my best friend, and that's the way it is. If you're goinna be my girl, you're just goinna have to accept that."

"Well maybe I don't want to be your girl," Amelia remarked.

Before anything else could be said between them, the doors opened again, revealing Mr. Fulcher bathed in the light from the common area. "Tracy, I brought-," he noticed Derek and Amelia. "Miss Gants, Mr. King," he addressed them sternly. "You're not supposed to be in here. If you don't want a detention…

Derek shot a hateful look at the corner where I was concealed, but even knowing that he couldn't see me, I felt guilty. I felt like I'd been eavesdropping, which I had been, technically, but it wasn't on purpose. I certainly hadn't wanted to hear that conversation. "We're leaving," Derek remarked. He stalked to the door without seeing if Amelia was following behind.

In French, Derek was visibly agitated. He sat with his teeth clenched the entire period, staring down at his notebook. Even though he looked unlikely to change that position, I checked myself from looking his way, trying to pretend I didn't notice his mood. Hard to ignore, though, were the words that I'd overheard. Amelia was nice. That's what everyone thought of her, how I would have described her, too: nice. Amelia was nice. She was a nice person, who could condemn and make judgment on 18 million people, without even knowing them. During the course of an argument people screamed things, I knew that, but underlying those words were the thoughts that gave them life.

This was the judgment that I faced every time I stood before someone new that was white. This was the thought process that made Mrs. Dressler move my desk off to the side and give me a different test than the rest of my classmates: the idea that we were just not like them. I was sure that in her own world, Mrs. Dressler was a nice woman, and so was Amelia. It made me wonder, though, how you could smile in someone's face, but think this about them quietly, and still be considered nice.

In true high school fashion, by second period the next day, the news had spread: Derek and Amelia had called it quits. In true best friend fashion, Patrice cornered me outside of my fourth period class that same day. "So you goinna do it?" she demanded, without so much of a hello.

I pretended to be very occupied with looking for my English text. "Do what," I wondered.

"You haven' heard? Derek and Amelia are in Splitsville."

My body reacted to her words before my mind did because a smile started to grow before I noticed. I quickly covered up the action with my hand. "Are they?" I questioned. My surprise was genuine because despite their words in the auditorium, I didn't think that they were terminal. That they had broken up, though, gave Derek a few points in my book. He'd stood up for his best friend, and that showed a condemnation of her beliefs, right? Well…maybe not entirely. And though their break up caused me to smile unexpectedly, it didn't make me any more anxious to want to go and talk to him. "You said you'd talk to him if they broke up," she reminded me. "And now they have."

A few days later, before I'd made up my mind about whether or not I was actually going to talk to Derek, I was heading out of Mrs. Diece's room when I heard Derek call my name. I stopped so he could catch up, my heart already doing laps in my chest. I hated how fast your imagination could create scenarios in your head in the span of time it took for someone to take a few steps your way.

"Yes?" I remarked, my voice hopefully void of emotion.

"Were you-," Derek began and stopped. I merely waited, not sure what I was waiting for. I could have admitted to being in the room, but that wasn't about to happen. "Amelia and I broke up," Derek blurted. He didn't sound like he was singing the *Hallelujah Chorus* over that pronouncement. He sounded miserable, actually. Was it odd that I was sad he was upset, even though I was happy for the cause?

"I'm sorry to hear that," I remarked, wondering why I said those words. I wasn't sorry at all. But what else was I supposed to say? Good? I'm glad? Patrice probably would have wasted no time in telling him that she'd been crushing on him, but that wasn't me. It was kind of insensitive, wasn't it?

He blinked. "You are?" he questioned. I wondered at the tone of his voice. Did he want me to not be sorry?

"You guys made a nice couple." *Stop. Stop talking now.* Somehow my mouth didn't get the synapses that my brain was sending to it. "I hate that it didn't work out." Derek fidgeted, but didn't say anything. Standing in front of him, I realized that I wasn't about to say anything, either. "I have to go," I remarked. I didn't even have the presence of mind to at least come up with a reason for leaving.

"Hey, Trace?" Derek questioned. I paused, looked at him. He looked back with no hints peeking out of his gaze.

"Yea?"

"See you around," he said, halting whatever it was he'd been about to say. From the way he hesitated, I could tell that that wasn't what he'd wanted to say. So then what was?

— 18 —
"Patient Lovers"

The Gordon door swung open at my knock, and an unhurried Marcus appeared. Even though I'd been looking for Patrice, I was glad that he'd answered. Marcus slouched in the doorway when he saw that it was me. "Patrice isn't here," he informed me, no need for formalities. "She's out with that fool boy that she got caught up with," he added.

Until he said 'fool', I thought he was talking about Clark. "Oh," I remarked. "Is she out with Darnell?"

He nodded before shaking his head. "Sometime I just don't understand her," Marcus declared. "She just keeps trading up one fool for another. I wish she had your good sense."

"I wish *I* had my good sense," I decided. "How've you been?"

"Same as always," he said, casually. "You know how life goes."

"How's work?" I questioned.

"Work."

"School?"

"Work. It's all the same," he remarked, "they just switch the names up on you so you get confused about it."

"You working tonight?" I wondered

"Nah, I'm off. Just watching some tube."

"Will you tell Patrice I came by?"

"Why don't you stay and watch with me?" he suggested. He opened his stance up so that I could walk past him, inviting me in.

I hesitated. "I don't want to interfere with your Marcus time."

He snorted. "You really say that, T-girl?" he wondered in amusement, using Sean's nickname for me. "Come on. *Lost in Space* is on."

He didn't wait for me to accept his invitation, turning to go back inside. He knew that I would follow behind him, and of course I did. I could see where he'd made himself comfortable earlier, and instead of taking back his spot, he made room for me. I stretched out beside him, and there was something about it that reminded me of the way Nicole had fallen asleep against Derek. It was easy. Everything about Marcus and I was easy; natural. Unlike with Derek, who everything always seemed like a struggle.

"So how're things with you? Still making me proud?" he wondered lightly.

"No earned B's yet," I replied. I didn't tell him about Mrs. Dressler's treatment towards me, because I realized that I didn't have to. Part of the reason Marcus and I didn't talk all that much when we were around each other was because we understood each other so well that our silences were just as meaningful. Marcus had probably experienced everything that I had, and more, during his three years at Mason.

He gave me a hug and a squeeze. "That's my girl!" he cheered.

The commercial ended, and Marcus' attention was reclaimed. While he watched the show, I watched him, paying more attention to Marcus than the program. In the middle of a laugh he caught me staring at him, and his open-mouthed laugh fell into his little half smile.

"Why you keep looking at me, kid?" he wondered. I looked him in the eye, and it elicited the same response that it normally did.

"I don't know," I remarked.

He chuckled throatily. "Doing stuff without knowing why, innit that what gets folks in trouble? You had ta have a reason."

"Yes," I agreed, "but I don't want to tell you what that is."

"Admiring my good looks?"

"Of course," I responded with no hesitation.

Marcus postured for me, smiling. "I knew you was diggin' me," he teased. I laughed along with him, letting my eyes journey along his own. I'd never tell Patrice this, but Marcus was my first, real, honest crush. I'd had a crush on him practically since the day I met him, and it wasn't hard to understand why. Marcus was like the embodiment of everything that I think a man should be: intelligent, honest, compassionate, charitable, attractive...he was *my* ideal. But my crush on Patrice's older brother was one of those crushes that you knew you'd never do anything about, never allow to grow or to develop into anything other than that.

Patrice's family was everything that mine wasn't, and everything I thought family should be like. I used to try to imagine what it would be like, growing up in the Gordon household; having big brothers to look out for me, to fight with, and to teach me stuff like how to drive, or how to change the oil, or the names and purpose of the parts of the engine so I didn't get cheated if I brought my car into the shop. I knew that Marcus (and Sean, too) would go to bat for me if I needed them to, but it wasn't really the same as having actual brothers, or having an older sister to look up to, borrow things from, make secrets.

So I used to have fantasies of somehow keeping my family, but being adopted into the Gordon family, and of course if that happened, Marcus and I couldn't get together. So, I chose the fantasy over Marcus, and Marcus simply remained my ideal. Besides, Marcus was older, more mature and sophisticated, and no matter how mature and sophisticated I got, I could never be mature and sophisticated enough to be with him. I always felt slightly shy around him. But still, being around him didn't elicit that same response I got when I looked at Derek. Why couldn't I have a big brother crush on Derek, too?

"Do you remember your first crush?" I questioned over the next commercial.

Marcus chuckled, but seemed unsurprised by my question. "It's kind of hard to forget," he remarked. "Seventh grade, Iesha Gates. She was the one the Temptations sung about in *The Things You Do*." He sang a few bars of the song, ending with a laugh. "She was the cutest little thing you ever saw. Skin like chocolate, eyes that you could wade in, generously proportioned," he said honorably, grinning, "the whole package. I was determined that she was goinna be *my* girl. When I finally worked up the nerve to talk to her, I yelled at her, and pushed her down."

I couldn't help laughing at the image. Marcus chuckled along with me. "Needless to say, she didn't want nothing to do with me after that," he admitted. "Who you have a crush on?" he wondered. "Me?"

"Of course I do, Marcus, you know that," I said honestly.

He smiled securely. We both were playing, but we were both serious, too, and we knew that the other realized that. He, too, realized that I was as much off limits to him, as he was to me: I was his little sister's best friend.

Without thinking much about it I questioned, "Do you remember falling in love?"

He nodded more soberly. "I 'member that too," he stated. "Are you in love, Trace?" Marcus questioned, seriously.

"I don't know," I responded.

"First love," he remarked. He squinted at me. "You old enough for that yet?"

"In my opinion, no," I said, speaking aloud the first words that came to mind.

"All right," he said, seriously. He rubbed the tops of his thighs, and what he said next was the reason why I liked him over his brother. "Well, let me hit you with some fatherly advice: high school's a difficult time. You're ready to be an adult, but the people around you treat you like a kid. Your body gets all excited and stuff, and guys, 'specially older ones, say all kind of pretty words to make you feel older and prettier, so to you it sounds like love, and girls look back at you in all sorts of pretty ways, so it looks like love, too, and when they touch you...it even feels like love. But it's not. It's never as serious as it seems to be in the moment that you're living it...but when you're living it...," he paused in contemplation, "*man*, you think that they are your everything. Can't even see around them. Can't think past them. Afterwards, you miss them like crazy, too."

I figured that Marcus was talking about his ex-girlfriend, Pearl. They'd broken off their three year relationship a month before we'd started at Mason. Everyone'd thought that they were going to get married. I guess Marcus wasn't exactly over her.

"Not helping any, am I?"

I smiled up at him. "Of course you are," I assured.

"So, you goinna tell me about him?" he questioned, leadingly.

"Nothing to tell," I remarked.

"Aw," Marcus remarked, placing his arm around my shoulders and giving me a quick, secure, hug. "It's okay, Tracy. This too shall pass."

Maybe, but it didn't seem like it was in any hurry.

Derek stayed in my thoughts, clouding them. I ran and reran that last conversation through my head, made up the words that Derek hadn't said. I tried to picture myself taking a page from Patrice's book, and just having the nerve to go up to him and talk to him, but I couldn't really see myself actually doing that; I wasn't that courageous. It didn't matter if I liked him, I was certain he didn't like me, not that way. And that's what truly mattered. Why make a fool out of myself for no reason? *But…what if?* What if *what?* 'If' was Patrice's world. There was no if in mine; there was no scenario that would put Derek and me together. And no room in my life, even if there was.

When I got home, I pulled out my schedule and chose some random assignment to get started on. That lasted all of five minutes before the images returned, and once again I was thinking about him. *This has got to stop!* I chastised myself. I wrote his name on the top of a sheet of paper, and paused. I started writing, at first listing all of Derek's faults, but then it changed to all the things I liked and thought I felt about him. Halfway towards the bottom of the paper, it got narrative, as if I was talking to him.

When I was done, I re-read over everything, got out another sheet of paper, fixed the grammatical errors, leaving out the worst of it. I re-read over the piece of paper, again, and imagined looking at Derek, telling him this. No doubt the smile that always seemed to be on his face would appear, and he'd look at me in barely concealed amusement as he said something like, "I'm flattered that you feel that way". I shook the image from my mind, re-read over the paper again, and got out another sheet. I wrote Derek's name on the first line, and paused, staring at the wide expanse of empty paper. My words had the power to turn it into anything. "I like you," I wrote. I read the words, and reread them, before having a good laugh at myself.

Why was I treating this whole situation like it was life or death? I was allowing myself to blow this out of proportion, allowing my imagination too much sway. Why should I be so afraid of expressing an emotion that everyone else expressed a dozen times a day? It was high school. You were expected to have a crush. On Monday, I decided, I'd talk to Derek after class. He might laugh in my face, but I'd at least be able to say I was honest, and no matter the outcome, after that, it'd be over.

I almost crumbled up the sheet of paper, but I decided not to. Instead, I very carefully folded the piece of paper into a square to remind myself of my resolve, put it inside one of my notebooks, and absolutely refused to think about him for the rest of the weekend.

On Monday, my concentration was pretty much non-existent in all of my classes. I ended up in my French class without remembering how I got there. I had absolutely no idea what Mrs. Diece said, or what we were supposed to be learning, and when the bell finally rang, I jumped, startled. I knocked my folder off the desk, and watched it fall into the path of the person who was walking past me.

"Y'alright, Tracy?" Quinn questioned, as I scrambled to recover the spilled contents. He bent down to help. Before I could reach the note that had slipped out, Quinn's hands beat me to it. He started to hand the note to me, and for the briefest second I thought that Quinn would give it back. But then he noticed Derek's name.

"Can I have that please?" I questioned of him. Quinn looked from the paper, to me, and to my chagrin Quinn turned and said, "Hey, Dare? Tracy's got something for you!"

Up until that moment, I'd always thought of Quinn as a decent guy.

Derek turned around, and my face burned in embarrassment even as I said sharply, "Give that here!" I reached for the piece of paper, which was the wrong thing to do, because Quinn easily held it away from me. Turning slightly so that I couldn't snatch it from him, he unfolded the paper, and his eyes scanned over my words. In a high-pitched voice that was supposed to be an imitation of mine he read: "Dear Derek, I think you're the sexiest man alive. I want to have your babies. Come take me...desperately your love... Tracy."

My face burned as they cracked up. Derek smiled in confusion. "What? Let me see that?" he snatched the letter out of Quinn's outstretched hand before Quinn could offer it to him. He pushed O'Neal out of the way, too, as he read the note. I don't know why I was still standing there, but I didn't move. I looked for something, a flicker or *something*, but Derek's expression was impassive. When he finished reading what little there was to read, a wild-eyed smile claimed his features. When his eyes locked on mine, though, they were unreadable. After a few seconds he looked back at his friends.

"Oh, yeah, she's hot for me," he said to his two buddies. I pushed past the three of them, making my legs move and keep moving. I fought down the urge to knock down both Derek and Quinn, and for good measure, O'Neal, too. I even thought about skipping out on the French Club meeting later that day, but I wouldn't give Derek the satisfaction. As usual, I arrived early, and was surprised to see Derek already in the room. He was leaning against his desk, his arms crossed over his chest. I was certain that he'd been waiting for me to come in.

"What do you want, Derek?" I questioned, waiting for the worst of it.

He gave me his twisted smile. "You like me, Trace?" he questioned. I met his gaze. I was amazed at how good I was at things academic, but when it came to people I didn't possess the same aptitude. Not for the first time, I wished that I was good at quick responses and wasn't so emotional when it came to this boy. I realized I had two options: I could say 'yes' and let the chips fall, or I could try to save face and lie. Even though I'd made up my mind to say something to him, that note hadn't been the way I wanted to do it, especially not with Quinn and O'Neal looking in.

Standing in front of him now, though, I just couldn't bring myself to say anything. I took in his stance, his smile, his eyes, and forced a laugh. "It was only a joke between me and Patrice," I lied. "You weren't even supposed to see it."

He pushed off from the desk he was leaning against and covered the space between us. I think my heart skipped a beat as he walked toward me, stopping only a few feet away. "I see," he remarked after a long minute had passed. "So you and Patrice talk about me?" he questioned pompously. He seemed so sure of my answer that it was almost insulting. Did I really like him? Really?

"Don't flatter yourself," I responded. "It was just a joke."

Derek studied me. "Alright," he said, devoid of any discernible emotion. "Okay." He stood there staring for a moment longer before he took a seat across the room, leaving me standing where I was.

— 19 —
"The Letter Writer"

Quinn and O'Neal had a field day about the letter. Two days later, I walked into the room to find a note sitting on my desk. The name at the bottom of it was Derek's, but I recognized the sloppy handwriting from the D papers O'Neal usually turned in when we graded homework assignments. The two of them laughed until they cried, and Mrs. Diece finally got sick of them giggling and gave them both detentions.

The next couple of days didn't get any better. Quinn and O'Neal couldn't resist the urge to make a joke about it whenever the opportunity presented itself, and it didn't take long before the whole class knew I had a crush on Derek. Even worse, Roy found out about the note, and he said something in passing that was so vulgar and derogatory that if someone hadn't walked between the two of us, I would have clocked him. I actually considered Sean's earlier offer, and thought about having him come up to the school to take care of the lot of them, but I didn't want Sean to get in trouble, and possibly arrested, because if I asked him, he would do it, and think about the consequences later.

I hated all of them, though, that's for sure. It didn't matter that in all likelihood, Quinn hadn't even read the letter. It didn't matter that I hadn't said anything more revealing other than that I liked Derek, either. The hurt was still there. What hurt even more than their teasing, more than the whispering behind my back, or the looks of disgust by the black students, the winks and nudges from the white guys who passed by, worse than all of that was that I knew, finally knew, that Derek didn't like me back. That I was singular in my feelings for him. I tried to tell myself that I didn't need him, that I was better than him, that he would have just been a distraction, but of course none of that worked. Life wouldn't have been what it was if it had.

I was at the school late one day, helping Mr. Colben set up a lab for tomorrow's class, when I heard the sound of approaching footsteps. I wouldn't have stopped working if I hadn't recognized Derek's voice as he questioned, "Mr. Colben?" I fought the urge to look up then. "Sir? Can I talk to you for a minute?" Derek wasn't his usual jocular self. He seemed far more humble than I was used to seeing, and I suspected that he wanted to speak to Colben about his grades. The end of the year usually had a lot of people suddenly more serious about them.

Colben took off his work gloves. "All right, Mr. King," he said stiffly. "Miss Burrows, can you finish setting up?" Derek looked at me, noticing me for the first time. He scowled. "No problem," I responded, still ignoring Derek. The two of them stepped out into the hallway and I continued working. I was just about finished, when Mr. Colben came back with Derek still with him.

"Allow me a moment, Mr. King," Colben directed, going into his office. Derek leaned idly against one of the lab tables, steadily not looking at me. This was the first time that we'd been alone together since the note incident. After Derek and Amelia got back together, things had started to die down, but then, on Valentine's Day, a rose had been jokingly placed on my desk, and I'd gone off on the three of them, giving them all a sound tongue lashing. Derek and I hadn't spoken since

He was the one to break the silence. "What're you doin' here?" he demanded, as if I had been the intruder.

I decided to go for cordial. "I'm helping Mr. Colben set up the lab for tomorrow's class," I responded, pretending to be absorbed in my work.

He scowled. "You're always doin' somethin', aren' you?" he questioned, almost angrily.

His near anger instantly changed my mood. "Why does that bother you?" I shot back.

"It doesn'," he said defensively.

Mr. Colben came out of his office before anything else could be said between us. "I have composed a list for you, Mr. King," he declared. "I expect everything on it to be completed before grades have to be turned in."

"Yes, sir," he said, gratifyingly. "What about tha lab?"

Mr. Colben shook his head. "I simply don't have the time to make up a whole lab. We're doing our last one for Bio I tomorrow, and Chemistry on Friday. I just can't fit it in." Derek nodded. "Thank you for this, sir," he remarked. I pretended that I didn't watch him leave. Mr. Colben returned to setting up the lab, going over what I'd done in his absence to make sure that it was done right. I'd been setting up the labs all year. I knew it was.

It took me a few minutes to find my voice. "If you need me to, I can monitor a lab for you."

Mr. Colben took his time looking up. "What was that, Miss Burrows?"

"I can monitor Derek's lab for you," I repeated hesitantly. "I can set it up myself, and clean it up when we're done. I'll even grade his lab report if you need me to."

Colben looked at me in cold speculation. "That would be a lot of work for you to do. I'd hate to see you waste your time."

"Why would it be a waste of my time?"

Mr. Colben switched to his instructor mode. "Because every year, I always get a dozen or more kids that have been slacking off during the year, come in and make a million promises to get a passing grade. Unlike some of the teachers around here, I don't give out grades. You get what you earn from me, and I don't make it easy for those who slack off to make up the work; it wouldn't be fair to those who do what they're supposed to do during the year, like yourself. I made the same deal with Mr. King that I make with all those that come to me at the end of the year: in order to make up anything, they have to make up everything, and I won't take any work unless they complete all of it. I've found that most people don't bother. It's not worth their time. So *you* would just be wasting *your* time in monitoring a lab for him since in the end it will all amount to naught."

I waited for some time to pass before I said, "If you don't mind, I would still like to, even if it won't, sir."

Colben seemed disappointed by my response. "It is your time, Miss Burrows. I have a faculty meeting on Wednesday so I'll be up at the school until five thirty. You can do it then. But this is your ship. If you want to help him, that is your business, not mine. You will set up and clean up the lab, go over his lab report, and it is up to you to tell him that you will be monitoring a makeup lab for him because I won't."

"Yes, sir," I responded.

"You surprise me sometimes, Miss Burrows."

Sometimes I managed to surprise myself.

I was hoping to run into Derek sometime before French class, but I didn't, so I had to wait until the end of class to tell him about the lab. As usual he was flanked by Quinn and O'Neal. "Derek?" I questioned, as he was walking out of the room. He paused, which of course caused his friends to stop, too.

His eyes narrowed. "What?" he demanded. There was nothing friendly in either his voice or stance, and for a second I thought that Mr. Colben was right about this being a waste of time.

"Can I talk to you for a second?" I gave a significant look at Quinn and O'Neal. "Alone?"

"Oooh...Tracy wants to speak to Derek," O'Neal chorused.

"Alone," Quinn snickered.

I rolled my eyes. "Grow up," Derek said to them before I could.

"Ouch, burned!" O'Neal laughed. Quinn shoved him, and O'Neal pushed him back as they exited the room.

Derek stepped back from the doorway so those behind him could leave. I caught a few of our classmates giving me a speculative look, one girl even going so far as to pretend to have trouble with her belongings, hesitating in the hopes of hearing something salacious. Derek watched her, rather than look at me. "What is it?" he questioned in a none-too-friendly tone. I held out the balled up piece of paper he'd left outside of Mr. Colben's classroom. "You dropped this yesterday."

He looked angrily at the paper in my hands, making no move to take it. "I don' need it."

I still held it towards him. "From what I understand, Mr. Colben gave it to you so that you can pull your grade up so you can graduate on time."

He glowered at me. "Have you evuh heard of mindin' your own business? If you want to gloat about that, go ahead. I don' care," he hissed. The straggler finally walked past us, giving each of us a look before she exited.

"I am not here to gloat about anything," I told him.

He shoved his hands in his pockets. "Well what do you want, then? I don' need that list. Did you get uh look at it? I miss uh coupla assignments and he gives me uh whole years' worth of work just to make it up. Grades have ta be turned in in three weeks, and it doesn' mattuh anyway cause tha labs count as uh fourth of your overall grade. Unless I can make up tha lab I missed, it don' mattuh what I do. So go ahead and have your laugh."

"I don't see anything funny," I stated. "I'm not here to make a joke. Mr. Colben told me to tell you that if you wanted to make up the lab, you could do so Wednesday, after school."

Derek's look didn't change. "He said that?" he questioned, skeptically. "What made him change his mind?"

"He just said that if you wanted to make it up you could."

"I bet he did. That hard ass probably wouldn' extend uh hand to his mothuh if she were drownin'," he said harshly.

I knew that Mr. Colben was probably one of the least liked teachers around the school, but so far he was proving to be one of my favorites. He had been the one to approach me about the fellowship that we'd spent the majority of the year working on, and though he was very stern, and often critical, he was that way towards everyone. I recognized that I'd probably never outwardly gain his approval, accepted that, and instead worked on learning as much as I could from him.

But the one thing that Mr. Colben was, was fair, and Derek's unfounded attack on Mr. Colben's character brought out my temper. "Don't blame Mr. Colben for your actions. It was you, not him, who didn't come to class all the time, who missed homework assignments, and who slept through some of your classes. Be happy that he cares enough to let you make up your work at all."

"Cares?" Derek demanded. "Did you look at that piece of paper?"

"Yes, I did, and he's just making you adjust your priorities. Since you decided that his class didn't matter enough to you to give it your time during the year, he's making you decide now what's more important to you: graduation, or your time at the moment? If you knew that overall your labs counted as a quarter of your grade, why would you miss one?"

— 176 —

"Because I didn' understand tha material, and I wouldn' have gotten uh good grade on it if I'd taken tha lab."

"But you *would've* gotten a grade, and that would have made a bigger difference in Mr. Colben's mind than just not showing up for it at all! And if you did not understand the material, you should have put more work into it. Mr. Colben's here twice a week, every week, to offer tutoring assistance to anyone who comes to him for help. How often have you come?"

He bit down on his lip. I knew the answer to that because I'd been here. "Hey, not everyone can suck up to tha teachers tha way you do," he said under his breath. "I don' just have things like that; some of us have to struggle to get through their classes."

As usual, it seemed like Derek knew the exact thing to say to get my blood boiling. "Excuse me?" I demanded, my eyes narrowing. "I *don't* get good grades because I suck up to my teachers. I *work* for every grade I have. How smart you are has nothing to do with you going to class, with putting effort into your work."

"Yeah, well I'll remembuh that next time," he said sarcastically. "Look, I'm goinna be late for my next class."

"I don't get you, Derek," I called at his retreating footsteps. "I really don't. If I was in your situation I don't care if I didn't get to sleep until graduation. If there was even the possibility that I could graduate with my class, I'd take it."

"Well you'd nevuh *be* in my situation, now would you," he questioned. "What do you know about havin' ta work hard for somethin'?"

For a second I didn't know if I'd heard him correctly. "What do you mean what would *I* know?" I demanded, barely taken care to keep my voice down. "I want to go to Harvard for God's sake, Derek! Do you think that I'm just going to blink and find myself there? Good grades aren't enough… Do you have any idea how much money it's going to take to get through undergrad and law school? My mom doesn't have that kind of money, so how do you think I'm going to get it?

"You know, I'm getting *really* tired of people thinking that I just have this easy time with everything I do; that things just happen for me! Yes, I may be smart, but I *work hard* for every grade that I get, and I make the grades

I do because I go over every assignment, every paper, every lesson, until I know that I know the material. Being smart is only half the battle; I have to be perfect! Every time I get over an obstacle, it's like one more moves in to fill its place.

"It's *always* hard being different from your peers, no matter the reason, but people like to treat you like a leper or something if you're smart." (In the black community, you were trying too hard to be white, in the white community you were getting uppity). "I've been made fun of for as long as I can remember because of the way I talked, or because I know what I want to do with my life, and people don't like that so much. I'm different, yes, but I'm not going to let that stop me from getting to where I want to be.

"So, *don't* tell me that I have things easy, because I don't, and if you'd gotten off of your metaphorical ass and tried a little harder this year, you wouldn't be in this situation in the first place."

Derek just looked at me in quiet surprise, and I wondered what had made me go through this little tirade. Why did I let him get to me so much? My voice softened considerably. "Yes, Mr. Colben gave you a lot of work to do, but you have three weeks to complete it in, and he is allowing you to make up the lab, so why don't you do yourself a favor, and do the work? Even if you don't get it all done, at least you know you tried." I paused. "I'll even help you, if you want."

Derek's lips curled into a sneer. "Wouldn' that be *cheatin'*," he said mockingly.

"I'm not offering to do the work for you; I said I would help you."

"Why? So you can rack up some more brownie points for yourself?" he demanded.

"It seems to me that the only person who is tallying up my brownie points is you."

"Why would you want to help me?"

"I'm only trying to be a friend."

He stiffened. "Yea, well no thanks."

"Suit yourself. I just thought you could use the help." I turned to walk away.

"I'm not an idiot you know," he said fiercely. "I'm *not* stupid. I got offered uh scholarship! To uh good school! That means that someone out there thinks that I know tha right stuff."

I stopped, surprised by his words almost to the point of being offended. "I've never said that I thought you were stupid," I responded. "God, Derek, don't you see how special you are? Why don't you start acting like you believe it?"

"Did Mr. Colben really say that I could make up tha lab," he questioned as I turned to walk away.

I nodded. "Yes, he did."

"Okay. Tell him I'll be there?" I nodded.

On Wednesday, after Derek finished his lab and was helping me clean up the materials, he told me that if I wanted to help him with his work, that'd be all right, he guessed. I knew it was the closest he would get to asking for my help.

It turned out that it wasn't just Mr. Colben's class that Derek had fallen behind in; he had an equal amount of work to do in two other classes. I made up a timetable for him to follow so he could get everything done and turned in. Derek had just gotten caught up in the tedium of the work. He wasn't stupid, just unmotivated. His insight into stuff was incredible, but he didn't like to do the work. I could understand that, but sometimes you just had to grit your teeth and buckle down. Besides, it was his senior year, the last year of school that he was forced to go through; I never understood the concept of giving up at the finish line.

"So where's your scholarship to?" I questioned on the last day that we were working together. He'd been sketching idly in his notebook, and even though I hated people reading over my shoulder, I glanced over at what he was doing. His sketches were a little too good to be considered average.

"What?" He looked up, unexpectedly, and since I was leaning in, it brought his face very close to mine. I was momentarily distracted by the sudden closeness. I had to pull away a little.

"Your scholarship?" I repeated. "Where's it to?"

He grinned so broadly that I wondered why I hadn't asked him before. "This arts school in Georgia," he answered proudly. "It's uh good school. They have uh very good art program there."

"That's great!"

He sat back in the seat, the enthusiasm surprisingly draining from him. "It's not Harvard," he stated.

I wondered why he said that. "What does that matter?" I questioned.

"You wouldn' want to go there."

"I'm not an artist," I reminded him.

"You write, don' you?"

I self-consciously put a hand over my notebook. "I'm not going to school for art."

He looked at the hand covering my notebook. "It's uh really good school," Derek said as an afterthought. He picked up his pencil, but he didn't write anything. "So, why were you here when I came to talk to Colben? I know you aren' gettin' tutored."

I was agreeable to the change of subject. "Actually, I am, somewhat. Mr. Colben has been helping me with a fellowship."

"Oh." He thought about those words. "Well I guess I know why you chewed me out so much." He smiled, slightly. He picked up his pencil again, and again stopped. "So, what's next aftuh I finish these questions?"

I checked the list, but I knew I didn't have to. "Nothing," I responded. "After this, you're finished."

"No, I'm not," he said in disbelief. I showed him the sheet of paper. He read it over more than once. "We're really finished?" Those words sounded so empty when he said them.

"Yes, you're going to graduate. Congratulations!"

Derek sat back in his chair, less enthusiastic than I thought he'd be. "Huh," he remarked. "You sure?"

"Positive."

"Guess this means you get to get rid of me," he remarked. He didn't sound happy about that.

"Guess so," I responded. "I have a club meeting in a few minutes, and you should be good with finishing this without me, so I'll see you around, I guess." I stood up, collecting my notebook and books together. My hand touched the envelope I'd left in my science book, and I pulled it out, silently, warring with myself because the last time I'd done this, it didn't go over so well.

I sat the envelope on the desk beside Derek. "What's this?" he questioned.

"A graduation gift," I responded.

His hand touched the envelope in a way that made me wonder if he knew what was inside. He didn't look up, though, hiding behind the cover of his bangs. "Tell me somethin', Trace. That note? Was it uh joke?" There was hesitation on his part, and I didn't know what his face looked like because I wasn't looking at him. "Was you just tryin' to make me look bad in front of my friends, or… did you really mean what you said?"

It didn't occur to me to lie. "I meant it," I said, slowly, cautiously giving him a glance.

His face wrinkled in…frustration? Confusion? "You hate me," he stated plainly.

"I don't hate you," I clarified, "I thought you were a jerk."

He laughed, softly. "Gee thanks, hon, for that clarification. You've uh way wit' words, you know that?"

"You asked," I reminded him.

I looked up to see him nod. He smiled, slightly. "You're right, I did."

"If it makes you feel better, I don't still," I remarked to my surprise. The words drew his eyes to mine, and that familiar little well of emotion rushed to the surface, causing my mind to clear, my face to blush.

"No?"

"I was wrong," I admitted. "I still think you can be a jerk sometimes, but after I got to know you, I guess my opinion's changed." I should have stopped talking at that, and under normal circumstances I would have. But Derek was graduating in a few days: I might not ever see him again. I wanted to say what I had to say to his face, lay it all out there as honestly as possible. I didn't want to still be mooring over him after this year. When he was gone, I wanted the feelings to go with him.

"Ever since the French Club convention…I've felt like something connected between the two of us, like we could see each other. I-I've never felt that way with anyone else. When I look at you, it's like I'm seeing who you really are." I waited for Derek's laugh, or for his mocking smile, or for him to say he didn't feel the same, but he didn't say anything. "And since then, that feeling hasn't gone away; I'm not sure why. I guess...I love you."

His eyes actually flickered at those words, and I suddenly felt like an idiot for saying them. After all, we weren't even really friends, much less anything more. Before this we hadn't talked in months. So what'd I expect: him to gaze deeply into my eyes and tell me that he loved me too? That he felt the same way towards me? As I stood there, it couldn't have been clearer that he didn't.

"I should go," I remarked. "Good luck, Derek." He reached for my hand, stopping short of touching me. "Thanks, Trace," he said, softly. "For tha help."

I nodded, blinking.

On my way out, I chanced a look back at Derek. He was staring at the envelope that I'd left. After a very long moment, he placed it in the front of his book. I ducked around the corner, trying to get lost before he could read what I'd written.

To you as you Graduate:

We forget, too soon, the paths we took
When we first learned to crawl.
The joy we'd get over the small stuff,
When the world was new,
And we wanted it all.

Already forgotten are the ancient lands,
Of childhood myth and lore.
We no longer spread our wings to fly,
And treasure hunting soon becomes a daily chore.

Gone, it seems, are the kingdoms of Kings and Queens.
The Fairy Tales and Leprechaun gold.
Narnia's gates have been closed for ever.
And the 'Jolly Ole Santa Claus', is just old

Instead of myths and fairy tales,
We think to colleges and careers,
And what our life will have to give
With each passing of the years.

True, with age comes wisdom and maturity,
Insight into grandeur things.
Yet, still sometimes life does not turn out right
And we can lose sight of what we dream.

So even though we become older,
And put away those silly childhood things;
Remember that no matter how old you get:
Never be afraid to dream.

Congratulations to the Grad.

Derek

This is probably the hardest thing I've ever written, but I have to write it because if I don't, I feel like I'll spontaneously combust or something. So here goes: I was wrong in my original opinion of you. I've enjoyed the parts of you that you've let me get to know. You've made me laugh, you've made me think, and, I admit, you've made me cry, too. I don't know what you feel about me; I guess that will just be one of those things I have to accept not knowing. I'm fine with that just as long as you know what I feel for you. I love you. I want you to know, too, that I believe in you, and I care about you. I hope that you discover that you don't have to be someone else in order to be liked; being yourself is enough.

I want to wish you good luck at school. I truly mean it when I say that you're special; I see nothing but great things coming from you. I pray that you always remember that all dreams, no matter how small, are significant, and no dream, no matter how large, is unreachable. Shoot for the stars, and never be afraid to dream. You have a tremendous light in you; I would hate to see it dim because you lost yourself along the way. I hope you make every moment count. I'll miss you, and I'll never forget you. If you ever need anything, even just someone to talk to in the middle of the night, I'll be there. Good luck in all you do.

Love always,

Tracy C. Burrows

— 20 —

"Craters of the Moon"

"Tray?" It was the amount of concern in my friend's voice that made me look up. Until she said my name, I hadn't realized that I was just sitting there, staring at the page in front of me. I'd been holding on to my pencil so tightly that it had made an indention in my fingers, but it hadn't made any sort of mark against the empty page. I must have been a sight if Patrice had actually looked up from her wardrobe. "What's goin' on? You haven' said anythin' for tha past couple uh hours."

"Nothing to say," I said moodily.

"Does this nothin' have anythin' to do wit graduation? Are you goin'?"

"I don't know."

"You on' know?" she repeated. "Derek graduates tonight! You on't want ta see that?"

"I don't know!" I exclaimed in frustration. "I want to go-," but I didn't want to continue to make a fool of myself. I'd poured my heart out to him, and he'd said nothing in return. That spoke volumes. "I don't know what I want right now." Well, that wasn't entirely true. I wanted for this whole crush thing to not be so hard. Why couldn't I just forget about him?

Patrice clucked her teeth at my response. "You know, T, for someone so smart, you're clueless half tha time."

My sentiments exactly. "Thanks," I said, sarcastically.

"Nah, I mean it. I mean come on, you like tha guy, you helped him ta get there anyway, he's goin' off ta school, and you may not see him again. What's tha problem?"

"I don't want to ruin his night," I responded.

"You're probably tha only person he *wants* ta see, Trace. I've seen tha way he looks at you. When you're around, he don' see no one else. He's in love wit you."

Her words nearly brought my hackles up. "Why do you say stuff like that?" I asked, frustrated by her certainty. I hated that she was always so adamant when it came to love. "Why are you so sure of that? Why won't you just admit that I don't mean anything to him?"

"'Cause I know that he's in love wit you," she said with that certainty that was frustrating. Why couldn't she be the kind of friend that would tell me that I was being foolish and to get over it?

"How?" I demanded. Patrice looked too long at her wardrobe. "Patrice?" I called.

"There're just some things you just know," she said, vaguely.

I shook her words away. "That's not good enough! Other than your intuition, how do you know that? What evidence do you have? The way he looks at me? I've never seen him look at me in any way other than in derision. He doesn't like me! Why can't you just admit that?"

Why did she always have to be so self-assured about feelings that I just couldn't see as being there? Why did I believe in her self-assurance? Why couldn't I just accept what was staring me in the face? "Why?" I implored.

"Because he's told me otherwise, okay?"

Her statement was so unexpected that for a full minute I wasn't sure I'd heard her correctly. It took me another full minute to find my voice. "What do you mean he *told* you?" I demanded, my heart temporarily stopping.

She sighed, giving up on her clothes for the moment to face me full on. "I mean that he *told* me that he liked you." It felt like the world spun beneath my feet.

"When?"

"At a basketball game back in February. I ran into him at tha concession stand, and I mentioned tha fact that you and him were in tha same fifth period. And then I said somethin' like, 'You know my girl Tracy likes you', and he got this *huge,* corny, smile on his face, like he couldn' help it, and says, 'I know'. I forgot what I asked him next, but his answa was somethin' like, 'I really like her uh lot, I like spendin' time wit her,' and some othuh stuff, maybe somethin' about how smart you were, and all that. I don' membuh it all, but trust me, he wasn' short on what he felt, and I know for a fact that he said he liked you," she concluded. And then her soft lines disappeared, and she gave me her talking-to-idiots face, "and God, Trace, he didn' even have ta say it. It's so obvious. The only person who don' see it is you!"

I stared, wondering if I should be mad at my best friend. A dozen emotions crowded my mind as I tried to process what she'd said. "Why haven't you told me this?" was the question that managed to come through.

"He asked me not to," she said simply.

"He was probably joking around, and you didn't pick up on it."

"You didn' see how he was lookin' when he said it."

"He didn't mean it," I decided.

She let out a frustrated sound. "See what I mean? You don' want ta believe that he likes you! I would *love* for Darnell ta feel for me tha same way that Derek feels for you, for him ta look at me tha way he does you! And tha thing that kills me is you don' even see that you have it; you just wanna ignore it!"

The brokenness in her voice gave me pause, a reason to really hear what she was saying. "If all that you said was true, why does he act the way he does when he's around me?" I asked. "Why would he tell you all this, and not me?"

She shrugged. "He didn' have nothin' to lose by tellin' me," she answered, simplistically.

It was hard to connect her words to Derek's actions; he wouldn't even look at me. "I think he was working you over," I said, dismissively.

Patrice shrugged in the same careless way. "I know what I saw, and I'm pretty good at feelin' othuh people's emotions. I know you'll regret it if you don' at least say good-bye ta him, and he probably will too. Just go see him graduate. The Civic Center's pretty big. He won' see you unless you want ta be seen."

"I have to think about it."

"You know what your problem is, Trace? You think too much."

I didn't make up my mind to go to graduation until the moment Patrice was leaving to go, and even then I still had doubts about it. Patrice was right about the Civic Center, though. It seated at least twenty thousand, and there was no way Derek would be able to pick me out of the crowd. I watched him receive his diploma, and started to leave, but I had to go back. I wanted, needed, to at least say good-bye to him.

I made it back in time to see the pit fill up with the graduates and their family and friends. Derek stepped into the pit almost directly in front of me. He looked at me, I looked at him, we made eye contact, and then he just walked off.

So much for saying good-bye.

To say that I was glad that the school year was finally over would have been an understatement. Sophomore year just seemed kind of pointless, like they just sort of put it in there to take up time. Next year, though, things were going to be more serious. I only had two more years left before I had to make my case for why I should be allowed to attend school at Harvard, and I didn't intend to waste that time. I needed to make sure that I really stood out.

Instead of doing this summer program, I audited two classes at AAMU. I also obtained some higher level math books, and worked and reworked through the books with a man at the church who was a math teacher at Forest Lake College. I subscribed to the *New York Times*, the *Post,* and the *Journal,* kept on top of who was expected to run in the upcoming presidential election, and read through the latest scientific journals so I could keep current with the information I would never find in our outdated textbooks. To improve my English and basic writing skills, I gave myself a different essay topic to write on each day. I came up with lists of vocabulary words to study. I even got a job at the library, which essentially meant that I was being paid to read all day.

The days passed by pretty quickly. Before I knew it, the first summer session of school was nearing an end. Near the end of term, I'd just gotten off of work, practically just walked in through the door, when the phone rang. I dropped a few books in my haste to answer. "Hello?"

"Hello, Tracy!" A falsely cheerful voice exclaimed, and for a moment my heart stopped beating. "It's dad." I stared at the base of the phone as if it was a dangerous thing that might jump up and bite me. I wondered if more time had passed than I thought, and it was suddenly September.

"Tracy?" my dad questioned. "Are you still there?"

I found my voice. "Yes, I'm here. Err...Hi, dad!" I hated how chipper I sounded, especially compared to his return greeting.

"Hi munchkin, how're you?"

"I'm doing well, how are you?" I questioned very formally.

"Couldn't ask for better. How's your summer going so far?"

"It's…okay," I allowed.

He didn't waste any time in getting to the point. "So, I've been thinking: why don't you come out and visit me this summer?"

"Visit?" I questioned. The notion seemed foreign to me. I hadn't seen my dad since I was ten.

"Yes," he continued. "I'll show you around town. We can catch up. How about it?"

I wondered where this was coming from, or if my mom had solicited this call from him; certainly he couldn't have called just because he wanted to see me.

"I wish you'd have called sooner, dad. I already signed up for classes this summer at the college."

He was momentarily taken aback. "You're in college already?"

I sighed because it showed how little I actually talked to this man. "No, dad, not yet. I'm auditing some classes this summer."

He seemed cheered by this news, which made no sense to me. "So the classes aren't for credit then, correct?"

"Right."

"Well, I was really looking forward to seeing you. Are you enrolled in both semesters or are you just signed up for the first one?"

"The first one," I answered, even though I'd signed up for both summer terms.

"Well that's great, then! How about you come out after term ends, and you can spend the rest of the summer here? How does that sound?"

I wasn't sure how it sounded. "It sounds…*great*, dad."

"When do you go back to school? September?"

"August."

"August? Gosh that's soon isn't it?"

"Schools in the south go back sooner."

"Oh…right. Well that'll give us at least a month together, right?"

"Yes, sir."

"Great. I'll see you when the semester ends. Call me back with the exact date so I can get you a plane ticket."

I hesitated. "I'd rather take a bus or train," I remarked.

"Okay, just call me back with the date so I can get it."

"Okay," I responded.

Even after I replaced the phone, I was still mildly in shock. It wasn't that I hadn't talked to my dad since the divorce. I had. Like clockwork, every year on September 12th and December 24th, he would call at six and we'd talk until seven. My dad and I'd clocked in twelve hours of phone conversation since the divorce…so we talked. But not once in six years had he called me on any day other than December 24th or September 12th. I got that long distance calls from Denver were expensive, but postage cost less than $.10.

I wondered what my mom would think about my dad's sudden interest when I told her about the call. She always made it a point to never talk bad about my dad in my presence so she pretty much did not talk about him at all. It wasn't like she had a reason to talk about him that often, though. He simply wasn't in my life enough to say anything about.

I told her about my conversation with dad as soon as she got through the door, and she seemed as surprised by it as I did. She looked at me over the day's mail. "If you want to go, I'll get you a ticket for the Greyhound."

"Dad said he'd send me a ticket," I said in answer.

"Is that what you want to do?"

"I haven't seen him in years," I said in response.

She considered my words. "Well, then, maybe it's time you did see him again."

Like I said, she never criticized him in front of me. And dad never spoke ill of her in the two hours a year that we talked to each other. I think a lot of the time they pretended that the other never existed. I wondered what in the world made them get married to each other in the first place. Neither of them spoke of the other as if they had ever loved each other. I used to think that they'd married because my mom had been pregnant with me, but I'd checked their marriage certificate and they were married for a year and a half before I was born. Whatever it was that *had* been there, though, no longer was. That was obvious.

— 190 —

"Yes, ma'am," I said in agreement.

And that was that.

The day after classes ended, I got on a bus to Nashville, where I boarded a train to Colorado. When I arrived at the station, I was met at the terminal by a well-dressed man with a sign with my name on it. I paused in front of him long enough for him to ask, "Are you Miss Burrows?" I knew there was no purpose in looking around, but I did anyway. I nodded. "Mr. Burrows asked for me to express his apologies on not being able to make it, and to give you this." He handed me an envelope that contained a small note of apology, and a key to my dad's house.

I followed him out to the awaiting car, trying to mask my disappointment. My dad, Mr. Benjamin Burrows, was a man that stuck to his word. So far in my life he had yet to break a promise to me because he only made promises he knew he could keep. *"Be careful of the promises that you make to the Lord,"* he'd quote, *"for you do not want your thoughts to make you a liar,"*.

If he said that he would do something, you could trust that he was going to do it, end of story. In retrospect, however, he only did the things that he said he would do. So I never expected any more from him than what he said he would deliver. And he never said he would pick me up at the station; he'd said he would send me a ticket. I spent the ride to his house staring at the partition between me and the driver, looking at the landscape that passed us by, praying that coming out here wasn't a mistake.

As we neared my dad's home, I couldn't help but think about Peter Seeger's song *Little Boxes*. The suburban neighborhood that he lived in was the kind of place where you had four choices of floor plans, two for the mailbox, a choice between one and a half baths or two, and very little choice for anything else. It was all very cookie-cutter, but far nicer, and more spacious, than our own house in Wilmington. I'd never really paid attention long enough to know, exactly, what it was my dad did. I knew he was broadly classified as an engineer, and he worked with electrical things, with computers, but that was pretty much the extent of my knowledge of his work. Well, that, and that the job afforded him a certain lifestyle.

Before the divorce, we'd lived in a house like the one my dad lived in now. We'd gotten a new car every two years. My mom and I belonged to the East

St. Louis chapter of Jack and Jill, I took ballet, jazz, and gymnastics. We used to attend Cardinals games every other weekend, or we went on day trips to the riverside, to movies, biking, or to symphonies. I didn't realize that this was considered privileged until I no longer had it. I didn't even know that this was considered different from the lives most Blacks had, either, because we'd spent so much time in the city, where there was not only a high black population, but a wealthy, or at least solidly middle class, black population. I'd spent enough time around kids that had fathers who were doctors, or were engineers like mine, or were in the military, to think that it was normal. I'd been raised to the DuBoisian standard, the Talented Tenth. I hadn't known that my dream of being a lawyer was impossible until I'd moved down South.

The driver helped me with my bags, wished me a good day, and was off. I let myself inside, and after I put my things away in the guest bedroom, I went on a tour, trying to glean who my father was from the items he had filled his home with after my mom and I were no longer a part of his life. Despite the pictures of me that faced the door, it was easy to tell that he lived by himself. It wasn't that his house was unkempt: his house was clean and very organized. The furniture matched and was tasteful, but not ostentatious, yet there was something undefinable that said that this was the home of a bachelor. I wondered if he ever came home to this empty house after a long week of work and wondered if there was anything missing in his life.

It was after seven by the time my dad made it home. When he saw me, he looked slightly surprised, as if he'd forgotten that today was the day that my train was supposed to arrive. After an awkward moment, he gave me an even more awkward hug. "Hey, munchkin, you surprised me. Geez, you've gotten big!" We were now very near the same height. "I didn't realize you'd gotten so tall!" I wondered if he felt any regret that he hadn't been around to watch me age, that most of my memories didn't have him in it. Did he ever think about those kinds of things? "How was your trip?"

"It was okay," I responded. "No problems."

He seemed cheered by that small fact. "That's great. I always hate those roller coaster flights. Not a big flier, you know?"

"I took the Amtrak, remember, dad?"

"Oh, that's right!" he remarked. "I forgot. Have you eaten? Tell you what, give me a moment to get out of my work clothes, and we'll go out for dinner. You can catch me up on what has been happening in your life while we eat. How's that sound?"

"Sounds great, dad," I said.

At the restaurant I sat watching my father, familiarizing myself with his face and features. My mom didn't know it, but I still kept my parents wedding picture in my room, away from her sight. In the intervening years, he hadn't changed much in appearance from the picture. He was still a very handsome man in a 'no touch' kind of way. He was a very light brown, with black hair that was always kept short, parted, and brushed back. If he were to allow it to grow out, it was noticeably wavy, but he never allowed his hair to grow, so you wouldn't know that. His hazel eyes were surrounded by the slightest darkening of his skin, and were topped by two, thick, bushy eyebrows. Beneath his high-cheek bones, and framed by a thin, English mustache, was the mouth that I couldn't remember stretching into a smile very often, and a chin that was wide and devoid of any hair.

My dad was considered to be black and a quarter Indian, and even as a kid, I knew he cared way too much about his looks. He was proud of the lightness of his skin, that his hair wasn't 'nappy', that he wasn't just black, but mixed; as if that fact mattered to anyone but him and his family. They all held on to that quarter Indian part of their heritage as if it made them better than the average black person, as if that elevated our family to some different plane. I wouldn't mind that attitude so much if he actually embraced the heritage, but he didn't; just the genetics.

His attitude made me often surprised that he and my mom had gotten married, because I would've thought that my mom was too dark for him, had too many black features, took too much after my Grandpa. But maybe it was enough for him to know of her past. Or maybe they had once honestly been in love and none of that had mattered.

"So, how has school been for you?" he questioned.

The question was easy enough to answer, unlike the ones that left gaping questions as to why he was no longer in my life. So I answered without pause, "Things are going well. Senior year I'm going to dual enroll," I said, quickly, remembering that I had already said that. I filled him in on my grades, about the clubs I was in, about the college that I wanted to go to…stuff we discussed over the phone that I was sure he didn't remember.

"Do you remember your cousin Vinny?" he questioned at some point. "He lettered as a sophomore, and he's got a lot of scouts looking at him now. Your Uncle Wally keeps on telling me how he thinks colleges will be begging Vinny to go there."

"I can't say that I have scouts looking after me," I responded. "But I'll graduate in the top ten, though. I may even be the valedictorian or the salutatorian," I added. It was unlikely, not because of my grades, but because the school board wouldn't allow it.

"That's great, Tracy," he responded. "Keep up the good work!"

As the summer progressed, I began to remember what it had been like growing up with both my parents. When I was younger, my dad and I spent so much time together on the weekends because he was missing so much during the week. My dad, like my mom did now, spent a lot of time away from the house. He wasn't someone who could just completely put work aside, but he did manage to spend some time with me while I was there. In fact, he seemed to be trying to make up for lost time. It was nice that he wanted to spend time with me when he could, but I would have settled for just one real, serious, sit down conversation with him, one where he actually listened to me and heard what I was saying. Or even one warm hug, one moment where he said, "This is my daughter," with pride in his voice, and no need it to back it up with some sort of accomplishment.

— 21 —
"The Unexpected Visitor"

While I was in Denver busy visiting my dad, my best friend became a licensed driver in the state of Alabama. She wanted to be the one to pick me up from the train station when I got home, but her parents didn't think that that was a good idea, so instead she was waiting at the curb when we got back from Nashville, ready to take me out joyriding. "Uht oh," she exclaimed as my mom and I were getting out of the car. "Look at you!" As an afterthought she said, "Hello, Miz Burrows."

"Hello, Patrice," my mom remarked cordially. "How are you doing?"

"All right, ma'am."

My mom nodded at her. "Don't forget to call your father," she told me on the way into the house.

"Okay," I responded. I made the call before Patrice and I carted my two bags into my room and began to unpack my stuff. "How was your dad," she asked, once the door was closed.

"He was my dad," I responded. I couldn't honestly say that I'd been sad when the two of us said our good-byes. I loved my dad, but it was so awkward being around him, and *I* felt awkward about it because it *was* awkward to spend time with my own father.

Patrice evaluated my response. "Did you at least have fun?" she wondered.

"I learned a lot," I replied.

I could see her repeating my words back in her head. "That's not what most folks would say."

I shrugged. "My dad's complicated. We did a lot of things that were fun, but fun wouldn't be the adjective I would use."

The last article of clothing got placed in its drawer, and after a brief stop in to say good-bye to my mom, we got into Sean's car. Patrice paused to put on her sunglasses, scarf, and riding gloves. "Do I look like Audrey?" she questioned.

"Oh yes, darling," I assured her.

I'd been driving with Patrice before, so the thought didn't scare me as much as I thought it would. I was actually envious. Even though my 16th birthday was only a month away, I knew that I wouldn't be getting behind the wheel of a car any time soon.

"So, it wasn't fun, but did anythin' interestin' happen? Is he seein' someone?"

"Not that I know about."

"A man that attractive?" she questioned in disbelief. I knew she had a mini crush on him; she thought my dad looked like a black Clark Gable.

"Nobody came by the house, and no one called," I answered. I'd been a little surprised by that fact because I'd kind of assumed that had been the reason for his sudden invitation. "I didn't meet any of his 'special' friends, either, though I was kind of expecting too," I admitted. "Why else would he ask me to spend the summer with him? It just seems too parental."

"Maybe just ta see you?" I didn't remark. "So why isn' he datin'?"

"I didn't ask."

A thought must have occurred to her. "Would you have a problem if he did start dating someone else?"

I'd never really thought about it. "I never see him, why would I have a problem with it?"

"Because you'd have a step-mom. Wouldn' that be wild?" I shrugged; I doubted I'd see her, either. "Does your mom go around wit anyone?"

"I think that she thinks that it would be a sin to, you know, since she got divorced."

"What d'you think?" Patrice asked.

"I try not to," I told her. "Why all the questions?"

"You've got nerve! Mostly everythin' you say's a question! I'm just curious, you know. I always wondered what it would be like for your parent's ta be divorced."

"It's no picnic," I asserted, "I doubt that you'll ever have to worry about that. I can't remember my parents ever looking at each other like your parents do."

"Girl, my folks fight just like everyone else," she informed me. "You just have ta think 'bout it tha way Marcus told me. I got tha old folks. When Abdul and Sean were growin' up, they couldn' do *nothin'*. They've mellowed out since they got ta me. Bein' a parent, like marriage, takes time, I guess."

I guess. "I doubt I'll ever get married," I said, thinking about it. Being around my dad this summer had made me realize something about myself. I would probably spend just as much time, or more, away from my family, if my ambitions took me to where I wanted them to go. I had no intention of bringing a family into that. I think that the people you live with deserve your time and affection, and my career ambitions wouldn't really allow me to give them that time. If I had a family, I didn't want to be distant towards them, so I didn't really intend to have a family of my own. My Aunt Joanne, my mom's older sister, didn't, and she was doing just fine.

"Everybody gets married at some point," she said dismissively. "It's like nature and stuff."

"Not everyone," I stated. "I'm not going to."

"You probably right, seein' as you don' like guys too much."

"They're unnecessary," I asserted.

She smiled to herself, and by her grin I could tell that whatever it was that she found amusing was a whopper. "Oh, yeah, that reminds me. Guess who I ran into!"

"Who?" I couldn't help but ask, hoping for only one answer.

She seemed in tune with my thoughts. "I'd tell you, but he's unnecessary," she teased.

"Who?" I repeated, complete putty in her hands.

"Derek," she said, casually. "I seent him at Brewster's Hobby Shop."

I tried not to let my feelings show. "When?"

"I think a coupla weeks ago. He said, 'Hello'," she stated very deliberately.

"I'm surprised he wasted the breath," I muttered.

She ignored it. "He ast 'bout you," she added, watching for my expression out of the corner of her eye. I almost looked at her, but didn't want to rise to her bait. "He wanted ta know what you're up ta," she continued, "and when I seent you again ta tell you that he said 'hi'. So, Tracy, Derek says 'hi'."

I let a smile tease my lips. "Did he really ask about me?" I posed.

"What'd I say?"

"You could just be teasing."

She smiled. "I thought you was ovuh him."

"I am."

"You're funny, T, but in all seriousness, he did ast 'bout you."

I tried to play it cool. "Uh huh."

She rolled her eyes at my reaction. "You can play fool all you want, but you know you still like him. The two uh y'all are goinna get married some day," she predicted.

"And pigs are going to learn how to do new math. Are you still talking to Darnell?" She did not frown or anything, but there was instantly a change in her demeanor. I immediately felt bad for bringing him up.

"Coupla times," she admitted. "He comes by my job ta see me. Says he still wants ta be friends." With a huge effort to change the subject she said, "While you were at your dads' we got our schedules!" And that quickly talked turned to the upcoming school year.

Over the summer I decided that junior year was going to be the *it* year for me. It was my personal goal to score in no less than the 91st percentile when I took the college boards, and now that I was a junior, I could finally start applying for most scholarships. I also wanted to make a bid for student government (even if I didn't get it), make it onto the exec board of at least one of the clubs I was involved in, and I was going to make all A's, no matter what. Graduation was shockingly close, and I wasn't going to let it catch me unprepared.

Patrice seemed to be just as determined to make the most of this year. Even though I was still taking mostly all college prep classes, Patrice and I had a few classes together, and she had even decided to take a foreign language. She indulged me in making study schedules and doing vocabulary drills. She joined a service group as an extra-curricular, even declared that she was swearing off guys for good…or for the first few months, at least.

The only fluff in her schedule was her 3rd period. She was an office aide. It was a perfect match for her because it expanded her repertoire of gossip past just the simple rumor mill of the privileged and the popular; she was now privy to the gossip of everyone in the school, including the faculty and staff. Patrice and I had 4th and 5th periods together, and while we were supposed to be paying attention to what the teachers were saying, Patrice usually recanted the day's gossip, which I unashamedly enjoyed hearing.

In what seemed like an annual ritual now, the second week into the school year, Mrs. Rupert called me into her office to talk about my schedule. I took my seat, and waited for her yearly assertion that my goals were too ambitious. Mrs. Rupert seemed less than thrilled to have me sitting across from her once again. "I see that you have overloaded your schedule with a work load that, quite frankly, seems near impossible, and I fear that you won't be able to handle," was her greeting. She no longer had a cookies-and-milk smile for me, and I wondered why she disliked me so much.

"I've managed to keep an A average for the past two years," I informed her.

"Yes, and it makes me wonder how you've managed *that*."

Her words reminded me of the unfounded accusations of cheating that I had to deal with last year. I was certain that it'd been Sam who'd complained to Mrs. Dressler; I guess he'd gotten tired of me always outscoring him on every test.

I frowned at her, but said nothing. "Miss Burrows, if you insist on this path that you have started down, I have no choice but to remind you that we take academic dishonesty *very* seriously around here. If you're caught-,"

"I don't cheat-," I interjected.

"- we will be forced to expel you from school, and that will, of course, go in your permanent record and then where will you be?"

We stared at each other over the gap that separated us. I remembered thinking, freshman year, that I'd just have to someday prove this woman wrong. Sitting here now I realized that women like her were never wrong. Even if I graduated number one in my class, she still would remain unconvinced of my abilities, no matter my scores. In her mind the only way I could have achieved them was to cheat.

"Yes, ma'am," I remarked, picking myself up from my seat without waiting to be dismissed.

It was only a few minutes to the next bell, so instead of going back to Physics, I went to my locker before heading to Warner's class early. Patrice must have waited for me outside of my third because she was almost late to class, sliding into the room just as the second bell was ringing. Mr. Warner, who had a far more relaxed attendance policy than most teachers, did not even look up as Patrice entered the room, grinning from ear to ear. The look she wore either meant that she had run into some cute guy in the hallway, or that she had just heard some really juicy gossip.

I gave her a questioning look as she slid into her seat beside me. "Oh, Mrs. King!" she greeted. "You have a visitor!"

"Very funny," I remarked, not in the mood for her teasing after Mrs. Rupert and my conversation.

She tried to look serious, but the grin dominated her face. "No, really, you do," she insisted. She'd purposely left the door open, and my eyes slid over to it, before looking back at her. Curiosity got the best of me. I knew who she wanted me to think was out there, and I felt like an idiot as I got up from my seat and went to the door.

I was expecting the hallway to be abandoned, so I was completely caught off guard when I was met by a pair of laughing blue eyes. "Hey, Trace," Derek greeted, nonchalantly. He was resting against the wall as if there was nothing unusual about him being there. I was too taken aback to say anything; a smile already creeping up on my face. It was all I could do to nod and curl my fingers in a wave.

Derek opened his arms in a gesture that said 'come here and give me a hug' and after I got over my initial shock of seeing him, I obliged. I walked into his awaiting arms, and they wrapped around me in a secure embrace. For a moment, the rest of the world felt like it dropped from around us. Already my morning was washed away, swept down the river, and forgotten. Who cared about Mrs. Rupert and her condescension when hugging Derek felt so *good*? He had the perfect feel, the perfect smell, and he felt so firm, so sturdy. I couldn't say if his hug lasted a few seconds, or a few minutes, and I didn't care either way. I just enjoyed being in his arms.

When we did finally separate, it was too soon. He was still wearing a smile, and I was positive that I was too. As hard as I tried, I couldn't stop smiling, but for the first time, when I looked at him, I didn't feel as if the feelings were just one sided.

He was too cute, I thought to myself.

"How've you been? What have you been up to?" he questioned, eagerly. His brow furrowed as he seemed to be searching for something, and triumphantly he questioned, "Comment vas tu?" It took me a moment to find my voice, or even remember how to talk.

"Uhm…ça va bien?" I answered. *Très bien!*

His eyes found purchase in mine. "How was your summuh?"

"My summer?" I repeated stupidly.

"Yeah, your friend said you went to Denver."

"Yes!" I said a little too eagerly. "I did!" Silently I was thanking Patrice for helping me out with this conversation. "It was great!" And suddenly, inexplicably, it was. "I went to see my dad, and we went to see one of his sisters who just had a baby; she was so cute! You had to see her. The baby." When I realized I was babbling I stopped, blushing. Derek's smile grew. "How was yours?" I managed to get out.

"Good. Busy, but good. *Really* good," he emphasized. "It was really… illuminatin'."

"Patrice said that she ran into you."

If it was even possible, Derek's smile increased. "Yea?" he asked.

"She did…," I affirmed. "So what made your summer so good?"

Derek's smile turned mysterious. "Uh lot of things," he remarked, just as coded with his words as he was in smile. "Atlanta's uh great city."

"Oh, yeah I forgot you're going to school there." *I forgot?* As if that were really possible. "So…what are you…I mean, I thought, when does school start?"

"Next week," Derek answered.

"So when're you leaving?"

Did I imagine the sudden look of bashfulness that flashed across his features? "I'm not," he answered, slowly. "I decided not to go to that school in Georgia aftuh all."

His words didn't fit in with a summer's worth of thoughts; despite that he was standing in front of me, in my head he was already gone. "Why not?" Honestly, though, I didn't care. He was staying here!

He gave a casual shrug. "I decided to go to AUB instead. It's cheaper, more practical, closuh to home."

"I thought you said that you had a scholarship," I remembered.

"I did," he remarked, giving a slight nod, "but my parents are goinna shoulder half of it; I'm goin' pay for tha rest. AUB's tuition's not so bad."

"Do you know what you're going to major in?"

He seemed amused that I was asking, and I realized that it was probably because he wouldn't have asked me that same question in this situation. "Accountin'."

Accounting? That was definitely a surprise. I couldn't see Derek as an accountant. They all seemed so stuffy; I just couldn't picture it. "Oh. So… um…what brings you around?"

This, too, seemed to amuse him. "I came by to see Mrs. Diece," he explained. "I'm tryin' to refresh my French. I want, well I's thinkin' 'bout it anyway, but I'm tryin' to get to France eithuh this summuh or tha next. I thought it'd be nice to visit. First stop on my trip 'round tha world."

His words brought on a blush as I remembered his hand touching mine in the car that night. "That sounds fun," I think I remarked to that. If he was to ask me about running off with him right then, I don't think I'd have been able to say no.

"I'm just happy Mrs. Diece is takin' tha time to walk through this wit' me, 'cause it might be uh good idea for me to be able to speak tha language fluidly."

"That might help a little bit," I agreed.

"Since I's up here," he continued, "I thought I'd visit wit' some of my old friends, check on you kids. Are you in Warner's class right now?" I nodded. "You're not missin' anythin' important are you?"

We both knew I wasn't. Warner didn't even take attendance half the time. He lectured for fifty minutes straight, but the tests came straight from the book, not from his lectures. I could easily miss one class and that was probably what Derek was hinting. To both of our surprises, I answered, "Yes."

Derek frowned slightly at the words. "Oh?" I wondered how that one syllable word could sound so suggestive, hold so much promise.

I held a brief, inner fight with myself. "I probably should be getting back," I realized.

Derek looked off balance. "Yeah...well, I'll c'ya around, okay?" I nodded. He hesitated for the briefest of moments. "It was great seein' you again, Trace," he said, giving me a quick half-hug. I was disappointed; I wanted the real thing. I couldn't believe that I said that I was actually missing something!

"See you," I got out. He waved before I went back into the classroom.

— 22 —
"The Anatomy Lesson"

I slid a piece of newsprint into my best friend's hand. "What's this?" Patrice wondered, barely glancing at the article.

"Read it!" I insisted.

"How about you just tell me-,"

"Thurgood Marshall gets confirmed to the US Supreme Court," I read off excitedly, before she had even finished her sentence.

She didn't get it. "Okay…" I just looked at her, until… "Wait, is this like lawyer from tha NAACP Thurgood Marshall?"

"Yes, chief counsel of NAACP, one and the same. First black elected to the United States Supreme Court!" The triumph that ringed my voice was as exuberant as if I were reading my own confirmation.

Patrice didn't catch my elation. She turned over the paper as if it contained some sort of coded answer. "What's this prove?" she questioned.

"Nothing, Triece! It proves that nothing is impossible! The Supreme Court! That's the country's highest court!"

"He's still a man, though," she said, diminishingly.

"There're female lawyers," I informed her. "It's only a matter of time before one of them makes it to the bench."

She still looked doubtful. "Maybe, but how many uh those lawyers are Black?"

I considered. "There's Constance Motley; she's black, and not only is she a U.S. judge, but she was once the borough president of Manhattan, which is almost like being the mayor of one of the world's largest cities. And she's not the only one. I don't know how many of us there are," I declared, deciding to include myself in that category. "I'll count them for you once I pass the bar!" I said, exuberantly.

"What's the bar?"

"It's the test that each state gives to prove that you have the legal know how to be a lawyer, sort of like a certification. It gives you the right to practice. I'm telling you, Patrice, nothing is too far out of our reach; even NASA believes that they can send us to the stars!"

I was overly giddy at the news of Thurgood's appointment, and wanted to know why my friend wasn't as excited about this news as I was. It was big, it was life altering, it meant things really could change. I'd been following Mr. Marshall's, pardon, *Justice* Marshall's career for a long time; in my opinion there couldn't have been a better choice to fill Justice Clark's vacated seat. With Marshall and Warren on the bench, and Johnson in office for another term, we might just be able to complete the work that JFK started before he was assassinated.

She merely grinned at my enthusiasm. "I'll take your word for it," she responded. "Is Derek comin' up ta tha school today?" Her question caught me too quickly to try to fight the smile that spread across my lips. "I guess that's a 'yes'," she noted.

"He might be," I responded, trying to reel in my eagerness a little. I was always a little upset with myself for allowing myself to be so enthused by his presence, but it was almost automatic. I liked Derek. I'd been expecting him to make one or two trips up to the school, before giving up on his lessons with Mrs. Diece, but he seemed like he was dedicated to improving his speech. On top of his course load at AUB, he was at Mason every Tuesday and Thursday during Mrs. Diece's planning period, and while he graded papers for her, the two of them would hold conversations in French. Some days Derek stayed at the school past Mrs. Diece's planning period, and he had lunch with Patrice and me after, though honestly, it seemed that he was really having lunch with Patrice because she was responsible for most of the conversation.

She had none of the same complications as I did with talking to him: to her he was just a guy. To me, well it was bad enough when I thought that Derek *might* know what my feelings for him were; it was worse knowing that he *knew* what I felt. Even though we never brought it up, our last conversation before graduation and the note I'd written were always at the back of my mind. I wondered if he read them, wondered what he thought about them, wondered why we *didn't* talk about it. But why rock the boat? I was just content with him coming up to the school.

Patrice smiled at my unbridled joy, but then something in my grin caused her to frown. I felt the smile slide from my face at her expression. "What's wrong?" I questioned.

She shook her head a little too quickly. "Nothin'."

It wasn't a normal nothing. "Patrice?" I questioned with concern.

"I, I was just thinkin', it's nice. You two…"

I suddenly understood, and I was hugging her before her tears even started. I knew those particular tears; she'd developed a cry specific solely to Darnell. "I wasn' goin' to see him anymore," she whispered into my shoulder, "and I wouldn' ask if it wasn' important, but I need a favuh, Trace. I told Mrs. Taylor that I'd watch Nicole, but Darnell called me, yesterday…," her voice trailed off. She looked at me, pleadingly, as if she was trying to get me to understand. "He wants ta see me," she said, smiling sadly.

It was odd to see how happy and sad that small fact meant to her. Seeing those conflicting emotions on my friend's face made me dislike Darnell that much more: he knew exactly what he was doing to her. And Patrice knew, at least a small part of her knew, that he was no good for her (or in general), but he seemed to be like a drug to her. I wanted to tell her how much better than him she was, remind her about all of her best tributes, and that she didn't need anyone like him in her life. Instead all I said was, "I can watch Nicole."

"You're tha best, Tracy, you know that?"

"That's what I keep hearing," I responded, feeling a little sick inside.

Mrs. Taylor was in her usual hurry when we got to her house, but she stopped a moment to talk. Nicole, she explained, was sick and running a fever. Orion wasn't available to baby-sit, and Mrs. Taylor didn't want to leave her by herself when she was feeling so miserable. If she got any worse, Patrice was told to call the next door neighbor, but she didn't think that there would be any problems. Mrs. Taylor hesitated on the doorstep (she and Patrice were paradoxes of anxiety), but after going back into Nicole's room and kissing her goodnight, she headed off to work. While Patrice went to the window to wait for Darnell to show up ("Oh, I hope he does"), I went into Nicole's room to check on her. She was curled up in the fetal position and trembling, sleeping fitfully. When I touched her forehead, it was sweaty and she felt a little warm to the touch.

In the living room Patrice was pacing the floor, jumping at every car that drove by. Finally the sound she was waiting for happened. She started for the door, but paused, remembering to at least wait until he knocked. "I'll see you latuh, Trace," she called over her shoulder as she left.

When Patrice was gone, I poked my head into Nicole's room again to reassure myself that she was okay. Leaving the door ajar so that I could hear her in case she woke up, I got comfortable on the Taylor couch. I picked up the scientific journal I'd brought over with me, locating the spot that I'd last read. There was a knock at the door, just as I was getting to the most interesting part of the article. Reluctantly, I got up to answer it, and was instantly rewarded for my effort: Derek was standing on the other side!

Even though things had gotten a lot friendlier between us, I tried not to get too excited about his presence, and decided to hedge my bets. "Orion's not here," I informed him as soon as I opened the door.

He gave a chuckle. "Hi, Tracy. How're you?" he questioned deliberately.

I smiled. "Sorry. Hi, Derek," I returned.

He invited himself in, and I closed the door behind him. Derek took in the room at a glance. "Where's Nicole?" he wondered.

"Sleeping," I replied.

"Sleepin'?" He looked at his watch. "It's only 6:00."

"She's sick," I explained.

His expression changed at those words. "What's wrong wit' her?" he wondered anxiously.

"Just a normal cold, I think. She was okay when I last checked on her."

"D'you mind if I go see her?"

"She's asleep," I stated, but he was already heading toward her room. He didn't go in, though, just stood in the doorway, watching.

She made a piteous sound in her sleep, as if she knew of her audience, and he winced. "Are you sure she's okay?" he questioned, anxiously.

I nodded. Derek's shoulders relaxed slightly. A fraction. I thought the amount of concern he showed for her was touching; he really did treat her as if she were his little sister and not his friend's. "She'll be fine," I declared. To emphasize my words, I went back into the living room, and after a few minutes Derek joined me on the couch. He relaxed gradually. "She really will be all right," I assured.

He looked at me through his anxious gaze, his eyes refocusing. He laughed. "Guess, I worry too much, huh," he decided. "I just hate she's feelin' bad."

I put a reassuring arm around his shoulder. He looked over at me, which made me realize how incredibly close we were. I must have shifted uncomfortably or something because Derek stood back up, and I slid down to the floor in front of the table.

"I think Orion's working tonight," I remarked. I didn't really want him to go, but his presence was always a little disarming.

Derek had moved to the doorway. He leaned against the jamb, watching me. "I know," Derek returned. "I saw that you was ovuh here; just thought I'd say hi."

"Oh," I managed, pleasantly surprised by his words. I allowed a small smile to cross my lips. "No big plans for tonight?" I questioned.

His eyes didn't stray from mine. "Not really," he answered. "I just thought we could hang for uh while."

"Mrs. Taylor says boys aren't allowed in the house while she's gone," I said with a smile.

He shared the joke. "That don' include me, though," he assured me.

I wondered at that statement. "She doesn't mind the time that you spend around here?" I questioned, seriously. Even though Nicole was only eight, it was hard to imagine that Mrs. Taylor was that accepting.

Derek paused to consider the question. "Possibly, but I think that she's adopted uh kind of grudgin' acceptance of me. She's gotten used to seein' me 'round tha house ova tha years."

His words reminded me of how mixed-matched he and Orion seemed to be. "How did you two became friends?" I blurted without really thinking that maybe that question might be a little personal. The fact that they were neighbors didn't seem enough of a reason to bridge the distance that was between them, but Derek referred to Orion as not just another friend, but his best. He may have even broken up with a girlfriend because of him. You didn't see very many friendships like that around here.

He gave a casual shrug to a not so casual question. "How does anyone become friends?" he posed, contemplating the words. He looked at me, and his eyes flashed mysteriously, before darkening in thought. "I think O's simply learned to tolerate me ovuh the years. He started puttin' up wit' me cause of his sistuh, I think."

His words didn't exactly follow the conversation. "Why would he put up with you because of Nicole?" I wondered.

He gave me a shy look. "Not Nicole," he corrected. "Meda."

As far as I knew, Orion only had the one sister. "Meda?" I questioned in confusion.

"Orion's twin...you nevuh wondered why me and Nicole are so close?"

I had. "I figured that it was because she was your best friend's little sister," I replied to his question.

He paused, considering, as if he were trying to work through something difficult. His eyes slowly lowered to meet mine. "Orion's not Nicole's brother, Trace, he's her uncle. Nicole's my daughtuh."

There was a beat that passed while I contemplated what he said. "Your daughter," I repeated, disbelieving.

He seemed suddenly embarrassed. "It was uh...*happy* accident. Andre was 14, and I was 12, and just discoverin' sex. I didn' even know that I had tha power to get someone pregnant, but it turns out I did. Meda died in child birth."

I tried counting backwards in my head, trying to see if the numbers worked out. How old was Orion? Derek? He wasn't old enough to have a kid Nicole's age, was he? There was no way that that was possible, I decided. I didn't believe him. "Nicole doesn't look anything like you," I stated. Actually, skin color notwithstanding, she and I looked more alike. You wouldn't look at me and her and think that we were closely related, but there were some small similarities between us.

"That's like sayin' that uh child's not yours because both of tha parents are blonde, and tha child came out wit' black hair. You don' look like your mom, and I look nothin' like my dad, and anyway, looks don' exclude her from bein' my child."

"No…it doesn't…," I agreed, "but I still don't believe that Nicole's your daughter."

He chuckled. "That's because I'm lyin'."

"I knew it!"

"I had you goin' fo uh minute there, didn' I?"

"Andromeda," I said piecing it together.

"Don' Orion and Andromeda look like they could be names for twins?" he questioned, idly. "Honestly, though, me and Orion became friends 'cause we was always gettin' stuck togethuh; our moms would baby sit for each othuh all tha time. They both worked, my daddy was gone a few days every week when he had to sleep at tha firehouse, and Orion's daddy used to be gone for months at uh time when he had to go on tour."

"And Nicole?" I questioned, and he automatically knew what I was asking.

He shrugged. "She's just had me hooked since birth. Uh few weeks aftuh Nicole was born, Orion's mama got really sick. She was in tha hospital, so Orion was left to take care of his sistuh. Mr. Taylor was away, so my mama'd stop in, as did some of their church folk, but mostly it was just him.

"I know she's dramatic now, but as uh baby," he held up his hands to demonstrate, "she was just like tha quietest thing, slept most of tha time for tha first coupla months. I was ovuh here, and Orion'd just got her to fall asleep in his arms, and instead of rippin' into him 'bout always bein' stuck watchin' his sistuh, like I'd planned, I asked him if I could hold 'er, and he gives me this look, like he's summin' me up, like we ain' been friends since *we* was in diapers. Eventually, though, he hands her ta me, tellin' me how to hold her. She was sleepin' when he was holdin' her, but she wakes up from bein' jostled. Those big gold eyes settled on me and *man*…I tell you, it was love."

He smiled reminiscently. "There's somethin' 'bout babies that can win ovuh tha hardest heart, and without even thinkin' about it, I start talkin' to her. Lettin' her know how much her big brothuh, and her mama, and her daddy love her, and that she's protected, and that if any guy evuh comes messin' wit' her, if Orion can' take care of it, I will." It was written all over his voice how much that one moment changed him. Without conscious thought, I was imagining him holding Nicole, cooing over her. I think I liked the image a little too much.

"Orion overhears me, and looks at me, and he's like 'That uh promise' and I'm like, 'On my word', and he says, 'Tha way you'd want everyone to treat her, that's tha way all women should be treated'. And I got what O was sayin' to me, and I've been livin' up to it. Tryin' anyway. Nicole's had me hooked 'round her finguh since that one moment, and she knows it."

"Who knew you could be such a sweetie?" I questioned, trying to shake the image from my head.

He smiled in recognition of his weakness. "It's only to her," he responded.

In the silence following his statement, I picked the journal back up, burying my face in it to try to get rid of the image of Derek holding a baby. "So, why aren't you out tonight," I questioned, idly. "Isn't that what you young folks do on Saturday nights?"

"And I see you're ovuh here babysittin' Nicole," he noted. "Again."

"Only so that Patrice can go out."

"How is it that she keeps forgettin' that she's supposed to be babysittin'?"

"She doesn't forget. Darnell called her and it seems like whenever he calls, she goes running."

"It don' sound like you like tha D-man much."

"D-man?" I said, disgusted. "I don't."

"Why's that?"

"I tend not to like any guy who would proposition me when he's dating my best friend," I said without thinking.

"Darnell hit on you?" Derek wondered and without being able to look at him I couldn't tell if he was scandalized, angry, or amused by that piece of information. "What'd *you* say?"

"Are you serious?" I questioned. "Patrice is my best friend, and our friendship matters a little bit more to me than that. And with *Darnell*? Come on!"

Derek chuckled. "Shoot, he's uh nice lookin' guy, ain't he?" I recognized that he was teasing me now.

"Yes, and he knows it!"

"Nothin' wrong wit' uh little confidence," Derek asserted.

"No...," I agreed, "if it were a *little*."

"I thought you *liked* football players...I mean there was Shelton..." I wondered if I imagined the slight hint of jealousy there. "What evuh happened to tha two uh you, anyway?"

"Nothing happened to the two of us," I responded.

"You guys're still togethuh?" Derek questioned in surprise. In the back of my mind I wondered why it should bother him if we were.

"No. Shelton and I didn't date," I said in answer. "I don't date."

There was a pregnant pause from him. "Your mom won' let you?"

"No...my mom allows me to make my own decisions," I responded. "I just don't date. I choose not to."

He looked at me as if the words were hard to comprehend. "Why's that?"

"I don't want to get pregnant," I said baldly. There was nothing from Derek after this statement, and I figured I had shocked him with my bluntness. When I glanced at him, though, he was looking at me, trying very hard not to laugh.

"Your mama must think you're tha perfect daughtuh if you believe that you can get pregnant just from goin' on uh date," he snickered.

I flipped the page. "I've had both Anatomy and Biology, so I know you don't get pregnant from going on a date," I returned. "It's what happens on dates that I'm trying to avoid."

He tilted his head to the side. "And that would be," he wondered, his voice mocking.

"Humans are biological creatures," I responded, shrugging. "They're designed to procreate. Dating is merely a pretense set up to facilitate that predetermined end."

The look he gave was confused. "What's procreate?" he wondered.

"To reproduce. Naturally, we seek out intimacy; it's only our social consciousness that keep us from yielding to our biological leanings."

He blinked on that one. "So, you don' think that people date, I don' know, just ta spend time wit' someone, you know, cause they like bein' 'round them?"

"I'm sure," I said, sarcastically, "I'm sure that right now Patrice and Darnell are out 'liking' each other," I scoffed, "and I'm sure that's the reason you were dating, and are dating, the girls that you've dated; because they were great conservationists." He looked somewhat embarrassed. "The reality is that all of the things that we look for in a partner, a mate, are just about passing along our genes; even who we're attracted *to* is biological. It's our body's way of seeking out who it thinks our best DNA pair will be."

Derek sat in quiet contemplation for a moment. "That's ridiculous, Trace," he decided, "even from you."

I looked up enough to shoot him a hostile look. "No, it's biology," I reiterated. "I've been reading this article… "The Biomechanics of Love"." It was actually a really informed, well-written piece that posited that love was essentially a biological phenomenon. "It explains how it's all simple coding and programming with chemical reactions in order to reinforce that programming." Like Huxley's people in *Brave New World*.

"Everything, from the embarrassed giggle, to that sudden rush of blood to your face that causes you to blush, the acceleration of your heart, the emotion that wells up when you meet their eyes…,"-the way you think that in one second you've found absolution-"is merely biology. The hypersensitivity to key areas in your body is adrenaline being pumped into your veins; it's your body's way of gearing you up for that one, carnal act, which is there to ensure the continued existence of the human race."

His mouth stood open. "So what are relationships, then?" he questioned.

"Societal constructs, though personally I think that they're just man's way of attempting to control. Men naturally want to have sex. Women naturally want to have sex. Women bring new life into the world, and men envy that. They can't control the means, though, so instead they attempt to control the method in order to feel as if they are more involved in the process. Men make rules in order to attempt to control what's going to happen anyway, to restrict it so that they can prove that it was their attributes that got a woman to submit: their virility, strength, daring…and not simple biology. That way men can believe themselves to be mighty conquistadors."

"And women?"

"Get to see them show off."

I realized that Derek was staring at me even after I finished talking. "What?" I demanded, uneasy.

He was shaking his head. "You think you've got it all figured out, hunh?"

"No," I disagreed, "but simple observation correlates the facts. That's what science does; finds explanations for the world around us."

"No, it finds ways for you to not relate to the world around you. Have you ever even *been* in uh relationship?" Derek questioned. "Ever even gone on uh date?"

For some reason I was offended by his question. "I don't need to go on a date in order to know that it's all about peacock feathers and shiny plumes. If it wasn't, why do we gawk at movie stars? Why is it that the best looking girls are the ones who get asked out the most? All you have to do is look at the animal kingdom in order to get your answer."

"We're *not* animals," he said, fiercely.

"At our very core we are. Emotion is merely base instinct."

"Do you honestly believe that?"

I tried not to shrug. "I'm just telling you what the article said, but it kind of makes sense."

He shook his head. "So you don' date, 'cause you don' want to chance tha career that you don' have, on tha possibility of havin' uh child, so, what then, you're nevuh plannin' on havin' uh relationship? Of connectin' to any one?"

"I can't say never," I responded, thoughtfully. "It'll happen someday because eventually we all fall prey to our biological leanings, which is why we get married, but until I'm in a place where I can consider that, I try to resist as much temptation as possible."

"But for what point?" he demanded, hotly, and I was surprised by the show of emotion. "What's tha point of you spendin' all uh your life 'readin' 'bout life instead of actually livin' it? You only have this one life to live, why waste it in theory instead of actuality? What're you even livin' for?"

I was unsure of where this sudden passion came from, but my answer was ready made. "So that other people have the option of an easier life," I remarked. "So the next generation doesn't have to work so hard. I think we should all be equal benefactors to the American Dream and since I'm not, I want the people behind me to be one step closer to achieving it."

"But you do realize that you're tryin' to create uh world you don' even want to pass on to your children?"

"I can't say for certain that I don't want kids," I said pragmatically. "I just can't see myself as being a mom."

He seemed searching for something in my gaze. "And where does love fit into all this biology?" he wondered.

"Sometimes I think love is just a cohesive emotion meant to emotionally bind two people together in order to present the most ideal condition for the rearing of their offspring."

"*What*?" he questioned, unsure if he'd misheard me.

"It's imaginary," I said in layman's terms. "It's just a tying agent, like glue, so that the child ideally has more than one person to take care of it, to protect it."

"And you really believe that?"

"It's plausible," I returned, with a shrug. "The sole motivation for all organisms is the continued existence of their species."

"You're only sayin' this because you haven' been in love before," he said with conviction.

I looked at him. "I've been in love," I remarked, unflinchingly. "He didn't love me back."

Derek didn't back down from his gaze, either. "Maybe it's because you're tryin' to relegate your feelings into uh mere matter of chemical reactions instead of acknowledgin' that those feelings were actually somethin' real," he returned. I realized he was angry. "God Tracy," he hissed, suddenly, pushing off from the wall. "You and your damn logic! You think that there's an answer for everythin', don' you?" He angrily took the magazine from my hand. "You read too damn much, you know that? Those books aren't goinna put you any closuh to tha truth than watchin' life through someone else's eyes will!"

"It's simple science," I said reasonably.

"No, it's uh reason not to relate to people! Tha thought that there are things out of your control scares you so much that instead of acceptin' that some things just happen, you've found somethin' to explain it away, and you like it because it makes things *easy*," he accused. "Do you really, honestly, think that tha guy who wrote that journal knows everythin' about tha meanin' of life?"

"Doctor Rothburg doesn't claim to know everything-,"

"Out loud, maybe not, but silently in his head I'm sure he thinks he does. And who tha hell is 'he' anyway?"

I started to list some of his credentials. "I mean, it wasn't like he just came up with this theory out of thin air, Derek, it's based on what's observable, what's quantifiable, research-,"

"Yet, he has no real experience to back it up, I bet."

"They don't publish work that doesn't have merit-,"

"Life experience," he spelled out for me. "If this doctor is even married, I bet he's so convinced that he's right about what makes humans tick that he barely even *touches* his wife. I'd expect *him* to be so sterile, but I can' believe that *you* can just turn one of tha most...*beautiful* experiences in life, into somethin' so mundane, how y-you can just demean all tha interactions that take place between two people as if they are simply functions of biology."

"They are, though-,"

"No, they're not!" he actually shouted. "How can you ignore what your heart tells you, but take as gospel tha words of all these old sterile guys who've nevuh had one true human connection? Who can' understand their world so they have to dissect it, and dissect it, and dissect it to tha point where only *their* truth remains, just so they can sleep bettuh at night? Who have nevuh truly experienced anythin' dynamic, so they turn everythin' incredible into tha mundane in orduh to make them feel bettuh?

"If you honestly want to know what love truly is: listen to Jerry and Betty sing "Let it be Me", look at art, read uh poem. Go out and experience tha world, people, get out uh your head and your textbooks sometimes, or you're goinna end up just like tha ones who write those texts: old and alone, so convinced of how *right you are*! Until you do that, you know nothin'!"

— 216 —

My temper flared at his assertion. "Just because *you* don't understand-,"

"I understand perfectly that all you're lookin' for is somethin' to distance yourself from real emotion-,"

"No-,"

"Yes, you are, but I'm sorry, sweetie, it don' work that way. You don' get to not feel just because it becomes inconvenient. You don' get to lessen *this* just because it's hard." He pointed at the magazine. "Tell me what good does it do to know how tha body responds to stimuli, if you've nevuh actually been stimulated? A scientist can' tell you what love means," he said, passionately. "He can say that he knows tha inner and outer functions of how tha body works, but if you don' *feel* anythin', those words are just useless. We're *not* just chemical reactions! We're not...we're not goddam *machines* movin' mechanically along."

He shook his head. "I don' know, maybe you are," he said, in disgust. He tossed the magazine down, and turned as if he was going to storm out of the house, but he didn't. He turned back around and kneeled on the floor in front of me. "You can talk disconnectedly all you want about tha emotion involved when you meet tha eyes of someone you're attracted to," he looked me in mine, "but unless you've *felt* that total, *helpless*," his voice trembled, "pull, from tha person that's sittin' across from you, or you have that one instance where you just connect-" he snapped his fingers, and I startled at the sound. "Where *every* part of your body is just so excited about bein' near them, that you tremble from head to toe, you can' talk about feelin'.

"You can *talk* about tha feel of skin touchin' skin," he went on, his finger absently trailing across my arm, raising patterns on the flesh, "but until you've *felt* uh rough hand hold you so softly that it seems like uh contradiction...," his hand moved to gently stroke my cheek. "Until you've actually felt that blush, you know similar to tha one that's spreadin' 'cross your cheeks...," his fingers traced the bridge of my cheekbone, "it's meaningless. Go 'head and tell me about tha acceleration of your heart pumpin' blood to your cheeks, to my fingertips, tell me that heightened sensitivity is just nerve endings. That this force between two humans, this actual *connection*, this feelin' of only wantin' to bond, to touch-," his free hand found mine. "To kiss them," he whispered. "Tell me it isn'

— 217 —

real," he implored me, "that it's just programmin'." His eyes held mine and stubbornly refused to let go. "Say it," he urged, pleaded almost, his face way too close to mine for comfort.

"You *can't,*" he asserted at my silence, "because unless you've evuh felt *this*, then it all means nothin'." He pointed vaguely in the direction of my magazine. "*That* is *just* science. But *this*, Tracy," he said, fiercely, "*this* is actual chemistry."

As the set of his features changed, I realized that my heart was pounding so hard it seemed like it wanted to jump out of my chest. I could hear the blood pumping in my own ears. Derek leaned forward, as if to kiss me…and a sudden noise from Nicole's room pulled me back to where I was, back to my senses. I pulled myself from his hands as I jumped up eagerly to go check on her.

Nicole had gotten tangled up in her sheets and it must have woken her. I untwisted her sheets, remade the bed, and just for good measure, took her temperature and replaced her water, in order to give my heart time to return to its normal pace. I sat with her until she fell asleep again, and only after I was sure that she was completely under, did I go back into the living room where Derek was looking wholly uncomfortable on the Taylor's couch. He jumped up when I came in.

"Hey, um…," His voice faltered.

"She's fine," I said, only to have something to say.

"Trace-,"

"I-I think you should go, Derek." I allowed my voice to take on a note of reason. "Our voices are probably what woke her, and she needs her sleep."

"Why can' we talk?"

"I don't want to talk," I dismissed. "You…should go."

He gave me a hard stare, but after a moment he stood up. "O-kay," he remarked. "Okay." Before he walked out of the door, he paused long enough to say, "And just so you know, Trace, I did love you. But I guess that's all meaningless right? Merely biology?"

And then he was gone.

— 23 —
"The Diner"

Frankie was pulling his car to a stop in front of our house, when I walked up. He got out and leaned against the vehicle to wait for me to catch up to where he was standing. In the past year Frankie had really filled out, and most people had to look up to him now, me included. He flashed me his smile, and I very nearly scowled. Ever since Frankie started dating Cecilia, things had kind of changed between us.

"Hey, Frankie," I dredged up, as friendly as possible. It was odd; we'd both grown up, but in two different directions. I wasn't liking the new Frankie, either. Now that he had finally grown into his looks, he didn't look so awkward anymore. The girls were now giving him a lot more attention than they had before, and he was quickly moving to the point of being insufferable. Whenever he came around now, I felt more acutely the differences in our financial standings, and I was beginning to see just how one-sided our relationship truly was. He'd been over my house countless times; I couldn't say the same about his. I seriously doubted, too, that he would have talked to a guy I liked for me, and we didn't hang out in public that often anymore.

It seemed that our relationship had run its course. I'd feel bad that I was beginning to feel this way about a friend who I was once as close to as Patrice, but considering the way Frankie treated me almost grudgingly now, as if he *owed* it to me to still be friendly, I didn't feel too bad.

He smiled toothily at me, and invited himself in. He commented on my lack of treats (my mom had recently gotten a raise so the cabinets were stocked and there were all sorts of sugars hiding around, but I wasn't sharing that fact with him), and fell down tragically on our sofa. "You never have nothing good," he grumbled.

"What brings you around?" I questioned, trying to put the proper amount of courtesy, mixed with the slightest trace of annoyance, into my voice, hoping to convey that I didn't like the intrusion. He either missed the point, or completely ignored it, instead propping his leg up and balancing his hat on top of his knee, showing off his short, dark, curly hair.

"Thought I'd come'n see you," he declared. "Want to go for a ride?" Translation: *Want to see the cherry Mustang my rich Dr. Daddy bought me, and by the way, where's your new car? Or old one? Don't you even have a license? Well I guess that's a good thing 'cause girls shouldn't be on the road anyway.*

"No, thanks, Frankie, I've got homework."

"Man they sure work you hard over at Mason, huh? It's all of them accelerated classes you taking." His words irked me. Even though, with a little work, he could have done just as well in an accelerated class, Frankie had so far only taken basic level classes. It bothered me on a very elementary level that Frankie and I had the same grades, but he hadn't had to work half as hard for his. I guess for him it just wasn't worth putting in the extra time.

"Just trying to get to college," I remarked.

"Mama said that you scored pretty high on some test or something, while back. Still trying to get into that school you always going on about?"

"Harvard, yes, that plan hasn't changed," I responded.

"I don't see why you wanna go there so bad: it's mighty expensive and how *you* going to pay for it anyway?"

I glowered at him. "There's this thing called scholarships," I said testily.

He leaned back, ignoring my mood. "You'd *want* to be a scholarship student? I wouldn't. Be around all those folks that got more money than you. Your rags ain't as decent, and they know stuff that you don't, have hobbies that you couldn't imagine. *I'd* be embarrassed; why'd you want that? That's what a man's for. Ain't you just going to get married anyway?"

"Was there actually something you wanted?" I said, trying my best not to get angry and kick Frankie out of the house in a way that would do irreparable damage to our friendship. On second thought…

I smiled. "I didn't intend on getting married, no," I declared.

"You're odd, you know that? You're pretty enough, so that's alright, but you're going to mess around and end up so no man's going to want to marry you, 'specially if you keep with that nonsense about Harvard, and going 'round with them White boys." He gave me a look like I should be ashamed of indiscretions I never had. I was merely amused that talk about me had made it to the Academy.

"Seriously, Frankie, was there something you wanted? I have a test coming up that I needed to study for."

"Testy," he said, breezily. "You know you ain't much fun no more. I'm just telling you the truth. Make things a whole lot easier on yourself, once you realize that. No guy wants a girl that's too smart."

It was like a flash of lightning, how quickly the thought occurred to me, but it was irrefutable. Our friendship, Frankie's and mine, was over. Not just different, not just changed, but actually over. It made me sad. I didn't kick him out. I let him turn on my set and complain about the fact that we hadn't yet gotten a color TV like he had (and unless we earned one turning in our S&H stamp books we wouldn't be getting one either), and I listened to him go on a little bit about Cici. He was in the process of trying to figure out if it was worth getting back with her, when Patrice walked into the house, slamming the door heavily in her wake.

"You'll nevuh guess what he's done now," she demanded, steam practically coming off of her body. Her head swerved and she saw Frankie, who had a smile on his face in anticipation.

"How you, Patrice?"

"Don' 'How you', Franklin, like we chums or somethin'," she snapped.

"What's got in ta you?"

"Don' act like you on't know. Boy, you faker than those earrings yo mama claims is pearls."

He sat up in his seat, his hat falling to the ground. "Don't you say nothin' bout my mama," he remarked.

"Ain't said nothin' that ain't true," she shot back. "What choo doin' sinkin as low as Marbury Street, anyhow? Watch out, else them white folks goina start ta realize you actually Colored."

Frankie looked at me. "You just going to let her talk to me like that?" he demanded.

"You got somethin' ta say, you say it ta me," Patrice remarked, before I could answer him.

Frankie looked pointedly at me. "All right then, fine!" he scooped his hat off the ground and pointed it at me. "Y'all used to be decent, but then you goinna start acting out just so you can be like this here friend of yours. Go head, see how far it takes you!"

He slammed his hat on his head, and left the house angrily. I expected Patrice to burst into a fit of giggles at his departure, but when I looked over at her, she looked like she was struggling not to cry. "What's the matter?" I questioned.

"What're you doin' tonight?" Patrice questioned. "You on't got anythin' planned do you?"

"I was going to do some studying for the boards, why?" I questioned, trying to figure out why she sounded tentative.

"You want ta go ta tha football game wit me?" she questioned hesitantly. "Darnell came by and he said that he wanted to meet me at the game."

Oh. Well that explained some things. "Why are you even still talking to him?" I questioned, not unkindly. I hated seeing the way Darnell treated Patrice; she was worth so much more than that. I wish she could see that.

Patrice shrugged. "He called," she responded. "I told him I didn' want ta see him."

"So then there's no issue."

"I doubt he took me seriously though," Patrice added. "Well, I mean, he says he's goinna be at tha game, and he wanted ta talk ta me. He says I'm tha only one who really understands him, and I wanted ta go to tha game anyway."

I looked at the conflicted expression on her face. "I'll go," I said after a moment.

Patrice smiled, sadly. "Thanks," she remarked. "Be ready by six. I want to be there by 6:30."

I was almost certain that this meant that by the time the game started at 7:00 she would be wrapped up in Darnell's arms, but I was wrong: it took Darnell longer than 30 minutes to find us, no doubt hindered by the folks who wanted to pat him on the back over his performance so far at UNA... and the girls who he felt obligated to talk to as he passed. It took until after kickoff for Darnell to find us, but by the start of the second quarter he had an invitation to sit, some nachos, candy, and his arm around my friend's shoulder.

When Patrice left to go to the bathroom, Darnell took the time to tell me, "you know, if you wasn' so frosty to everyone, maybe you'd have somebody for yo'self, and you wouldn' be all in Patrice's relationships."

I didn't look at him. "If dating means having a guy like you," I returned, "then, no, thank you."

Darnell smiled an oily smile, winking at me. "Tha offuh still stands, you know. All you'd need is one really good night to change your perspective," he declared. He ran his finger along the length of my arm.

I waited until I had more control over my emotions before I responded. "When hell freezes over, I'll be sure to take you up on that." Darnell only laughed and when Patrice came back he made sure that he sat as close to her as possible.

After the game, I got dragged along to Chase's, a popular Mason hangout. I sought out a familiar face, any familiar face that would take me away from Patrice and Darnell, but I had no such luck. Halfway through the meal I used desert as an excuse to get up from the table. I was still waiting in line when Derek walked in, surrounded by a group of guys. Two of them were recognizable from around school, though I didn't know their names, another was Quinn, and bringing up the rear and looking inherently sulky was Roy.

I'd been about to say hi to Derek, but seeing Roy changed my mind. While I stood there, not sure if I wanted to be noticed, Quinn left to go talk to a friend, and the rest of them got in line behind me. Any hope of them not noticing me was quashed almost immediately. "'Ey!" I heard Roy say loudly. "That's Tracy, ain' it, Dare?"

I watched the young couple at the front of the line count out pennies. "It *is* Tracy!" The only part of me that reacted to him was my ears, which burned red. "Tra-cy," Roy said, this time his words were aimed directly at me.

I turned to look at him. "Hello, Roy," I said, politely.

He ignored me, though, turning slightly toward his group. "Hey, Derek, lookit, it's Tracy!" I looked at Derek, too. He was looking rather intensely at his feet. To one of the guys Roy said, "Tracy's in love wit Derek; ain' that right, Tracy?"

He turned toward someone, but I didn't see who since my eyes hadn't moved from Derek's still form. "She wrote him this big, long, love lettuh," he went on, "sayin' that she'd do *any*thin' fer him!"

"I'm glad to see that you've matured since I last saw you, Roy," I said, biting back hard on what I really wanted to say to him. My anger at Darnell was quickly shifting to him as his voice rose.

"Oh, ho, now don' you get all feisty wit me, gal!" Roy joked. "I ain't Derek", he chuckled. His voice adopted what was probably supposed to be a sultry tone. "Though I wouldn' mind uh bit uh what you gave him." He winked, and the two guys with him laughed.

"Shut *up*, Roy," Derek said, finally opening his mouth, but still he refused to look at me. "Cut tha crap, okay?"

"Hey, I don' blame ya fer takin' her up on that offuh, I would uh. Nothin' ta be shamed 'bout. That's what they there fer, anyway. They like it, ain't that right, Tracy?"

Patrice appeared at my side, stopping me from doing or saying any of what I wanted to. "You know, Roy," she said to him calmly, "you're a pretty cocky somethin' for someone who nevuh has a girlfriend, and needs at least three othuh guys 'round ta make you feel tall." The two guys with Roy coughed into their hands, looking away. "No wonduh you have ta make fun uh people when they really like each othuh, cause ain' no one round here likin' you!"

Roy's face burned red, and I could see the anger rising in him. "Hey, just 'cause he wuz tryin' ta get a piece of this gal don' mean that he liked her," Roy yelled back. I missed what either of them said next because the only person I was paying attention to at the moment was Derek. I kept waiting for him to say something, anything, to do something, but he staunchly remained silent. I think Roy said some slur aimed directly toward Patrice, because she looked like she was about to deck him. Derek finally did something, then, stepping forward. He placed a hand on Roy's shoulder.

"Would you kiss yo mama wit' that mouth, Roy? And what'd she tell you 'bout fightin' wit' ladies?" he questioned, laughing. "Why you tryin' ta make trouble?" Derek's eyes brushed mine for the briefest of moments, his look cold. "That's not how you get uh woman to like you, kid. Where'd Quinn get to?"

Without a word to me, Derek steered Roy to where Quinn was, leaving the two guys behind to order for them. One of them looked at me in speculation. He winked. Patrice grabbed my hand before I could smack him.

As we were leaving, I heard the sound of Derek's laughter in accompaniment to Roy's. "Come on," Patrice said when I paused. "Let's just go."

I had the whole weekend and Monday to think about Friday night. I thought I'd calmed down about the situation, but when I saw him again, I felt a familiar sense of anger boiling up inside of me, fighting back against the wave of tears that seemed to be trying to break through. I can't believe I'd said I loved this guy. When I looked at him standing in front of me, his hands stuffed in his pockets, I couldn't help but see the guy that I'd first seen in Derek: the cocky son of a gun, full of bravado and swagger, thinking that everyone was supposed to be immediately charmed by him. Why had I ignored that first impression? First instincts were usually the correct ones.

Derek looked chaste when he appeared in the common area. He was smart enough to not immediately try and sit down. "Mind if I sit," he questioned. He had let Roy read that note, I realized. He had to have. Roy wasn't even in Mrs. Diece's class, so Derek had to have been talking about me. To *Roy?* Who else had he shared my feelings with? How much had he been laughing at me behind my back?

I looked at Derek steadily. "You can do whatever you want," I remarked. He sat down. I stood up.

"Tracy, wait-," he called after me. I turned and looked at him, and it was enough to silence him. I wasn't one to make a scene in the middle of the lunch room, especially over a boy, so I put my tray up, and Derek followed me into the hall. "Listen, about Friday…" he tried to get out.

"Save it."

"I understand why you're angry at me, and I'm sorry. Just let me-"

I cut him off. "No, Derek, you *don't* understand. That's the problem. I *like* you, okay! I *more* than like you. You know when you stopped by at the beginning of the year? That made my week. Sometimes just thinking about you is enough to make my day, and that was my stupidity for allowing me to feel that way about you; for foolishly believing that we were even friends."

"We *are* friends. We're-"

"No, we're not!" I yelled at him. "Friends stand up for their friends, and they don't let scum like that little piece of trash Roy say what he said to me! And you just let him say it! You let your friends think that I slept with you or something! You didn't say anything, Derek; you didn't say one blessed word, not one word! You just stood there, and then you laughed like it was all some big joke to you! Well it's not fun or funny to me. You have no idea what this feels like, so no…you don't understand!"

"You're *not* uh joke to me, Trace; I just didn' want you to become one to those guys."

"I didn't hear you say *any*thing, Derek."

"Tha guys I was wit' were uh bunch of crass idiots who wouldn' understand, and I didn' want-,"

"Those crass idiots are *your* friends so what does that say about *you?*" I posed. "Let me save you the trouble, Derek. I'm sorry if you're embarrassed to be my friend, but I'm perfectly content with who I am. I am not going to convince you to try to like me."

"Will you listen-,"

"No!" I shouted. "I've had enough of you! I have this year and the next in this stupid place, and then I'm gone! I don't need any more distractions."

"Is that what I am?" he demanded. "A *distraction?*"

I continued to ignore him. "I have class."

Derek grabbed for me when I turned to move away. "Will you listen for one minute!"

"Take your hands off of me!" I said, pulling away from him so fiercely that he took a step back.

He held up his hands, but didn't try to touch me again. "Just listen to me, Trace, will ya?" he pleaded.

"I don't care about anything you have to say," I said, firmly.

"Tracy?"

"I have class," I said, sharply. "Good-bye."

I left him standing where he was. It was sheer force of will that I didn't look back.

— 24 —
"All Broken Up"

It took Derek two weeks to realize that I wasn't going to bend, and that I meant what I said about him being around, and then he stopped coming up to Mason altogether. As with everything about Derek and I, my feelings following our 'break up' were illogical. We hadn't been dating; he had just been a friend, and not even that, if I thought about it. Derek had done exactly what everyone had said he would do; I put my trust in him, and he betrayed it.

Okay, maybe *betrayed* was too strong of a word, but it was the only one that I felt fit. He'd cut me down, chosen his 'own kind' over our tentative friendship. Chase's had been one of the first times since I'd known him, that I saw Derek as being inescapably White. It was one of the first times that I saw his color.

Seeing that night again, and again, and again in my thoughts, I reviewed every moment of our relationship. It was all tainted now. Any time we'd joked together, or had a moment, the time he almost kissed me…he had never been sweet, kind, worth liking. He'd always been a jerk; I'd just been blind to it.

But what was his goal, though?

To make me think that he liked me?

To get me to have sex with him so he could brag about it to his friends? Well he picked the wrong person for that.

But then, why? It seemed a lot of time and energy to waste just to have a laugh, and was he really that big of a sleaze?

Did he really not have anything else to do with his time?

Then *why?*

Why?

I wrote another poem to commemorate how emotional, and senseless, and illogical falling in, and out, of love is. Like a Dickenson poem I titled it after the first (and only) line of the poem. It was called "Love's Hell (But it makes for great poetry)".

I can't believe that I ever thought I'd liked Derek! Even worse, I couldn't believe I really thought I loved him, that I saw depth when I looked into his eyes. There was no depth; I'd just saw what I wanted to see: that despite his faults he was perfect, despite his flaws, he was beautiful, despite his attitude, he was gentle. Maybe I'd just wanted to fall in love, so I allowed myself to think it manifested where it hadn't, picking an unlikely partner who I knew wouldn't reciprocate the feelings. Maybe love really was just a manifestation.

I was *so* ready for the high school years to be over with! I was beginning to wonder if high school was just in place to erase as much of your soul as possible, so that by the time it was over, you were all geared and ready to be what corporate America wanted you to be.

"I'm never falling in love again," I declared, when I met up with Patrice at the end of one particularly long Thursday. My friend didn't even so much as crack a smile. She was still wearing her practice clothes from softball. "I need you," she remarked. Her face looked flushed, but there was a determined set to her features.

"You're babysitting again?" I wondered automatically, since that particular choice of words usually followed her asking me to baby-sit for her. I had trouble reconciling that desire with the set of her features, though.

"No," she said, quickly. "I want you ta come wit me somewhere."

"Okay. Where?"

"Pincer Street," she said, watching for my reaction. Pincer Street ran parallel to the train tracks that separated us from Whitesburg, and was the official marker for the end of the Black District. It was the first street of the area everyone referred to as Duke's Hole, called such after the most prominent building on the street, The Duke. The neighborhoods near the Duke were known as the Hole, and it was a kind of an unspoken rule that kids from 'good' families, families from the Trick or neighborhoods like ours, didn't take up with those from the Hole.

"Why do you want to go to Duke's Hole?" I questioned. It didn't mean that I wouldn't go, but I knew for certain that her parents had put a restriction against it. I'd heard her and Marcus joking several times about the time that Sean had started drinking there-shortly after dropping out of school-and Mrs. Gordon going down and giving him a beating in the middle of the bar.

"Stacy said that Darnell's been at tha Crown and I-I want to see him." I wish I could figure out what it was that she saw in him, but then, I couldn't figure out what I saw in Derek, and it seemed like falling in love meant falling for the one most likely to break your heart. "T, I think, I think I might be pregnant."

For a moment I think the world stopped turning. I tried to figure out if Patrice looked pregnant. She couldn't be pregnant. "What makes you think that," I questioned slowly, careful not to let any emotion enter into the words as I spoke them.

"I'm late." She'd whispered the words, her eyes reflecting the fear she felt. "What 'em I goinna do?" she wondered. "I-I have ta see him."

Patrice and I waited at the school until the normal after school crowd had pretty much disappeared, before we made like we were going to one of the shops in the Trick. There were only a dozen or so blocks that divided the Trick from Duke's Hole, but there was a stark contrast between the two places. Duke's Hole wasn't the same as the shops in the Trick. If any one of the places in the Hole was set on fire, no one from the churches would come out to help clean it up. The business there made no attempt to look kempt and uniform, or even very welcoming. The street was only paved near the Duke, and most of the grass was gone due to people parking their cars on top of it. The buildings, too, seemed more like row houses, and there were even a few with busted windows, or one's boarded up. At this time of day there weren't many patrons, but at night I imagined the street to be packed with people looking for a little relief from the misery of the day.

The Duke's reputation wasn't entirely bad: any musician traveling the Chitlin' Circuit would make The Duke one of their stop-ins-Ray Charles had played there a few times, even-and anyone with an ambition to be a musician learned all the top covers there. The problem wasn't the music, it was the attitude that the place exuded. The Duke served alcohol to anyone who was old enough to walk through the doors, sold reefer and LSD, and it seemed like every weekend someone was getting arrested from the place.

More insulting than its policies, though, were its owners. Unlike the Trick, where mostly every business was black owned, most of the establishments in the Hole weren't owned by the Community, they were owned by the Whites who believed that all colored folks wanted was to have a good time, and tried to milk every penny from those 'good timing folks' that they could get. The houses that made up the surrounding neighborhood, mostly owned by the same people who owned Pincer Street, were substandard, poorly maintained, and overpriced.

The Crown was one of the last bars at the end of Pincer Street and it, at least, had all its windows still intact. But that was the highest commendation you could give it. Its salt and pepper door stood slightly ajar, allowing you the smallest taste of the music that was playing inside.

"You don' have ta come in wit me," Patrice remarked. "I just wanna poke my head in, anyway."

I nodded. She did as she said, poked her head in the door, and her body soon followed. I stood in the middle of the sidewalk, feeling terribly out of place. Since it was still relatively early, there weren't many people milling about, still nursing old hang-overs probably. The street wasn't entirely empty, though, and I felt uncomfortable just standing there. Patrice was in the Crown long enough for me to start to worry, to consider going in to check on her, but I stayed where I was. A few minutes later she came out, Darnell slouching behind her. He looked drunk, which wouldn't surprise me. I wondered why he wasn't at school.

They passed some words together before they broke apart, and he went back into the bar. I was dying to know what had transpired between the two of them, but Patrice didn't say much as we walked the length of Pincer to cross over to Crutcher Street, the start of Glennwood Heights, a neighborhood of mostly apartments and government houses. Patrice had some friends who lived off of Rita, and it was a plausible enough excuse that we'd gone to visit them. We took the long way back to the Trick, before eventually heading home.

The sun was starting to go down, and I thought about the homework that

I had to get done. My mind was on nothing else until we neared Patrice's, and I paused because something didn't feel right. Patrice felt it, too, because her feet slowed, and when I looked up, I saw why: the Gordon's car was parked in front of the house. Mr. Gordon was never home at this time of day. He always left early, got home late.

The door opened as Patrice started up the walk, and I'd forgotten all about him, and his ban, until I saw him with his belt off. Patrice must have remembered about the same time I did, because she froze where she was. "Bet' keep walkin', Sissy," he said to her in a steady voice. Patrice involuntarily stumbled forward, the same time I started to back down the walk.

"Not so fast, Tracy, some uh this heah be for you, too," he let me know. "Come on, Sistuh."

Patrice's eyes went wide. "Daddy, let me explain!"

"You can come'n talk all you want, aftuh you come get what you got waitin'."

"Daddy!" she protested.

He snapped his belt in the air. "I done tole you that I don' want none uh y'all at that place. You done got it in your head to go, I'm goin get it in your ass that when I say you on't go nowhere, that means you on't go. Don' make me wait here," he instructed. "Thuh longuh I's waitin'-,"

Apparently, Patrice knew the end of that sentence. Shaking, Patrice walked past her dad into the house, and Mr. Gordon stared me down, waiting for me to follow. I thought about backing away, taking my chances with my mom and never being able to go over to the Gordon's again, but the look on Mr. Gordon's face was enough to propel me inside.

The door wasn't even closed properly before his belt went whistling through the air, the hard leather strap finding purchase on Patrice's bottom. I winced as if I'd been hit, and Patrice squirmed, trying to avoid the sting of the next blow. I was in no way anxious to feel his strap against any part of me, but after seeing Patrice dance around, I kind of wished I'd gone first. I think, too, Mr. Gordon's hand worked harder the second time around.

"If I *evuh* catch you," his eyes went from Patrice to me, "at Duke's 'gain, I'mma skin y'all alive, ya heah?"

We both mumbled our, "Yes, sirs," and feeling really resentful of Patrice and Mr. Gordon, I went home to work on my homework. My mom came into the house as I was sitting dinner on the table. She didn't say anything to me until we were sitting across from each other.

"I heard Ebbert had some words with you," she said, staring at me over the dinner table. Somehow her words caused my behind to sting even more.

My face burning, I looked up. "Yes, ma'am."

"About?" she wondered, sternly. I was still upset about the indignity of it: I was being punished for something that I didn't do. Of course my mom didn't have any words about Mr. Gordon issuing a spanking, either. In the kids versus adult world, Mr. Gordon had every right to spank me, and a whooping by any person in the community other than your parents often resulted in two. Like if the teacher switched you for acting up in class, you were nearly likely to get it again when you got home from school. My mom didn't spank often, but she didn't seem upset about Mr. Gordon doing so, either.

"He told us not to go to Duke's Hole-,"

"And you thought you should?"

"No, ma'am," I responded.

"Then why'd you go?" she reasoned.

Before I could defend my actions, I figured I wasn't much of a friend if I placed blame on Patrice. I didn't have to go, even if she had begged me. "I don't know," I answered.

My mom crossed her fingers in front of her. "Do you know why we don't want you any where near any of those *filthy*, low-rate bars?" I was all ready to say 'yes, ma'am', but apparently she wasn't looking for my answer, yet. "The Trick is a part of our community. The dollars that we spend there, go back to the community. *Those places* do nothing but destroy community. The buildings are in disrepair, they promote drinking and smoking, they encourage truancy, promiscuity, they break down the family unit, and they're White owned, which means that the revenue generated there helps to benefit their communities and helps to keep us down.

"You remember that the next time you decide that you want to go down there, if you so choose. I won't stop Ebbert from taking a strap to you again, either, and if you went down there to be with your friend, which I suspect is the real reason, you remember, too, the consequences of doing something just because your friends are doing it."

She paused to take a breath and waited. "Yes, ma'am," I mumbled.

"Now after dinner, you will go over to the Gordon's house, and apologize to Mr. Gordon for your disobedience. You should thank him, too, for caring enough about you to even *be* angry at you." My jaw dropped as I wondered where her logic came from. Why on earth should I be happy that it hurt to sit down? "And then I don't want to hear another word about it, do you understand?"

"Yes, ma'am," I said, softly, biting down on my lip. This entire situation was grossly unfair. Between the injustice at school, the trouble with relationships, and the problems with parents, I was sick of this whole teenage thing. It's been a ride, but I'm ready for the end, thank you very much.

— 25 —
"Portrait of a Man"

With the exception of Bann's Music Jam in September, and the State Fair in July, FanFaire-Bakersfield's annual arts festival-was one of the biggest outdoor events that took place during the year. It was billed as a family event and was free to the public, so it was one of those events that people made it a habit of going to, at least one of the days that it was in town. It didn't have much appeal to the teenage crowd, though, since we were too old to still get a kick out of seeing our artwork on display, and not quite old enough to get into the more serious aspects of the festival. So it was surprising, and a little suspicious, when Patrice expressed interest in going.

When we arrived, there was already a fairly decent crowd represented for it to be the middle of the afternoon, but FanFaire wasn't the state fair, or the music festival, when people came during the nights and evenings. FanFaire's peak hours were between 12:00 and 4:00 in the afternoon; everything was closed and locked down by 7:00. 8:00 on Friday night.

For the most part, we worked our way in between the gates, ignoring the booths and the acts, occasionally stopping to talk to a classmate or friend of Patrice's. For some reason Patrice seemed a little uneasy, or anxious maybe, and kept shooting glances over her shoulder.

"Who are you looking for?" I finally questioned.

She shook her head too quickly, smiling at the doubting look I gave her. "No one," she tried to assure me. I didn't buy it, though, because she was obviously expecting someone. "Have you talked to Derek, recently?" she wondered far too casually for it to be a subtle attempt at a change of subject.

"I haven't talked to him since that night at Chase's," I said a bit irritably.

It wasn't her that I was irritated at, just the circumstances. It was like the same forces that had once put him everywhere that I didn't want him to be, had virtually erased his entire presence off of the face of the planet. I hadn't run into him anywhere since our 'break up', which was flat out frustrating because I still felt like I hadn't given him enough of my mind. And even though I was still mad at him, still hurt by what he'd done, I'd still wanted to see him again, convinced that if I did see him, or talk to him, it would be enough to kill any remaining feelings that I had left for him.

"Oh," was her only response to that statement.

"Hey Patrice, Tracy," an engaging voice greeted. We both scanned the crowd, and as my eyes settled on Alex Layton, I felt sure that I had figured out who Patrice had been looking for. Alex was one of those rare guys that Patrice liked and I actually approved. He was very down to earth, goal-oriented, and respectful, but more important than any of that was the fact that he actually treated my friend like a friend and a person, and not like some object. He'd been in the picture for a while, but Patrice had always been too caught up in Darnell to take notice of him. Now that Darnell was completely out of the picture (and she wasn't actually pregnant, Thank God!) I was seeing more of him.

"Hi, Alex!" she chorused, a look of pleased surprised breaking over her face.

He grinned back, just as pleased to see her. "How are you two doing?" he questioned, cordially, turning his attention to acknowledge me as well. "What brings you out today?"

Alex had this quality about him that made him absolutely adorable when he frowned, or drew his lips into a line. He was a preacher's kid, but not wild like they usually turned out to be. He was a nice guy. He wasn't a sleaze, an ass, or all in to himself. He listened to Patrice when she talked; he cared about her friends. He was a complete 10, and I hoped Patrice would actually hold on to him, but to be honest, I was a little less than pleased to see him today. The last thing I wanted to contend with at the moment was Patrice and another beau. I'd thought it was just going to be me and her for once.

"Just thought we'd see what it's all about," Patrice remarked, her eyes once again sweeping the crowd. "We were just about to go check out the booths, actually."

I gave her a sideways glance, this time making no pains to hide my suspicions. FanFaire was separated into two sides: the part closest to the library was mostly in the street, and it was where you'd find the events for the younger crowds, the stages, the plays, and the artwork from the elementary, middle, and high school art departments. The other side of the park was where the 'real' artwork was displayed by the professional artists. This is where you came if you wanted to buy actual artwork by local artists, instead of just cheap souvenirs. Not that she couldn't be trying to broaden her horizons, but as the only thing in her bedroom that could even be construed as artwork was the postures she had of The Drifters and The Temptations, I just didn't buy her sudden interest.

She took one of my hands, and reached for Alex's with the other. She steered us across the lake, past where a string quartet was playing classical music. The music made me think about Nicole, which had me thinking about Derek, and I bit down on my lip, wishing everything in the world didn't remind me of him. She and Alex made small talk as Patrice snaked her way through the booths, amid stares that we all ignored, stopping with a sudden sense of purpose. She gave a slight glimpse at the metal works in front of us, and gave another sweeping look of the crowd. "I want funnel cake," she said, incongruously. "Alex?"

He looked just as confused as I did. "Okay," he said, slowly but agreeably.

"We'll just be a moment," Patrice said to me. "Wait here."

"Patrice!"

She pulled Alex off into the crowd with her, and I grinded my teeth at her hasty departure. If this had all been some elaborate scheme to meet up with Alex, it'd been a bit much, and if she was just going to ditch me, she could have just as easily not asked me to come.

While I waited for my friend to return-I decided to give her five minutes-my eyes fell to the objects that were displayed on the table in front of me. They were these weird metal creatures, statues that were distorted almost to the point of being unidentifiable. One, in particular, caught my eye. It was a large feline with glass eyes. A scene had been painted on the metal before the glass had been fitted, so you could see a ghost of what the animal might have seen. I stopped short of allowing myself to touch its face, just staring.

"Hi," an unsure voice said at my shoulder, and I felt my insides tighten, because I recognized the voice from just that one word. I was hesitant to turn, though, in case my ears were playing tricks on me, but they weren't. It was Derek! My body reacted of its own accord, and a familiar smile came automatically, without permission. As soon as I realized that the smile was forming, I worked to compose my features before I turned to look at him. Derek watched me shrewdly, and if he noticed my struggle not to smile at him, it didn't show.

All the words that I'd thought I'd say to him if I saw him again, vanished. Derek didn't quite know what to say, either, and his eyes fell on the table in front of us. "That one's my favorite, too," he said, nodding at the one that I'd been studying. I didn't know what to say, or how I should feel about being this close to him for the first time in months. My feet started to move, as if to walk away, but Derek stepped in front of me. "Please, don' go, Trace," he remarked, his hands rising as if to stop me. "I...I was hopin' that you'd come," he added, softly.

I appraised his stance. "Why's that?"

"So I could tell you how sorry I was...for what happened between us. I'd understand if you were still mad at me; you'd have every right to be, if'n you were, but...I'm sorry, Trace."

I was unnerved by the emotion in his voice. "You hurt me," I told him. "I wasn't mad, Derek, I was hurt."

"I know," he said, quickly, frowning, "and I can' apologize enough to change that. I...acted like an ass. I'm not uh confrontational guy, and faced wit' that situation...I chose wrong. I've known Roy for uh long time, and those othuh two guys...and I know that don' make it right. You were right when you said that I didn' treat you tha way that you should treat uh friend, and you *are* my friend, Trace. I'd rathuh spend time wit' you, than any of those othuh guys, any day of tha week. I've missed you." I may have scoffed at that. "I did!" he insisted.

He missed me!

Mentally I slapped myself.

"Yeah, and why's that?" I demanded stubbornly.

"Because no one aggravates me as much as you do," he declared with total honesty. "Or frustrates me, or can make me laugh tha same way." I contemplated his words. It was all the right words, but I didn't trust the right words. Not from him. You could make up the right words. "I consider you to be one of my best friends," he said to my surprise.

He waited for my response, but I wasn't going to give him the one he was looking for, namely that I cared about him. I wasn't going to be so casual with my tongue again.

"It won' happen again," he stated.

"It better not," I warned.

"Are we okay?"

"I'm not sure yet."

"Okay," Derek remarked after a few seconds passed. "Let me know when we are." He shifted as if he were going to disappear back into the crowd. "You don't have to leave," I said quickly, worried that he was going so soon. His smile was ready made, and I frowned at the sight of it. "I only meant that you didn't have to go, not that you were forgiven."

"I wasn' figurin' on leavin'," Derek remarked, "but I probably should go."

"Why's that?"

"I can' tell you unless you've forgiven me," he stated.

"Oh fun-ny."

"I try," he responded. "So how've you been?"

"The same. What about you?"

He shrugged. "Otherwise, alright," he remarked. "Been tryin' to get some things togethuh."

"Have you?"

He nodded, casually. "Yeah."

"How's school?"

He tried not to frown. "It is what it is. Coupla more years, I'll have tha degree my daddy wants me ta have, and I suppose I'll be bettuh for it." Derek finally relaxed the set of his shoulders, I guess realizing that if I hadn't gone off on him yet, I wasn't going to. I searched for something else to say, and couldn't think of anything.

Thankfully, before it could fall into that awkward silence, Patrice returned, smiling broadly at the sight of us together. "I see you found my friend," she declared. "And you're still alive, so I guess she's forgiven you."

A small smile tugged at the corners of his lips. "Just 'til I do somethin' else stupid," he joked.

"Yea, well you bettuh not, cause if'n you do, you got me to deal wit, and I ain't so forgivin'."

"Yes, ma'am," he chirruped.

"So did you two make up yet, cause I can' stand seein' Tracy wit her lip poked out all tha time."

"Pat!" I hissed.

He gave me a sidelong look. "You missed me?" he wondered. His voice didn't have that jaunty swagger; it was all genuine.

"Possibly," I said, stiffly.

Patrice gave an angry sigh. "Not possibly. You're all she evuh talks about, and personally it's gettin' annoyin', cause I on't think you're all that interestin', no offense. You two are hopeless, you know that? You care about her, she cares about you, hallelujah, amen!" she exhaled. More calmly she asked, "So, how've you been, Derek?"

Derek and I looked at each other, and started laughing at ourselves and my friend. His face burned from his blush. "Good."

"Tracy says you goinna be an accountant." Patrice looked like she was sizing him up. "I can' see you as an accountant. Accountin' is one uh those safe careers. You love danguh. Where's tha adventure?"

He chuckled. "Adventure don' pay tha bills when they cut you off in four years."

"I thought that accountin' was full uh numbers. How you fit all that in that dome uh yours?"

He seemed perplexed by that notion. "I don' know, but I'm tryin'."

Alex showed up carrying a funnel cake and an onion petal. Without a pause, she introduced the two of them. They eyed each other speculatively before nodding. Alex handed me the funnel cake. "How's school goin' for you," Derek asked Patrice, watching the transaction between me and Alex. I pretended I didn't notice how hard he was staring at Alex.

She gave the classic sigh. "Lord, they tryinna kill me!"

"What about you, Trace," Derek said, turning his attention back on me. I'd almost forgotten that I was still there. "Still gettin' A's?"

I shrugged. "Things're going okay."

"Quit lyin'," Patrice interjected. "Tracy's grades is perfect, as usual. She got an award a coupla weeks ago, first in tha city for some dumb test we had ta take. Why on't you tell him about *that*? Or tha project that you've been workin' on wit tha historical society? I mean you tell *me* about it *all* tha time."

I looked angrily at my friend, but Derek only laughed. "It sounds like you're doin' really well for yourself," he noted. "Still Harvard bound?"

"That's my goal," I remarked.

"Bet'cha find uh way," Derek remarked, and I wondered if the heat that flew to my cheeks was a blush.

"So what's new in your life?" I asked him, mentally kicking myself as I did. I'd just asked him that.

He seemed to be searching for something else to say. "I got uh new apartment," he said, with a shrug.

"Really?"

He nodded. "Yep, finally moved out from underneath my parents, it's goinna be really great. Right now, though, it still needs some work, but once I get all of that worked out…, you should come see it sometime."

"I should?" I questioned, not really knowing what else to say. I became fully aware of my friend and Alex standing there, and wished suddenly that they weren't. Patrice was in line with my train of thought, because she turned towards Alex, touching the top of his arm. "I just remembered I said I'd meet some friends." She looked at me. "I'll meet you back here in a few hours?"

"Okay," I said, agreeably.

"Have fun!"

Derek's smile grew after Patrice walked away, but neither of us had any words readily available. My eyes fell back to the objects of the table. "That's really neat," I remarked, mostly fishing for something to say. "It's like it's saying that inside of something ugly, or I guess distorted, there is something really beautiful, and the reverse is true, too: in something beautiful, there's still something ugly."

Derek grew in front of my eyes. "Yeah, that's what I's thinkin', too," he remarked, with something close to pride, maybe, in his voice. "You know, I know tha artist of this piece right here," he said. "Of all tha pieces in this booth, actually. I could introduce him to you if you wanted me to. Would you like to meet him?"

"I'd love to," I remarked, absently.

"Just give me uh second, and I'll get 'im for you."

He disappeared into the booth. When he came back he was wearing an apron and a paint stained hat. "I heard that there was someone out here that was interested in my work." He held out his hand, trying to conceal a grin. "Hello, I'm Dèréq."

"*You* did this?" I questioned in surprise.

"Yep," he responded, promptly. "You're lookin' at uh Dèréq original. Let me show you some of my othuh stuff."

We went inside the booth. The small space was dedicated almost solely to portraits; faces that seemed nearly familiar stared back at me, along with a definitely unmistakable pair of laughing blue eyes. The painting was part romanticism, part pop art, and part expressionism mixed together in a way that somehow worked. "You painted yourself," I commented.

"I was bored and feelin' very Van Gogh that day," he joked. "That's tha picture that got me that scholarship to tha Georgia School of Art."

"It's-," Derek seemed pleased at my loss of words. "Amazing."

To cover up my awkwardness, I looked away and my eyes alighted on another picture. It seemed to feature yellow as the dominant color, and it took me a moment before I was able to work out what it was.

"Sand dollars," I said in surprise. There were dozens of them spread out on the beach, but their shapes were almost lost because they were nearly indistinguishable from the sand. They only became distinct when you looked at their very center, or you looked at the ones near the surf. In the picture, there was a person carefully kneeling down among them, but it was impossible to tell whether it was a man or woman because all you saw was their shadow as they sifted through the sand.

"Yea." For some reason Derek blushed red, pausing to scratch the back of his neck. "When I's visitin' in Atlanta, I found this little café-we'll have to go there one day-and there was this man there. He was uh really nice guy, but it was kind of sad 'cause he was visitin' tha grave of his daughtuh. She'd died really young, but while she was alive, she loved to collect sand dollars. He'd told her once that it was tha currency of mermaids, so every time he'd come back from uh trip, he'd bring uh sand dollar back for her. Even aftuh she died, he'd still look for sand dollars, and every time he visited her grave, he'd place one on it."

When I looked again at the picture, I could see the yearning, the desperation of someone mourning the loss of a loved one taken too soon. "No wonder you got that scholarship," I said, awed. I looked at another one of his paintings, not realizing before how truly talented he was. "*Why'd* you not go to that art school?"

The posture he adopted was dismissive. "What am I goin' to do wit' an art degree?" he questioned. "Wouldn' be able to do nothin' wit' it."

"But if it's what you want to do...why go to school to be an accountant?"

"Do you really want to be uh lawyer?"

I was a little startled by the question. "I really do."

"Oh," he said, softly, surprised. "Well my daddy wants me to be practical, and he has uh valid point. Ain't no point ta goin to college if they ain't no return on your investment. He don' want me to have to have uh job like his; where he worries about dyin', or gettin' hurt, every time he hears that call. He'd ruthuh his boys have uh career."

"That *is* more practical," I agreed.

"Yeah, well," he shrugged. "So, now you know why I didn' go," he finished. Derek didn't seem as if he was going to say much more on the subject, so I continued looking at his work, wondering how I had missed this obviously large part of his life.

After a while, I trailed back outside to look at the cat. I decided that it was a tiger. There was no color to it, but it had stripes, and it was stretched out, almost as if in a pounce. It was probably one of the most unique things I'd ever seen. Derek, who had been following me, spoke quietly behind me. "If you like that one so much, why don' you take it wit' you," he questioned.

"I couldn't," I remarked. "I don't want to take anything from you."

He picked it up, and held it out to me. "I want you to have it, Trace," he remarked. "That way you'll have somethin' to remembuh me by."

"Are you going somewhere?" I wondered.

"No, but I might do somethin' to push my luck," he remarked. "Sides, I made it to be enjoyed, and you obviously seem to like it. Go'n take it."

"Really?"

"Yep."

"Thanks, Derek!"

"My pleasure," he remarked. He looked as if he was going to say something else, but a man came up to the booth, demanding his attention concerning one of his pieces. He sounded completely in his element as he described the painting, its inspiration, the materials he used. I listened to him talk, enjoying the sound of his voice. Although he often seemed cocky around school, this was true confidence that came out in his voice and manner as he spoke about his work. I listened to them for a few minutes longer, before I went looking for a pen and paper.

When Derek was finished with the guy that he was talking to, he glanced over at me, and saw that I was writing. He started to head towards me, but two more people came in, and he went to address them. We passed only a couple of words over the next couple of hours because people kept coming in to see him. I may have dozed off because I remember saying something to Derek, and then I felt his hand on my shoulder. "Hey," he said, softly. "Time to go."

I blinked twice, and yawned. "What time is it?" I questioned, automatically.

"8:20."

"Oh, wow," I remarked. "Patrice?"

"Came by. I told her I'd take you home."

"She wasn't mad was she?" I wondered sheepishly.

"No, it's all okay."

"Oh," I said again. "Well, then. How'd you do?"

He laughed softly. "Very well, actually," he remarked. "A lot bettuh than I expected. I wasn' expectin' tha sculptures to sell so well; I sold just 'bout all of them." I took one of the boxes that he was trying to juggle from him, and he smiled thankfully. "I feel like celebratin'. Want to go to tha Tadpole grille? My treat?"

"Isn't it too late for that?" As much as I wanted to spend time with Derek, I didn't want to seem too eager in that regards.

Derek reconsidered his offer. "How about an ice cream, then? I promise to have you home by curfew?"

"Okay," I consented.

Derek gave me a sidelong look as we walked toward the exit. "What do you write about all tha time?" he wondered. "Every time I see you, you have uh pen and paper in hand."

"Nothing really," I told him.

"Yeah, and I just scratch out images on tha edge of my notebook."

"Just stuff," I amended. "Nothing important."

"I love stuff! You ever think about usin' 'stuff' to help get you scholarships for college?"

I'd thought about it, but there weren't exactly a lot of scholarships for my writing. "I submit essays and papers for that, but no one wants to read what I write. It's just stuff for me, educational journals."

"Seriously, Trace. Be honest wit' me."

"It's just my observations, mostly," I consented. "Thoughts." We walked through the gates, Derek nodding at the guard on the way out.

"Well you seem to have uh good eye," Derek responded. "*I'd* be interested in readin' what you wrote. Mebbe someday you'd let me?"

The thought of Derek wanting to read something of mine both excited me, and sent butterflies fluttering in my stomach. "I have," I remembered, suddenly, and then when I really remembered what it'd been that I'd let him read, I felt slightly embarrassed. "That poem," I said, "well…if you've even read it."

"'Mind me to show you somethin', one of these days," he said, in response to that. "I think that you write beautifully, Trace. I'd love to read somethin' else. I'll let you see more uh my work," he offered as an exchange.

— 244 —

I reveled at the thought. "There's more?"

"Of course! This was just tha pieces I could bear to part wit," he said, lightly. "You'll have to come visit my studio some time. It's right downtown, coupla blocks from here on Washington Avenue."

"You have a studio?"

"Studio…apartment," he amended with a laugh.

"When can I see it?" I questioned eagerly.

"Any time you want," he answered, readily.

"How about after class on Monday?" I realized it sounded like a challenge.

"I'll be there wit' bells, Miss Burrows," he said without hesitation.

— 26 —
"Shot on Highway 51"

Derek was as good as his word. On Monday, he was waiting for me outside of my seventh period class when the final bell rang. He greeted me with a shrug and a smile. "I didn' know where you went aftuh school, and I didn' want you ta think that I'd cancelled on you or nothin'…"

Derek lived only a few minutes from Mason, in a building downtown that had once sat above a now vacated bakery. The entrance was off an alley, and was little more than an aluminum door with a metal grill protecting it. Since the bakery was no longer there, it seemed more ominous than it must have been when there was the smell of fresh baked goods wafting up from below.

Derek paused in the entrance way. "I should warn you," he cautioned, "you have to have uh bit of an imagination. It's not much." He switched on the light. "Bienvennue le Chez Dèréq."

I had to compliment Derek on his use of the word 'apartment' to describe the place. It was just one giant room with a kitchen and a bathroom. The walls were all concrete and there were five pillars-four cement, one metal-placed seemingly at random around the room. Off to the side was a set of rickety looking stairs. They led up to a loft where Derek had placed a mattress on top of a plank and milk crates. Other than a few more crates for storage, two bean bag chairs, and a red couch that seemed like it was falling apart at its seams, there was no other furniture.

"I told you, it takes some imagination," Derek reminded me, nervously. "But I think that it's great for uh first place. It was uh real dump when I got it," he added. I imagined the dwelling worse off than it was now, and found that I had a lot of trouble picturing it. "I'm in tha process of cleanin' her up," he went on. I noticed on the furthest wall, the largest wall, white primer served as the only decoration.

"It's not much, I realize," he shrugged, "but it's somethin'. I'm out of my parent's house, and this place has real potential." He looked around as if to reassure himself. "Besides, I get to live here for free. It belongs to uh friend of my daddy's. He's been tryin' to sell tha place, but no one wants to buy it as is, so while I get this place to halfway resemble somethin', he'll let me stay here for free. All I have to do is pay half for materials, and when he sells this place he'll give me uh split of tha profits. It's uh hell of uh deal."

He correctly gauged my reaction. "I know that you're thinkin' I got tha shaft end of it, but you're wrong. Just give me uh couple of months, and I'll prove it to you."

I took note of the word 'months'. 'Months' was an almost guarantee that I would be seeing more of him. I realized that Derek was waiting for me to say something, so I said, "You've definitely got your work cut out for you."

Derek only smiled. "I nevuh run from uh challenge," he declared. The look he gave me made me wonder if he was just talking about this place.

"So where do you do your painting?" I questioned. "You're supposed to be showing me your great works of art.

He steered me over to a little alcove that had sunlight streaming down liberally from the skylight; a perfect place to paint on a sunny day. There were three easel's set up, two paintings propped against them, one unfinished. Surprisingly, I recognized the inspiration for the unfinished painting. He noticed my attention and nodded at it. "I'm attemptin' to do uh tribute to *White Fence*, do you know Crichlow?"

"I know his painting," I remarked. Ernest Crichlow's *White Fence* was a painting of a group of black boys who were standing on one side of a fence, crowded together. In the foreground there was a white girl, who stood on the other side, alone, not looking at them.

In Derek's painting, on one side of the fence stood a lone black boy, while three white kids stood on the other side, two of them standing back while the third cautiously approached the fence. Instead of metal, Derek's fence was white and more of the kind you'd see in a garden, but high enough to come to about mid-chest. The biggest difference, though, between the two paintings, wasn't the change in the look of the fence, or in the sexes or number of children, but that in Derek's fence there was a gate. One of the forward white kids' hands went to open it, while the other rested on top of the hand of the forward black boy.

"I've only seen his work in magazine articles," he explained, as I took everything in. "But in *White Fence* and a few of his othuh paintings, Crichlow uses fences as uh metaphor for how Blacks and Whites relate to each othuh. I wanted to kind of play wit' that idea. I-I know it's not as good as Crichlow's, his was brilliant-,"

I cut him off, mid-stammer. "Derek, it's...," I cleared my throat, "really, really good. How often do you get to paint?"

He sighed. "Honestly...not that much. Really I's surprised that I could get enough togethuh to feature at FanFaire, what between school, work, and this place, I hardly have any time." He glanced around quickly. "I don' mind, though."

I followed his eyes to the far wall. "What's going to be there?" I wondered.

Derek gestured. "I want to do uh mural. This big Serengeti type of scene, but you're just goinna have to wait to see it; I can' really explain it to you."

"It's going to cover the whole wall?" I questioned, my eyes tracing the structure up to the roof of the studio.

"That's tha idea."

"It's a big wall," I remarked.

He nodded in agreement. "Yea, it is."

"How do you expect to paint it all?"

He seemed like he'd just been waiting for me to ask. "You want to see," he questioned, giving me a devilish grin.

"What are you going to do?"

He pointed at the wall. "I'mma show you how I'll paint it all, watch!"

Derek climbed up the stairs to his loft. He stepped from one of the crates near his bed, up onto the guardrail, steadying himself before he bent his knees and launched himself across the room. My heart stopped for a few seconds as he fell, only noticing the rope he was aiming for once he'd caught it. He pulled himself up so that he was straddling the rope. Once that was done, he started pulling on another rope that was parallel to the first one. A jerry-rigged artist bench rose along a pulley system until it was flush with Derek's body. He swung from the rope, to the bench, and the bench swayed unsteadily on the wires even after he was seated.

"You could have warned me that you were about to do that," I yelled up at him. "Thanks for giving me a heart attack!"

"Sorry," he yelled back, really sounding sheepish. "I do it all tha time though; you have nothin' ta worry about."

"Do you really have to be on that thing?" I questioned.

"I can only stand so tall," he said, lightly. Easy for him to joke; it wasn't his heart pounding in my ears.

"You could fall!"

"It's not like I'm ten stories up or nothin'. It'd be uh short fall if I did, and even I'm smart enough to land on my feet. 'Sides, I'd be more upset about tha wasted paint." He worked his feet back and forth so that the bench swung even harder.

"Don't do that!" I yelled.

He continued to swing. "Do what," he questioned, innocently.

"That!"

"Why? Am I scarin' you?"

"Yes, you are, now stop!"

"Would you care if I fell, Trace?" he wondered, casually.

"Not if you don't have sense enough to stop!" I yelled at him. The bench continued to sway. I turned my back on him.

"Okay! Okay...look, I'm stoppin'!" When I turned back around, the bench was swinging considerably less. "Look, I'm stopped. Happy?"

"I'd be much happier if you came down," I remarked. He lowered the bench down to the ground, laughing as he stood in front of me. "You couldn't think of anything better?" I asked.

"I could've," he said, lightly, "But this's more fun!"

"You're incorrigible!"

"Eh," he said, casually. "It's good to know that you care 'bout me, though, Trace," he remarked.

"Of course I do," I said to my surprise. "So, don't be so stupid."

He motioned toward the stairs. "Come up to tha loft so I can work while we talk."

I just shook my head. "I have to go."

"You just got here!"

"I have homework," I explained. I'd only planned on spending a little time with him, an hour or two, tops, so that I wouldn't be setting myself up for a disappointment in case Derek had only planned on having me over for a short time. Derek had apparently planned on spending more time together than I had. "You've got all night to do it," he protested.

"It might take I'll night," I asserted.

"Yea, like it would evuh take you all night," he responded. "You goinna come back tomorra, at least?" he questioned hopefully.

It made me happy that he wanted me to. "I've got HH." I didn't try to mask my regret at the words. Derek didn't attempt to cover his either.

"Wednesday?"

"Church."

"Thursday?"

"Patrice has a softball game," I answered. Derek seemed like he was waiting for something. When I realized what it was, I supplied it readily. "Why don't you come?" I questioned. Derek's smile was instant, but then he started to laugh. "What?" I asked.

"Should be interestin'," he remarked.

I tried to imagine what could be interesting about a softball game. "Why is that?"

"You'll see," he assured me.

On Thursday, Patrice rode over to Chatham with the team, and I rode over with Marcus. By the time we got there, Alex had already staked out a few seats for us. He was sitting with Lina, a guy named Damien, Pauline, and Pauline's little brother, Bo-bear (real name Charles). Lina seemed about as happy to see me as I was to see her, but her gaze quickly shifted from me, to give Marcus an appraising look. Marcus noticed, and, giving a smile, put an arm around my shoulder. We sat down on the bench in front of them, and I could almost feel Lina scowling at my back.

Derek showed up a few minutes later. He saw Marcus with his arm around me, and he paused for the briefest of seconds, before giving a nod to Alex. "Hey," he remarked. I looked back to see Alex return the greeting, and the rest of the group gave Derek an appraising look. "*Who*," I could tell by the way that it was said, that Lina had pointed at me, "invited tha White boy?"

Derek ignored her words. He sat down on the other side of me, his shoulders hunched over as if he were upset, and I was sure that it had little to do with Lina's comment. I gave Marcus a sideways look. "Mark," I whispered. Marcus' eyes rolled from me, to Derek, and he frowned, but he took his arm from around me. Derek's arm didn't suddenly move to take his place-not that I expected it to-but his posture, at least, improved.

I got what Derek meant about the game being interesting when the girls came out onto the field. I'd forgotten that Derek and 'the blonde at first' used to date until I saw her walk onto the field. Carol's eyes scanned the crowd appraisingly, before they stopped on him. Briefly they moved on to me, pausing in recognition before they made it back to Derek. I remembered suddenly that the reason the two of them had broken up was because he had practically stood her up on Homecoming because he'd been with me (well Nicole, really). I was certain he hadn't told her that little tidbit.

She smiled his way, though. "Hey, Dare," she called enthusiastically. He waved, smiling a nervous, somewhat forced, smile. "What're you doing here?" I recognized the unmistakable hope in her voice. I tried to dredge up whether the rumor mill said whether or not Carol was dating anyone at the moment. I knew, because I'd been there, how much Carol hoped that Derek had come to see her.

"Came to watch tha game," he remarked. "How're you?" She opened her mouth to answer, and he turned towards me. "Be right back," he said quickly. He walked down the bench steps to go up to the fence, and she jogged over to meet him. I watched their body language, and Marcus watched me, pretending that he wasn't.

"This that same White boy?" he questioned under his breath.

"What white boy?" I wondered innocently.

Derek came back a few minutes later, and sat back down beside me. It might have been my imagination, but I think he was sitting closer than he had been before he left. "What'd she want?" I wondered.

He shrugged. "She asked if I wanted to meet her somewhere aftuh tha game's ovuh."

"What'd *you* say?"

He looked at me in confusion. "I told her I'd already had plans," he remarked. "You don' get to get rid of me that easy," he added.

The game started with Chatham at bat first. From first base, Carol had a good view of the bleachers, and she kept glancing over. He steadily pretended that he didn't notice. Two innings went by uneventfully. In the bottom of the third, Patrice was up to bat again, and we cheered loudly when she took the plate. She smiled at us, adjusted her stance, and waited for the pitch. As the ball went whizzing towards her, a black sedan pulled into the parking lot. For some reason it caught my eye, pulling my attention from the game. I followed it as it made its way towards us, stopping abruptly at the fence. A well-dressed, red-headed man got out, and strode up to the mound with a sense of purpose. One of the umpires noticed him and whistled the current play to an end. This brought in the rest of the umps, and of course the coaches came running over, too, yelling at the unexpected interruption.

They held a small conference while the rest of us wondered what was going on. The head umpire (or whatever he was called) stood out on the pitcher's mound and addressed the crowd at large. "Please, if I can have y'alls attention!" Gradually silence fell as people quieted, wanting to know what was happening. By now it was obvious that something wasn't right. Unease settled on our little group, and Bo-Bear intuitively whispered, "Look like it time to go," just as the ump said, "This game has been called due to emergency circumstances. Please make haste to your vehicles. Thank you."

A few people looked up at the darkening sky, as if expecting rain, but mostly everyone looked confused. The rest of the girls went up to the coach for an explanation, but based on the looks on their faces as they left, I could tell he probably didn't say anything to them other than what the umpire had just said. A little ahead of the game, Patrice had already started tossing things into her bag, and came rushing out to meet us.

"What's going on?" Lina wondered.

Patrice shrugged. "That's Chatham's principal," she stated. "All Coach said was that tha principal said that tha game had ta be rescheduled and we're ta go home."

The words were barely spoken when Carol came sprinting over. "Dairy, can you ride me home?" she wondered. "My dad's not here, and I don't have a ride."

Her question seemed to make him uncomfortable. "Err, sure," he remarked, looking at me. "*You* comin', Trace?" he asked, pointedly.

"I'm going to ride home with Patrice," I remarked. Patrice nudged me. I ignored her.

One of the umps walked past our little group. "Get on, y'all, no loiterin'," he remarked authoritatively. "Get in your cars, and go on now."

"Here, Carol," Derek remarked, tossing her the keys. "You know my car." He turned to me. "Trace?" I paused. "See you tomorra aftuh school?"

"Yea," I remarked. He hesitated for a slight second to spontaneously touch my cheek, before he went to his car. Patrice pulled me toward Alex's as Chatham's principal looked like he was about to swoop down on us, an especially stern look on his face.

"Why you lettin' that twit move in on yo' man?" she hissed in my ear.

I looked across the lot at the two of them, wondering why I hadn't gone with Derek. It was too late now. I crowded into the Pastor's sedan, and Alex started the car. "What do you think's got them all upset?" Damien wondered.

Alex shrugged. "Weather, maybe," he stated, though none of us actually thought that that was the case. Patrice turned on the radio to the soul station, to help eliminate the unease that had settled around us, but no music issued forth. We'd tuned in, in the middle of a news broadcast or something, and Patrice was about to click the radio off when something caused her to stop. "Did ya hear that?" she questioned in a whisper, just as the words the announcer had spoken seemed to translate to my ears.

She turned up the radio, and it was the only sound in the car; I don't think anyone even drew breath as the announcer continued, "*...we got word, about an hour ago, of rumors circulating that the injured party was with Dr. King. Memphis police have only moments ago confirmed that the victim is in fact Dr. Martin Luther Ling, Jr. Reverend King was pronounced-*"

The air turned stale as the voice continued. "He didn't say dead, did he?" I questioned. "He said wounded…or arrested right?" There'd been a passing article about a rally in Memphis…

We all listened without a breath passing between us. "He said dead," Damien confirmed.

"He didn' mean our King," Patrice decided. "It couldn' be."

It was.

Even though Patrice cut the radio off as if to cancel the news, as we drove through town it only confirmed what we'd heard. People dashed from their houses to their neighbors, spreading the news. It was like the day that we found out about Kennedy. We'd been in school, then, in Alex's mom's classroom, ironically. It'd been Mrs. Layton to tell us that our President, *the President* of the greatest nation in the world, had been killed, and not by some foreign opposition, not by an anti-capitalist, but by one of our own. And a nobody at that.

But this news hit a little harder than Kennedy dying because King wasn't as untouchable as the President. Reverend King had dined in some of our homes. He was a southern boy, raised on collards and hog, and born from that same rhetoric. Before he had become well known across the country, he had been known around the towns. Many of the educated black men in Bakersfield had attended school at Morehouse; Frankie would tell anyone who'd listen that King and his dad used to play pool together on Friday nights when they were in college together. My mom and I had listened to him speak when he came to Forest Lake College a couple of years ago. I'd shaken his hand.

He was dead.

You could feel the tension that pervaded the streets, even through the steel of the car. It was like our city, our state, our country even, had merely been teetering on the precipice for a long time. The news of the death of Dr. King was like a dry brush; all that it needed was a spark to set it off.

And then someone lit the match.

Thankfully, though, not in Bakersfield. No, Bakersfield was the type of city that's too green to really burn, but just across the river in Decatur-where its inhabitants were overloaded from the toil of the factories and the grim reality of the everyday-King's death sent the city up in smoke, and it erupted in violence. In Chicago, too, with its gray, and concrete, and that wind to spread the flames, Watts with its large, black, invisible middle class population, Boston, in my aunt's neighborhood of Roxbury, where the people were currently overburdened over busing and school integration, in Detroit, Oakland, Harlem, Washington, and many other cities around the country, violence broke out.

Alex dropped me off at my mom's church. It was the logical choice: by the end of the night the churches, and Duke's Hole, were going to be the most crowded black establishments in Bakersfield. When I met up with my mom, she was stone faced, her features carefully blank. She was always reserved with her feelings, and even in this moment she didn't let those feelings show. Mostly, she just seemed to tremble, and I couldn't tell if it was from fear, anger, or a little bit of both. We stayed at the church well past midnight while Pastor Pride preached overtime, and the choir sang, and people stared dully, not really hearing any of it.

I went to school the next day, but many didn't. It was understandable why they chose not to. The tension was so palpable in the hallways that you could almost see it, feel it, taste it in the air. It was like everyone was waiting for the wrong person to say that one thing that would end the fragile peace that Mason High has existed in since the police got sent home. Uncharacteristically, Principal Vaughn got on the bullhorn to address the student body. He assured us that Mason *would not* have any problems, that we were a model school, in a model city, in *God's* South, and that we would not react in *that* way.

Surprisingly, he praised Dr. King's unwavering faith in the Almighty, called him a great man whom "you may not have agreed with, but should still respect". He talked about how we should all learn how to live together, and respect each other, and our differences, because God had made us all the way he wanted us to be, and he wanted us to share His love for each other. He ended by saying that if there was even one instance where we did not conduct ourselves as 'the ladies and gentleman I know each and every one of you to be,' prom would be cancelled, and every extracurricular activity would be suspended for the rest of the year. Who knew if his threat meant anything to anybody, but there were no fights on school grounds.

I made it through about half a day before I went home. In the house, I turned on the radio to WJAB, and listened as details that had already been stated a thousand times before were recanted and said differently. I half-listened to other people talk about the aftermath, who had killed him, who was suspected of really killing him, what this meant, and how people were reacting. When the DJ read off some of his last words, I got chills. Had King known he was about to die? How did someone just walk into that knowledge willingly?

When I got tired of being alone, I went over to Patrice's and we watched the colorful images that they put on the news. The images the media brought to us of the troops that were moving into the capital, and the fires that consumed Washington, D.C., momentarily had us confused: was this the capital of *our* country, or another battle over in 'Nam incorrectly labeled?

Dignitaries and traveler's fled from our borders, fearing their lives. Foreign newspapers wondered if America was on the verge of a second Civil War. Many watching the violence didn't understand, but then how do you understand the frustration of a people who were raised on the same promise of America that white children were, only to grow up to find that, for us, it wasn't true? Really who but the Indians, the native peoples of this country, really understood what it felt like to hear promises, year after year, only to have those promises to be rescinded, year after year? Or feel the frustration of hearing daily how our country was the champion of the world for freedom, and watching a war being fought in that name, yet all the while not being able to indulge in the freedoms that we were trying to gain in other countries? Or of being told to wait, that this wasn't the right time, wait, it's not the right place, wait, it wasn't the right atmosphere, and then, when things seemed to be changing, changing for the better, one of our leaders is killed, in cold blood, and once again it seems like we were being told to wait?

Ernest Chambers' words about how we were taught in schools that Patrick Henry was a patriot for his dissent, yet our heroes were simply trouble makers, kept ringing in my head, over and over, like the insistent ringing of a church bell. It was no wonder why people were being violent. It seemed like a harsh tribute to Dr. King's method of non-violence that his death seemed to be a catalyst for it, but people were frustrated. People were scared, and people were angry. Even the looting I almost understood. We were being denied everything else, including the means to get the items legally, so why not take what you *could* get, how you could get it?

At least this is how I understood it. But I was only myself, one person, 16, and trying to understand what was hard to understand. I stood staring at myself in the mirror for a long time trying to figure out what it was about me and my skin color that caused people to react so violently. I couldn't understand how my life, my actions, my ambitions, could be viewed as a threat. A threat to what? What was it about skin that made someone want to kill someone over it?

So far in my life, I hadn't had anyone I was close to die. I was thankful for that. I wondered, though, how long that would last. Did I take for granted that the lives of the people I loved were just as fragile as Reverend King's? Was it naïve to think that despite his hot-headedness, Sean would always come home, that Marcus would always be there to offer me guidance? Would it really take something as dramatic as another civil war before we could find peace with each other? Was that really the only way that things could work themselves out?

And if it was, how many people would have to die in order to make that happen?

A week passed.

As long as I didn't read the Times, it got better.

Another week passed, and the news became like a dull ache. Already I was used to it. Eventually there was that realization that death was just a natural course of life, and I didn't even know this person, only knew of him. Slowly, eventually, he faded from the 'Man of the Movement' to just another man.

I was coming out of school by myself one afternoon, and got a shock to see Derek standing across the street from the carport. He looked off, and I wasn't immediately able to place why, until I realized that it was because he looked so serious. Our eyes met across the distance, and he watched me warily, trying to gauge what I was thinking.

"Hi," he said, hesitantly, once we were closer. I associated it with the same tentative greeting he gave whenever he knew he had done something wrong. I wondered what he had done wrong. Slowly, in stages, and then suddenly, it dawned on me that he was trying to figure out if I was mad at him, or if I hated him. It didn't make sense to me until I remembered the events of the past few days: Fanfaire, the game, Carol. Did that mean that he had stood me up? Did something he shouldn't have done with her? Otherwise he would have known that *I'd* stood him up; I'd forgotten all about meeting up with him.

I suddenly remembered, too, that a small tragedy had just taken place in our country, and his look had nothing to do with what I thought it did.

So what was he worried about...that I didn't like him anymore? He held open his arms, an invitation, and I accepted it, letting my arms wrap around, and be wrapped around, by him. "How're you?" he questioned in my ear, once the space between us had narrowed a little. "I called," he let me know. "Six times. I was here."

"I didn't stay," I explained. "Patrice and I ditched, and we went to church later. We didn't get back home until after midnight."

"Y'all right?"

I allowed myself to get wrapped up further in his comforting embrace. "Still a little bit shell shocked," I admitted, not knowing how much I could say, how much I *should* say. That hesitation was, in part, the reason why you didn't see very many black and white teenagers or adults still friends after that certain invisible age; because there were some things that just didn't translate. Even for the Whites that supported King, to them it was sad, maybe even a tragedy, but for us this was far more personal; King could have been any one of our brothers, our cousins, our neighbors.

It didn't matter, either, that while blood was pumped in and out of his veins, some didn't like him, believed that he was more for Whites than Blacks, or that he was too passive, too aggressive, not passive enough, not aggressive enough, that he was stirring up the waters, or that the Movement was effectively over. It didn't matter that many disagreed with him, or even hated him and what he stood for...he now became immortalized, a martyr for the cause, *our* cause. For equal rights, equal protection, for equal access to the dreams that we went to sleep every night envisioning. King was our royalty. He was the Noble prize winning minister, from a humble background that had helped to shape the rest of the country, maybe even the world. He was our Gandhi. One man, standing at the front of the tanks of oppression, Christ-like, telling the world, "Peace, be still."

"It's like Kennedy all ovuh again, isn' it?" he questioned to my surprise. "My daddy just come home today. He's been at tha station ever since it happened. Mayor Tamer said just in case, but we're alright here, aren' we?" he posed. I thought about the Trick being set on fire while the firefighters sat by and did nothing, or the accusations that arose every time I did well on a test. The whispers of speculation that followed me after it came out that I liked Derek. The conjecture that grew now as people saw me and Derek talking, a little closer to each other than the space that we allowed black and white to exist in. I could understand being frustrated to the point of violence.

"Are we?" I posed.

"I mean it's Bakersfield," Derek reasoned. "It ain't Watts. My daddy really liked Dr. King," he added. "He hates violence…says he sees it every time he goes to work, and he admires anyone who can envision uh world without it, even if it is just uh dream." Derek's father was a firefighter. Had he been one of them in the crowd the day that the Trick was set on fire? How would *he* react to his son and me?

We kind of just stood there for a moment, searching until we found familiar territory. Derek hugged me tighter, pulling me deeper into an embrace. I hugged him back. "I guess we just have to find uh way to all get along," he declared.

We went back to his place. Almost as soon as the door opened, my eyes alighted on Derek's painting, still sitting on the easel. "Will it really always be this way," I wondered, aloud. "If we're always going to be on opposite sides of the fence, what's the purpose of fighting? What are we fighting for?"

Derek considered the question seriously. "It's about tha individual relationships," he remarked. "People get told they hafta do somethin' they don' want to do it, but if they have uh reason to, it's different. My mom and Orion's mom became friends. All it took for that was an apple pie."

My eyes stayed on his picture. "But how close are they really?" I mused.

He shrugged. "How close is anybody really?" he questioned philosophically. "Who says Crichlow's painting has anythin' to do wit' race merely because there's Black and White represented in it? '*Somethin' there is that doesn't love uh wall*'," he quoted Robert Frost. "Good fences make good neighbors, right?"

"But why?" I returned. But wasn't that the question that everyone wondered? "What's so scary that we need to wall ourselves off from each other?"

This one was more introspective; I didn't expect an answer. He surprised me by answering anyway. "Maybe it's cause we're all just goin' along, just barely managin' to hold ourselves togethuh, and we know how fragile we are, and we're worried that if we let too many people in, they'll know it, too, and use it against us."

"If we're all like that, why work so hard to pretend we aren't?"

"Force of habit?" he guessed. "Fear of bein' preyed on for showin' our weaknesses? Isn' that why we fall in love? Because we find someone we *can* be weak in front of?"

I contemplated his words. "What makes you weak, Derek?" I questioned of him. "What's got you afraid?"

His face twisted as if he were about to smile, but decided against it right before he did. "You, uh lot of tha time," he remarked, honestly. He tilted his head towards me, his eyes intense. "You?"

It took me a moment to vocalize the fear that dogged me almost every day. "Never being good enough," I finally answered.

— 27 —
"Angry Landscape"

Derek and I spent the rest of the afternoon talking, and when it started to get dark, he took me home. I was back over at his place the next day, and it didn't take long before spending time at Derek's became somewhat of a routine. He cleared space for me to work, and made room for my stuff, so I didn't have to cart it back and forth every day. He even kept the cabinet stocked with my favorite snack.

While Derek worked, painted, or did repairs, I did homework, or worked on essays. We didn't say much to each other, most days, just enjoyed spending time in the other's company. I was on his typewriter tap-tapping away one afternoon, and didn't notice that Derek had come down from the loft until I looked up to notice him watching me. He was leaned against the wall, a Coke in his hand.

"What?" I wondered, once I noticed him. He shook his head. "Just watchin'," he answered, as if that were the most natural thing in the world. "What're you workin' on?"

I looked at a line I'd just written. "Nothing really," I responded. "School work."

"No you're not," he dismissed, easily. "You don' look like that when you're workin' on school work."

"No," I challenged. "How do I look, then?"

He toyed with the can in his hand. "The way you look all the time: like you're tryin' to figure out the correct way to say somethin'. When you write, just because, though, it's like you're searchin' for somethin', 'stead of just tryin' to figure on how it ought to sound, and when you discover whatevuh it was you were searchin' for, you can see it in every line in your face. When you

— 261 —

get amused by somethin' you wrote, your eyes twinkle. When your lips turn down, I assume it's because somethin' unpleasant happened in what you were writin', or you lost tha thought for tha piece you were workin' on."

I think I just sort of gaped at him, wondering how much time he spent thinking about me, and how had I failed to realize he was making observations. "It's not often that I get to see you so unguarded," he added. "It dazzles me."

I searched for a response, but all I could think to say was, "I'm not guarded."

His eyes still held that intensity. "Yes, you are," he stated. "When you write, though, it's different. Everythin' just kind of eases out. Otherwise, it's like you analyze everythin' too much."

"I don't analyze everything."

"You do," he said, unapologetically. "When aren' you lookin' at things every way from sideways?"

"I-I like to observe things," I said haltingly. "I wouldn't say that I analyze everything, though."

"You do," he said, firmly. "It's just how your brain works."

I thought his statement was unfair considering that amount of scrutiny he'd apparently had me under. "Aren't you analyzing me now?" I demanded.

Derek shrugged. "I'm an artist. That's what I do. You have to know tha tiny things about people if you want to portray them properly, and the best way to do that is to observe. It's amazin' what you can see when you let your eyes wander."

His eyes wandered along my features as he said the words. "Like what?" I questioned, wanting to shift the conversation off of me.

Derek considered. "Well…there's always that one person that's watchin' back, or tha one who walks through life wit' their head down, that one kid who thinks that life is still an adventure. You learn a lot when you just observe, and if you're tryin' to reflect tha world back to someone, you have uh lot to take in."

"So how does that make you any different from me?"

He flashed me a smile. "When'd I evuh say that I was?" he asked. "I just don' put myself above it all." He held me off, "And before you try to say that you don', you do, too. It's like you eithuh don' want to be tainted, or you're scared of what'll happen once you just let go."

I tried to relax the defensive stance of my posture. "That's because I can't ever just let go," I responded. "I kind of have to put myself above it all. Everyone can't take the world as simply as you do," I said in a non-antagonistic way.

Derek shrugged. "It's just life," he remarked. "No one makes it through alive; might as well enjoy it while it's here."

"Why do you think I don't enjoy things?" I questioned.

"You don' listen to music-,"

"I can't dance-,"

"You don' watch TV-,"

"I don't have the time for it, and it's so happy go lucky." Everyone on TV had such perfect, unrealistic lives, that didn't even touch on true reality. Not mine, anyway. "Watching TV just reminds me of what I don't have, and it makes me miss my dad," I said. The dads on TV were all married and full of wisdom…and they talked to their daughters for more than two hours a year, as if they really cared about them. There were no real problems, but plenty of easy solutions.

"You don' go bowlin' or skatin'…I've nevuh seen you truck."

"Why do you spend your time painting?" I questioned, turning the conversation on him. "It's not what's considered normal?"

He looked towards his easels. "It's what I love to do," he responded.

"Why?"

His brow furrowed. "I don' know," he realized. He gave a sudden smile. "Maybe it's just my programmin'."

I smiled in return. "Well there's your answer: it's just the way I was made. So, what're you looking at when you're painting?" I wondered. "Where do *you* go?" When Derek worked, it was like he was in a trance. It would have been interesting, I thought, to be able to see what his eyes looked like, but usually all I got to see were his shoulders as his fingers traced their way across the wall.

Derek seemed a little thrown off balance by my question, but that was okay because he had already completely knocked me over. "I guess I see what part of me I'm tryin' to express when I'm workin'. There are things I can' say, that I can' come up wit' tha words to express, so I use uh pencil, or uh paintbrush, to get them out properly," he shrugged, looking slightly embarrassed. "What do you see when you write?"

I looked at the paper in front of me as if it contained some hidden message. "Not really sure," I answered. "Sometimes I miss getting lost in the pages of fairy tales and fantasy. When you're a kid, there's nothing in the world that you can't do, no one that you don't trust. I've always been treated like I'm so mature; it's expected of me to get things right, to be serious, to be the achiever. When I write, I don't have to worry about grades, or about what people will think. It's the one thing I do that will not be critiqued or judged. I cannot fail anyone. I cannot disappoint."

There was some connection in the look he gave me over my words. His fingers twitched at his side. "I feel tha same, sometimes," Derek admitted, "but I *want* people to see my work. I want them to see that *I* did this, and by them admirin' it, they're really admirin' me, you know? Who doesn' want admiration?" he questioned rhetorically. He paused, giving me a sidelong look. "That stuff you were sayin' in Colben's classroom that day? You've been waitin' uh long time to say it, haven' you?" he questioned.

I thought back to the conversation, to the words that I'd said. "No," I replied. "Just waiting for someone to hear it."

I went back to writing. I thought he was going back to his easel until I heard the grill slide open. "It's really comin' down out there," Derek declared from the hall. I looked over. Derek's form was posed in the doorway, silhouetted against the graying sky. "It's goinna be uh long time 'fore it stops," he added.

"Did you have somewhere to be," I wondered, responding to the conversational tone in his voice.

He shook his head, "Nope," he declared. He looked back at me before closing the door and walking back over to where I was. "Your look changed," he noted. "What're you workin' on now?"

I paused, slightly embarrassed that he could read me that well. "It's an interest letter for summer school," I answered.

"Summuh school?" he repeated. "What they have you teachin' tha place now?"

I laughed. "No, I've enrolled in this special summer program."

He shook his head. "Summuh school, Trace? You don' take breaks do you? You're like tha hardest workin' person I know." He deliberately put his hands on top of mine. "Take uh break," he said, suddenly.

"I can't," I remarked.

"You nevuh quit, do you?"

"Don't know how," I replied with a smile.

He pulled my hands from the typewriter. "Come," he directed.

"Come where?"

"Let's go to tha park," he said with a certain amount of determination, the thought clearly just entering his mind.

"It's raining!" I reminded him.

"Doesn' mattuh."

"Later."

"Now," he said, seriously. Staring me down, and holding my hands loosely, he coaxed me out of my chair and out into the hall. It was raining just as hard as it had been a few minutes ago.

"I'm not going out into that!"

Derek smiled. "You're beautiful, Trace, did you know that?" he questioned entirely out of the blue.

"W-what?" I stammered, wondering if I had heard him right. He gave a smile...before pulling me out into the rain. "Derek!" I screeched. He danced out of reach of my hands, enticing me to come further out into the street. I went running after him, and he took off down the sidewalk, pausing every now and then to taunt me, or to kick at a puddle, sending water flying. We were quite alone; this part of downtown never saw much foot traffic, and no one was driving in this rain.

He pulled me into an alcove suddenly, and before I could protest he was holding a finger to his lips. "Look," he whispered, pointing. A few yards down from where we were, there was a couple who were also enjoying the rain and solitude, a slight more than we were. "See, we're in good company," he

— 265 —

remarked. Derek and I looked at each other, and laughed, before continuing on with our play.

When we got tired, and were both thoroughly soaked through, we went back into the studio, still laughing. He hugged me loosely in the entrance way, getting me wetter. "Oh, look at you," Derek said, brushing water out of my eyes. "You're soaked."

"I'm going to get you back for that!" I promised.

Derek gave a crooked laugh. "I wait," for some reason he paused, and in that same second, I realized the closeness. "In expectation," he whispered.

His words trailed off, and we just stood there, looking at each other, barely breathing. His mouth opened, slightly, his eyes scanning my own. He leaned in close, unsure, but then he paused, blinked, and the spell was broken. He turned to go up to the loft to change, and for a stunned moment, I just stood there by the door, confused.

From the loft, Derek threw down a towel, a pair of his jeans, and a t-shirt for me to wear. I retrieved them, and changed into his clothes, wringing out my hair the best I could.

"Do you have any rubber bands?" I called out.

His appearance was sudden. "What?" he questioned. Although he'd changed, his hair was still wet, but it was slicked down for once so that it didn't hang into his eyes, and the word handsome came to mind.

"I need a rubber band. For my hair."

Derek didn't seem as if he heard me. He stared, looking like he was cataloguing my features. His hands casually went to brush back a few strands of my hair. "Why don' you evuh wear your hair down?" he questioned.

I self-consciously touched my hair. "What's wrong with my braid?"

"Nothin'," he said, as he disappeared into the kitchen. He came back with a rubber band dangling from the end of his finger. "You just look amazin' when it's down."

Derek walked back into the 'living room' and plopped down on his couch unceremoniously. "So tell me about this summuh program you're doin'."

I looked up from my silent contemplation of him. "It's just a chance for high school students to take some college courses before they get to college. Every summer, some of the most prestigious schools in the country do this scholar's program where they invite upcoming juniors and seniors to attend classes specifically engineered to them." I sounded like the brochure.

He looked slightly impressed. "So you're goin' be takin' college classes?"

I nodded. "Maybe," I corrected. I sat back down at the desk. "If I get in. I found out about it last year, but I never applied. When I was offered a position in the program this year, I couldn't pass up the opportunity again."

"Why didn' you do it last year?" he wanted to know.

"Money, mostly: it's kind of expensive."

"How bad?" he questioned.

"$1,350."

His eyes widened. "For tha summuh?" he demanded, incredulous.

"For five weeks," I amended.

"Is uh cruise included in tha package? A new car? Are classes on tha beach or somethin'?"

I shook my head. "You're paying for the prestige," I explained. "It's a tremendous honor to be able to do the program. Some really impressive schools are involved in it: MIT, Georgetown, I think Yale... I mean the list is really notable. Plus, you get high school *and* college credit for the classes you take; you get to meet with the admissions board of the school you get into, take tours of the campus-,"

"And that all sounds great, but won' college be expensive enough?"

"Yes," I said with a nod, "but if you get accepted into this program, you can essentially write your own ticket to any college in the country. And if I get enough scholarships, it doesn't matter how expensive college is."

"Do you have tha money to go this year?" he said after a moment of silent contemplation.

I looked down at the papers stretched before me. Last year I'd been really excited about the nomination until I saw the price. One of my biggest fears was getting into Harvard, only to not be able to go because I couldn't afford it. "Not really," I said softly, hating whenever money came up. "But they offer scholarships, and my mom said that she might could put up the money for whatever the scholarships don't cover. She just won't be able to assist me as much as she would have for college."

"Uh gamble worth takin'?" he questioned.

"Pretty much. Spending the money now could actually mean that we'd have to pay less in tuition later."

Derek picked up the topmost paper in front of me, his eyes briefly taking in the descriptions of the campuses. "So, which one of tha 'Nation's most prestigious schools' will you be goin' to, Madame Burrows?" he questioned over the brochure. "Does tha almighty Harvard participate?"

I blushed, feeling caught at something. "Yes, it does, *and* it accepts females for this program."

He studied the lines of my face, but what he was trying to divine I couldn't say. "What's your deal wit' Harvard?" he demanded.

"What do you mean?" I questioned.

"Harvard for tha summuh, Harvard for undergrad, Harvard for law school? That sounds like uh lot of Harvard, don' you think? Why do you want it so bad?"

The way he'd phrased it made me seem almost obsessive. "It's the best school in the country," I stated.

"One of tha best," Derek corrected. "And that's not what I'm askin'. Why does it *mean* so much to you? I've nevuh once heard you say that you want to go to Yale, or Stanford, MIT."

"MIT is an engineering school."

"Stop tryin' to change tha subject, Trace, you know what I'm sayin'."

I shrugged. "I've just never really wanted to go anywhere else."

"Why?"

"I don't know," I admitted. "I just haven't."

"Anyone tell you that you have to go to Harvard?"

"No."

"Anyone tell you that you couldn' make it?"

"Everyone says that," I responded, "but I've wanted to go to Harvard long before someone was there to tell me that I couldn't." I think, though, that being told that I couldn't make it just made me want to attend the school that much more.

"What if you don' get in?"

"I know I won't; Harvard doesn't allow females to enroll. But there's

Radcliffe until law school, and I have no reason not to believe that I won't get in there."

"Why's that?"

"Because I have to believe that if I know what to do, and I do what I'm supposed to, I'll get the result that I'm aiming for. If I don't, I'll adjust my aim, and try again."

Derek looked very tired, suddenly. "And what if somethin' happens that you can' help?" he questioned quietly.

"Like what?" I wondered.

"Like *life?*" Derek posed. "There are just some things that you've no control ovuh. People die, people get injured, laws inhibit or doors close for no reason."

"I don't deny that," I replied, and I wasn't. I knew that there were things just not available to me as a black woman. That's why I spent so much of my time trying to find the way to get past that. I might have hated Mrs. Rupert, but I was glad to have her in my life because she was a constant reminder of what I was consistently up against. I knew that, in all honesty, I probably wouldn't make it in to Harvard. I didn't think that Harvard was going to change their policies just because I really wanted them to. That someone was just going to accept me because I willed it. But I did hold onto the belief that eventually things would change. And while I was waiting for that to happen, I didn't really see anything wrong with dreaming, or with working as if that dream was an actual possibility.

"I just think that if you prepare, if you know the rules, and if you are ready for things to go wrong, if you expect and anticipate change, then you're more likely to succeed in life. I know that there's a fair chance that I'm not going to, but I'm going to keep at it until I do, or until I run out of energy."

His response clouded his eyes, but he didn't express it. "Fair enough," he said, for the moment dropping it. "So are you goinna apply anywhere else next year?"

"Of course I am." I remarked.

Derek gave a sly smile. "Just in case?"

"I'm going to apply to cheaper schools, in case I somehow can't come up with the money to pay for Radcliffe, or in case I don't get in to Radcliffe for some reason."

"Do you know, yet, where else you're goin' to apply?"

"I've pretty much settled on U Conn, U of Penn, George Washington University, the University of Chicago, and Boston University."

"None of those sound like they're close to here," he noted.

"That's the general idea," I agreed.

He paused over my words. "What's so wrong with tha schools here?" he questioned.

"Besides the fact that they're here?" I asked.

"Yea, besides that," Derek questioned a little too sharply.

I gave him a speculative look as I answered. "Well, if for some reason or other I don't get into Radcliffe this time around, I want to go to a school that will help prepare me to go there when I apply to law school."

"I'm sure people from AAMU have gone to Harvard. A&M-,"

"Is a wonderful and historic school," I supplied. "But does not offer an accredited political science program, and it, and AUB, are too close to home."

It seemed like those particular words offended him. "What's wrong wit' home?" he demanded. "What's so wrong wit' here?"

I thought it was obvious. "We just got a crash course in what's so wrong with this place! In case you missed it: if you have the unfortunate luck to be born a minority, dare to step out of your place and you risk being killed. The Governor, the highest elected official of this state, stood in the doorway of the state's top university and officially barred Blacks from higher education. If you follow that symbolism across the state, Wallace not only barred admittance to the University of Alabama, he barred admittance to all institutes of higher learning, and the jobs that could result from the obtaining of a higher degree. What hope is someone to glean from that?

"I hate it here," I said, bluntly, looking at him. "I guess since you've lived here your whole life you wouldn't know what it feels like to be completely settled where you are, and then get thrown into a completely different environment. Even if we discount race, living in Illinois was a lot different than living here. Granted, Bakersfield may be better than most other southern cities, but before I came here, I was never looked at to fail based on nothing more than the color of my skin. At least not this blatantly.

"That's not something that's just easy to get used to," I asserted, "especially moving from where I moved from. Even as young as kindergarten, it was expected of you to excel. I didn't go to a private school, but if you even got a C+, the counselors came and talked to you about it, no matter who you were. Those that showed a high aptitude were moved into more challenging classes. They got you thinking about college at a young age.

"Here, our guidance counselor encouraged students to start off taking Pre-Algebra, and go the Algebra I, part I, route. You do that and the highest math you will have taken by graduation is Algebra II. Most colleges want you to have taken at least Trig/Advanced Math before you graduate, which means that you're going to be behind from the start.

"It just feels, sometimes, like there is no encouragement to succeed here, like everything is a celebration of mediocrity. I understand that college isn't for everyone, but they're setting students up to fail long before they get to decide whether or not they want to succeed. I don't like that."

"That's high school, though. College is different. College is for tha people who want to be there."

"You don't want to be there, Derek," I reminded him. "So there's a fallacy in your argument. The south moves differently, you can't deny that."

"It does move slowuh," he agreed. "But it don' mean it's uh bad thing."

"For many, no, but for me that slowness drives me crazy. You know there are people here who were born at Bakersfield Hospital, grew up on the same block their parents grew up on, went to the same schools, and have never once been out of the state? The thought of that type of life scares me."

"*I* was born at BH, and I go to tha same high school that my mothuh went to. What's so wrong wit' that?"

"It doesn't show growth," I insisted.

"When my mom went to Mason, it was an all-White school," Derek remarked. "It's mixed now, so it *does* show growth. And bein' restless doesn't show growth eithuh. It just means that you flee from stability."

"I'm not fleeing from anything!" I said with an unintended scoff. "It's just that the notion of being exactly where I am 20 years from now, 30 years from now, terrifies me. And your point about your mother just serves to illustrate another. Blacks and Whites might go to Mason, but it'd be a stretch to call it integrated. Present company notwithstanding, how often do you see Blacks and Whites interact with each other socially? We don't, not really, and as long as we don't these feelings that we have towards each other aren't going to change.

"What would I even have to look forward to, staying here? Half the time I get treated like it's the second coming because I know how to read, and the other half I spend trying to defend myself. Defend who I am, defend my ambitions, defend wanting to go to college in the first place, never mind wanting to go to Harvard, or be a lawyer. People were downright offended when I was the cities highest scorer on the state exam."

"People have problems wit' *anyone* who is smart, Trace. You said so yourself, rememuh?"

"That's not the same thing," I replied.

"So it's uh problem; what're *you* goinna do about it? By leavin', all you're doin' is what everyone else does: lookin' for somethin' bettuh out there instead of improvin' things at home."

"So, is *that* why you came back," I remarked somewhat sarcastically. "To improve things at home?"

He looked caught off guard, and he shifted uncomfortably. "No, I had my reasons," he said evasively.

"Which were?" I prodded.

Derek got quiet. After a thoughtful silence he declared, "This is where I'm supposed to be. This is my home."

"Well, it's not mine," I responded. "It's easy for *you* to call this home, you're white and male. You're right: this is where you're supposed to be. You can make what you want from your life. *You* can disappear if you choose. You can walk through a crowd, anywhere, and not be seen. You can go skiing, or to a play. You can go to the beach, or leave the country, go to college, go to the bank, or just go see your favorite team play, without anyone noticing. You can take a test without anyone questioning the result. I can't.

"You can be whatever or whoever you want. Me, I've got this spotlight trained on me, all the time, waiting for me to slip up, to fail, to show I'm not as smart, or as confident, or as determined, as I am. You try feeling comfortable when you have to live like that. I've got one shot at success, just one, and if I slip, if I even show a sign that I might, people are eagerly waiting to put me back in the place they think I belong.

"Maybe it won't be like this forever," I conceded. "I pray that it won't be like this forever, but this is the reality of the world that we're living in *right now*. Until things change, I have to go where I'll at least have a chance of success, of *dignity*. I don't get that here."

Derek seemed as if he'd stopped listening. "I guess not," he remarked, letting the matter drop. "So what were your othuh reasons for not doin' this program last year?" he questioned. "You said that money was uh big part of it, meanin' it wasn' tha only part."

I had to adjust myself to the sudden switch. "I was worried that I wouldn't get into the program," I responded hesitantly.

Derek considered my answer. "Can anyone apply to do this program?"

"No, I mean, I guess they could, but you receive the information because a teacher nominates you."

"But you received this information, and you didn' think you would get in?"

"There are a lot of exceptional people in this country."

"Yes, and you're one of them; in my mind tha best." I felt my face redden. "I can' believe that you were worried about that." He flicked his hand, dismissively. "In all seriousness, Trace, you're brilliant. You should have more faith in yourself."

"It wasn't that I didn't have faith-,"

"Then...?" He nodded to himself. "You were afraid that if you didn' get into tha program then you wouldn' get into Harvard, eithuh," Derek stated intuitively, hitting the truth. "Is that it?" I nodded reluctantly. "So, does this mean that if you *do* get into Harvard's program then you'll get into Harvard when you apply?"

"There's no real guarantee of that since the standards for admission in the summer program are not the same standards for getting in during normal enrollment. Besides, Harvard shuttles all of their women over to Radcliffe."

"And how far away is Radcliffe to Harvard?" he questioned in speculation.

"Same teachers, same clubs, same classes, and they leave a certain number of seats in their law school specifically for women coming from Radcliffe."

"So, you're goinna go to Radcliffe when you graduate here?"

I smiled to myself. "I'm still hoping that Harvard will start admitting females before I graduate, but if not, I will."

"And if you go to Radcliffe for undergrad that greatly improves your chances of goin' to Harvard for law school."

"It doesn't hurt," I responded.

"Congratulations on your acceptance to Harvard," Derek declared.

— 28 —
"The Summer Project"

When you're sixteen years old and into politics, your age can be your biggest vice. Even though I still had five years to go before I could vote, I still kept up with the debates and the candidates that were running, because the upcoming presidential election was one of the most exciting that history promised (okay, maybe not *the* most exciting, but it was certainly pivotal). It was the first national election that blacks would have the right to vote in, en masse. It was also the first national election that I followed fervently.

I believed, unflinchingly, that the best candidate for president was the current president. Johnson was exactly what the country needed right now. Despite that we were still in Vietnam, the things that he'd been able to accomplish domestically, especially the legislation he'd passed in order to advance civil rights, was worth commendation. But, the war was damning, and people expected him to be just like Kennedy, and he wasn't. I was convinced, though, that if he could just get reelected, he'd be able to prove that he was the best choice, but unfortunately I was strongly outnumbered in this opinion; even his own party disagreed with me.

To me, the choice that the Republicans seemed to highly favor was far more incompetent than Johnson ever showed himself to be, and was the antithesis of the current change we were seeking. I didn't like Nixon, but I didn't really think he had much chance of winning, either. Nixon was a snake in the grass; he'd proven that while he was still Vice President. And even though I'd mostly sided with the Republican view in the past, I just couldn't see a Republican becoming president; not in this election anyway. The momentum was certainly with the Democrats. The Dems would end the war, bring the boys home, and, just for good measure, extend equal rights, equal access, and equal justice to every American citizen. The question, though, was which Democrat.

McCarthy had the experience and anti-war stance, Humphrey, the support of the politicians, labor unions, and more of a concept of what being president entailed, and Bobby…Bobby was JFK's brother, and people still felt cheated about the abrupt end to our Camelot president's reign. He was also a staunch Civil Rightser, and I believed that he would stand up better against Nixon in debate, too. After all, Bobby was better looking, more charismatic, and a Kennedy had already beaten Nixon once…

While the candidates were gearing up for a promising political summer, and state by state we got closer to knowing who the Democrat presidential candidate would be, I got my acceptance into Harvard's summer scholar's program. With the acceptance in my hand, it finally felt like I could let out the breath I'd been holding in since I started high school. It took every ounce of restraint I had not to march into Mrs. Rupert's office to show her the letter. The thought of what awaited me over the summer, though, was enough to humble me into telling only my family, Patrice, and Derek.

A few days before I was supposed to be leaving for Boston, I was over at Derek's, as usual, finding busy work in order to help the time pass by. Derek was at his easel, and he must have been thinking about the piece that he was currently working on all day, because once he sat down, his brush didn't still. I loved the way Derek looked whenever he got lost in his work, and I kept getting lost observing the occurrence.

He paused, suddenly, turning towards me, laying his brush down for the first time in hours. "You're leavin' for Boston, soon, right?" he questioned.

"On Friday," I replied. I surprised myself by how detached I managed to sound speaking those words.

He seemed preoccupied by something. "How long you goinna be gone?"

I tried to figure out the meaning behind the cadence of his tone, his posture, his questioning. "I'll be back the week before school gets back in." I thought I mentioned this at some point, but I might not have. Although

Boston was pretty much the only thing that I'd been thinking about for the past couple of days, I didn't bring it up around Derek all that often.

"You're not leavin' *this* Friday are you?"

I wondered where the sudden change in his expression came from. "I am," I responded. "Why?"

"You didn' see tha article in tha Sunday papuh, did you?" he questioned, eagerly. I shook my head. He went digging through his pile of old newspapers until he found what he was looking for. He walked over to me and showed me a clipping. "Look at what tha Boston Museum of Fine Arts will have on exhibit!" It was a passing article in the "Things Round the Country" segment from the Sunday paper. He read over my shoulder as I looked at the article. "Paintin' in France, 1900-1967!" he said aloud, while I read. "Chagall, Kandinsky, Picasso...," there was awe all over his voice. "God! To be there!"

I remembered how he'd once claimed to have joined French Club just so he could see McMillan's works. "Why can't you be?" I questioned, gripped by an unexpected sense of spontaneity. Derek was an adult after all; he didn't have to ask his parents' permission. "I'm sure my aunt'd have no problem with you staying with us," I offered, "and you can take a few days off of work, can't you?" I had an added burst of inspiration. "You can use the money you're saving for your trip! It might not actually be France, but it'll have some of its artists."

That teased a smile from Derek's lips as he contemplated that. As he looked at me, though, his look changed. I shifted uncomfortably beneath it, looking away.

"I could do that," he said, slowly, after a few minutes had passed. "I could just work a few extra shifts when I get back to make up for it."

"Well, then, it's done," I decided.

On Friday, my mother's church friend, Mrs. Parker, drove my mom and me to the train station early in the morning. Even though my mom said that she was coming along so that she could see her sister, I knew it was because she wanted to make sure that I got to Boston okay. Despite that I'd managed the trip to Denver without complications, I guess there was something about being let loose in Boston that gave my mom some pause. I wasn't going to complain: as long as I got to spend the summer unfettered, I didn't mind her coming along for a few days.

At the station, when my Aunt Joanne greeted me, she wrapped me up in a hug so fiercely that it lifted me off of the platform, but the hug that she shared with her sister was far stiffer. She gave her a smile, and a "How are you, Sibby?" and my mother's returning answer was just as stiff.

While they caught up with each other in their own way, I mapped out the places I wanted Derek to see when he got here. He was only coming for a few days, and I knew that the museum was going to take up a lot of the time, but I wanted him to have a chance to do a little sight-seeing while he was in town, too. Maybe I could make him into a convert.

Tuesday, we went to dinner at my aunt's favorite restaurant, Bob the Chef's, before we went to see the new Hitchcock, *Vertigo*. While my mom and her sister stayed up late, chatting, I turned on the radio and listened to election news updates. I went to bed with Bobby reigning victorious in the California primary. When I woke up on Thursday, it was to news that he was dead.

It was one thing to see King, the leader of what was effectively a war, murdered, or even the leader of a country, like the president, but this, Bobby's assassination, was completely unexpected. After seeing how our country reacted to the death of King, I was expecting an angry backlash, riots, protests; especially from the student population. I wasn't prepared for how my mom would handle the news. She started packing. "Mom?" I questioned at the sight of her haphazardly throwing my things into a suitcase. "What're you doing?"

She gave a heavy, resigned sigh. "I'm sorry, Tracy," she said, "but I can't leave you here with things like this. We're going home."

At her words, I saw my plans crashing around me faster than I could draw in breath. "We can't go back to Bakersfield!" I protested. "I'm already here!"

She wouldn't look at me. "It wasn't like I'd planned this. I don't want you in the city right now. Maybe next-"

"There is no *next* year, mom!" I pleaded. I could see it so clearly: if I didn't do the scholar's program, I wouldn't get into Harvard, and if I didn't go to Harvard... "What do you possibly think's going to happen?" I tried to reason.

She paused for the briefest moment. "I don't know," she admitted, "and that scares me. The world went crazy when King was murdered." We'd both read the letters that my aunt had sent about the reaction in her city, following King's death.

"Robert Kennedy isn't King-," I tried to get her to see.

"No, but this is their-," meaning the Kennedys, "city."

I went tearing through the brownstone, and in my haste to find my aunt, I accidentally trampled on her Greyhound, Duke's, tail, causing him to start howling. Joanne came out to see what had caused the commotion, and I threw myself in her arms. "She's threatening to not let me stay," I practically wailed.

After listening for a few minutes, my aunt put a comforting arm around my shoulder, trying to get me to calm down. "Relax. I'll talk to her."

She didn't do it right away, wisely, I guess. She let some time pass, and I paced up and down the apartment, giving the occasional glance outside, while my mom continued to pack away my future. I finally heard my aunt go into the guest bedroom, and I didn't like to eavesdrop, but the situation called for it.

I don't know how the conversation started, but I heard my aunt calmly question of my mother, "What do you think's going to happen, Sibby?" My mom said something that I didn't hear in response. "And you think they're goinna attack *Tracy*? What's she got to do with anything? I can take care of her, Sibby. I won't let anything happen to your baby."

"You can't even take care of yourself, Joanne!" my mom shouted. "How are you going to manage to do that?"

I'd never seen my aunt mad, so I didn't know what the face she gave my mom looked like; I could only imagine. "I did a fine enough job of it when we were growing up," Joanne remarked, soberly. "And I happen to like my life," she added, without any sense of bitterness or anger. "Nothing's going to happen to your child while she's with me."

"What if something does?" my mom demanded, and I didn't like the sound of fear in her voice. I wouldn't admit it, especially not to her, but I *was* a little scared about being away from what suddenly looked like the safe confines of my hometown. But I wasn't going to give up the chance to study at Harvard for anything.

I stopped listening, in case some other words should fly that I didn't want to hear. A lifetime later, the two emerged from my aunt's bedroom. My mom looked haggard from her packing frenzy. I looked to my aunt for some kind of clue, but she just stood watching her younger sister. "You have to call me every week," my mom instructed, "and write every other day." I started to smile. "And you better not find yourself in anything you don't belong being in."

"Yes, ma'am!" I agreed. I failed to reel in my excitement: I could stay!

My mom's train left Boston the same day that Derek's bus arrived. Exactly a week had passed since I'd last seen him, and until I saw him getting off the bus, I hadn't realized just how much I'd missed him in that little amount of time. Derek was like my own private island, a solace in the middle of the chaos that was currently surrounding us. His tired eyes lit up across the terminal when they made contact with me, and he waved. He'd dressed up for the trip, and in his brown trousers, green button down, and with his hair swept back almost neatly, he looked either like he was heading to school himself, or like he was heading off to war. All he needed was a rucksack. He'd even worn a tie.

"You made it!" I greeted cheerfully.

"Orion had to drive me to Chattanooga, just so I could make this bus," he informed me. "How're things here?" he questioned.

"Our political arena has practically turned into a veritable war zone," I remarked. "But other than that-,"

I could see Derek trying very hard to conceal a smile I knew had nothing to do with my words. "It's not funny, I know, it's just-," and he shrugged, not offering an explanation, just hugging me. I could relate to his words; the presidency and the fate of this country was in question, but…here he was!

The next day, as soon as it was late enough, we were off to the Boston Museum of Art. At the entrance to the exhibit, Derek casually reached for my hand before exclaiming grandly, "France est le lieu pour l'art et l'amour." Senselessly, I found myself giggling at his words, my hand practically shivering in Derek's grasp. I prayed he wouldn't notice.

The theme of the exhibit paralleled Derek's words. It wasn't an exhibit of French artists, just those who had been inspired, drawn to, or had been in the country at some point, at some time. In low voices we spoke about the works in French as much as we could. Although I'd heard Derek speak French a thousand times, there was something about the accent that he adopted that held me enthralled, left me hanging on to every word.

Being with Derek simply made the experience. Even without the fake accent and the hand holding, I wouldn't have gotten the same experience had I come here by myself. Part of what makes art great, I think, is getting to see how other people respond to it, and Derek's responses were just so open; so pure. He took nothing for granted. I'd passed by Max Ernst's *Flower Shell* and *Shells with Flowers* without giving it much pause, but seeing how much it grabbed his attention made me go back for another look to see what features of it I'd missed.

What the exhibit lacked in a cohesive theme, it more than made up for in sheer amazement. There was hardly time to see it all. I stood, awed, in front of Kandinsky's *Composition VII*, unable to move for a very long time. Seeing me so enamored with the painting, Derek whispered what he knew about it, and I half listened, overcome, finally feeling what Derek must have felt looking at McMillan's work. We'd had talks before about Derek's love of art, but I don't think I'd ever spent much time putting myself into his world before. That day at the museum, freshman year, I'd gotten an idea, but if that day had been merely a taste, today I got the full buffet. If I hadn't been in love with him before, today would have sealed it for me.

We spent the whole day at the museum, and the next, leaving only a little time for me to show him around before, sadly, Derek got back on the bus to go home, leaving me with nothing but a promise that he'd write, to hold me until I saw him again. In between *Paintings in France,* and the start of the scholar's program, despite my mom's mandate, I got adventurous, and explored the city alone. One of the best things about Boston was that you could hop a bus, a train, or the underground, and go just about anywhere. It was hard to believe that after all this time, next year-I refused to believe that I'd be anywhere else but here-I would actually be living in Boston, somewhat on my own. It was hard to wrap my head around the idea that when the semester started in the fall I'd be starting my last year of high school!

When the start of the scholar's program finally arrived, my aunt escorted me over to Harvard's campus on her way to work at MIT. Already, by the time we got there, the common room of Straus Hall was overcrowded with high school students. I checked in and got a name badge, found out my rooming assignment, and had just enough time to get my suitcase put away before we met back in the common area. We were briefly introduced to the master of the hall and the resident dean, before the head counselor/tutor, a way too perky brunette named Marty, took over.

"Thank you for joining us this summer," he began once the murmurs had died down. "Congratulations! Look around you: you are surrounded by the best and brightest minds from all across the country." There was a mix of smiles that ranged from nervous to cocky, and a scattering of applause. "Welcome. I advise you to take every advantage offered, and make your summer count. To help make the most of this program you've all been assigned to a counselor and a peer group. Your counselor will be your key to the campus, to your events, he is your mentor, your scheduler, your life raft. If you don't know something, ask your counselor, that's why they're here. Your peer group will be the ones that you share your meals with, study with, and pass your free time. They will mimic your housemates for when you're here in the fall, so make connections wisely."

He talked for about an hour, his smile not disappearing even once. Before we were dismissed, we were giving an itinerary for the next five weeks, the names of our tutors, and our class schedules. I was surprised by how familiar some of the kids already seemed to be with each other, and that familiar tension I always seemed to get when teachers made us divide up, started to surface. It felt too much like my first day of school after we'd moved to Bakersfield, and I paused to question whether I had maybe made a mistake in coming up here.

"If you don't want to seem as if you don't belong, don't act like it," a voice near my shoulder instructed. I turned towards the speaker. "First summer program?" the girl wondered of me.

Even though she didn't seem like the friendliest person, I inwardly breathed a sigh of relief at the contact. "Yes," I responded. "Is it that easy to tell?"

"Let's just say, it's not hard to miss," the girl responded. "Just act like you belong and you'll be all right," she said, assuredly. "People respond more to confidence than competence, anyway. I'm Stephanie Fulbright, for the business program." Confidence permeated from every inch of *her* 5'4 frame. It reminded me a little of Derek, but I wouldn't exactly classify what she exuded as cockiness. Was there something beyond cocky?

We shook hands. "Tracy Burrows. Political Science," I replied.

"Oh, are you planning on going into politics?"

"Not currently. I'm pre-law."

"Well, you should," she directed. "The political landscape is changing, and the only way to make sure that your voice is heard is to be the one doing the shouting. Where're you from?"

There was only the slightest hesitation before I said, "Alabama."

"You don't sound like you're from Alabama." The way she said it almost sounded accusatory. "Your accent doesn't sound southern."

"My family moved there when I was younger."

"Well that makes more sense," she decided.

Stephanie didn't stay long, anxious to move on, but that sense of nervousness didn't crop back up after her departure. I forced myself to relax. I *belong*, I kept telling myself. I wouldn't have gotten in if I didn't. By the time we'd been arranged in a circle and were going around to do introductions, I was convinced of it.

Classes began first thing on Monday morning, and didn't still for a moment all summer. My favorite class was "Movements in U.S. Government". Unlike back home, where the teachers talked and we listened, we didn't just sit in class impassive. The first lecture wasn't even given by our professor, Dr. Ferguson, but was an interactive lecture by Dr. Howard Zinn, a professor at Boston University. His lecture on the role of civilians was so engrossing that I didn't glance at the clock even once during the two and a half hours that he lectured. Dr. Zinn talked about history and politics in a way I hadn't heard anyone other than the men at the barbershop talk about it. We talked about the politics of economics, the politics of war, even the politics of perceptions.

"You have to remember," Professor Zinn ended the class on, "it is the one who wishes to tell the story, that makes history, so it's not necessarily that historians omit facts, it's that some things fail to make it into the narrative that the person writing wishes to tell."

Dr. Zinn's words were magnetic, but Dr. Ferguson was just as passionate about his subject. For possibly the first time in my life, I was sitting in front of a teacher who posed, in an academic setting, the questions I'd always wondered privately, but didn't ask. King's death, Bobby's death, well, really the current political arena that we were in as a whole, left gaping questions about our future that weren't easily answerable, but provided plenty of fodder to be discussed in class. And luckily, those questions came at a time when I was in the proper medium to seek out the answers.

There was no topic that was off limits. Subjects that were hushed, brushed under the rug, not talked about, not even hinted at back home, were made public discussions in the classroom. We were encouraged to challenge authority, to seek out answers instead of just believing what we were told. We actually discussed the theories of different governments instead of assuming that ours was the absolute. We discussed Chavez and the Migrant Farmworkers strike. The Chicano Movement. The Indian American Movement. In "Contemporary Literature" we discussed the New Negro Movement in conjunction with the Harlem Renaissance.

All summer I got to be around adults, teachers, who didn't say that children should be seen and not heard, or should blindly follow the lead. Instead they encouraged us to think, to speak, to act. I'd always been teased for the amount of questions that I asked, but here there was nothing else but questions. My classmates had not only read the assigned readings so that we could get intelligent discussions going in class, but they also kept current with the news, they read outside sources, knew what was going on with the world, and weren't so quick to accept what was 'established'.

Like many of my peer group, I saw the college campus as a forum for figuring out what ailed the world, and I saw Harvard at the forefront of discovering the cure. There was no challenge before us too large. We were going to end the Vietnam War, Colonization, the Apartheid in South Africa, bring peace to the world, and all of the other things that you think you can achieve when you're young (and almost end up achieving because you don't realize it's impossible).

The future was a tangible thing. It existed beyond the Fab Four and the Beach Boys, bell bottoms, wigs, and permed hair; past the current movies or actors. We thought about the years ahead, to the 70s, and even the 80s. We were the generation that couldn't be told no, and there was so much work to be done. It was frustrating that I was only here for the summer, but I assuaged that feeling by reminding myself that in only a year's time I would be back and joining my fellow undergraduates in making a world that we weren't ashamed of; that we could pass down to our kids one day and say, "Look at what we did for you!"

Nothing is impossible when your 16.

I'd applied to the scholar's program for the boost it would give me academically, but I wasn't aware of how much knowledge I'd get outside of the classrooms, nor how much I'd enjoy my fellow classmates. Back home I'd gotten used to being around people of a certain type; a certain characterization. Just about everyone in my peer group was pretty close to the same economic status that I was. Even those like Frankie didn't live too high above where me and my mom rested. I'd grown accustomed to that.

The scholar's program, however, employed people from all walks of life. A lot of the students that I was attending classes with were wealthy, had known luxuries that I could only imagine, yet there were also students who had much less than I had, too, and while I understood well what it felt to be poor, some of my peers described instances of true poverty. The program enrolled people from all races, ages, religions, and socioeconomic status; the only common denominator was that we were all upcoming juniors and seniors in high school.

It delighted me being around them because I wasn't used to being around people who were so motivated. I wasn't the only person at Mason who had high ambitions, no, but this was truly the first time that I was around people who not only had ambitions that most people couldn't envision, but also had well thought out plans, and the means to achieve them. Stephanie didn't have vague notions about her future, she had a set course from which she didn't plan to deviate an inch. Like me, she'd known what she wanted to do from a young age, but she had plotted her academic career far more than I would have thought to, down to which professors she should take or to avoid, and what classes were acceptable electives. (I wondered if her lists included people that she could befriend, too, but she was the one to initiate our casual friendship, so maybe I'd passed some test).

I was able to keep up with the assigned work, but I occasionally felt the gaps in my education. The philosophies of men like Nietzsche, Goethe, and Machiavelli were referenced often, but had hardly been required reading at Mason. My Grandpa had been instrumental over the years in helping me to fill in a lot of the gaps, but even still my peers had read books and studied philosophies that I hadn't, had attended lectures and seminars, and gone to museums, their whole lives. Sometimes it felt like I was mentally running, just to draw even. It was difficult, but well worth the challenge. At the end of the program I felt like an athlete must feel after an especially intense work out: drained, but immensely satisfied.

— 29 —
"Mother and Child"

I stayed in Boston until the week before classes started. When I arrived back in Bakersfield, I was surprised by how overcome I was at the sight of my mom. I nearly bowled her over with my hug when I got off the train. Her shock from my reaction was still marked on her face once we stepped away. "To what do I owe this honor," she remarked.

"I missed you," I enthused. For good measure I gave her a solid kiss on the cheek, which made her blush.

"Did my sis treat you horribly?" my mom inquired.

"No, ma'am!" I assured her, "Aunt Joanne is incredible!" My aunt was that rare person who could die tomorrow and no one would feel bad about her passing because she lived fully every day of her life. She was somewhat of a rarity, even in the changing climates. She was a single woman in her 40s, had never been married, and didn't have any kids. A very happy old maid. It was perhaps for this reason that I'd always felt more connected to her than to my own mother. I admired my aunt for not getting married, for choosing to live her life the way that she wanted to. Getting to spend the summer with her had just reiterated how alike we were…but, oddly, it made me feel strangely sentimental towards my mom.

"Your sister is so neat!" I informed her. "We saw *Hello, Dolly!* She took me to some other plays, too, and we went to a bunch of museums, and I got to see Grandpa again!"

There was a slight hesitation, but she kissed me on my head. "I missed you too, Tracy," she remarked, stiffly. "Now let's get you home to your friends so they can stop harassing me. By the way, whatever happened to Frankie?"

On the drive to our house, I caught my mom up on the things that I'd seen, done, heard, and learned over the summer. I'd had to update her every weekend to let her know that everything was okay, but that had merely been obligatory. So now I filled her in on what I hadn't told her in our brief calls. There was a lot that I hadn't been able to tell her about because there had been so much crammed into those five weeks that I didn't have the time to write it all down.

"There was this one seminar that we sat in on that talked about using puppets to teach inner-city kids basic life skills, like counting, and the ABCs, but on TV!" I said, telling her about the workshop we'd done with Professor Gerald Lesser. After Dr. Zinn, I think that was my favorite moment of the program. "At the end of the workshop, we'd been given a demonstration, and afterwards, we'd even gotten the chance to participate.

"Thank you so much for letting me stay," I concluded.

When we got home, I called Patrice and Derek to let them know that I was back. I'd lucked out with my friend: she was home and came over almost as soon as we'd hung up. Since we hadn't talked for practically the whole summer, we had a lot of catching up to do. Before we had much of a chance, the doorbell rang, and my mom very stiffly informed me that I had additional company. Patrice looked at me questioningly. "Were you expectin' any one?"

"It's Derek," I told her. Her look became even more questioning. I didn't answer the look. "Come with me?"

In the living room, Derek was seated and looking very formal sitting across from my mother. As soon as I walked into the room, though, he sprung up, smiling.

"Hi," I greeted, returning the smile.

"Hey!" he said, excitedly. He started to cover the distance between us, looked at my mom, looked at Patrice, and with a lot of restraint, sat back down. He nodded at Patrice, and finished answering whatever question my mom had asked him. He kept shooting glances over at me, though, until my mom finally excused herself. He was quick to jump up, again, once she was gone. He hugged me tightly to him. "God, I've missed you," he said with longing, momentarily lifting me off the ground. "How was tha rest of your vacation? How was Boston?"

As promised, Derek had written often, but they had usually been these short, two sentence notes that'd probably been written on his way out the door. My responses to them were usually just as short, so there was a lot that hadn't managed to make it into our quick, bi-weekly two-line notes. I didn't realize how anxious I'd been to hear the sound of his voice until that very moment. I wanted to fill him in on every point that I hadn't, but I didn't want to just blow off my friend. "I'll tell you everything later," I promised.

"Okay," Derek remarked, easily. "So what's tha plan for tha day'?"

We waited for Alex to show up before we walked down to Chase's to have lunch, and it wasn't long before we were joined by other friends or classmates. We killed daylight, and spent most of the afternoon at the Trick. When it was starting to get late, Derek and I went over to the studio, and I could definitely tell that he had spent a lot of time on it in my absence. The place looked completely transformed.

With only the aid of a set of counters and shelves that rose about waist high, he had turned the awkward pillars into a sort of room inside of a room. They, and the shelves, had been painted a dark blue color with the smallest fleck of yellow paint here and there. The lone metal pillar was painted all black and had strategic holes placed in it for lighting. The carpet that Derek had chosen for the floor was a deep-set, pale blue that he assured me would not readily show stains, and would work with any furniture that would be brought in, no matter the color.

Derek had also worked on the kitchen. He turned it into its own distinct room instead of having it flow from the main room the way it used to. He had placed tile in the kitchen, and set in some cabinets so it felt more like a real kitchen now. I was really beginning to see the place's potential.

"How did you do all this in so little time?" I had to ask.

Derek's smile was almost tired. "By not wastin' uh single moment of my time." He perked up, suddenly. "I almost forgot. I've got uh surprise for you. I made you somethin'."

"You made *me* something?" I repeated.

"Yep." Derek pointed to a far corner, and stood back for me to admire his handiwork. The *something* was a desk. It was this weird metal creation with a piece of thin, smooth, concrete that served as the writing surface, a bookshelf for storage, and a flat piece of metal with padding for the bench. "Go 'head and sit down," Derek urged. I did, and discovered its true secret: the desk had been tailored to me. The place to put the pens, pencils, and other odds and ends was exactly an arm's length away. The bookshelf was level with my eyesight; the bench was exactly the right height off the ground.

I stood up and found myself in Derek's arms. "Wow, Derek! This is just neat! Thank you!"

Derek looked as surprised as I felt, but he didn't hesitate to hug me back. "I like to hear that kind of praise!" he remarked. "So, you like it?"

I gave him an extra squeeze. "It's perfect," I informed him. "I love it!"

"Well, thanks Trace," he said, warmly, "but be forewarned: I had ulterior motives when I made you this desk. I didn' do this purely out of tha goodness of my heart." I waited for his explanation. "I expect you to write great works here, so that when you become famous someday I can say that *the* Tracy Burrows once wrote her masterpieces on uh Dèréq original."

I shifted in his arms to better look at him. "I hate to disappoint you, *Dèréq*, but I don't intend to publish any masterpieces."

He shrugged casually. "Well then that's even bettuh. You'll have to sign tha desk anyway, so once you leave, every time I see it I'll know that I was once tha sole ownuh of greatness."

There was an uncomfortable moment in which I did not trust myself to respond, and we both realized that I was still in his embrace. I pulled back, and gave a laugh. He smiled at my discomfort. "I missed that," he declared. His hand darted out to touch the curve of my face. "It was uh long summuh," he informed me. I couldn't have agreed more. "I'm glad you're back, Trace. You're my muse."

The night before the first day of classes, I was on my way over to Patrice's house when I ran across my mom in the den. She had a dozen or so old shoeboxes spread out in front of her, quietly sifting through them. I paused, watching her work. "What're you doing, mom?" I questioned.

"I've been trying to get the shed in order," she said, distractedly. "Been meaning to for years, just never could find the time. I got a little started while you were gone-" her voice trailed.

"I would've helped if you waited until I got back," I remarked.

"I'm not done yet," she responded.

I momentarily glanced at the door before going all the way into the room. I sat down beside her. "So what are we doing?" I questioned.

"I've been sorting old photographs. That box, there, has some of your old baby pictures in it."

I pulled the closest shoe box toward me, lifting the lid. The first picture I came across was me in fat little pig tails and a polka-dotted dress that I knew that my mom had made for me. I was sitting on her lap, anxious to turn the page of the book she was reading. "You were always like that," she said softly. "As soon as you could walk, you'd run ahead to see what was coming around the corner; you'd always wanted to turn the page to see what happened next."

I smiled, sitting the picture down, moving on to the next. I stumbled onto old pictures of me when we still lived in Illinois, old pictures of my next door neighbor, Brian, family pictures of my aunts, uncles, and cousins, on both sides of the family. In one of the boxes, there were pictures of my parents as children, and I paused to take in one of my dad. He was standing beside his parents looking extremely serious at 4, at 7, at 9. No matter how young he looked in the photos, he had had the same pose and the same serious face. In a picture with his brother and his two sisters, all four of them looked like carbon copies of each other. My dad's dad looked like he took no nonsense from his kids, and his kids looked like they gave none back.

I wondered what it must have been like for him, growing up. He and the rest of the family were big braggers. His family had a lot to be proud of in a time when many didn't have anything. I had several relatives who were teachers, some who were doctors, a more distant relative of mine was a minor actor, and there was even a politician in the family. There was no room to be average on my dad's side of the family, and I speculated at times that my parent's divorce had something to do with the fact that there was nothing tremendously special about my mom (from his family's view point, not my own). She was only pretty, not beautiful, and a housewife.

I stayed on their family picture for a long time before I moved on.

The next box I touched brought me to the early years of my parent's relationship, first when they were dating, and then when they were married.

I got a shock when I realized how happy the two of them had once looked together. They actually looked like they'd been in love, once. I wasn't used to seeing that look on either of their faces.

Hidden beneath this particular set of photos were old, folded, pieces of paper, yellowed with age. I picked one out at random. "He used to write me letters all the time," my mom said, looking over my shoulder. "We met at a church function and somehow we just connected. When he was leaving a couple of months later, he asked for my address so he could write to me once he got home. I didn't think that I'd ever hear from him again, but sure enough, a week later I had a letter in the mail from Ben."

This was the first time I heard my mom say my dad's name like that, or even at all, really. Since my parents divorced, it had always been 'your father': 'Tell your father that I need to speak to him', or 'tell your father I said 'hello'. I could not recall another time when I heard her call him Ben.

She held her hand out for a letter, which I supplied. Her fingers traced over his words. "We wrote each other religiously for a few years," she went on. "He'd make trips to see me whenever he could, and then one day he came to Boston with a ring, asking me to marry him." She still sounded surprised by the action. I tried to think of my parents as they must have been in that moment. The young part was easy enough, but the in love was what was hard to picture. "Ben was just so different than any other boy I'd met. He was *dignified*." I kept looking through the pictures as she talked. There were a lot when they first got married and when I was born, but then they sort of just tapered off. The last box was filled with random pictures of a jaded couple who'd had a kid together.

"What happened?" I questioned. In the last family picture we'd taken before the divorce, the smiles had been fixed, vacant.

"Benjamin wasn't ready to be a father, and I suppose I wasn't ready to be his wife. My Papa was a very affectionate, open, encouraging man. I expected Ben to be the same, but that just wasn't Ben's personality. We both tried, though," she said earnestly, her eyes meeting mine imploringly. "I cared strongly for your father, and I believe that he had for me, it just wasn't enough to make it work. It seemed the more we tried, the more strained the relationship became. One day I said to him, 'I don't think this is going to work', and your father agreed."

I still had the photo in my hand. "Did you love him?" I wondered of their relationship. The only emotion that I'd seen from my mom about the divorce was nearly right after we'd moved, and I'd stumbled into the house to see her crying to *Teardrops on Your Letter* playing on the record player.

"I loved the idea of him," my mom said. "He was someone that I thought I could believe in."

I was about to ask how you could love the idea of someone, but I didn't wonder about it very long because I'd been trying to convince myself for a long time that I'd only fallen in love with the idea of Derek: the idea that someone could be that great, sweet, and sensitive beneath all his other layers. I hadn't yet stopped believing that about him, but what happened when I did; if I ever did?

I met my dad's cat-eyed gaze. "I thought love was supposed to be forever," I said more to myself than to her.

"I did too," my mom said softly. I didn't have the full story, but it sounded to me like both of them had just let the marriage go because they were too scared to admit that the other person meant so much to them. Did they not have any reason to stick together? Was the love that they had felt for each other just completely gone? And what about me? Was I not enough to keep them together? Was I not a reason to stay?

My mom looked at me like she knew my thoughts. "Tracy, we were together for so long because of you," she said, softly. "But your father, Ben, he just didn't know how to be a husband, and instead of asking him to stay long enough to figure it out, I got so angry at him for admitting that to me that I just let him leave."

"Do you miss him?" I questioned.

She was silent for a long time. "More than anything else, I miss that he has missed so much of your life. I know how great an influence a father has, and I'm just glad that I was lucky enough to get a kid who I didn't have to worry too much about." She paused. "I sure do wish that I hadn't had to do all this alone," she added.

I let some time pass before I questioned, "Do you ever think about dating again?"

She shifted, and I wondered if the question had made her uncomfortable. "I don't think that I've gotten over your father yet," she responded. If I were younger, that statement probably would have sent wheels of scheming in motion where I envisioned ways of getting my parents back together...but I was too old for that. I was at the age where I knew that it wasn't going to happen.

"What do you think about Derek?" I blurted. I didn't know what made me ask, and once the words were spoken I was kind of embarrassed that I had.

My mom quietly appraised my expression. Her eyes focused. "I'm not sure I like you spending so much time with that White boy," she declared. "He's a man, and men only want one thing, especially White men who hang around Black girls."

Her frank words were startling as I realized that she was applying them to Derek. I don't think I'd ever thought about it from her viewpoint, and I don't know why it'd never occurred to me how uneasy the thought of the two of us being the two of us might make her. There was so much worry a mother had for her daughter, and I tried not to give her reasons to worry about me; I hadn't paused to realize that Derek could be one of those worries. "Mama, Derek's different," I tried to assure her. "I-I think I'm in love with him." It was one thing to admit that to Patrice, or even to Derek, and another thing completely to admit that to my mom, especially considering the relationship I had with mine.

Her look became clouded; she hadn't liked those words. "I was watching him when you came into the room," she remarked, "and I thought, 'this guy is in love with my daughter'. It wasn't a happy thought." She didn't look pleased with herself. "It's not that I don't think that he's a fine enough boy," she said, hastily. "But like I said, I don't like it. Love's wonderful when it's just between you and someone else, but when other people get involved, things change. I don't think the world is as kind as you would like them to be towards two people in love. Especially down here."

Her words unexpectedly caused a spark of anger to flare within me.

"Why'd we even move *here* in the first place?" I demanded. "Why Bakersfield? Why didn't we stay in Wilmington, or move to Connecticut, or Boston, or California? Why'd you have to move here?"

Her decision had never made much sense to me. Why would anyone *choose* to come to a place that was segregated?

Her voice remained calm in response to my heat. "We couldn't afford to stay in Wilmington. Not in our house, not without Ben. I wouldn't have wanted to, anyway. I guess we could have moved to the city," she said, contemplatively, and I could tell by the way that she had said those words that it had never occurred to her. "But East St. Louis and St. Louis were too big, too dangerous, too open for a single mother to want to raise her daughter in alone, and the last thing a woman who's a parent wants to do is return home to her father's house after a failed marriage."

"That still doesn't explain why *Bakersfield*."

She looked startled by my words, giving me a confused look. "My grandmother grew up here," she said, surprisingly. This was news. Since my grandmother had grown up in Atlanta, I'd always assumed that's where her part of our family was from. "Did I never mention that?" No, she hadn't. My mom retrieved an old photo album, talking as she searched through it. "She moved away to Georgia for a few years, but moved back after my Uncle Robert-he's who *your* Uncle Bobby's named after-died. While she was alive, though, we'd come here to spend our summers. After the divorce, I didn't know where else to go, so I moved here."

"You never told me that."

"It never came up," she responded, "but that's why. I don't know if you remember, but we were going to move when Ben's project ended in Wilmington, anyway. Ben got offered a position at the Arsenal a few days before he got the one in Denver. I told him he should take the job in Bakersfield, and he remarked that he'd move to the South when hell froze over."

I wondered if this was their final fight; if they had just decided to call it quits instead of moving on together. Even now I had trouble pinpointing the moment when I was told, or finally realized, rather, that there was no point in waiting up for him, anymore, because daddy wasn't ever coming home. I do remember that he left when we were still in Illinois, and we had stayed in the house, just the two of us, for a few months before we'd finally moved south.

"So, you moved here because this place held good memories for you?" I tried to imagine how that could be possible.

"I wouldn't entirely say that," my mom remarked. "I used to hate coming down here, honestly. Nana was a very bitter woman. She liked Joanie the best because she was the lightest, and she liked your Uncle Bobby because he was named after her son. She was indifferent to me most of the time, and was absolutely horrible to Papa. She couldn't speak to him without mentioning how dark his skin was. She forever blamed him for mama dying. I can't say that I was too sad when *she* died...," her voice trailed.

"Then why move here?"

"Because it was familiar," she said simply. "My great-grandmother was still alive at the time, too, and I did like *her*, very much."

I tried to conjure up some memory to go with her statement, but that first year had all been such a blur. I couldn't remember much about it except for the confusion over the move, the sudden hunger and feeling that there wasn't enough, the feeling of standing out when school started, and, of course, Patrice.

"I don't remember her," I stated.

"I don't imagine you would have. When you were younger, she scared you because she was blind by the time you met her. We'd stayed with her when we first moved here, but then she died."

She handed the photo album to me. "That first picture, that's my grandmother, Regina," she leaned over and flipped the page of the album for me. "And those are her parents."

I looked at the couple, only mildly surprised by them. The woman in the photograph looked nearly white, especially in contrast to the man she stood beside, for he was very dark in comparison. The man was extremely handsome, and obviously where the looks in the family had come from because the woman wasn't very pretty at all. She was plain, almost homely looking; had she been fully white, she probably would've never married. I felt bad for her, not necessarily for her looks, but because of the color of her skin. How unpleasant it must have been for her to look one race, told that you were another, and not know where you were supposed to fit in. It was hard enough for me just being considered light skinned and having my features. But at least I had some color. She, on the other hand, could've easily passed for white.

I tried to dredge up some memory of my past with her in it, but simply couldn't.

"My great-grandfather was Brewster, and the woman is Sibyl, like me. She, Sibyl, told me that the reason she married Brewster was because he was so dark…so her kids would have some color, and maybe a place in the world. Sibyl's grandfather was a White man, and her mother and father were two of those by-products of one of those house servant factories. It was *my* daddy who actually explained to me what they were, but during slavery, light skinned house servants were sometimes valued, so a man had this idea to 'create' them.

"Big Sybil once told me that she hated her skin so much that she used to cry herself to sleep at night. Said she used to pray that God would make her darker, but Nana Regina was the opposite. She'd always claimed she loved her daddy, but she hated every little bit of her that looked Black. She was *so* mean to Papa," she repeated. "I had to ask Big Sibyl why, once, and that's when she explained to me about how her mother had come into the world. About skin in general.

"The Christian part of me, the part that believes in a better world, a better future, wants to tell you that it doesn't matter. That it's just skin, and love will triumph over it all, but I've seen the damage that skin's done to my family, alone, and I think there's too much between us to ever really get along.

"I don't like the feelings that you have for this boy. I don't want you to get hurt by him. It's hard to imagine that any of them hold true feelings, when they've done so much to us. Them setting fire to the Trick, they only needed a reason: Pollie was just convenient. They didn't do it because he caused that accident, they did it just because they could. Because they don't think that we should have nice things, or should find any sort of peace or enjoyment in life. They're raised from the time they're children to look down on us, and as much power as love's supposed to have, I don't think that's something that you can so easily overcome."

She suddenly looked at me, and I was trying very hard not to look at her. "I know you don't want to hear this," she acknowledged, "but I'd rather you hear me say it to you now, instead of finding this out for yourself once it's too late."

"Derek wasn't one of the one's down at the Trick that night, mom. He's not like that."

"Until he proves that he is," she predicted. Her words brought back images of that night at Chase's. He'd apologized, and I'd let that be enough, but was it? Would there always be those opposing sides? Was there really this invisible fence between us that would forever keep us from coming together?

Silently, we went back to separating photos. The two of us started on another one of the albums before either of us noticed the time, and I remembered that I'd been on my way over to Patrice's. My mom wished me a good first day, and I said good-night to her with the conversation still on my mind. Was I setting myself up for heartache by entertaining the thought of Derek? She made it seem as if the answer was an inevitable 'yes'.

— 30 —
"Figure on the Bed"

The next morning we pulled into Mason's parking lot at 7:40. Instead of heading into the common area, we lounged around in the side parking lot with the other seniors and idly talked about our summers. For once, instead of heading to my first class, or disappearing into the library, I stayed and talked, sharing my summer with my classmates. I walked around proudly with my new hairdo, wearing store bought clothes that my aunt had gotten me on our trips to places that they'd never even heard of before.

Very few people talked about the more tragic events of the summer: Bobby dying, the riots, the rising student movement, and why would we? When JFK died, for maybe three or four days, life seemed to simply stop. But then it went back on again. People don't easily forget how to laugh, to smile. You pick up a Coke, marvel at the taste of it, and it doesn't even register that while you're drinking it, 47 people died in Watts. Your best friend could have died 10 days before the President rolled through your town in his presidential motorcade, but you would still jockey for position in the hopes that maybe *he* will look at *you*, and smile your way.

So we talked about the things that mattered more to us, and for this one instance, I happily joined in. When the bell rang, none of us were anxious to leave. We had the timing of the bells down by now, and knew that you didn't have to rush just to get to class on time. That there was time to finish up a conversation.

My new schedule this year actually held some promise, and my first class of the day was guaranteed to be the most challenging one that I would take at Mason: AP US Government. After seeing the syllabus, though, I wasn't too worried about the class. While Mrs. Ross talked about the course aims for the semester, I took in my classmates. There were only five people from the senior class who had decided to brave this one. I'd had at least one class with each of the people before, at some point or other, but save for their names, I did not know much about any of them. It occurred to me, now, how odd that was.

During the summer, I had known the names and future ambitions of everyone in my peer group within a few days. I knew where they were from, what their parents did, and what career track they were doing during the summer. Sitting there in class, halfway listening to Mrs. Ross talk about the philosophical origins of our constitution, I made a conscious decision to get to know and relate better to my classmates, even though in the back of my mind I knew that the chasm that separated us would only get wider as time progressed.

I was dual-enrolled this year, so by noon I was done with classes at Mason. Even though we'd gotten out early, Derek was already waiting for me in the carport when I got out of class. "How was your mornin'?" he greeted me. He looked me over, and looked again. "You look great," he observed.

I blushed as I slid into the seat. "Thank you," I remarked. "It was interesting."

He started the car. "I think that that may be tha first time I've evuh heard anyone say that 'bout tha first day of school. What made it interestin'?"

I turned towards him so that I could see him better. "What did you want to be when you were little?" I wondered, not directly answering his question.

"A fireman," he said, without thought. He sat straighter at those words. "Just like my daddy."

"And now?"

"Apparently an accountant," he answered. "Why do you ask?"

"Do you think you would have wanted to be a fireman if your dad hadn't been one?"

"Course I would 'cause they're tha coolest guys in tha world."

"Why don't you still want to be one?"

He scratched the side of his cheek. "My parents want me to have uh bettuh life; not just be some workin' stiff for all of it. Why? What'd you want to be when you was little?"

"A lawyer," I responded.

Derek smiled. "That figures," he remarked in a tone that sounded a lot like admiration. "You hungry? I've convinced mama to make her little boy lunch today, so unless you have othuh plans, I thought we could go ovuh to the 'rents."

"Did you tell your mom that you were bringing company?"

He looked at me from beneath his thick lashes in a way that brought a blush to my cheeks. "No," he said, slowly. "I told her I was bringin' you."

Since Derek and I didn't really spend time talking about our families, I didn't really know what to expect from his. All I knew about him, in that way, was that he had a younger brother named Denny, who was in the 7th grade this year, and that his parents were still married. At our arrival Mrs. King met us at the door with a plate of crispy squares, the very picture of domesticity. Although he was thinner, Derek looked strikingly like his mom. They were the same height, and had the same eyes and hair. Her smile seemed more formal, compared to the abandon that claimed her son's features whenever he smiled, but their laughs were similar.

It was her day off, he informed me, but she didn't seem slightly bothered that her son was coming over. She seemed genuinely happy to see him, actually, and fawned over him for a few minutes before she released him. "So this is Tracy?" she stated, looking me over from head to foot. "You know he does nothin' but talk 'bout you," she informed me. "So, tell me everythin', so I can see if it's true."

I wasn't quite sure how to respond. I looked over at Derek for guidance, but he only gave a lazy little shrug, and Mrs. King leaned on me until I started talking. When I told her that I was a senior this year, the first words out of her mouth were, "Do you know that Carol Torcette? She was *such* a sweet lil thing. I just cain't figure why tha two uh them evuh broke up." I hid a smile because I was indirectly one of the reasons why the two of them had broken up. "Derek always likes tha nicest girls; I for tha life uh me can' figure why he's single."

Derek gave me a sideways look at this one, wiggling his eyebrows, and I almost started giggling. I was curious as to the nature of what Derek had told her about me, but judging by her words I was sure Derek hadn't put me in any sort of romantic context. Or maybe he had, and his mother was just ignoring it.

After lunch there was more of that strange plurality: she continued to tell me about how great a guy her son was, as if hoping I would pick up on it, but continued to extol the virtues of his old girlfriends. Mrs. King brought out the photo albums, and had just gotten started on them, when she had to leave to pick up Denny from school. Derek volunteered to do it, so I went along with him, eager to meet the youngest member of the family.

Derek's little brother shared Derek's eye color and nothing else. His hair was dark, too, but closer to brown, and his features were more round, like his mother's. He and Derek talked all the way from the school, to his parents' house, and when we got there we ended up staying a while longer because Mr. King was home now, and Derek couldn't leave without spending time with his dad.

"I didn't know lunch would last that long," Derek apologized when we were finally alone in the car, heading away from the north side of town. "But I thought you two should meet."

"And why is that?" I wondered.

The smile that teased his lips was easily readable. He shrugged. "It got me a free meal."

We were going to go straight over to the studio after we left Derek's house, but on the way I remembered something I needed to take care of, so Derek took me home. He hesitated in the drive, as if he didn't know whether or not to wait. "I'll only be a minute," I assured him.

His door opened. "Can I use your restroom?"

"Go out back," I teased. He made like he was actually going to do it, and I called him back to the house. I gave a quick glance behind me, scanning the neighborhood. I wasn't really concerned about the neighbors, but I didn't want their words to get back to my mom. Derek bounced on the balls of his feet, reminding me of his need, so I showed him where the bathroom was before I went into my room to look for the information I needed for a scholarship application that was coming due.

"So *this* is tha inner sanctum of Tracy Burrows," Derek declared from the doorway, his voice filled with pretend wonder. I hadn't heard his footsteps, so his voice startled me. The hairs on the back of my neck stood on end at the sound of it, and I found myself suddenly nervous. I think it might've had something to do with the thought of Derek being in my room. If by some chance my mom was to walk into the house right now, she'd probably skin me alive…yet there was still a part of me that was actually happy to have him in my space; maybe because there was something forbidden, and extremely personable, about it. "I think I should feel privileged," he declared wondrously, walking towards me. "What're you doin'?"

"I remembered some papers I had that needed to be mailed soon for a scholarship application. I should only be a minute."

"Okay," he responded, looking around. He walked over to my wall, briefly giving a glance at the news photos I'd collected over the years: of students sitting at lunch counters, Emmett Till's disfigured body, and of Civil Rights workers protesting, of Dr. King, and Huey P. Newton, and Rosa Parks. Many had been taken from newspapers my Grandpa sent, but there were a couple I'd collected from the *Bakersfield Times*.

Derek stopped in contemplation of a poster board I had taped up in the middle of the images. "*Gideon v. Wainwright*," he read off. "What's all this?"

"Court cases that I think are pertinent to Civil Rights," I replied.

"Why're there numbers on them?"

"It's the case's docket number…for when they go to court. You know like docket number 379 U.S. 241, Heart of Atlanta Hotel v. United States, et cetera. It's just a way for the courts to keep track of all the cases," I said with a shrug.

Derek continued to read even after I was done explaining. "I know some uh these," he remarked. "Plessey v. Ferguson…Loving v. Virginia," he paused, abruptly. I didn't look at him at his pause, but I wondered what expression his face carried; if he knew the significance of that particular case. Loving v. Virginia had just been decided the year before, and had struck down the laws that prohibited interracial marriage. "I membuh Dad mentionin' that one," was the only mention Derek made of it, though. "What's this one, Missouri ex rel. Gaines v. Canada? The state of Missouri sued Canada? Can they do that?"

— 303 —

I laughed, slightly. "Cy Canada was the registrar at the University of Missouri," I explained. "Gaines helped to break open upper education to Blacks and other minorities." Gaines had been one of the cases Thurgood Marshall had brought before the Supreme Court. "In the late 1930s, Gaines tried to enroll in the University of Missouri's law school; he was denied admission solely because he was black. Although it set legal precedent, the original case was eventually dropped because the plaintiff disappeared during the trial. His whereabouts are still unknown."

Derek nodded as casually as I said it. "What's Co…rim…mat…tu? What's uh Corimmatu? Zoo?"

"Korematsu v. U.S. attacked the constitutionality of internment camps. In 1943, Hirabayashi v. United States upheld that a curfew affecting only Japanese Americans was constitutional. They weren't exactly progressive cases, but Earl Warren, the attorney general of California at that time, was one of the biggest pushers of the internment legislations. I guess he had a change of heart in later life."

"Who's he?"

"Warren? He's the chief justice of the Supreme Court who handed down the majority decision in Brown v. Board of Education," I explained.

Derek looked as if I were speaking Greek. "Was Brown important?" he wondered.

"We'll see," I said in answer. "It decided that 'separate but equal' was inherently unconstitutional because it created a wholly unequal feeling of inferiority, but it was passed in '52, and here it is 14 years later and most schools are still segregated."

"Mason's not," Derek remarked proudly.

"No, it's not," I agreed. "On paper anyway."

He turned back to my poster with the court cases, and I turned back to my desk. "So why d'you keep all this?" he questioned after a moment had passed.

"I find it interesting," I remarked with a shrug. "We're poised on a turning point in history: the arts are changing, education is changing, mindsets are changing. Look at where this country was with Plessey, to where we are right now. In fifty more years, look at where we can be: women and men making the same wages, all races living in mutual respect and appreciation of one another, workers in more control of their future?" Reality took my enthusiasm down a notch. "Okay, so maybe not fifty years, but the legal system has been, and is going to be, one of the biggest proponents of that change."

"So law is goinna change tha world?" he questioned, teasing.

"Why not? At one point laws helped to divide it; they should be responsible for fixing it."

"And you're going to be the one to do it," Derek remarked.

I smiled. "I know that I'm not going to change it all by myself, but with time, all things change. Children grow up, and they adopt different ideals from their parents as their experiences guide them. Warren had a change of heart, and you know something? Rosa Parks wasn't trying to change the world when she sat down; sometimes great movements are born for no other reason than because someone becomes too tired to move to the back of the bus."

Derek's progression moved him to my bookshelf. He read the titles off the spine of the books. "Carter G. Woodson," he said aloud, pulling the book down. "The Mis-education of Tha Negro." He flipped to the middle of the book, read something, and then placed the book back on the shelf. Beside Woodson's book was Voltaire, followed by some bound papers written by Booker T. Washington. To the right of that was my collection of Charles Dickens, and beneath it I had my Rousseau, Shakespeare, Hughes, Alexandré Dumas, a man who my Grandpa was intensely fond of, and my two well-read novels by Chinua Achebe.

Most of my books had been Christmas and birthday presents from my Grandpa since the Bakersfield library had only recently allowed Blacks to have a library card. For years, I'd had to make do with the small church collective library in the Trick. The collective, my Grandpa, and the occasional book from my mom and aunt, had helped to fill in the void that not having access to the main library left.

"Hung Lou Meng? What's this?"

I squinted at the book he pulled out. It was gray, noticeably dingy, and only one of several volumes. I had a translated copy of parts of the story, but the copy that he picked up was in Chinese. My aunt had hunted it down for me, and even though I couldn't read the language, I held on to the Chinese copy with the vain hope that one day I'd actually learn how.

"It translates into *Dream of the Red Chamber*," I attempted to explain.

He reacted to the word 'red'. "Communist literature in your bedroom, Trace?"

I laughed. "Not 'red' as in Commie, Derek. It's supposed to be a very popular Chinese book series written long before Marx came on the scene."

"What's it about?"

"I don't have the full story, but it's mostly about family, sacrifice, scholarship, and...religion. It's really hard to describe."

"You've a lot of books," he noted.

"I read a lot," I replied.

"I see," he said, wryly. He turned away from the bookshelf to look at me. "So where're your posters of tha Beatles and Sidney and Mickey?" Derek questioned, teasing. "Your pillow with tha Monkees on it?"

"Why am I supposed to have a pillow with monkeys on it?"

"Not monkeys... *The* Monkees. You know," he started flailing his arms, "'Hey hey, we're tha Monkee's, people say we monkey...'" His hands fell back to his side. "Nothin'?"

I laughed. "Am I supposed to have those?" I asked.

His head nodded vigorously. "Well, *yeah*," he said certainly.

He replaced *Dream of the Red Chamber* and picked up another book, lying across my bed with it, looking quite comfortable. I realized that I shouldn't be this casual around him, that he shouldn't be in the house without my mom being home, and even if he was, he certainly shouldn't be in my bedroom, lying on my bed. If one of the neighbors had seen us come in together, there would be gossip as to why I was entertaining a white boy alone. There'd be gossip even if Derek weren't white, but that tidbit just added more fuel to the gossip flame.

"I'll only be a few more minutes," I remarked.

He shrugged. "Take your time."

"What's that?" I asked.

"1984. I's supposed to read this for one of my classes." He turned over on his side, the book still in his hands, but he was facing me now. "What'd

— 306 —

yer mama do if she walked in and saw me lyin' on your bed?" So he *wasn't* without an appreciation for the intimacy of the situation. I wondered what thoughts he was currently entertaining.

"Kill you, probably," I said, just as casually as he'd asked the question. "I'd get grounded. She might even get a switch," I added.

"Bet she don' know how to switch good," Derek remarked. "Didn' get much practice on you."

"I bet you're wrong," I replied.

"I used to get beat all tha time," he stated, honestly. "My dad doesn' like to hit any more than necessary, but I always earned 'em. Playin' on uh trestle bridge, jumpin' off of uh train, that type of thing. Bet you nevuh did nothin' like that," he challenged.

"I've never been stupid enough to play on a trestle bridge, no, but me and Brian got into our share of things when we were little."

"Brian?"

"My best friend in Illinois," I remarked.

"Like what?" he challenged. "I don' believe for a second that Miss Tracy evuh did nothin' to make mama mad."

"There you go making losing bets again," I remarked.

"Alright, well tell me somethin', then, and none of that wimpy girly stuff counts."

"I've never really done any of that 'wimpy, girly stuff'," I asserted. "So, no worries there."

"I'm waitin'."

"Okay," I remarked, thinking. "Once, during the winter, when we woke up, there was like snow everywhere. Me and Brian were up at first light, and while we're out playing in this waist high snow, we hear rumors that overnight someone had buried a treasure underneath it, and there were signs up all over the neighborhood, leading to the treasure. Without telling anyone, me and Bri spend all day looking for it. When we got back to the house, my mom nearly threw out her arm wearing me out. The only time she paused was to let me know that anyone could have put the signs up, and that that was very stupid. I kept trying to get her to understand that it wasn't anyone, it was *magic*."

Derek's body shook, biting down hard on his lip, trying very hard not to laugh. "So was there actually uh treasure?" he wondered.

I nodded. "Yep. Bobby West's dad had buried a little box full of quarters in the snow, and then put up signs that led up to the box."

"Did you and Brian find it?"

"No," I said regretfully. "Henry Carrol did. Me and Brian kept getting drawn into snow ball fights, and of course we had to sled down every hill we came across."

"That doesn't count," Derek declared, after a moment.

"Let me see *you* stay out all day with waist high snow and freezing temps! Schools here get shut down if there's even the possibility that snow might fall at some point. And anyway, I didn't say that was the most adventurous thing that we did, that was just the type of thing Brian and I used to get into. There was this one time that we took our sleds up to the roof of Mr. Hatcher's barn and sledded off of that-,"

"Still not-,"

"...when there wasn't any snow on the ground," I finished. "Brian broke his leg."

Derek looked slightly impressed. "I bet you got beat senseless for that," he said, giving an appreciative nod.

"Nope; *I* didn't get in trouble at all because Brian kept it secret that I was up there with him, too. And I didn't break *my* leg," I had to add.

Derek thought about it, a smile playing on his lips. "Who went first?" he questioned.

I gave Derek a devilish grin. "He did."

"And you did it *aftuh* he broke his leg?"

"Well...I didn't know it was *broken,* and, I mean I was already on the roof...and then there was that time we once rode our bikes into the lake. That was pretty fun. We didn't get caught doing that, either, but it took the rest of the day to fish the bikes out, and we had to rub them down with oil so they wouldn't rust."

"You really did those things?" he wondered.

I nodded. "Why do you sound so surprised?"

"Because I didn' know you had it in you, Trace. Who knew you knew how to have fun?"

"Just because I don't enjoy your brand of fun, doesn't mean I don't know how to have it."

"Evuh done any drugs."

"No." I glanced at him. "I assume that you have by the way you asked that?"

He shrugged. "What about cigarettes?"

"I tried it once when I was little. But they're gross."

"Pinch some baccy. Liquor?"

"No."

He grinned, his smile going from ear to ear as his face turned red. "Do tha horizontal polka?"

"I can't even do the vertical polka, much less the horizontal one," I responded.

"I can break you into both," he remarked, joking. I was sure it was a joke anyway. I didn't say anything to that. I turned back to my work, and Derek picked the book back up, but that didn't last too long. He rolled off the bed and came and stood behind me. "What'cha workin' on?"

"The same thing I was working on a few minutes ago."

"You're not bein' uh good host. I'm lonesome ovuh here."

"I can call Patrice to come over."

He pulled me up to my feet. "I don' want Patrice. I want you." He held on to my hands, swinging them. "Come play wit' me, Trace…"

For a brief moment, I forgot what I was doing. I met Derek's gaze, my brown eyes meeting his playful blue ones. Every cliché in the world cropped up to mind concerning his eyes, but they really did remind me of water. Not like the frosty, freezing, water of the Pacific, but more like the calm, softer, tamer blue of Florida, just without the splash of green.

"You have the oddest eyes," Derek remarked, cutting into my thoughts of his. "They're like three different colors."

"Everybody's eyes are three different colors," I remarked smartly.

"Quit bein' an ass. I mean like your eyes are like dark brown, light brown, and hazel. Like tha hazel separates tha two browns, it's weird."

"It only looks like that because of the light. Sometimes they look dark gray, or light brown, or dark brown." It was an inherited trait, something I got from my dad's side of the family. We all seemed to share these cat-like hazel eyes. (My Uncle Wally's eyes were so clear that it was sometimes unnerving to look at him).

"I like them," he decided.

"I'll pass that along to my father," I returned smartly. "He'll be delighted to know that."

"Are you always this sarcastic?"

"No, not always," I remarked, "just when the proper occasion arises." I turned away from him and his eyes.

"So I don' get it: why d'you study so hard if'n you're so smart? I mean you could pass your classes wit' your eyes closed. Why d'you do all this? Why d'you read these books, and memorize dates that no one's goin' to ask?"

"Why not? I find it all interesting," I remarked. "And it will help me out later on."

"When you're this big, high powered attorney, knockin' heads around, kickin' butt left and right?" He did some fake fighting moves.

I laughed at his theatrics. "That's right. My ultimate goal is for them to someday make me into a *Barbie Doll*. Career-Action Tracy."

"With Kung-Fu grip," Derek added, a note of amused admiration in his voice.

— 31 —
"The Kiss of Life"

Patrice came up to my locker, just as I was about to slam it closed. She leaned against the adjacent one. "They're doin' a special skate night at tha rink down South Parkway tomorrow night," Patrice stated. "You comin'?" She asked it in a compulsorily way; as if he already knew the answer I'd give, and was just asking because she should.

I adjusted the books in my hand. "The Parkway? Since when do you go to," I realized I didn't even know the name of the white rink. "What about Pink's?" I questioned. Pink's was our rink, the one in the Trick.

"It's a bunch uh us from tha float committee, and they wouldn' feel comfortable at Pink's."

"And you'll feel comfortable at Figure 8's?" I wondered, the name suddenly coming to me. Figure 8 was on the south side of town, an area we didn't frequent if we could help it. "Why do we always have to be the ones that give?"

She shrugged. "Supposedly Figure 8's got tha bettuh floor," she remarked. "And bettuh skates."

"You have your own skates," I pointed out.

She shrugged again. "Look, Trace, they're goin', so I just thought I'd go too; don' make a federal case uh it."

"Is Alex going?"

"Well, duh," she remarked, as if that was a given.

"I don't want to be a third wheel."

"So, bring someone. Bring Derek. Y'all togethuh now, ain't you?"

My lips pulled into a frown she wasn't really supposed to see. "No," I said flatly.

She gave me her best 'don't bs me', look. "Y'all ain't done nothin' yet?" she questioned, doubtfully.

"Something like what?"

She rolled her eyes. "Use your imagination, girl," she directed. "Seems like every time I talk ta you, you're at Derek's, or you're wit Derek, and girl who could miss tha way y'all look at each othuh? If I didn' know bettuh I'd say y'all's about to go at it every time y'all in tha same room togethuh. Is he your boyfriend or what?"

"Since that hasn't come up between the two of us, I'm going to say that he's not."

Her hands went to her hips. "Y'all ain't kissed?"

"No." We hadn't. On occasion there was a touch, or we'd hold hands, he'd open the door for me, which meant that we were what? Friends? Something more than that? I loved him, obviously, and there was some strong feelings on his part, but was it love? My heart told me that we were much more than friends, yet he hadn't even kissed me yet. Was I not kissable? "I think he came close once," I responded. "But that was mostly out of anger."

I started down the hallway, and Patrice followed. "Girl, that's tha best kind!" she remarked with a laugh.

"Have you and Alex kissed, yet," I wondered, just for the sake of making conversation.

It was her turn to frown. "That's all we evuh do," she said, grumpily. "This is tha first time I've evuh dated a saint!"

"Shouldn't you be a little thankful for that?" I wondered. Alex came with a lot less drama than Darnell. "I mean saints don't throw wrenches in your future plans."

She didn't agree. "Saints be tha ones who get it in they heads ta get married right aftuh graduation," Patrice remarked. "You should want me ta be wit tha bad boys."

"Have you given any more thought to college?" I questioned at her words. "Graduation isn't that far away. We're not freshmen anymore."

She casually dismissed my words. "I can barely get past tomorrow. So, you comin'? Alex's got a cousin our age. I can tell him ta bring him along, and there's always Preacha."

— 312 —

That would probably be really awkward. I hadn't really said more than a passing word to Ricky since sophomore year. "I've got homework," I remarked.

"Trace," she grunted. "This's our last year, girl! Next year you're goinna be a million miles away, and we're nevuh goin' be able ta hang out like this no more. Put tha books down, just for a little while. It ain' like you can' afford a coupla B's."

"No, right now, a couple of B's *will* kill me. After January, I promise, I'm all yours. For the last semester we can do whatever you would like."

"Why's that?"

I smiled. "I apply for college in November."

I think I was as ready as it was possible to be. I had ranked all of my teachers according to how well I did in their classes, and how well of a recommendation letter I thought that they'd write. I had my test scores submitted, I even had the applications filled out and ready to go; I just had to wait for the admission season to open up so I could send them.

I felt pretty confident. My transcripts were good, and I'd had enough teachers who liked me-most of them had, actually-to get a couple of good recommendation letters. I'd secured a character witness from the pastor of my mom's church, my school record was blemish free-except for that bogus cheating scandal (which hadn't made it onto the record)-and I had some pretty great academic work outside of what was considered standard. I'd achieved a 675 on my boards, I'd taken college prep courses, I had four years of a foreign language, I already had some undergraduate credit thanks to the scholar's program, and I was on the list of notable high school students for Science and for English. I'd spent my entire high school career doing what I was supposed to, as best as I could. Come spring we'd see how it'd turn out.

I changed my mind about the skate party and decided that if my mom could spare the dollar, I'd go after all. I only had a light homework load, no club activities, and Derek had to work. I rode with Patrice and Alex in the pastor's car, and wished for the first time that I had a car of my own; or at least got to drive my mom's every now and then. All of the boys in the neighborhood started driving as young as fourteen, and even most of the girls were able to convince their parents to let them drive every now and then, but not me. It was the one area my mom didn't feel I needed the independence.

Figure 8 was thoroughly on the white side of town, and probably a favorite hang-out of the Chatham and Barclay kids. The rink was definitely an upgrade from Pink's. Pink's was mostly loud music and dim lighting, and you had to compete with the adults who frequented the place. But Figure 8 was freshly painted, full of color, light, and, of course, the requisite loud music. I vaguely recognized *Dance to the Music* blasting over the speakers, and Patrice started swaying to the beat nearly as soon as we walked through the doors.

I paid my $.25 skate rental fee, got a locker, and stashed my stuff inside. Patrice and Alex waited patiently for me to put the skates on, but I waved them away as soon as our other classmates were on the floor.

Once I was laced up, I tried it out on the carpet before even attempting to move out onto the floor. Easy enough, I told myself. Balance. Eight wheels had to be as stable as two feet. Maybe. With no conscious recollection of a decision to actually move onto the floor, I found myself suddenly on it. I thought about everything I knew about aerodynamics and motion, realized that that would do me no good, and just did my best to stay on my feet while everyone in the rink skated around me.

Just when I was confident that I'd gotten the hang of it and felt like being adventurous, I realized that my arms were suddenly wind-milling because I'd begun to lose my balance. I braced myself for the impact, but instead of falling on my behind, I hung suspended in the cushion of someone's arms. I looked back, and into the smiling face of my savior. "Looks like you're falling for me, Tracy," Damien said.

I returned the smile. "Thank you, Damien," I replied. "Perfect timing." He laughed, familiarly.

Damien, who had longer than average dark brown hair and eyes to go with his deep-brown mahogany skin, was a friend of a friend; one of those classmates that I'd had at least one class with every year. I knew he was on the college tract, like me, but we hadn't spent much time talking to each other in the past. "Well, you looked like you were in need of a hand," he stated.

"I'm lucky you had two," I replied wittily. He sat me back on my feet, and I wobbled a little. I grabbed hold of his arm to steady myself. "Guess I'm not very good at this."

"Nah," he said, easily, "you're perfect." It didn't escape my notice that he was being purposely flattering, and I didn't mind. "You just gotta spend more time here."

I smiled in response to his charm. "I'm not much of a skater," I admitted. "As you can see." I wasn't really embarrassed about that, but I felt as if I should be.

He extended a hand, along with another smile. "S'okay, I'll show you," he offered. There was only a slight pause on my part before I gratefully took his hand.

It turned out that Damien wasn't much better at skating than me, which somehow made him a great partner. He kept me on my feet, didn't go too fast, and didn't mind going slow when I needed to. The thought struck me that I probably shouldn't be having as much fun as I was having, but that thought didn't trouble me for very long. I didn't end up on the floor again for the rest of the evening, and I even played some of the skate games, Damien close by my side. I only sat out when they did the *Hokey Pokey* on the rink floor, convinced that that would've just been pushing my luck.

"Hey, so's this is just a thought," Damien remarked, as he helped me out of my skates. "If you're maybe not doin' anythin' for Homecomin', how'd you like to be my date to the dance?"

Homecoming? Was it really that late in the semester? I had to do a mental calculation to calm myself down, because it wasn't time for Homecoming, not yet; Damien was just an early planner. It made me smile to myself. "I wasn't planning on going to the dance," I remarked.

"Okay," he said, quickly, easily. I don't think he actually expected me to say yes anyway. Even though we'd had classes together, we'd never really talked outside of normal classroom conversations. I wondered what compulsion had made him ask me to the dance.

"How about prom?" I suggested.

"Really?" he wondered, trying not to sound so surprised.

"If you're asking," I said clearly, "I'd love to go to prom with you Damien."

There wasn't even a moment of hesitation on his part. "Tracy, will you go to prom with me?" he questioned eagerly.

"It's a date," I remarked. I realized my smile was still there as he skated away, and I was pleasantly pleased. It wasn't until May, but I had a date!

Patrice skated up to me, stopping easily in front of me. "You and Damien were lookin' really cute out there," she noted.

"I had a blast, 'Triece," I informed my friend, eagerly, anxious to tell her my news. "And *guess* who has a date to prom!"

She easily connected the dots. "Prom? Really? You and Damien?"

I nodded, vigorously, still tickled by the idea. "He wanted to go to Homecoming, but I told him I wasn't going, so I suggested prom, and he asked me!"

"Why aren' you comin' ta Homecomin'?" Patrice asked.

"Because I can't dance…"

"So, learn! No one's born bein' able ta dance; they work at it. They watch *Dance City Music Hall*, or their big brothuhs or sistuhs, or they copy TV, or they just make uh fool of themselves, by themselves, until they figure: what tha hell, I'll just do it! This is our last Homecomin.'"

"So, it won't miss me not being there. I'm going to prom, though, and I'm counting on you to help me not make a fool of myself by May."

Patrice pretended like she was studying me. "Hon, I don' think that's goin' be enough time," my friend teased. Her brow furrowed, suddenly, at a thought that just occurred to her. "What do you think Derek'll say 'bout you goin' out wit Damien?"

"Well since we're 'just friends', he shouldn't have a problem with it," I stated.

"Yeah, okay," she dismissed. She started skating backwards away from me. Show off.

After my visit to Figure 8, I was convinced of two things: one, I needed to learn how to skate, and two, I needed to learn how to drive. Marcus would have been my first choice in a teacher, but since he was living in Nashville, he wasn't really an option. I don't think Sean would have the patience, and I wasn't really sure why, but I was hesitant to ask Derek to teach me. I think it was because the act seemed kind of intimate to me for reasons I couldn't pinpoint.

I hadn't lied to Patrice when I said that Derek and I really hadn't done anything so far. Either Derek was a saint himself, or he just wasn't in to me in a physical way. Even though he did boyfriend things all the time, I didn't connect that word to him, and wouldn't. Until he said it, I wasn't going to think of him in that way.

A few days after we'd gone skating, Derek's car was waiting in its usual spot in the car lot when I got out of class. We'd gotten out a little late, so Derek had decided to park. He was listening to the radio and alternately playing air guitar and wheel drums along with the musicians. His head turned right at the moment I walked up, and as his eyes locked on mine, he grinned. "How was class," he wondered through the open window, his hand still raised to slap the wheel.

"Mrs. Ross loaded us down with homework, but other than that it was good. You?"

"We learned about unearned accounts and accounts payable." He yawned to emphasize just how exiting he thought the material was. His fake yawn elongated into a real one as I got into the car. He blinked.

"Tired?" I questioned.

His mouth snapped shut as he smiled. "Little. Long night carried ovuh into an early mornin'. You know how it is."

Derek had taken up another night job on top of the repairs for the studio, school, and the job he already had. "You're not overdoing it, are you?" I questioned. "Why're you working so much?"

For some reason he blushed. "How else am I supposed to pay for this trip to France?" Until he said those words, I'd forgotten all about his former pretense for coming up to the school.

"So, about that trip," I questioned. He was already grinning. "You don't come up to the school anymore," I stated.

"No time," he said promptly.

I was already certain of the answer, but still I questioned, "Were you ever planning a trip to France?"

"Course I was...one of these days," he remarked. "I still figure on goin',

— 317 —

but only once you can come wit' me. Otherwise, it wouldn' be worth tha trip."

I allowed myself a smile. "And why's that?" I questioned.

He reverted to his favorite French accent. "Par ce mon français es terrible. 'Sides, Trace, who else can I count on to fill me in on all tha important historical facts 'bout tha Louvre, and tha Seine, and tha French Quest for Independence, or whatevuh?" he made it sound like those things were dire to know for the sake of such a trip.

"So, you were only coming up to the school..." I led, wanting him to admit that he'd been coming up there to see me. I never pushed it, but I suddenly wanted some sort of validation for our relationship.

"To see Patrice, duh! Who else would I come up to tha school for? Am I headin' to tha studio?"

"Actually, I've got a couple of errands to run. I've got this big project for school, and I need supplies, so if you want to drop me off, or if you don't mind chauffeuring me around?-"

Derek kind of grimaced. "I kind of have something at the studio I want to get done before I go into work. Why don' you just drop me off when I have to go in, and that way you can use my car while I'm working?" he suggested.

I wondered if he realized that he was offering to leave me in custody of his vehicle. "I don't know how to drive," I admitted. I realized that it would have been the perfect moment to ask him to teach me, but I didn't.

"How do you not know how to drive?" he asked.

"My mom's never let me drive our car. She's worried I'll wreck it."

Derek allowed himself a grin. "Smart woman."

I punched him in the arm. "Oh, you're a regular Flip Wilson, aren't you?"

He blinked at the reference, his eyes crinkling. "Oh, so you're not entirely oblivious!"

"I turn on the TV every now and then."

I realized that we'd stopped. "Trade seats wit' me," Derek said, suddenly.

"Why?"

He gave me a tortured look. "Because you're too old not to know how to drive. Come on, hurry up 'fore I come to my senses."

"You're volunteering to teach me how to drive?" I questioned, making sure I understood him correctly. I'd spent the last couple of days trying to work up the best way to ask him to do this very thing, and he was volunteering for the task? It was irritating, and frustrating, and amazing, all at the same time, how in sync we were sometimes. "I thought you said you had something you needed to do."

"This is more important," he stated. "Have you at least taken Drivers Ed?" I shook my head. I hadn't wanted to give up one of my more challenging classes to do it. "Guess you wouldn' have," he said, answering his own question. "Okay, quick crash course," I wondered if those words had been deliberate. "On tha baseboard you have your break, tha clutch, and tha gas. Clutch is on the left, break is in the middle, gas is on tha right. Your gear shift is right here," he placed my hand on top of the stick, and went through the positions, showing me how to shift gears.

"Steerin' wheel," he said, nodding at it. "Tha proper position for hands is at 10 and 2, but if you hold your hand at 12," his hand clutched the top of the wheel, "it leaves your right hand free to either hold your sweeties hand," he briefly reached for mine, "or to put an arm around them. That's why I prefer cars that don' have bucket seats; that way she can slide right next to you." He'd said all this in a rush. "Okay, switch with me," he directed.

He slid up so that I could scoot behind the driver's wheel, and he moved awkwardly over into the passenger seat. He pulled the seat belt around him. It was the first time I'd seen him wear it. His nervousness made me slightly more nervous. "Can you show me again?" I questioned, hoping he wouldn't laugh at me. He didn't, just went through it all again, slowly.

"Got it?" he questioned.

I nodded, mostly to myself. "I think so," I responded. I positioned my feet the way he'd said to. "Like this, right?"

"Yea. And your hands?"

I knew that he was talking about the ten and two position, but I placed my hand on the top of the wheel, and with a daring that I didn't know I possessed I declared, "You're going to have to get closer, though, if you want me to put my arm around you."

To my surprise, Derek undid the belt, and slid over on the seat, underneath the bar of my arm. The sudden closeness was momentarily distracting. When I turned towards him, it brought my face dangerously close to his. Surprisingly I found a piece of his face that I didn't have memorized; four freckles on his nose that I hadn't noticed before, a slight scar above his lip that was nearly insignificant. His tongue darted out to nervously lick his lips. He gave an uncomfortable little chuckle.

"Hi," I whispered, softly, my voice higher pitched than normal. Was that my heart racing? Derek seemed to wonder the same thing, or maybe I'd spoken the words out loud, because his hand went up to touch my chest in the spot over my heart.

"Hi," he said back, just as awkward, just as unsure, and I wondered about it: surely he'd been here before. I knew better than to think that Derek was a virgin, and if he was, at the very least he had spent enough time parking for this to not be new to him. At the moment we were close enough to each other that we could have kissed; wasn't that what happened in moments like this? I realized, too, that I could make that decision, that I could cover the few inches between us, press my lips to his, and…

The awkwardness stopped me from doing that. How'd people do this? Kissing was like dancing: I didn't have any practice with it, and I certainly didn't want to do something wrong. As a blush colored my features, our eyes met each other's. For a long time, eternity maybe, we just stared at the other, having a conversation without any words being spoken. In that moment there wasn't a lie or line that he could have said without me knowing the truth of it. It was far too easy to read the desire that burned in his gaze, and tensely I waited for the feel of his lips against mine.

The spell was broken by Derek's yawn. The connection between us terminated, and we were back to what we were: two young adults sitting in Derek's car, me behind the wheel.

"I guess I shouldn' distract you like that when you're tryin' to drive," he remarked. His humor returned to his voice and he chuckled, because that's what he usually did.

Derek gently took my arm from around his shoulders, and placed my hand back on the steering wheel. He tucked a strand of hair behind my ear, and embarrassingly, goose bumps appeared where his nail accidently grazed the skin. "We'll work your way up to that," he assured, a hint of amusement in his voice. "For now, I'd be comfortable wit' both hands on tha wheel."

He gave my hand a quick squeeze to let me know that he wasn't being dismissive; I knew that, still, why hadn't he kissed me? Was he thinking about the time that he almost had, back at Nicole's? Was he just being friendly, and I misinterpreted everything? I didn't think that was the case, but still, he hadn't kissed me. Derek and I were always around each other. My best friend thought we were dating. I wondered if Damien would have kissed me by now.

It was funny how I suddenly needed verbal confirmation about something that his eyes had already stated; odd that there seemed to be a judge outside of the two of us, as if they mattered. As if anything other than Derek and I...I stopped that thought process right there. That...*that's* where girls got in trouble. That idea was a fairy tale, one where 'Happily Ever After' was assured, as if there ever could be such a thing. Of course there were other things that mattered: school, work, other relationships. College. Harvard. Boston. I didn't want a relationship anyway, I had to remind myself. So really I should be happy that we hadn't gone any further than where we were currently.

The moment was past, anyway, and I turned my attention back to learning how to drive; on navigating the empty lot. I jammed the clutch down to the floorboard, lightly eased off of it, and remembered at the last moment to push down on the gas. The car lurched forward, shockingly fast. I tried to shift into neutral at the same time I slammed on the brake. Derek winced as the car rocked slightly, coming to an abrupt, bumpy stop. "Ah geez, well there goes tha transmission," he chided.

"Sorry," I mumbled.

"S'okay," Derek remarked, patiently. "You're learnin'. Didn' really need it anyway." His thumb rubbed the pack of my hand. "Just remember: finesse." I pushed the clutch down to try again, but didn't feed the car the gas quickly enough, and we stalled out. "Gentle, Trace," he instructed, as he leaned over and restarted the car.

I did my best to think around his hand touching mine, trying to focus.

Clutch…slow release…gas. I had to fight the urge to slam on the break, reminding myself that I was protected by the tons of steel that surrounded us. I wished, almost, for something between me and Derek, too, to make me forget about his body sitting ramrod straight on the seat beside me. "Are you that scared of me crashing your car?" I questioned.

He swallowed hard. "Not scared of that a'tall," he replied. "Of you crashin'," he clarified. I forced my eyes to keep looking forward, and not at him, though all I really wanted to do was look at him. He must have finally realized that his hand was still on top of mine, because he moved it suddenly, and I did look at him, then, but only briefly. "Keep your eyes on tha road," he directed. "I'm still here."

I guess once I finally realized that I wasn't going to crash, I was able to relax enough to enjoy the feeling of being in control of the vehicle. By the time Derek was hinting that he had to be at work, I couldn't say that I felt confident that I wouldn't total Derek's car, but he left it with me, anyway, so either *he* felt confident in my abilities, or he was good at pretending.

Once I dropped him off at his job, and was left alone with my thoughts, I spent an inexcusable amount of time thinking about that moment where we could have kissed…and imagining just how good of a kiss it would have been.

— 32 —
"Found Objects"

It wasn't Derek's car, but a dinted and very rustic looking Chevy pickup that was waiting for me when I got out of class on Friday. It was hard to tell, since most of the original paint had rusted away, but I think the truck had once been green. Derek was leaning against the side, but straightened out when he saw me, giving me what I started referring to as his 'afternoon smile', this slow, simmering smile that made his eyes twinkle. I called it his afternoon smile because it was the smile that greeted me when he picked me up from Mason.

Derek handed me a piece of cloth as he held open the passenger door for me. "Put that on," he directed.

I held the bandana up against my body. "Somehow, I don't think it's going to fit," I said with a smile.

He rolled his eyes. "Put it ovuh your eyes," he directed. "I wanna show you somethin'."

"How am I supposed to see anything if I'm blindfolded?"

He waited. "Come on, Trace! We're wastin' daylight, here."

I hesitated in the doorway. "Give me a hint so that I know what I'm going into."

Derek surprised me by lifting me into the cab. He smiled at my shock. "Now, if I were goinna tell you where I's taking you, do you really think I'd blindfold you first?" he questioned. He made sure my hands were clear before shutting the door.

I leaned across to open the driver's side door for him. "How do I know you're not going to do anything to me? After all, my mom told me never to be alone with dangerous boys."

Derek laughed his way off the school grounds. "I'm dangerous," he scoffed.

"Who's truck," I wondered as we rattled along. The truck might be built to withstand an atomic explosion, but no one was about to accuse it of providing a smooth ride.

"Daddy's. I needed tha extra space." At his words, I checked the bed, but whatever was back there was obscured by a tarp. Derek nodded at the scrap of fabric I still held in my hands. "Are you goinna put that on or what?"

"I'm not sure if I trust you that much," I declared.

He steadied the steering wheel with his elbows, placed his right hand over his heart, and held his left hand up, palm toward me. "I swear I'm not goin' to kidnap you, torture you, or cause you to lose your virtue in any way, Tracy Burrows," he recited.

"You forgot to say that you wouldn't cause me bodily harm, either. The way you phrased it, dismembering is still possible."

He shook his head. "I should've brought uh gag, too," he mumbled. I folded the bandana into a rectangle and tied it over my eyes. "Thank you," Derek remarked. And then much too casually he questioned, "How's school?"

"It was school," I answered after a beat passed. I wondered if he saw the look I gave him.

"What'd you learn?"

"Why Edgar Allen Poe should never be allowed to read bed time stories to little kids."

"Poe, hunh?" he questioned darkly, giving a very sinister cackle. "What's your favorite?"

"What's my favorite what?"

"Poe poem?"

"I don't really have one," I said after a moment of consideration.

"How can you not have one?" he questioned. "It's Poe! Is that because you just like all his work, so you can' determine which is your favorite, or cause you just don' like poetry?"

I laughed. "Something in between the two," I answered. "Why, what's your favorite?"

There was an odd, but short, pause. "It's not one of tha more popular ones," he stated evasively, and I wondered if I imagined the blush in his voice. "So what's your favorite non-Poe poem, then?"

I thought about it for a second. "It's a tie between "Richard Cory" by Edwin Arlington Robinson-,"

"I know him," Derek declared, surprise in his voice. "Well, obviously not personally, but he also wrote "Miniver Cheevy", right?"

I was surprised he recognized the name. "Yes, he did."

"I like him!" he asserted. "His poems usually have tha theme of watch out for each othuh, 'cause you nevuh know who might need someone to be there for them. He reminds me of my daddy. Who's he tied wit'?"

"Paul Laurence Dunbar's, "Sympathy"."

"Every time we'd used to do somethin' wrong when we was little, Daddy would read us uh poem of his called "Debt", you know, to remind us of tha consequences of our actions. I don' know "Sympathy" though."

"It's about relating to a bird that's been caged," I remarked, reluctantly. I was glad that I couldn't see Derek's face at the moment, but I wondered why he was quiet for so long.

"Well, I can' say that I'm surprised," Derek responded eventually. "Favorite book?"

"Why all the questions?"

"I'm just makin' conversation," Derek responded, a smile in his voice. "I thought this was uh little bit bettuh than commentin' on tha scenery."

"A book called *Their Eyes Were Watching God.*"

"Haven' heard of it."

"I'm not surprised."

"Why, cause I'm White?" he questioned, lightly. "I knew Paul Laurence Dunbar, didn' I?"

"Yes, you did, and no, it's not because of that, it's because it was written before our time, and it wasn't well received by Hurston's peers when it came out. You'd have to specially order it to get it."

"Is it uh book I should pick up?" he questioned.

"You're more than welcome to," I encouraged. "I liked it a lot. I think that it's a book more for women, though. If you really want to read it, I can let you borrow my copy. It was my grandmother's, so you'd have to be very careful with it. What's yours?"

"Tha first book you publish; bound to be my favorite," Derek responded without hesitation. "What 'bout favorite music?"

"You're not going to answer?"

"I already told you what it is," he said seriously. "Music?"

"Bach's Cello Suite 1." He laughed at that making me wish that the blindfold wasn't there. "What?" I questioned.

"Nothin'," he said after a moment. It's just, you're you, that's all. I guess you're really into classical music."

"I can't say that I'm 'really' into it, but it does one up mostly everything modern because classical music has the benefit of being without words that most people can understand, so whoever's listening to it can determine for themselves what the words are. I'm pretty picky when it comes to music. I usually know within the first fifteen seconds whether or not I'll like something."

"That's all you give it? Fifteen seconds? Isn' that limitin'?"

"That's usually all it takes," I remarked, wondering if Derek could hear the smile in my voice. The road suddenly got rougher beneath the tires, and I wondered if that meant that we were no longer on paved road.

"Is that tha same for tha people in your life? Fifteen seconds, too?"

"Well, no…people are more complex. I give them at *least* fifteen minutes."

"You're pullin' my leg."

"Actually, yes, I am."

"So Cello Suite 1 is your favorite song-,"

"And "You Really Got Me is yours"," I blurted without thinking. I blushed as I said it, and hoped he wasn't looking at me.

"How do you know that?" he questioned, and I tried to pick out the emotion in his voice. Wonder? Surprise?

"Tanya Newsome told me."

"Tanya? Quinn's little sistuh?" I nodded, not knowing if he could see the gesture.

"She told you what my favorite song was?" That and a lot of other things actually. We'd shared a class together last year, and she gave me a *lot* of unsolicited information about Derek. I really wished that I could see his face. It was hard telling how he felt about that when I couldn't see him.

"She kind of has a crush on you," I admitted. I wondered if telling him that was a betrayal of trust. "So she talked to me about you all the time." She hadn't known that I had my own feelings about him, too, and even though I didn't solicit the conversations between us about Derek, I still absorbed the information greedily, especially during those months that we weren't talking.

Derek made a noise in the back of his throat. "Tanya had a crush on me." I turned to him at that, even though I couldn't see him, because in my head I could see the little half smile that must have been on his face.

"What's that noise mean?" I wondered.

The sound of his smile grew at my words. "Nothin'," he replied, loftily. "We're almost there."

The truck gave a shudder at his words. "Where's *there* exactly?"

"You'll see in uh few." Even more casually he wondered, "You finish up your paper for Rochester's class?"

"All that's left is to make my final copy," I responded, "unless you want to do that for me?"

"Seriously, Tracy?"

"I'll do the bibliography for your paper for British Lit if you do," I replied, offering a trade. "You have better penmanship than me."

"That sounds like it would come dangerously close to cheatin'," Derek said with a smirk I recognized even without seeing.

"You love bringing that up, don't you?" I questioned.

"I do," he said gleefully.

A few minutes later the truck stopped. Derek got out and helped me down, holding on to my hand even after my feet were firmly planted on the ground.

"Can I take the blindfold off now?" I questioned.

"No, we've got uh lil bit of uh walk."

I didn't like the idea of having to walk without being able to see. "I don't want to fall."

Derek gave my hand a little squeeze. "You won't," he assured me. "Trust me, sweetie, I got you." We walked in silence for about a minute before Derek cautioned, "Careful, there's uh log." I felt it out with my feet, making my way over it with Derek's help.

A bird call came not too far overhead. "Where *are* we?" I questioned, again.

"Quit bein' uh baby, we're almost there."

His words made me adopt a whiney voice. "I'm not being a baby, but my feet hurt and, and I'm tired...are we there yet?"

He chuckled. "It's uh shame you're tha only child," he teased, "you'd make uh great little sistuh. It's just uh little bit farthuh," Derek directed. We stopped after a few more minutes. "Are your eyes still closed?"

"I can't see anything around this bandana you've got me wearing," I responded. "So what does it matter?" He didn't say anything, merely waited. "All right, yes, they're closed!"

I could hear him lift his hand. "How many fingers am I holdin' up?" he questioned.

I pulled the bandana up enough to see over it. "Three," I responded.

"You cheated!" Derek accused. I pulled the piece of cloth back down over my eyes. "Thank you," he remarked, and I wondered if he rolled his eyes. His footsteps moved behind me, and I felt his fingertips on the bandana, but he didn't pull it off. "Hmm," he remarked, apparently distracted by something.

"What?" I questioned.

His finger trailed the base of my neck. "I nevuh noticed this line," he murmured. I shivered as it moved cautiously from the top of my spine to the dip right above my collar bone, before tracing that too. "Beautiful," he said, softly. Not being able to see him, I felt hyper aware of every inch of my body in approximation to his. I felt the soft whisper of his breath, millimeters away from my flesh, as he breathed in and out shallowly. I could tell that his heartbeat had increased by how quickly the little puffs came.

I turned towards him, lifting my fingers to remove the piece of cloth. Derek's fingers moved too, and he helped me untie it. The cloth fell between us, revealing him standing in front of me, his face holding a confused look mixed with...even I could see the desire that was there; I'd have been blind to miss it. A few stray strands of his hair had fallen over his eyes, so, impulsively, I raised my hand to comb them back. His hand reached up to cup the hand as I did, and as he held it, I thought that he was going to kiss my hand, but, of course, he didn't. Maybe I really was unkissable.

"We're here," he said, unceremoniously, but where 'here' was, I wasn't quite sure. Physically, we were in the middle of a field, and I struggled to see what Derek had dragged me out here to see, but there was absolutely nothing.

"Where are we?" I finally had to ask.

"Nowhere."

I was confused. "O...kay?"

"I brought you to see this," he added, walking towards the one thing that stood out: a huge, old, oak tree.

"It's nice..." I said, hesitantly. Derek just laughed at my confusion. "I picked this tree specifically for its branches. Evuh since I showed you how to drive, it had me thinkin': what else haven' you learned how to do yet? So I brought you out here to help you tick off anothuh one of your life goals today," he offered, grandly.

I ran my hand along the coarse bark of the tree, trying to figure out what he possibly had in mind. "And what goal is that?" I wondered.

"No one should be allowed to graduate from high school without havin' uh tree house to their name," Derek declared seriously. "So we've got tha weekend, if you're up for it."

I was dumbstruck. "You brought me here to build a tree house?" I wondered, skeptical.

His smile vanished. "You think that's stupid?" he questioned quickly. "I just thought..."

"No," I said, just as quickly, anxious to eliminate the response that my words had created. "I just can't believe...that you would think to do that."

After a moment of hesitation, he smiled in relief. "Yeah, so I've got planks, I've got nails, I've got uh saw...I'll even let you use my hammer...," he held it out to me until I reached for it, and then he pulled it back to his side. "Mebbe. I've cleared my schedule, so darlin', I'm yours."

Derek started back to his dad's truck, and I followed behind him. "I can handle it," he remarked, but I wasn't having that.

"Anything you can do, I can do better," I told him.

"Honey, I can do anythin' bettuh than you," Derek remarked in a sing-song voice. He did a little jig, before jumping into the air, executing a high-kick ballet-type move. He smiled an exaggerated smile as he ended with a spin, throwing his arms wide on the landing, the way you always saw the Olympians do after they finished with their floor routine, as if he were expecting flowers. It was anything but graceful, but at least he'd landed on his feet.

I raised an eyebrow at him. "Nicole," he offered as explanation, as his arms fell to his side. "You don' know how many times I've had to be Frank Butler to her Annie Oakley. Wait here, I'll be back."

"I want to help," I insisted. "It'll make unloading go by quicker."

Derek looked like he wanted to protest, but then thought better of it and just smiled, reaching for my hand. He released it only once we reached the truck. I stayed on the ground while he jumped up onto the bed, and started handing down materials to me. When the truck was unloaded, we dragged everything to the tree, and spread it out on the ground beneath it, before we got to building. We worked through the day, only pausing to eat. When it got too dark to continue, Derek took me home, promising to come back to pick me up first thing in the morning. By the early evening on Saturday, the structure was almost finished, and by Sunday afternoon everything was sanded smooth and painted.

Derek had designed our little tree house to look like a scaled down version of a real house, including windows, a balcony, and a porch. "All it needs is uh little picket fence," Derek declared, when we were finished. We stood back to admire the work. "I think it come out lookin' pretty good."

"*Pretty* good?" I questioned of his choice of words. Derek's design had been far better than 'good'. "It's a masterpiece."

He gave his usual chuckle, but I could tell he was proud of my assessment. "You know: uh person only technically creates one masterpiece in their lifetime. Tha phrase was used for apprentices. Like an apprentice carpenter would make uh table or somethin' to present uh piece of work to his master, called tha 'master piece', and if it was good, perfect, whatevuh, then he would no longer be an apprentice but uh master. Did you know that?"

I nodded. "I might have heard that before," I answered.

"Hunh," Derek said with a frown. "One of these days I'm goinna teach you somethin'."

"What do you mean? I wouldn't know anything about building if it weren't for you. You teach me something new just about every day." I was amused by how much he tried not to smile at those words.

I climbed up the ladder while Derek showed off and climbed the rope. He balanced on our little balcony rail before making an oddly graceful jump onto the roof. I wasn't as acrobatic, and he had to help me out a little bit for me to get up there. I leaned against the branch that ran through the house, admiring the view that surrounded us.

"So what number is this?" Derek questioned.

Because of the way we were sitting, I had to lean forward to look at him. "What?"

"What life goal is this?" he stressed, "Try and keep up, Trace."

"Oh, right." I tried to think of something quickly. "Umm...five."

He snorted. "Five? What comes 'fore this?"

"Mastering the potty...I think that's pretty high up there, talking, taking my first steps, and learning how to ride my bike."

"And aftuh that's graduatin' from high school, goin' to Harvard, changin' tha world..."

"I don't have to change it," I remarked. "It'll still be spinning when I'm done. What's on your list?"

"My list? Hmmm... Are we talkin' uh hypothetical list, or things that we actually plan on doin'?"

"The first."

"Hunh? Well, I wouldn' mind doin' some crazy Evel Knievel type thing like jump uh line of cars wit' uh motorcycle. Or, I'd love to know what it feels like to save somebody's life. My daddy's pulled uh man from uh burnin' buildin' before. I've always wondered what that must feel like." He held his hands up to his face, examining them. "He's held othuh people's lives in his hands. How can you not like uh man like that?" he posed rhetorically. He gave me a sudden sideways glance, his look unexpected and intense. "You nevuh asked."

I was confused by the statement, the change in his expression. "I never asked what?" I questioned.

"If he was one uh tha ones down there that night." The words seemed almost like an accusation, but there are some questions that you just don't want to know the answer to. "He wasn'," he said fiercely. "He was at home. He wouldn've just watched y'all's businesses burn," he said certainly. "If'n eithuh of us had been there, we would've been helpin' to stop tha flames." He looked up at those words, to catch my reaction. "If you evuh think to doubt that 'bout me, don'. I'd always be there by your side." There was no question about the protectiveness in his voice, the security of which he promised. As quickly as it sprang up, though, it was gone, and with the ease that I'd grown accustomed to, he changed the subject back to something lighter. "So what else's on your list?"

I wasn't as quick; it took me a moment to catch up to the change in the direction. "You already ticked most of them off for me," I reminded him.

He turned, angling himself so he was sitting completely in front of me. "Ah, come on!" he enthused. "Hypothetically, if there were no limits, what'd you want to do?"

"No limits?"

"None."

I took a minute to really think about it. "I'd like to jump out of an airplane," I said, and I could read the surprise on Derek's face. "The thought of flying terrifies me, but a controlled fall…completely different." I thought some more. "Go over Niagara Falls in a barrel, and this is one of the weirder ones but," I shrugged, "I've always wanted to crash a car. Not like a fender bender type deal, but a full on crash, like you see in the movies."

"Well, you are uh woman," he said with a smile and a laugh. "Crashin' is just second nature."

"Oh…fun-ny. You're as bad as that Volkswagen commercial: *so cheap you can afford to replace whatever she chooses to use to break, even the breaks.*"

"Who knew you were such uh dare-devil, though," he questioned.

"If it's not exciting, what are you doing it for?" I returned.

"Very true," he agreed. "You know you're strange, don' you?"

"Thank you, Derek."

He looked frustrated. "I didn' mean it like it was uh bad thin'. I wasn' tryin' to be...oh what's that word? If you weren' so smart, I wouldn' try to use big words 'round you. Malevolent!"

"Malicious?"

"Yes, that, I wasn' tryin' ta be mean spirited when I said that, I's statin' uh fact. You don' have tha same mindset as others your age."

"I don't want to go to the same places as others my age. I want something more from life."

"Too simple for you?" he posed.

"Not at all," I told him. "It's way too hard. It's too much pretending to be something that I'm not, of trying to fit in as someone that I'm not. It's like there's this pressure to place me inside this tiny little casing that they've designed for me to exist in. Ever since I got here, everyone's been trying to get me to not be me, like I shouldn't act the way I do, or I shouldn't talk the way I do. Or that I shouldn't have the goals that I do; that I shouldn't *want* to do certain things. There's so much out in the world to experience, why in the world would I want to limit myself to existing inside that small little shell? Besides, I like being me...I don't want to have to be anyone else."

Derek's hand reached for mine. "I like you bein' you, too," he remarked. "Nothin' wrong wit' wantin' tha freedom to be yourself. So what else?"

My voice became lighthearted again. "I want to travel," I continued. "Go everywhere, see everything. I want to write a book someday," I declared, surprised that I said that out loud because that wasn't really something I admitted to anyone; I barely admitted it to myself. "I know it's not going to make the *Times* list or anything like that because I just don't have that type of talent, but I mean the thought of someone finding enjoyment out of something that *I've* written; that one time, at least, I was able to get the words I meant out right."

Derek searched for something in my face. "What d'you mean?"

"I have trouble communicating sometimes," I said with a shrug. "Some people, like you, don't stumble over your words, but I do. I don't always say the right thing, at the right time, and I often don't say what I mean to. But when I write...it's different. And if I don't say it right the first time, that's why you have erasers and correction fluid."

Derek was quiet in contemplation. "Believe it or not, Trace, this smooth talkin', devastatingly handsome,"

"Tremendously humble..."

"*Stoically* humble guy sittin' in front of you ain't always able to express himself in tha way he would like to eithuh. That's why I like art. It helps those of us who are socially impaired." He grinned at me, and changed the subject. "So, I've uh question for you?"

"Just one," I teased.

"For tha moment."

I pretended I was bracing myself for the worst. "What's the question?"

"Didya really not like me just cause I asked for your help on an assignment?"

"You asked me to help you *cheat*," I corrected. "And I didn't like the way you asked, like it would have been my honor to help you. You were so unabashedly arrogant; it seemed like you kept trying to get under my skin."

Derek chuckled. "I was," he admitted. "God, I loved teasin' you, Trace. You were like this full grown adult at...14?" I nodded. "Yeah, and you were always *so* serious, I couldn' believe that anyone could really be that serious about life at your age. But you would...smile...sometimes, for no reason, I guess when you realized that you were takin' life too seriously, and I just wanted to be tha one to put that smile on your face. I...I've nevuh been as foolishly dumb as I've been whenevuh it comes to you."

"And why is that?" I questioned, curiously.

"Cause I wanted to be wit' you so much, and I didn' know how to say it." He grinned a lopsided grin, shrugging. "So what changed your mind 'bout me," he questioned before those words could really sink in. "If you hated me so much?"

"Who said that my opinion's changed?" I questioned. I expected to see him ease into my smile at my joke, but he didn't, so I took it back. I guess we were being serious. "I didn't hate you; I just didn't like you too much," I clarified.

"But-," he prompted.

I thought about it, easily remembering the exact moment that I'd fallen in love with him; the moment he forever became changed in my mind. "I guess I'd have to say it was your eyes."

Derek studied my face for a silent second before he brought his gaze up to meet my eyes, his own searching mine. I kept waiting for the effect that that had on me to subside, but it hadn't yet, and I hoped it never would. As we stared at each other, I understood why lovers sometimes just got caught up in gazing at each other. It truly was like finding that eternal point of connection. And Derek really did have an amazing pair of eyes...you could get lost in them.

"I'm attracted to people's eyes, too," he declared, after a moment's pause. We had yet to look away from the other. Unconsciously, we'd both leaned in towards each other, and I took in the full effect of his face, inches from mine. Derek's breathing had grown uneven, ragged. His hand rose, to stroke my cheek, to remove a strand of hair from my face, to scratch his nose...but it stopped midway to its destination. He looked conflicted, unsure. "It's getting' late," Derek stated, his voice barely above a whisper. "Reckon we oughta be headin' home?" I realized that my eyes had gone from looking into his, to watching his lips as he talked, tracking on to their every movement. It took a second before I connected his moving lips to the words that he'd spoken. Home. The question hung in the air around us, as fat as the heat of a summer day.

"Probably," I realized. Home was really the last place that I wanted to be at the moment, which probably meant that it was where I *should* be.

He smiled, as if he knew my thoughts, his eyes twinkling even in the growing darkness. He stood up swiftly, surprisingly graceful, and extended a hand to help me to my feet. I placed my hand in his, and he tugged swiftly, to pull me up alongside him. I rose quicker than I expected, throwing us both off balance. As I stumbled forward, he shifted to catch me, his arms closing protectively around me. There was a moment, where one, or both of us laughed, but then, without any conscious recollection of how it happened, Derek's lips were suddenly on mine, moving cautiously, testing; unsure.

And then the realization hit me: *I was kissing Derek*! Or rather, Derek was kissing me, and I was just standing there dumbfounded with him doing all the work. There was really only one remedy to that. I could tell I surprised him when my own lips moved, trying to sync with his. But since I was as much a novice as it was possible to be in that respect, I stopped, not wanting to embarrass myself.

Derek pulled away in embarrassment. "I-I shouldna done that," he remarked.

I was dizzy. "Why shouldn't you have?" I wondered, confused.

Derek studied my face in the growing darkness. "I should've at least asked. Isn' that why you pulled away?"

"I pulled away?" I questioned.

"You didn'?"

We both laughed at the same time. "Hmm," he said, contemplatively. "Well, on that note-," Slowly, he brought his lips back to mine. My hands felt awkward by my side, so I experimented with where they should go. They started out on his shoulders, but eventually they ended up around his neck, and his went around my waist. As we kissed, I began to be more aware of his body, the way it felt against mine.

The sun went down before we came up for breath, and I blinked in the sudden darkness. Derek came back to himself at the same time. "I guess we really should be gettin' home," he remarked, airily. "You probably have some essay that you're supposed to turn in. I know you have that deadline for tha Wright Grant comin' up."

I nodded, softly, still tasting Derek on my lips. "I do," I said in agreement.

"Well, come on, then," he remarked. He jumped down, before helping me climb down from the roof. When we were on the ground, he reached for my hand. "I don' want to keep you from good money, honey." His movements seemed jubilant. Euphoric. Ecstatic. I flexed my vocabulary for words of happiness; there were so many of them weren't there? Rapturous, thrilled, bliss. Exhilarated. Joyous. This, I marveled, was love.

He paused in his stride. "You still confuse me to no end, Tracy Burrows," he declared, releasing my hand. "But it keeps me on my toes." He tossed me the keys. "You can drive," he declared, a jaunty swagger to his walk.

— 33 —
"Second Class"

Sometime during the morning, a light rain had started to fall. It came down sideways with just enough force to cover every seat in the carport, making sitting down impossible. *Where was Derek?* I huddled against the unexpected cold, leaning against one of the metal pillars, and tried to keep warm. As I waited for Derek's car to show up, I realized how spoiled I'd gotten. Even though the studio was only a mile from Mason, and easily in walking distance, since the start of the semester I hadn't had to wait on Derek to come pick me up. Not even once. I hoped something hadn't happened to him.

Five minutes later, his car came pulling onto the school grounds, and stopped in front of me. "Sorry, I'm late, babe," he said, getting out. "You wanna drive? I'm beat."

"Sure." Derek slid over on the seat, so I could get behind the wheel. "What happened?" I wondered. "Did your professor let you out late?"

"No, I just lost track of time."

The rain started to pick up a little by the time we got to the studio, and I got a pretty nice soaking on the way inside. I borrowed a sweatshirt from Derek, and hung my sweater and shirt over the radiator to dry, before I got started on my homework. I managed to finish with the last of my Mason assignments before I realized I hadn't seen Derek since I started doing homework. I climbed the stairs to check on him, only to find him stretched out halfway across his mattress, fast asleep. He hadn't even made it all the way into the bed. I laughed softly, adjusting him so that he was actually lying in the bed. I started to leave, but a compulsion pulled me back to watch him.

Even asleep his hair fell in his eyes. I moved to wipe a strand from his face.

At the touch, I felt a fleeting moment of possession. He was mine. I leaned down to place a very gentle kiss on his lips, barely touching them with mine, but still his eyes fluttered opened. He looked up at me, still half-way asleep, smiling in recognition.

"Ah, babe," he mumbled. "I'm not being much company, am I?" He moved as if to get up, but I pushed him back down.

"It's okay, Dare, get some sleep."

"I'm just tired," he mumbled.

"So sleep," I directed.

"But you're here," he protested.

"I'm always here," I returned. I sat down on the edge of the bed. Slowly his eyes closed, and his breathing became regular. With only the slightest misgivings, I took off my shoes and slid underneath the sheet to take up the empty space on the bed across from him. I leaned over to give him another kiss. "I love you," I stated, softly. In response, his hands blindly reached out to pull me closer to him. I lay there with his arm around me, watching him until my own eyes closed, and I joined him in sleep.

When I woke up, Derek's chest had somehow become my pillow. He was already awake, and quietly watching me. The hand that idly stroked my hair paused when he saw that I'd opened my eyes. "Hey," he greeted. "Sorry. I fell 'sleep on you. Thanks for keepin' me company."

"Anytime," I responded.

"I love you, too," Derek assured me.

"Do you?"

He nodded. "I do. Do you know why?"

I shook my head. "No, why?"

It was like there wasn't even a pause between my asking and his response. "I love you for your heart, your spirit. I love you because of tha way you smile when you say my name. I love you because you're kind, gentle, and courageous, and because you keep me in line." He pulled my hand up to his chest, to rest above the spot where his heart beat steadily. I watched my hand move up, and down, as he breathed in, and out. "I love you because you're in tha beat of my heart, and when I'm near you, my heart changes its rhythm just to match yours."

I watched my hand as it moved in synchronized rhythm with my own heartbeat. "Who knew you were so poetic?" I questioned.

He gave a goofy grin. "Just anothuh of my many talents," he boasted. He started to lean over to kiss me, but he paused. "Are you wearin' my shirt?" I nodded. He tugged on the collar. "That's anothuh thing to add to tha list. I love you in my clothes."

As much as I didn't want to move, eventually I got out of the bed, and went back downstairs. I changed back into my now dry clothes before I went to my desk to see what else needed to be done. I had a scholarship essay that I could write, and I had a study guide that I needed to get started on. I stared at both, as if that would somehow make them get done, but my brain was still half asleep, and since my mind didn't want to cooperate, I decided to procrastinate a little longer.

I pulled out and read over the news article that my Grandpa had sent me about the Tlatelolco massacre that had happened in the Plaza de las Tres Culturas in Mexico City, ten days before the start of the Olympics. He'd sent it because he correctly assumed that there had been little mention of the massacre in the local newspapers. What the Bakersfield Times had mentioned, however, was the classless act of 'disgraced' Olympians Tommie Smith and John Carlos. The article had come with a picture of the two of them standing on their podiums in their black socks, their heads bowed, fists raised above their heads. Patrice and I'd cut out their picture from the Times, and now we both had pictures of the disgrace hanging on our bedroom walls.

I finished the article, forced myself to at least pretend to get to work, and decided to start on the most difficult of the two tasks first. Derek finally made his way downstairs. I looked up as he lifted my feet so he could join me on the couch. Once he was seated, he pulled my legs over his lap, balancing his sketch book on top of them.

I glanced over at him, even as my pencil kept moving. "What're you about to start working on?" I asked.

"A house," he answered readily, as if he'd only been waiting for me to ask so that he could share that information with me.

"You're building a house now?" It didn't really surprise me.

"I'm makin' Nicole uh doll house for her birthday," he corrected, showing the diagram to me. Even on a sketch, Derek's talent was unmistakable. The top part was purely a blueprint, drawn to scale, the bottom was a detailed sketch of what it would look like from the front and side. "What d'you think?"

"It's very…," there was really only one word that came to mind, "rectangular."

"It's supposed to be," he assured me. "It's modeled aftuh uh wall house design by Ralph Price. I wanted to see if I could sight copy tha design; this gives me an excuse to try, and Nicole gets uh new dollhouse out of it."

"You're going to ruin her for every other boy in her life, you know," I cautioned.

Derek gave an older-brother smile. "I know," he stated, "but there's no one out there good enough for her, anyway." He looked completely serious when he said that, and absolutely adorable.

"It's going to kill you if you have all boys isn't it?"

He glanced over from his drawings, sizing me up. "I don' know. Do boys run in your family?"

Instead of reminding him I never intended to have any kids, I chose to laugh instead of trying to dissuade him. "My mom has a sister and brother, and my dad has two sisters and a brother."

"And I have uh brothuh," he said in contemplation. "So it looks like I'm lookin' at uh fifty-fifty chance that I'll get uh girl."

After the words were spoken, he seemed in thought for a long second before he started idly sketching in his book.

"Who built the one that you brought to Evans?" I asked.

"That one," he replied, distractedly. "Borrowed it."

I could tell that something suddenly clicked with him, because his body stiffened completely except for the arm that moved his hand across the surface of his pad, conducting a symphony on the paper in front of him. "Derek?" I questioned.

"Hmmm…?" he wondered, his eyes remaining riveted to the pad in front of him.

"I've got something important to tell you," I said with a sense of urgency.

"What is it, babe?" When I didn't say anything, he actually looked up from his work, gazing up at me from beneath his bangs. "Yea?"

"Just trying to break your concentration," I replied. He looked confused for a second, but then he smiled at me. He leaned over to give me a quick kiss before going back to his notepad. I left him to it, picking up my own pencil and letting my words flow without any sense of direction. I could always go back and correct them later.

For some time, we worked in companionable silence, but then I looked up to see that he'd stopped working on his sketch, and was steadily looking at me.

"What?" I wondered, a smile already claiming my features.

"I could draw you all day," he told me. "You've got this line-," he reached out, and traced a curve of my jaw. "Classic," he declared.

"Could you really," I questioned, as he sank back against the cushion.

"Could I what?"

"Draw me?" I remarked.

He gave me one of his wild smiles, mysterious and reckless. "Au naturel?"

"Yes, Derek," I said, sarcastically, "let me go strip right now."

He grinned down at his notepad. "I might could do it sometime," he decided. "Tha real question, though, would be if you'd be willin' to sit still long enough for me to."

Doubtful. "Oh, you know me so well," I replied.

He laughed as he stood up. "I'm fixin' me uh sandwich. You want one?"

"Sure," I responded. He kissed me on the forehead before he went off into the kitchen. I heard the refrigerator open, but the sounds that came after that didn't sound anything like meat being placed between bread, or a knife hitting the side of a mason jar. "I need to make a run to Earl's," he called unsurprisingly. "Wanna come?"

I checked the time. "How long do you think it'll take?" I called back.

He finally appeared with two sandwiches. He handed one to me. "Not that long," he stated, "in time for you to get to class. Yes?"

"Okay," I said agreeably.

We finished our sandwiches before we drove across town to Earl's

Hardware & Variety. While we stalked the aisles, Derek never quite grabbed for my hand, but he kept reaching over, as if he might when he thought I wasn't paying attention. Since there was little that I could do to help him with his task, I idly lazed around the aisle, pausing every now and then to contemplate an item on display.

I heard heavy, squeaky, footsteps join ours, and I looked up, surprised when I realized I recognized the person that they belonged to. As usual, Roy's clothes were wrinkled and dingy, his hair wild and in terrible need of a haircut. The man he was with was slightly taller, but looked just as slovenly. He was wearing overalls that were a size too big, a shirt that might have once been white, and shoes that were old, and nearly falling apart. The two of them were wearing identical looks of displeasure at the world, and it made me wonder if surliness was an inheritable trait. As they walked past me without taking notice of me, I noticed that Roy's dad walked with a slight limp.

Roy recognized Derek at the other end of the aisle, and he brightened. "'Ey man!" he said by way of greeting.

Derek gave a friendly smile, too. "Hey, Roy. How's it goin'?"

"It's goin'," Roy said. "Me'n Pop here are doin' some repair work on tha house. What 'bout you?"

"Pretty much tha same thing," Derek responded. "Tracy and I-," at the mention of my name, Roy scanned the aisle, looking for me, "-are doin' work on tha apartment." Roy scowled as I started to walk over, and Roy's dad actually looked at me this time, instead of pushing me into the background. The look was unfriendly, and his eyes narrowed as I got closer. I could see him stiffen.

"That gal still stiffin' round you," Roy questioned, as if I weren't present.

His father's frown became more pronounced at his son's words. "What's this?" the man questioned.

Derek looked from Roy to his dad, and took a step to cover the space in between me and him in an unmistakably protective way. "Actually, Roy, we're kinda wit' each othuh, and before I was kinda hangin' 'round *her*."

Roy contemplated his words contemptuously, giving me another hard stare. "You're one crazy sonsa bitch, you know that? All tha nice White girls

— 342 —

you get, and you goinna hang 'round wit this Colored filth? You uh fool. You're supposed ta sex 'em, Dare, not date 'em."

"Watch how you speak about her, Roy," Derek cautioned. "And know somethin'? It don' get much better'n Tracy."

Roy scowled. "Who you tellin' ta watch they selves?" he demanded, his hackles rising. "I ain' tha one that's some monkey lovin', race-traitor." He said a curse word, and something else I didn't care to hear. Derek's fists balled at his side. "I ought ta knock some sense into ya damn head til you realize what you are, and what she ain'. I always thought bettuh uh you," Roy declared.

Roy's dad looked at the two of us as if we were something foul, and spat on the floor. As if they couldn't stand to be in the same space as us, the two of them stalked off together, the heel of Roy's boots audible even after they were out of sight.

"Yeah, well I always did, too," Derek said at their backs. He looked after them for a few minutes, still as a statue, before he sighed heavily. He looked over at me, and swung his arm around my shoulder. "Y'all right?"

"Are you?" I questioned.

Derek's face scrunched up. "I know you don't think much of 'im, Trace, but Roy *can* be decent at times, he's just, let's just say he didn' grow up in tha most encouragin' of environments, if you catch me. But he's wrong 'bout you, and I just want to clarify that *we* are hangin' *togethuh*. I spend time wit' you because there's no one else I want to spend my time wit', okay?"

I nodded. Derek did too, then I guess he realized where we were, and where his arm was, and he took it from around my shoulder. He eased into a grin. "So, those fixtures..."

When we finished up at the hardware store, I decided that I didn't want to wait until this afternoon to check the mail, so I made Derek stop by the house on the way back to the studio. Illogically, I'd begun to look for decision letters as soon as I had mailed off my first packet, but that had been months ago, before Christmas, and I hadn't heard anything from Harvard yet. So any time that I wasn't completely immersed in my school work, I kept going over my entire high school experience, trying to figure out what I could have done different, worried that maybe I had set my sights a little too high like everyone kept saying.

When I got out of the car I had to mentally steel myself for the disappointment of not finding a letter inside. Today, there was a lot more mail than usual, and it seemed like the mailman had just haphazardly shoved everything in the box. I noticed the Harvard emblem peeking out from beneath the Burrows family newsletter, a religious magazine of my mom's, and half a dozen bills. For the moment time stopped, and I just stood there, staring at the emblem, afraid to open the letter for fear of what it might say. It was a large envelope (they would've sent a normal letter sized envelope if I hadn't gotten in, right?) but very thin. I weighed it in my hand, before turning it over and opening it. My eyes tracked only as far as the first line.

"Y'alright," Derek asked, pulling me a little out of the shock. I wondered how long I'd been standing there for him to have gotten out of the car. I nodded in recognition of his presence. "What'cha got?" he questioned, the VE-RI-TAS shield not registering.

"It's my letter from Harvard," I informed him breathlessly.

His whole demeanor changed. "What's it say?" he demanded.

I showed him the piece of paper. "I didn't get in," I told him, my voice shaking at the last word. I bit down on my lip to stop it from trembling.

He read over the letter, slowly, taking in every word, every sentence, before he looked back at me. He watched my face struggle with emotion. "Are you okay?" he questioned.

"I really wanted Harvard," I remarked, softly, the tears starting. I blinked. "I knew it was a long shot, but I'd still hoped-."

He broke our no-touching-in-front-of-the-neighbors rule, and rubbed my back. "There's still law school," he reminded me.

I made myself nod. "I know," I said, wiping my eyes, trying to sound more upbeat. "There is."

Derek hugged me to him. I grunted. He looked me in my eye. "You're really disappointed, aren' you," he questioned. He parroted my words from before. "Same teachers, same clubs, same courses, remembuh?"

His thumb wiped away a tear. I looked up at him. "Am I being silly?"

"You are," Derek assured me. He kissed my forehead. "Only difference is tha name, babe. It's still Boston."

"It's just that...I didn't actually think that I would...everyone kept saying…and," I was unable to finish my sentence. Even though I'd voiced my doubts to no one, inwardly I'd always questioned my ability to actually get into the school. It was the best.

"Course you'd get in," Derek said. He tried a smile. "*I* nevuh had any doubts. This is…," he waved the letter, looking back at it. "Trace, I'm… happy…for you."

I looked up at him within the circle of his arms, and it really set in. "I can't believe that I got into Radcliffe," I remarked. "We should go celebrate! I have to tell my mom and dad; I can't wait for Patrice to get home!" Derek's smile expanded, though it didn't convey any of the warmth and amusement it usually did.

"We *should* celebrate," he remarked. "And we will," he added. "I can', tonight, though. You have that test. I have to work, and I'm swamped all weekend…I overspent on my budget, and I have to pick up some hours… and, but soon." It might have been my imagination that his shoulders shook. "Soon. Do you need to go back to tha studio, or are you set here?"

I wanted to ambush Patrice with the news as soon as she got home from school, and I wanted to tell my mom in person. I exhaled out the breath I'd been holding. "I'm good," I responded. He nodded, pausing to kiss me on the cheek. "Okay. I'll see you tomorrow?" I nodded. "Bye."

Derek's lack of enthusiasm was lost in my own excitement. I called my dad while I waited for Patrice to get out of class, forgetting that he was still at work. When I told Patrice, she reacted the way I knew that she would, which meant that she was as excited as I had been about me getting in. "My best friend's goin' ta Har-vard," she said in a sing-song voice. "That's so neat, girl. And we're not goin' to be that far away from each othuh cause Boston ain' that far from Chicago, right?"

"Chicago?" I questioned, confused. "What's in Chicago?"

Patrice looked a little apprehensive. "Hopefully, me. Wit a job. I didn' want ta tell nobody 'bout it, cause I didn' want to jinx it, but I've applied for this program wit this magazine. It's like for people like me who don' know yet if they want to go ta college. I mean, I've been in school for 12 years now, and I'm not sure if it's my thing," she said as an aside. "But this program…tha company is an advertisin' and marketin' firm that wants recent high school grads ta come and work for them."

She seemed searching as she talked, explaining the finer points: she would be taking a few college level courses, and working full time. Only a handful of classes were mandatory, but the option was there, if she decided that she wanted to pursue a degree. She paused in her excitement, looking sideways at me. "You think it's stupid?"

Before she'd asked, the only thing that I'd heard was that Patrice was going to be taking college classes. "It sounds like it's perfect for you, Triece!" I said, excitedly. "Why would you think I'd think it's stupid?"

"Cause I know how much you want me to go ta college, and everythin', like you."

Her being like me had never been the issue. "No, all I wanted was for you to see that you have a lot of options out there. I think that this is going to be a real good thing for you!" We were hugging again, and I think I floored her with the amount of emotion I was showing.

"If I get it," she added. "But I think I will. My application was happenin', and I think tha interview went well."

"When did you *interview*?" I demanded, surprised that I was just hearing about this. I didn't spend so much time at Derek's that something this big should have escaped my notice.

"Two weeks ago, ovah tha phone."

"And you managed to keep this from me?" I marveled, wondering how one of the biggest gossips I knew had managed to keep something like this quiet. The two of us both had trouble keeping secrets from the other. "I'm impressed!"

"I've got my secrets, too," Patrice declared, smiling. "But we can celebrate me when tha time comes." She switched the topic back to my acceptance. "Right now I'm still trippin' ovuh you, girl! You really did it!"

When I got home from my classes, I told my mom about the news and, after one startled second where she did not know what to say, she told me that she was proud of me. My dad said the same thing, but without the hug and the tears. My Grandpa, my mom's father, told me that he did not have the words to express his elation, he was so proud, and my dad's parents sent me a check with a two word note: *Good job*. In my head, however, I could just hear them telling the rest of the family, "*Ben's* girl got into Harvard."

— 34 —
"The Dance"

M y acceptance to Radcliffe made it five of the six schools that I applied to, and though I had the money ready to go, and I knew which school I wanted to go to, I didn't immediately send back my intent form. Radcliffe didn't hold the same weight as Harvard, wasn't as easily recognizable, and I did get into Yale, too. It was only an hour away from my Grandpa, so I could visit him every weekend if I wanted to, and it was still close enough to Boston that I could still see my aunt.

Yale had given me the best offer, too, and was just as prestigious. It and Harvard were both consistently in the top five, usually in the top two. Boston was the larger city, though, and between it and Cambridge, it had more schools surrounding it. And I'd wanted to go to Harvard ever since I was little and my aunt had taken me to walk across the Quad. But even though it was *like* going to Harvard, Radcliffe felt almost like having to use the 'Colored Only' entrance to the train station or something.

Harvard and Radcliffe *were* moving toward full integration of the two schools, though, and maybe it'd happen while I was still there. One could hope. So I sent back my letter of intent, and once the sheer shock started to dissipate, I looked through the entire package that was sent, and examined the price tag of my Ivy League education. Inwardly I cringed at the mere sight of how much it was going to cost, but that was just an instinctive reaction.

On top of the other scholarships that I'd accrued over the past few years, I'd been named a National Merit Scholar and Radcliffe had awarded me a $900 a year scholarship. I had enough in other scholarships to cover at least three years' worth of tuition, too, if not the entire four by the time I graduated from high school. Possibly the only thing that my parents would have to pay for would be books, if that.

"So, I'm going to Radcliffe," I informed Derek when he picked me up from Mason, a week after I'd gotten my acceptance. He paused in my open doorway, giving me a kiss before he gave a laugh.

"I thought we already determined that," he remarked. "Wanted ta go there since birth or somethin' like that, 'membuh?"

"Well, yes, but I got into four other schools, too, so I just thought I'd consider all my options. My Grandpa lives in Connecticut, and Patrice will be in Chicago; it'd be silly to not at least consider them."

He contemplated those words. "So does that mean you'd consider uh school down here?"

I looked at him, surprised, because he knew how much I hated living here. "I didn't apply to any schools down south."

Derek seemed to be warring with himself over something. "Is it too late to?" he questioned pragmatically.

"I suppose it's not, but why would I do that?"

Derek repeated my own words back to me. "Considuh all your options?"

"I don't have many down here," I replied. "That's why I'm leaving."

He stared at the center of the steering wheel in quiet contemplation. "Right, I keep forgettin'."

*

"I *can'* believe we're graduatin'," Patrice said, as she removed a dress off of the shelf. "It's so weird. I mean, we've been sayin' it for years, but it's really happenin' now. In like a few weeks!"

"I know," I cheered. "I don't know what I'm going to do without you!"

Patrice shot me a look. "Please. Don' get all sentimental now! You know we're still gonna be close, and we'll write to each othuh every day." Patrice held up the dress she had been studying. It was silver and paneled, with big squares of black. "What do you think?"

I gave the dress a quick glance, my face crinkling. "For you or for me?"

"Me."

Patrice looked good in just about anything that she wore, but even she wouldn't be able to redeem that dress. "Eww...no," I declared.

"Okay, what about for you?"

I shook my head. "That dress wouldn't look good on anyone." In jest I picked up a short, red, cocktail dress. "What about this?" Her eyebrows rose and she grinned. "Oh, that is so bad ass! You should try it on!"

"My mom would have a conniption," I declared. "She wouldn't even let me leave the house."

"Con...nip?"

"She'd spaz out."

"What about a pink dress then?" We looked at each other and both started giggling.

A very stern looking woman crossed the floor. "Is there anythin' I can help you *ladies* with?" she questioned, tightly. The smile dropped from Patrice's face as her gaze shifted to the woman's. "No thank you, ma'am, we're fine," she responded, politely.

The saleswoman's return question wasn't as cordial. "What is it that you are looking for?"

"We're just looking," I responded.

Despite the dismissal, the woman still lurked, so Patrice and I pointedly turned our backs on her, and continued with our mission. After discarding a few more dresses, Patrice ended up trying on a pale gold dress, and I, a no-frills navy blue gown. Patrice looked absolutely gorgeous in the dress she picked, the gold complementing her brown skin very nicely. I waited for her to make the usual comment on how good she looked, but she was steadily looking at me. "What?" I wondered. "Should I go try something else on?"

"Heck, no, T, that dress is it! If you on't get it, you're outta your mind. It's perfect!"

"You like it?"

She nodded vigorously. "I *love* it!" she assured me.

"You don't think it's too clingy?" I wondered. I had room to move around in the dress, but it clung slightly to my form. I twirled once, just to see it flow around me.

"No!"

"And it's not too revealing?"

Patrice laughed. "Quit worryin'. It's perfect. All you need is a simple silvuh necklace or…does your mom have pearls?"

"I don't know."

"You should ask her. Big Ma didn' have a single cent ta her name when she died, but she had her a string uh pearls. It'd be so cute if you could find a carnation that color for your date, that's what Alex's goinna do…what's Derek wearin'? He's goinna love you in that dress." I must have looked guilty. "You're not goin' wit Derek?" she wondered in confusion.

"I told you I was going with Damien."

"*Still?*" she demanded.

"He hasn't said otherwise…"

"Does *Derek* know you're goin' wit Damien?"

"I haven't mentioned it yet."

"He's not goinna be thrilled by that," Patrice warned.

"I don't even think he's thinking that prom exists. By the time he'll realize that it does, it'll be a week before prom, and there won't be a single tuxedo left in the city! Besides, Mr. Vaughn said that there's no mixed couples allowed, and could you imagine the uproar if I showed up with Derek? Going with him would be a lot more complicated than I want to deal with on prom night, and it's my prom!" I said a bit stubbornly. It was the one thing that I was supposed to want to do, that I actually wanted to do. "I want to go, Damien is easy, and he likes me. He knows we're only friends."

"How would you feel if Derek was still in school, and he decided that he wanted to go to prom as 'just friends' wit anothuh girl? Or that'd he'd rathuh take a White girl wit him because it would be easy?"

Well, when she phrased it like that… "Pretty lousy," I replied. "But it's not the same, is it?" I posed.

"Ask Derek," she returned.

Patrice and I spent a couple more hours in the shopping center, killing time until I had to go pick Derek up from work.

"What's so heavy?" he wondered as we traded off seats. As I passed by him, he pulled me to him for a second to give me a kiss on the cheek, before he got in on the driver's side.

I didn't answer. "How was work?" He yawned in response. "Tired?"

He nodded, vigorously. "You've no idea," he told me. Derek had been pulling even more overtime than usual. I'd barely seen him. "They're tryin' to work me to death," he declared. "What'd you do today?"

"Me and Patrice went to Harrold's."

"Oh yeah?" Derek glanced at the empty backseat. "You didn' get nothin'?"

"I've got a dress on hold," I remarked. "For prom."

He smiled, either at the thought of me and a dress, or maybe because he was trying to picture me dancing. "Prom's comin' up?" he wondered.

"May 5th," I informed him.

"Damn," he mumbled, "I'm losin' track of tha days. *You wanna* go ta prom?"

I turned towards him. "Why do you say it like that?"

"I didn' think that you'd be into that type of thing. You don' dance, remembuh?"

"I thought every girl's supposed to want to go to prom."

"Yeah, but you're not like girls." He glanced sideways at me and then quickly backtracked. "Well, obviously you're uh girl, Trace, but you've nevuh done anythin' that you're supposed to. It nevuh seemed like your thing."

I shrugged. "Well, prom is my thing," I asserted.

Derek didn't respond to that, and I glanced over at him, only to find him looking steadily at me. "Well," he demanded.

"Well what," I questioned.

"Ain'tcha goinna ask?"

"The guy's supposed to ask the girl," I returned.

"Yeah, but I don' go to Mason," he responded.

I looked down at my hands, feeling uneasy. "Damien Lewin asked me if I wanted to go to prom with him at the beginning of the year," I blurted in a rush. I didn't look at him as the rest of it came out. "And I said I'd go with him."

I couldn't tell if he was still looking at me. "As in uh *date*...or are you guys doin' tha group thing?" Derek posed, and even without looking I could feel his discomfort.

"As a date," I responded, equally as uncomfortable.

"Oh," Derek remarked slowly. "So, do you *like* this Damien, guy?" he wondered, trying for casual.

"I wouldn't go to prom with someone I didn't like," I responded. I was possibly making this conversation a little harder than was necessary, but Derek deserved it, a least a little, because there were rules to this whole dating game, and he had never played properly. We had never put to words exactly what we were, and if I wasn't his steady, then he really shouldn't have a problem with who took me to prom.

"Come on, Trace, you know what I mean! Do you like him, like him… or do you just like him?"

I decided to be nice. "We're just going to prom together," I admitted. "If you don't want me to-,"

We were at the studio now, so there was no more avoiding looking at each other. "Come on, Trace, of course I want you to go to prom." He sat his books down in a chair, and turned to face me. "If you'd of told me, I'd of asked you."

"Sometimes it's just nice to be asked without telling," I remarked.

"Would it change anythin' if I asked you now?"

"I've already told Damien that I'd go with him," I responded. "It's kind of too late to back out of it. Everyone's already got a date, and Mr. Vaughn said that there was to be no mixing at prom."

"Then take Damien," Derek remarked, flatly.

"Are you upset?" I questioned.

"Of course I am!" he responded passionately, but without anger. He took his time taking off his shoes. His voice was somewhat muffled when he said, "I don' want you goin' to prom wit' someone else. I don' want you to miss your prom, eithuh. I don' want you to miss out on nothin' because of me."

"I won't go to prom," I decided.

"Trace, did ya hear what I just said?"

"I wouldn't be comfortable if you went to prom with another girl," I told him.

He squared off in front of me. "Do you love me, Tracy?"

"You know I do," I responded.

"Then that's enough for me," he said. "Go to prom."

"I don't want to anymore."

"Why're you bein' so stubborn, woman?"

"Because I know you don't want me to go; you just don't want to say that, and I don't want you to be hurt."

His hands reached out to cradle my cheek. "I *do* want you to go," he stated, sincerely. "I'm not blind, and I'm not stupid. I know bein' togethuh means missin' out on some things, but I don' want you to miss out on somethin' like this, Tracy. Go'n have uh good time."

It suddenly didn't seem worth it without him. "Why don't you come and invite Carol?" I suggested. "And I'll save you a dance?"

His brow wrinkled in confusion. "Why Carol?"

"I know you liked her the least."

He gave a sound laugh. "Honey, aftuh you, I like all my past girlfriends tha least." He hugged me to him, bringing his head down to touch mine, his eyes rising to search my own. He sighed. "It's like, no matter what, we're doomed, aren' we? I don' want to see you dancin' wit' Damien any more than you want to see me wit' Carol, or anyone else. I love you, you know that, right?"

"I do."

He kissed me softly, pulling gently on my braid. "Do you know *why* I love you?" he questioned. He didn't wait for me to respond. "I love you for who you are, for your heart, your spirit. I love you because you're kind, gentle, and courageous. I love you because you try, even when it's impossible." We started to move in a dance with no music playing. "I love you because when I'm near you, my heart changes its rhythm to match yours, and because our feet are nevuh out of step. I love you in uh way that's timeless, outside uh time." His lips punctuated his last word as we danced, swaying softly.

I hugged him around his neck. "Now, I really don't want to go anymore," I remarked.

Derek waited until I was looking at him again. "You'll go," he directed, "and you'll have uh great time wit' Patrice and your friends." His voice took on a completely different tone. "And you can dance, every dance wit' tha guy, who gives you tha eye, let him hold you tight," he held me tightly to him.

"Baby, don' you know I love you so, can' you feel it when we touch? I will nevuh, evuh let you go, I love you oh so much'." He continued to sing as we moved slowly, a half step out of beat.

"Go to prom," Derek whispered, softly. "You can dance…just don' forget in whose arms you're goinna be, and Darlin'," he twirled me, "save tha last dance for me."

— 35 —
"The Graduate"

Mason High's Prom was one of the last in the city. It took place a short amount of time before graduation, at the historic train station, a few miles away from Hunts Landing Park. Damien and I coordinated a few days before, and his boutonniere was the same color as my dress. When Damien saw me, his mouth dropped open in a kind of comical way, and I appreciated the reaction. Most of the time I felt like I existed in the background; I was overlooked frequently, and all too easily forgotten. It was nice being reminded that I was still a girl. And although I'm not usually vain, I was happy to find that Damien was not the only one who noticed me that night.

The whole night I was surprised by how much I didn't stick out. I kept expecting someone to call me out, to declare me a fraud, but no one did. We danced through just about every song that was played, and whether I was in tune or out of it, no one really noticed, caught up in the joy of their own moments. When we didn't dance, we talked, or took a breather outside, and I even danced with a few other guys besides Damien. At the end of the night, Damien walked me to my doorstep, and before he said good night, he kissed me on the cheek. As he got back into the pastor's car, I wondered, briefly, if I had missed out on some things by not being more social in high school.

On one of the last days of class before graduation, Derek was waiting for me out in the carport, in the same place he always parked his car. "How was class?" he greeted me with a kiss as I slid into the car.

"Torture," I moaned. "I keep telling myself that there's only four more days left to get through, but that translates into four days! Four more boring, pointless, days pretending like this stuff still matters." Even I had given up trying to place meaning on the last few days of school. Classes at AAMU had already ended for the semester, final grades had been submitted, and no new material was being taught in any of my classes at Mason.

Derek laughed fondly, nodding. "I 'member that."

"If you remember it so well, you wouldn't be laughing."

"Oh, I sorry," he mumbled, mockingly, making a pitiful face. He put on a fake old man voice. "But when you get ta be my age, young'n, you will laugh." He gave a preposterous little tinkling laugh, and I couldn't help laughing along with him. "Hey, don' see it as four *more* days, Trace. See it as *only* four days. Only four days to say good-bye to your teachers, friends, tha school you've spent tha last four years at, and will probably nevuh see again…"

"You graduated two years ago, and you still come up to the school," I pointed out to him.

"Yes, well, I'm tha exception. Besides, I've had my reasons," he asserted.

"And what was that."

He blushed. "Been trying to win back Carol aftuh all these years," he lied, giving my hand a squeeze before he kissed it. "Seriously, though, Trace, you know it was always you. I spent those last few days tryin' to work up tha nerve to tell you what I felt."

"And all that time you could have saved yourself the trouble by coming and talking to me."

"If I'd uh asked you back then, would you have been my girl?"

I didn't have to think about the answer. "Probably not," I realized. I wouldn't have believed he was serious, and I wouldn't have known how to handle those feelings if he was.

"See, God knew what he was doin'," Derek remarked. "He knew that you and me needed some time. Seriously, Trace. Don' take these days lightly. You've got four days to make it count." Derek stared at his steering wheel. "Four days."

"Derek? You're drifting."

His head shot up, and he bared a grin. "Sorry, I'm gettin' on in years." He pretended to wipe some drool from the corner of his mouth. "Just don' waste them, okay?"

I curled up beside him on the seat. "I don't really get what I'm supposed

— 356 —

to be feeling right now," I admitted. "Everyone keeps saying that life is so much different when you get out of high school, but I don't see it like that. I just see it as over."

"You're just goinna have to trust me when I say that once you have uh little time to look back, you're goinna realize why people keep sayin' not to be so anxious about it bein' done. Even though you'll be in school for forevuh and all," he teased, "it's still not tha same. You don' have tha same friends, tha same *type* of friends, you don' think tha same way. You start thinkin' 'bout things you nevuh *had* to think about."

"Like what?"

"Like, I dunno, do you have enough money saved up to tell tha boss you hate where he can go? Or, do you have enough money to covuh all your bills. Can you afford to live on your own? Do you want to start thinkin' 'bout livin' wit' someone else? Contemplatin' your future wit' them? Why don' these jeans still fit anymore?"

I barely heard him. His words had me thinking about life in Cambridge. "I don't think that I'll have those types of worries," I remarked. "I mean about bills and stuff. At least, not anytime soon, and what bosses have you wanted to tell off?"

He shrugged. "It's just different," he declared.

"I know," I remarked. "That's what I'm so excited about! I want to be back up north. I want to see snow again! I want the opportunity to live by myself, and take care of myself instead of always having to ask someone, or wait on somebody. And besides, it's not like I'm giving up any of the people that really matter to me. Pat and I will be friends until one of us dies, and you and I aren't going anywhere, are we?"

His head jerked. "What do you mean?" he questioned.

"Well…," I paused because, honestly, I hadn't really thought about the end of high school being the end of Derek and I. To be really honest, I hadn't thought much about Derek and I in that sort of context, period. "We wrote to each other and kept in touch when I was in Boston last summer. We'll keep in touch, right?" I was suddenly very anxious for his answer.

"Yeah," he said with no conviction. "Right." He changed the subject. "So how are you plannin' on celebratin' your release from this four year prison?"

"Patrice and her family, and me and my mom, are planning on going out to dinner afterwards, since we're graduating so early in the day. After that, I don't know yet. Pat and Alex are going to the Groovy-sponsored graduation party, which I don't want to go to, and a classmate of mine, Tammy, invited me to come to the Ritz with her afterwards, so I think that's what I'm going to do."

"You know tha party at tha Ritz always has like uh ton of alcohol," Derek informed me.

The party at the Ritz was a graduation tradition. I smiled slightly. "Yes, I know."

Derek seemed amused. "You're goinna drink, Trace? Really?"

I shrugged. "I graduate from high school once in my life," I declared. "Why not?"

"I just can' imagine you drinkin'," Derek responded.

"Was there something *you* wanted to do for graduation," I questioned, the possibility just occurring to me.

"You're tha one graduatin'," he said, quickly. "I'm just uh bystander."

"Oh sure! Bystander's don't grill you on who you bring to prom," I responded.

Derek grinned. "I's just bein' protective of you. You know how kids are these days. No boundaries."

"Uh huh. Well you're more than welcome to have dinner with me and my family."

Derek's eyes lit up. "It wouldn' be an issue?"

"Why would it be? You're like a big brother to me; practically family."

"Oh, is that what I am? Uh big brother?"

"Well, yeah," I teased. "You know since we're pretending that we don't like each other and all, the only other role that a good friend would occupy is the surrogate big brother. So, big bro, come have dinner with me and my family? You can even come to the Ritz with me later; it's an open party."

Derek looked me over, a smile playing on his lips. Meeting my eyes, he leaned in very deliberately and kissed me. "Okay," he decided, once he had pulled away. "It's uh date."

Against Mrs. Rupert's recommendations, I was asked to give a speech for graduation. I knew it was supposed to be a big honor, but I ended up putting off writing it until a few days before the event, not quite sure what it was that I wanted to say to a group of people that I'd never really taken the time to get to know. When I did finally sit down to write it, I thought a lot about the conversation that Marcus and I had had on my first day of high school, when he cautioned me about not being so anxious to be somewhere else, specifically what he said about transition.

Part of the reason that I had had so few close friends was because I didn't want the distraction. I didn't want to make friends with the wrong people, didn't want to be tempted to do stuff that would keep me from doing what I should be doing; keep me from getting into Harvard. There were plenty of kids who'd started school with us freshman year, who weren't graduating. I knew too many girls who'd gotten pregnant and/or married somewhere along the way; boys who left school to go work, to help put food on their family's table, or just because they'd had enough, because they had something else they'd rather do.

So, sure, I was awkward whenever it came to social situations, but mostly I just didn't want to be involved. Now, this close to graduation, I didn't really regret that; I'd accomplished from high school what I'd set out to accomplish. Not only had I (sort of) gotten into the school that I've wanted to attend since I was in the 2nd grade, I'd also found the money I needed to go there. I'd had an exemplary high school experience, it was just…I don't know. As anxious as I was…I was still a little apprehensive, and I knew a lot of it had to do with Derek. I know I hadn't spent a lot of time thinking about him being in my life, but the thought of him suddenly not being there was just as hard to imagine.

I ended up writing a kind of generalized version of what I'd written to Derek in the letter I'd given him before he graduated, and what I had come to figure out my last couple of years in school: high school was a foundation to help us become in part who we already were. I mentioned, too, how we all have our own talents, and that the future was limitless. I did pander a little, for the Mrs. Ruperts in the audience, toning the enthusiasm down some, humbling it, and adding a line or two about community ideals, societal norms, and how life was all about being balanced.

And of course I ended the speech the way any good high school speech ended: with well wishes for the future, and encouraging my classmates to set new standards. All in all, I thought it was a decent speech. Maybe not something that would have people talking about for years to come, but hopefully I wouldn't get booed.

Mason High's graduation was early in the afternoon on May 20th. We had a practice ceremony in the morning, and afterwards me and Patrice got breakfast and hung around at her place all day. We were too excited to do much of anything else, so we sat around talking idly until we were supposed to head back over to the Civic Center for the graduation ceremony.

Derek had said that he would be sitting dead center behind the cameraman, and when I got up to make my speech, I searched him out. True to his word, he was sitting right where he said he would be. I wondered how early he'd had to show up in order to get that seat. I looked away from him, seeking out my family in the crowd. Surprisingly, I was able to find them: my mom, Grandpa, uncle, and aunt. My Uncle Bobby had flown in all the way from California to make it to my graduation…but my dad hadn't. I tried to pretend that I didn't care, but it was impossible to ignore the one face that was conspicuously missing from the crowd. Top of the class, National Merit Scholar, and Ivy League bound, no less, and still it wasn't enough to make him proud enough to want to share the day with me.

Beside my mom and her family, sat the Gordon's. Although I'd told Derek it wouldn't be an issue for him to come to dinner after the ceremony, what if it was? Sean never kept his tongue about his opinion. Would he today?

That worry was just one of many that crowded my mind as I spoke, and I wasn't really paying attention to my speech, just reciting the words. I finished and sat down, then half-listened to the other speakers talk, wanting it all to be over. When my name was called later on in the ceremony, I got my diploma and waited for the rest of my classmates to do the same. Finally, though, the whole thing was over, and we were dismissed.

The East Hall of the Civic Center, where the graduation ceremonies were always held, was set up so that when the graduates left the hall, they walked out onto the outside balcony and down the huge double staircase into the 'pit', where friends and family members gathered to congratulate the grads.

On the day Derek graduated, I'd been the first person that he had seen when he entered the pit. Today, he was the first person I saw. I paused on the stairs for a moment, enjoying the sight of him searching for me. He caught my eye and gave me a slow smile. When I reached the bottom stair he ignored the crowd completely, and he hugged me tightly, possessively.

"Congratulations," he gushed when I'd gotten near enough to hear him. Oblivious to everyone else, we just stared at each other for a moment, before he kissed me adoringly. I loved this man, I thought fiercely as he held me. I'd spent so much time trying not to fall in love with him that this realization nearly took my breath away.

When he let me go, he handed me a bouquet of flowers and balloons. "I'm so proud of you, Trace," he declared.

"I love you, Derek," I responded.

He gave a startled smile. "I should get you flowers more often," he joked.

"How'd the speech go?"

"It was inspirin'," he declared with a straight face. "I loved it. I thought it was perfect."

"You're just saying that."

"No, I'm not," he said sincerely. "It was good. Maybe one of these days you'll realize how great you are. Accept it."

"I-I have to find my mom," I declared, as we were jostled by the crowd. He took my hand, and in the crush of people surrounding us, the gesture went unnoticed. Together we forced our way through the mass until we found her.

She, like most of the other parents, had positioned herself a safe distance from the pit, letting the graduates congratulate each other before taking their turn. When my mom saw me, she pulled me to her in a rare display of emotion, and kissed my forehead, muttering some incoherent words in my ear.

Patrice was next. She hugged me fiercely. "Can you believe it?" she shouted in my ear. We posed for pictures with each other, and our families, and then we found other friends and repeated the ritual. For about half an hour we sort of milled around making small talk with the adults, posing for pictures when it was demanded until Mr. Gordon reminded us that we had a reservation at the Garden Club; our community's version of the country club. I told my mom, Patrice, and her family that we would meet them over there, and I led Derek off to see my newest toy.

As part of a standing graduation tradition in the city, the bigger (and most expensive) of the graduation gifts, were displayed at the front of the Civic Center. It was a tradition that started years ago, when the owner of the local Ford dealership-back when there was just one-decided that a good way to promote sales would be to donate a car to the student that had the highest GPA in the city. Since then, proud parents paid a fee to display their gifts to their children, and the city's top dealerships donated cars to a few seniors each year in a sort of scholarship program.

I made my way through the assortment of brand new cars, a few Motorcycles, and the lone boat and camping trailer, until I stopped in front of a sky blue Triumph convertible with a sign that read: *Congratulations, Tracy!!! You've made us proud!!*

Derek gaped at the car in disbelief. "There's no way that's yours!"

"It is," I declared, proudly.

"This is uh TR4, Trace!" he announced as he gawked over my Triumph. "From uh standstill, 0-60 in 12 seconds flat, corners on rails, known to stop on uh dime. How tha hell did you get this car?"

I laughed at his enthusiasm, still giddy myself, but I'd had a two-day head start on knowing that this car was mine. "My mom's church was intensely proud of one of their own getting into an Ivy League school. They wanted to send me off in style!"

"That'll do it," he remarked. "This is so cherry!" Derek pronounced, walking around the car.

"You're drooling," I teased.

He laughed. "Sorry, but this is one solid car! Ain't no clown wagon, that's for sure."

I let Derek finish examining the car before we headed to the restaurant, where my mom, Grandpa, Aunt Joanne, Uncle Robert, Patrice's mom, dad, her dad's mom, an aunt, the Layton's, and all three of the Gordon boys were already waiting. Patrice and I were greeted by a chorus of "Congratulations," when we walked into the room with Derek and Alex in tow.

I remembered what Patrice had once said about Marcus not liking Derek only once I walked into the room and caught Marcus giving Derek a hostile look, before he came over and wrapped me in a bear hug. He mussed my hair-which I had worn down for the occasion-before sitting me back down, and repeating the procedure with Patrice. "I can't believe y'all are going be set out on the world," Marcus teased. "I don't know if the world will survive!"

I got hugs from Sean and Abdul, before they teased and made fun of their little sister good-naturedly. I enjoyed the dinner; enjoyed being surrounded by my family, and the thought was there that if my dad had come, it would have just made things awkward, and things were just so nice the way they were. I don't know if Derek was uncomfortable, but if he was, he was determined not to let it show. He got involved in conversations when the opportunity presented itself, and of course Mr. Gordon and my uncle spent a few minutes grilling him, but they were otherwise amicable.

Dinner ended when the Layton's had to leave to make Alex's graduation, and Patrice went with them. The Gordon's were going to sit through Alex's graduation, too, but my mom was ready to go home and spend some alone time with her father, brother, and sister. I was offered congratulations one more time, and was told to be safe and mind myself, my aunt giving me a wink as she said this.

Marcus came jogging up just as we were leaving. "Hey, Trace," he called. "Got a second for me?"

I stopped. "For you, Mark, I have a whole minute," I responded. Derek stepped back so Marcus and I could have some privacy. Marcus grinned down at me. "I'm totally blown away," he said in amazement. "It seems like just yesterday it was your first day of high school, and now you've gone and graduated. I know you're anxious to go partying and what not, so I'll be quick. I guess I could have given you this tomorrow, but you know me, I'm not very patient, and anyway, I got to be back in Tennessee."

He handed me two hastily wrapped presents. The bottom gift was a collage of pictures. Most of them were taken sometime in the past four years, but the center picture was one taken several years ago on Halloween. It was of me, him, Sean, and Patrice. She had dressed up like Nefertiti, I was Isis, and both of her brothers were supposed to be Tut. Patrice and I were 11, Marcus was 14, and Sean 16. I think Sean and Marcus were supposed to be going to some Halloween party, but Patrice had convinced them to dress up the way she wanted them to, and to hang around with us before they went. Patrice had always been able to get her brothers to do pretty much anything for her.

"Aw, look at you Mark!" I exclaimed, touching his cheek.

"Patrice made me include that," Marcus explained. "Said you'd get a kick out of it."

We both laughed. "I also got you this book of quotes so if you ever get overwhelmed while you're up there, you've got 365 wise sayings to help you get through whatever situation comes up. My number is on the back page, so if you have an emergency, or just need someone to talk to, you know I'm available."

I hugged him tightly, my throat tight. Tears filled my eyes. "Ah, thank you, Marcus."

Marcus sounded a little choked up when he said, "I gotta say this now, cause I won't get to see you when you leave for school, so be safe, be careful, be smart, and beat the pants off of all your classmates. I'mma be disappointed if anyone does better than you." He laughed and chucked me under the chin. "Love ya, kid."

"I love you, too," I remarked, my voice catching. If things went the way I planned, this may very well be the last time I saw Marcus. Surely there'd be weddings to attend, and that sort of thing, but this was the last moment that he would still be mine, that I'd still have any claim to him. The next time I saw him there'd be a woman beside him, maybe a baby in his arms. Life halted for no one.

Maybe he was thinking the same thing, because he suddenly shot Derek a look that was so reminiscent of the one that he had once given Omar that I laughed. "Be nice, Marcus," I admonished.

"Just be careful," Marcus said, louder than he needed to. "I'd hate to have to spend the rest of my life in jail because I had to kill someone for not treating you right."

I smiled and gave Marcus a big hug. "He's a good guy, Marcus, I promise. I'm going to miss you," I added.

"Me too," he responded.

We hugged each other slightly longer than necessary, and Derek warily watched Marcus until he walked away. "So, I'm guessin' he used ta like you," Derek remarked as soon as Marcus was gone. "Is he someone I should be worried about?" he attempted to joke.

"I've had a crush on him since I was in the fourth grade," I said. "Marcus is like a brother to me. *He* is a brother. Besides, what would you have to worry about?" I couldn't help but tease.

"That someone's gettin' uh little too close to my girl," Derek replied seriously.

"When did I become your girl?" I wondered.

"Oh, please, you've always been my girl," Derek remarked. "Everyone knows it."

"I've never heard you say it before."

"Like you didn' already know."

"Well, just so *you* know: you could have saved yourself a lot of trouble if you had just come out and said that yourself at some point."

He stood possessively in front of me. "Well, I'm sayin' it now. Do you have a problem wit' that?"

I smiled, kissing him. "Not at all."

"So, you know how you asked me if'n I had somethin' planned for tonight, and I said no?"

"Yes…"

"Well, I lied. I do. How long you plannin' on stayin' at tha party?"

"I dunno. What do you have planned?"

"Guess you'll have to wait long enough to find out, now won' you," Derek declared mysteriously.

— 36 —
"The Artist and the Model"

The party at the Ritz Hotel was almost as big of a graduation tradition as the cars at the Civic Center were. During the week of graduations, someone always booked the rooms downstairs and hosted a graduation party. The amount of alcohol floating around on the graduation nights could rival any of the bars in town, but as part of the deal, the sponsor(s) of the party always provided a designated van to cart home the inebriated, and since the drinking never got out of control, the police turned their heads on the recently matriculated seniors. It surprised me that Patrice had chosen the smaller Groverton High party to attend.

All night, I ran into people that I'd barely spoken to, and I was pleasantly surprised to discover that I wasn't as invisible these past few years, as I always imagined. I struck up conversations with people easily, as if we'd been friends for years. Because there were so many people around, Derek and I went mostly unnoticed, and he spent most of the night holding my hand. We even danced together a few times, although neither of us were very good dancers.

The party seemed to be winding down by the time I was on my third or fourth drink. By then, people were either heading off to different parties, heading home, or had gotten a room and were sleeping it off (and possibly doing other things that they may someday regret). I found Derek in the game room shooting pool with a guy I remembered graduating in his year.

"There you are," Derek noted when I came into the room. "You ready to go?"

I hiccupped. "Yep."

Derek tossed down his pool cue, and said good-bye to his partner. He draped an arm around my shoulders and steered me toward the door.

"What did you have planned?" I questioned.

"Stop askin'," he said, lightly. "You'll see." When we got closer to my car, Derek questioned, "Can I drive?"

I squinted at him. "Why?"

"Cause you've been drinkin', I haven', and it will kind of ruin tha surprise uh little if you know where we're goin'."

"I'm not drunk, you know," I remarked.

He smiled just the slightest. "Yeah, but I'm not sure that excuse will work when you're tryin' to explain to tha folks in Cambridge why you're goin' ta need them to hold your place until aftuh you've been sprung from jail. 'Sides, what kind of boyfriend would I be if I let that happen?"

I handed over my keys. He drove to his studio, and before Derek went up to the loft to change, he gave me my present. The gift was large, and thin, and wrapped in plain brown paper. I knew before I opened it that it was a painting of some kind. "This was too big to carry around tha Civic Center," Derek explained. "I hope you like it."

I unwrapped the package and just stared. Instead of seeing some astounding view of Bakersfield, like I was expecting, I was looking at a painting of myself. I was a little off center, half turned toward the front, a look of complete surprise on my face, mirroring the way I felt right now. The day was kind of overcast, the sun well hidden behind a bank of clouds. Around me there were pine trees, the only spot of green. There were also several indistinguishable shapes that were meant to be people, but the only one who stood out, besides me, was Derek. He was behind me and to the left, sitting on a picnic table, a sketch pad in his lap. His gaze was looking in my general direction. His face was not as in focus as much as mine was, but his eyes shone brightly, and I could read the expression on it, nonetheless, because I had seen it so many times in real life.

"This looks familiar," I stated once I found my voice. "Why does this look so familiar?"

"Do you remember junior year, well my junior year, when Mrs. Diece took us around tha school to name things in French?" I nodded. Vaguely. "Well that's when this is. When we stopped by tha baseball bleachers 'fore we went back in."

"How do you remember this?" I wondered in amazement. It was like looking into a memory. Derek went to his desk and rummaged around until he came up with a photo. He handed it to me. It looked just like Derek's painting with only a few differences. In the photo, Derek was looking directly at me, his expression glazed, his fingers curved around a pencil, drawing the beginnings of what I couldn't imagine. Still looking at the photo I questioned, "Who took the picture?"

"Ben," he answered quickly. "Stefferd? He used to sit one seat back, and to tha left of you." I remembered Ben, I even remembered him taking the picture. He'd called my name and snapped it, and I remembered being startled, but I hadn't thought of the moment since.

"How'd you get this?" I demanded.

"I asked for it," he said, simply. "I was there when he took it, and I thought it would be interestin' to paint."

"How long have you had this?"

Derek studied me for a small second, gauging my reaction. "Since Ben got it developed," he answered. He watched my face shift between expressions. "I'm goinna go upstairs to change," he stated, pulling his eyes from me.

I nodded, my mind still focusing on the two pictures. In Derek's painting he had somehow managed to capture every line, curve, and dimple of my face. Not that hard to do when you were working from a copy…except that Ben had snapped the picture a second, or two, too early, and had only caught half of my face. This painting was from memory. I recalled nearly every conversation Derek and I had had about painters and their motivations. Looking at his painting I could see how tenderly he had treated every line of my features. It seemed like there was love spelled out in every brush stroke.

"Are you goin' to stare at that all night, or are you goinna tell me how much you like it?" Derek questioned. I jumped, unaware that he'd come back down. "Are you cryin'?"

I quickly wiped my eyes. "No," I lied.

The smile disappeared as his look turned worried. "You don' like it?"

I found myself in his arms. "No, I love it Derek," I said, absently. "I-," I kissed him, overcome with emotion. "It's beautiful! Thank you."

He awkwardly put his arms around me. "Hey, so you goin' let me have tha photo back? I'm gonna need *somethin'* to remembuh you by."

"Oh, right." I handed him his photo. "Derek this was really, really, nice. Thank you. Was this the surprise?"

He raised his eyebrows. "Stop askin' or I'm not goinna give it to ya," he threatened.

We left my painting at the studio, and got back in the car. Derek turned south onto 431, and we drove in silence for a while with *Magic Carpet Ride*, then *Revolution*, being the only sounds in the car as we drove down the Parkway. We left Bakersfield behind, heading towards the small town of Dorton. My suspicions about where we were going were confirmed when Derek made a left, and a few seconds later the Tennessee River appeared on the right side of the car. *MacArthur Park* was just starting to play when Derek pulled to a halt in front of an old ruin of a mansion.

The house that we stopped at seemed almost symbolic of the town. While Bakersfield had flourished and blossomed, Dorton had quietly become a ghost of a town. The house we'd stopped at seemed like it had been something in its hey-day, but couldn't still boast of the same grandeur. The pillars were cracked and chipped, if they were even still there, half the porch was missing, the windows had been knocked out, and the doors boarded up. Derek and I had come to this particular house before, a few times. We'd stumbled across the place on accident, and when we'd found that it was deserted we'd gone through every room in the mansion, taking in what had once been.

Tonight, though, we didn't go inside. It was one of those near-summer-perfect nights that wasn't hot or cold, and held no clouds in the sky. The river flowed just feet away, following the same path that it had for thousands of years without regard to us, and since we were pretty much in the middle of nowhere, there was no ambient light to obscure our view of the stars that twinkled down majestically above us.

Derek took my hand, and led me around to the back of the house. "Wait here," he whispered, heading back in the direction of the car. He was only gone for a few minutes. When he came back he was wearing a jacket and tie. Music accompanied him as he walked toward me. "You promised me that I'd get tha last dance, so since I didn' get to escort you to prom, I thought maybe we could have uh redo. So, Tracy Catherine Burrows, will you be my date to prom?" I giggled as he solemnly held out his hand for me to take.

We danced closely together, wrapped up in our own world. The wind picked up just slightly, enough to disturb our clothes, and it was like we left the ground behind. Derek had never seemed so sure footed before, so graceful. Beneath his direction, I twirled and swooped, dipped and swayed, and I realized that for all my want of going to prom, Derek was what would have made it worthwhile. I let my head fall on his shoulder. How had I managed to miss how much he meant to me?

Eventually our feet stilled, and we sat down at the top most of the 26 Spanish steps that led down into the courtyard (one of the few parts of the house that wasn't completely in ill-repair). Derek leaned in to kiss me, but the angle was awkward, so we had to readjust ourselves, and we had a good laugh before he tried it again.

I was the first to pull away, but I stayed in his embrace, resting my head against his chest. I listened to the rhythm his heart beat played, matching it to mine. He shifted to make it more comfortable for the both of us, holding me securely to him. "I went up to Monte Sano Mountain on my graduation night," Derek said, softly. "Ky Johnson had been tha one to host tha party at tha Ritz, and he was determined to make it good. I went, and there I was, just graduated, partyin' wit' tha people that I'd been friends wit', and went to school wit' for years, and suddenly I no longuh wanted to be around them. So I sat out in tha parkin' lot, sobered up, and went up to tha mountains.

"I'd fallen in love with tha place when they took us on that field trip there in tha fifth grade." At the same time we both whispered, "Monte, say no," after a local legend, and laughed. "After that," Derek continued, "I'd *beg* my parents to take me up there. When I learned to drive, I'd go whenevuh I had tha opportunity. I loved to paint tha view from up there; I liked bein' there because it made me feel as if I were king of tha world: I was way up there, and everyone else was down here, in their borin', lackluster lives, not even realizin' how insignificant they truly were."

He paused, remembering. "But then I went up there at night. All you see is lights. You look up and you see tha stars. You look down and you see tha city. It's humblin'. I wasn' even one of those dots. I sat there thinkin', tryin' to figure out what Derek Lewis King really meant to tha world. I wasn' tha only artist out there, or tha only cute guy wit' dark hair and blue eyes; I wasn' even tha only Derek Lewis King in tha state, much less tha world. I was uh nothin' that'd just graduated. There were uh million guys, just like me, who'd managed to pass through tha world without even makin' an impact. It made me feel kind of small."

I kind of hugged him at those words.

He looked down at me and smiled. "And then, as I was sittin' there, I realized that tha real reason that I felt so bad was because there I was, on one of tha most important nights of my life, and tha one thing I wanted, tha one *person* I wanted to be wit', was nowhere around. While I was sittin' there wit' all of these thoughts runnin' through my head, I kept thinkin' on you. About our arguments, about what you wrote, what you screamed at me," he laughed. "Tracy, you've been one hell of uh ride, but it'd be uh lie to say I ain't enjoyed it. You've certainly made my life interestin', that's for sure. I can' imagine tha way I would have turned out, if I hadn' met you."

I reveled in his embrace. "Talk about flattery!"

"Was that uh little thick?" Derek questioned, good-naturedly. "I mean it, though, Trace. I don' know what I done to make you love me, but I'm glad you do."

"What's not to love," I questioned, looking at him. "You're adorable."

We kind of fell silent, and so we just sat for a while, not needing to say anything to each other. I listened to the steady beating of Derek's heart, concentrated on the feel of his arms around me, contemplating my newfound realization about how much in love with this guy I was.

"So when're you leavin'?" Derek ended the silence to question. He'd been quiet so long I thought he'd fallen asleep.

The date seemed so out of context in this moment that I had to actually think about it. "June 13th," I answered, after only a bit of a pause.

I felt him stiffen around me. "Why so soon?"

"I'm enrolled in the summer term."

There was a beat of silence. "You just couldn' wait, could you?" he demanded, and in his voice I heard more than a slight note of bitterness. He pulled away, suddenly, standing up. "*Why* do you hate this place so much, Trace? Why are you *so* anxious to leave?"

I watched him pace, confused by this sudden outburst. "I never wanted to be *here* in the first place," I answered. "Ever since we moved here, it's always been about getting away." Bakersfield was where everything in my life had gone wrong. Bakersfield was where I'd had to come to grips with my parent's divorce, where I'd had to learn *my place*.

"Well, hell, why even wait until June 13th? Why not just pack up your stuff and get out of this godforsaken place 'fore you become any more corrupted by this damn southern air?"

I was bewildered by this sudden change. "What's the matter with you?" I demanded.

"You mean you can' figure it out?" he questioned. "As smart as you are, and you still don' know?"

"No, I don't know, so how about you tell me since you're always so good at making up my mind for me!"

"Who knows what you think," he snapped. "Forget it." He jumped down from the wall and stalked off.

"*Where* are you going?" I yelled after him.

"Don' worry 'bout it," was his reply.

My head pounded as I squinted in the direction he'd disappeared, trying to decide if I should go after him. What was *with* Derek, anyway? Nothing that had been said between us was anything new. We'd had these same conversations over and over again. The words hadn't changed. Silently, I cursed him. He was like an endless roller coaster ride. One moment we could be coasting, the next I was rocketing around a corner, not really sure how to hold on.

I got up and walked the length of the deck, stopping to kick a stone. This was my graduation night for crying out loud! I was supposed to be celebrating the night, not seething. I considered leaving Derek to find his own way back to Bakersfield; it'd serve him right. I mean was a person not allowed to want something that wasn't right in front of them? Wasn't a baby's first inclination to reach? And I encouraged Derek, didn't I? Yet, Derek didn't even so much as congratulate me, or say that he was proud of me, for getting into Radcliffe.

When I got my acceptance letter he didn't even...I paused, remembering. He'd rushed off as soon as I told him. He seemed disappointed when I found out that I got in, no, that I was going to *go*...oh. I sat down.

But it's not like he'd ever came out and said that maybe he wanted me to stick around. Things had always been casual between us; hadn't he *just* labeled me as his girlfriend a few hours ago? He knew I was leaving since before we'd ever gotten involved, and until tonight a part of me had always treated 'us' as if it were merely a high school fling. He couldn't be upset if I was making plans for a future that didn't include him if he hadn't let me know that he wanted space in it. Not that there was any space. I was going to Cambridge. He was in school here. It'd always been that way.

I was still thinking about my sudden revelation when Derek came back. He sat down beside me. "I'm sorry, Trace," he remarked, sounding truly repentant. "I didn' mean to yell."

"Do you know what kind of life I'd have if I stayed here?" I nearly whispered.

"I know," he said, just as softly.

"There's no opportunity for me in Alabama. Even if I were to go to college at Alabama A&M, all that'll prepare me for is a lifetime of teaching. I want better than that."

"I know," he repeated.

"And even then the attitudes that prevail wouldn't allow that I have any dignity doing that. I want to be able to feel *proud* of myself, Derek, to not feel ashamed about holding my head up. You know how things are."

"I do," he said, agreeable. He gave a slight head nod that ended up dislodging a tear.

"There's just nothing for me here," I concluded.

"What about *me*, Tracy?" he questioned. "*I'm* here." His voice dropped a few more decibels. "I've been here, waitin' for you to take notice. It's not easy for me to say this; I'm not uh serious talk kind of guy, so maybe I haven' been as upfront wit' my feelings as you would've liked, but it's only because when I'm around you...I...I get tongue tied. I make uh fool of myself because I'm just so excited that I get to be near you, that I can' think straight.

"If you think I've been hesitant about us, it's because evuh since I started fallin' for you, I've been hearin' this clock tickin' away inside my head, countin' down our time togethuh. If you want to know tha real reason I didn' go to that school in Georgia, it's because I wasn' ready to leave. That's why I came back, why I was up at Mason all tha time, and why I'm standin' here, in tha middle of nowhere, beggin' you to finally see me!"

His hand slid into his pocket, and I didn't actually need to see what he pulled out to know what it was. "This night has been in my head for months, and I was tryin' to make things work out perfectly, but I'm not perfect. I don' speak beautifully; I can only tell you what's on my heart. I love you, Tracy," he asserted. "I feel juvenile when I'm around you, but I wanna grow wit' you. I know that there are so many things that are in our way, that all I have to my name is that small percentage of what we end up gettin' for tha studio, uh busted car, and uh few hundred in savings. I can' give you tha world… but I was wonderin' if maybe it was simply enough if I asked you to share your world wit' me?" He stood up, only to drop down to one knee. "Tracy, will you marry me?"

— 37 —
"Morning Landscape"

For a moment, I couldn't move. Stunned didn't even begin to convey what I was feeling. Once I'd regained my composure, I opened my mouth to say something, but nothing came out. I closed my mouth, tried again, staring at the ring so I didn't have to look at him. I wondered, idly, where he'd gotten the money to buy it, but then it all clicked. The money he'd been saving for his 'trip', the overtime. All of that had been for me. Was I really *that* self-absorbed? How had I missed that?

I knew that he was waiting, but I didn't know what to say. This felt like a dream. This was Derek, *my* Derek, the Derek that I'd had a crush on for practically four years, the Derek that I loved spending time with, the Derek that I'd fallen in love with. This was *that* Derek, asking me to marry him, in the moonlight, on my graduation night. It couldn't have happened any better than if I had written it to be that way. The first guy I'd ever fallen in love with was asking me to marry him.

So why wasn't I saying yes?

Because I knew there was no such thing as happily ever after.

I finally drew my eyes away from the ring, and I forced myself to look at him. If he could work up the courage to propose, the least I could do was make-eye contact with him, but it would have been a lie to say that it was easy. "I…I love you, Derek," I started, slowly. I was in no rush to say the words I knew I had to say. "I love you a lot. You're my best friend. You know that," his shoulders started to droop, anticipating what was coming next. I didn't want to finish, just so I wouldn't have to see the look that I knew was coming. "You know what I feel for you, and I would love for this to be real, but I know that you and I getting married just wouldn't work."

His face contorted, shaking off my words. "Why?"

"It just wouldn't, Derek."

He didn't accept that. "Why not?" he demanded. "Because I don' have enough money? I'm not ambitious enough? I'm not smart enough? I'm White, I'm uh Gemini, I have uh bad French accent? Why?"

"I'm seventeen!" I reminded him. "And you're not much older. We don't *know* what we want right now. You're just starting to figure that out, and I haven't even made it to the starting gate. I'm not ready to be *married.* We get married, and then what? We end up hating each other, getting a divorce a few years later, maybe drag a child into it? I don't want that, and I doubt you do, either. You said it yourself: you don't have much, I don't have much. We're both in school, struggling-"

"So we can struggle togethuh," he said, passionately. "When you care about someone, you don' let anythin' get in tha way!"

"But *everything is* in the way right now. Unless you want to move to Boston, we'd never have time to actually be with each other, and even then, I'm going to be busy all the time. You'll probably be busy all the time. And-"

"Don'," he said, cutting me off. "If you don' want to marry me, Trace, at least have tha courage to say that, but don' sit there and try to rationalize this away. Tha only thing that matters to *me* is that we're togethuh. That's all I care about. If that's not what you care about, then say that, but don' try to talk me out of somethin', then make it seem like it was my decision. *I* want to spend my life wit' you."

"Derek, you couldn't even admit that you were my *friend* in front of your buddies at Chase's," I reminded him. "You're telling me that all of a sudden you're going to start telling people that I'm your *wife?* I'm supposed to believe that you're going to stand up and defend us when people say that we're not supposed to be together?" Without meaning to, I was crying. I blamed the alcohol. "Damn you, Derek," I shouted at him. "Why'd you have to do this *tonight?* It's my graduation night! This was supposed to be *my* night!"

He grabbed for my hand. "You're leavin' me, Trace," he stated plaintively. "If I don' do it now, I don' know when I'm goinna have anothuh chance. I wasn' tryin' to ruin your night, sweetie, but I had to say this. This is how I feel for you," he whispered. "This is my heart, right here! Back when you still thought I was tha biggest jerk in tha world, I was fallin' in love wit' you. I told you, it's hard for me to put feelings like that into words. I'm not perfect; I've messed up. I'm sorry! But I love you. I love you," he repeated. "If it takes me sayin' that every day, for tha rest of your life, in orduh for you to believe it, I will. I love you, Tracy, and I want to be wit' you, only you, no one else."

I refused to hear those words. "And will you still love me when things are strained between us? After we've had a bad couple of months? A bad year? When the bills are overdue, and the car breaks down?"

"*Why* do you have to analyze everythin'?" he demanded in frustration.

"Because it's what I do! It's how the world makes sense to me. I understand emotions, but I have to deal with logic. The reality is that things are going to get hard. Things are going to be difficult; I want to know that you're still going to be there when things are no longer easy!"

He laughed abruptly, startling me. "Tracy, things haven' been easy since tha day I met you; tha fact that I'm still here should tell you that I'm willin' to work for us! I didn' mean that we had to go rush out and get married tonight. I would love it, if that's what you wanted to do, but I just want to be wit' you. No matter what happens between us, no matter what you decide about us or, or whatevuh, I will always love you. Even if we're not still togethuh. I proposed because…I just want you to slow down a little and remembuh that I'm here. You seem so anxious to get away, and I understand why, but I just want to know that I'm in your thoughts. I want to be uh possibility for your future, too."

We ended up staying out in Dorton until early in the afternoon of the next day. It was unintentional, but we'd spent a lot of time talking things out, and then we fell asleep together as the sun was coming up. It probably wasn't the smartest thing to do, but we didn't wake up dead, so it was okay. When I got back to the house, it was just my luck that Patrice was walking down my street when I pulled into the driveway. She paused to admire the car as I drove in, and as soon as I got out of the car she declared, "I'm in shock that that is yours, girl! You're goinna do it up big in Boston! You got that Ivy League thing down!"

I laughed at her enthusiasm. "Yeah; I just have to pretend that I have a house in the Hamptons, and that I vacation in Aspen, and I might be able to fool some people."

Patrice took her eyes off the car. She gave me an appraising look. "Awfully late night, don' you think?" she teased.

I rolled my eyes. "I bet you're just getting up," I returned.

"Actually," she clarified. "I've been up for hours, and girl, I swear those are tha same clothes that you had on tha night before!"

"They are," I admitted with a laugh, "and they stayed on my body all night."

"Mmm hmm…" She tried to give me a stern look, but it was broken up by her laughter. She hugged me sappily. "Congratulations," she declared. "We graduated!"

Her words seemed to impact both of us at the same time, and we stood in quiet contemplation of them for a few minutes. I had a brief flash back of Marcus and my talk on the day we started at Mason. "It's surreal, isn't it," I spoke, wondrously. Patrice seemed to be caught up in her own reminisces. I gave her a scrutinizing look. "So what did *you* do to celebrate?"

"You know Alex is preparin' for tha convent," she told me, "so I didn' *do* nothin' for real. It was-," she paused in the middle of her sentence. "What," she demanded, "is *that,* on your finguh?" Count on Patrice to notice the ring almost right away. My fingers flexed on their own accord. "Cause what it looks like," she went on, without waiting for me to say anything, "is an engagement ring." I said nothing. "T?"

"Derek asked me to marry him last night!" I admitted shyly, the smile growing on my face at the words. I actually giggled as the words manifested into the thought of an actual future.

She jumped up and down where she was standing. "Oh my *God*, girl, are you *serious?*" she questioned. "What 'em I sayin', course you're serious; you don' know how to joke." She started to crow, "Man, did I call this one or *what*? I am *so* good! I told you! You didn' want ta believe me, but I told you!" My words must have sunk in. "He really proposed?" she questioned. "I can' believe he proposed," she said, softly. "What'd you say? You must have said yes because uh tha ring on your finguh. So when're you guys gettin' married? I can' believe you're goinna be married before me! What about school? You're not pregnant are you?" It was amazing that she didn't collapse from lack of air because she didn't take a breath in between her words.

"No, I'm not pregnant, Pat, calm down," I cautioned. "Derek and I aren't getting married tomorrow…" I laughed a little uneasily. "Or any time soon. It's more of a promise than an engagement," I attempted to explain.

Patrice's look was confused. "What's that mean?"

I took a breath, thinking back over what we'd discussed the night before. "It means that things are pretty much going to stay the same: I'm going to Radcliffe, as planned, and Derek's going to stay here and work; finish his degree. When he graduates, he's going to move to Boston, and get a job while I'm in school. If we're ready to get married after I graduate from undergrad, then we will. If not, we'll wait, but we're going to live in Boston until I graduate from law school, and then, we'll see what's what."

"Sounds kinda complicated," she said after a moment. Inwardly, I had to agree, but it was the best solution either of us could come up with without admitting to ourselves, and each other, that it wasn't going to be cheap, or easy, and there was going to be a lot of time in-between visits. "If you're goinna do all that, why not just get married now?" Patrice asked.

That question had come up, too. "Cause I'm 17, Pat, and neither Derek, nor I, are really in a place to get married." I know that there were no guarantees in life, but I didn't want to even contemplate marriage before I had my degree. I didn't want to make my mom's mistake. Besides, if Derek moved to Boston, he'd have to find a new job; I'd have to move into the married dorms, which would mean I'd miss out on a pivotal college experience; part of attending Harvard was living in the dorms. I might even lose a scholarship or two if I got married.

And of course it would mean that we'd be married *now*, and despite my personal feelings towards Derek, I couldn't fix my mind on the idea of being someone's wife.

"So, what're y'all goinna do 'bout sex?" she questioned next. "Three years is a long time ta have to go without it. Unless you plan on puttin' out?"

Count on Patrice to think about that. "Hadn't planned on it, but who knows, I might change my mind," I said. "And anyway, Derek knows that, and it doesn't seem like he's unwilling to accept that. But I can knock out college in less than three years; I've got some college credit as it is, and I'm already going to school early."

"Yea, but still. This is kinda serious, Tracy! I can' believe he actually proposed," she mused. "Tell me everythin'," she demanded, "and don' leave *nothin'* out!"

Once we both had a chance to get used to it, we told our parents about the engagement. We talked to my mom first. Derek came over looking like a choir boy, his hair parted and slicked back, his clothes ironed so pristinely that they could cut paper. I'd only told my mom that Derek was coming over for dinner, but one look at him, and she sighed before a word was spoken.

He took my hand, and even though I'd taken off the ring, her hand went to look for the piece of jewelry that was missing. I could see Derek's nervousness, but I squeezed his hand in affirmation. If we couldn't do this here, we'd never survive a marriage.

"Mrs. Burrows, as you know, your daughtuh and I have become quite close to each othuh these past few years." Her eyes tightened, but I could hear his confidence grow as he spoke. His joy was unmasked in his words. I smiled in his direction, and he paused a moment to return it. "And tha more I got to know her, tha more in love wit' her I grew. On graduation night I asked Tracy if she would do me tha honor of givin' me her hand in marriage, and she accepted."

My mom didn't seem surprised, but she certainly wasn't overjoyed about the announcement, not that I expected her to be. I let Derek do most of the talking, and she seemed to listen, asked the questions that you'd expect a parent to ask: *"Where do you plan on living, how are you going to manage to pay the bills, have you thought about how hard it's going to be?"* We answered her questions, told her the things that we'd decided for ourselves. Mostly she just let us talk. Her parting words to Derek as he was leaving, though, were: "Thank God you're taking *some* time to think about it," in as sarcastic a tone as my mom could manage.

Of course she waited until she and I were alone for her true feelings to come out. She didn't yell, mostly because she doesn't yell all that often. Instead she merely questioned quietly, "Have you really thought about this, Tracy?"

It didn't catch me off guard because I was expecting her disapproval. I knew that most of her objections would be nearly the same ones that I'd had for myself, but I planned on standing by my decision. "Yes, ma'am, I have," I replied, politely. "Well, we haven't had the time to think *every*thing through," I admitted, "but we talked about all the important things."

She rubbed her temple. "And those are?" she questioned.

"Graduation, working, living arrangements," I recited, "when we think we'll get married...and we're not going to do it any time soon, mom, like we said earlier: we want to allow both of us time to get things in order."

"Then why even entertain the idea of getting married right now?" she questioned practically. "I say you two go your own ways, keep in touch, and *then* talk about marriage only after you kids have done a little more growing up, and each have something of your own." She shook her head. "You've always been much more level-headed than this, Tracy!" she admonished. "I never once worried about you making this type of mistake; that you'd trade in your future for some instant gratification that you'll spend the rest of your life paying for, especially now, a few weeks before you're supposed to be going off to one of the best colleges in the country-,"

"I'm still going to go to one of the best colleges in this country," I protested. "No one said anything about me not going to Radcliffe."

"No, but will your mind be where you need it to be? Will you be thinking about class, or will you be thinking about Derek? And no offense, but *Derek*...," she let the sentence falter, but what she didn't say spoke volumes. "And all of this over a silly little high school fling," she finished.

"He's not a high school fling," I protested fervently. "You say that you've always trusted my judgment; doesn't that mean that you should trust that I know the difference? I love him!"

"You have a crush on him!" she corrected, harshly. "You're 17 years old, and you've only had one boyfriend your whole life. You're way too young to know what love is. When you're a child, you hear nice words and nice gestures and you mistake it for love. And yes, I'll say it: you're Black and he's White, and that's going to put your relationship at a huge disadvantage right from the start because it *will* be an issue. People are going to hate you two *just* for daring to even like each other, and if you think that Boston is going to be any different than here, you're wrong."

"We know that."

"You think you do, just like you think you love him, but you don't really know better yet. People are cruel, baby, and there are so much bitter feelings between Blacks and Whites that you're going to always be in the middle with both sides demanding that you choose. Love and application are too entirely separate things. I loved your father, loved the thought of him, but that didn't turn into a viable relationship. I was just like you, then, with half of your potential. Back when I was your age, women got married, often before they even finished high school, and I swore I was different.

"But then I met your father, and I let him convince me that I didn't need to have something of my own, that I could depend on him. And what happened? He left me alone to raise a child all by myself!"

It would have been impossible to miss the bitterness that those words created. "Has it been *that* bad for you, mother?" I demanded.

She looked at me, realizing how I took what she said. "I don't regret having you," she stated. There was no fervent emotion to it, just a stated fact. "See past your youth for a second," she instructed. "You have such a bright future ahead of you; so much brighter than mine had been at your age. Get your degree. Finish law school. Have a couple of boyfriends, get some life experience, get something for yourself, and *then* think about marriage. But don't choose to settle for what is conventional and easy, just because you're afraid of saying good-bye."

"I'm still going to Harvard," I insisted.

"I'm not talking about that kind of settling," she responded.

It took a second for me to digest that. "Are you saying that if I married Derek I would be settling?" I worked out.

She brought her face close to mine, making sure that I was paying attention. "Where's Derek going in his life, except to jump on your train?" she questioned. "I know you're smart enough to know that your star is brighter than his, so yes, marrying him would be settling."

I started to protest, but she held me off. "I want to ask you something that I want you to think really, really, hard about. You don't have to answer now, either, because I want you to spend some time to really think it through." She waited until she completely had my attention. "If it came down to a choice between Derek and your career, which one would you choose?"

— 38 —
"The Railway Station"

A re they closed?"

"They're closed!"

"They're not closed."

"They are too!"

There was movement in front of me. "Okay, how many fingers am I holdin' up then?"

"Three," I said, confidently.

There was a second of silence. "I knew it," Derek responded.

"They're closed!" I assured him. "I just know you."

"Really?" he questioned. "You know me, huh?" He snuck a kiss, and it surprised me so much that I opened my eyes. We both laughed, sharing another kiss before Derek hissed, "Close your eyes!"

I closed my eyes again. Derek reached for my hand, guiding me across the room. There was a moment when he let go, took a few steps away, and I heard something cloth-like fall to the floor. "Okay, open them!" he said grandly.

I opened my eyes, expectantly. We were standing in front of the mural. "Hey," I exclaimed, staring at the wall. "You finished it!" Although I was over at the studio just about every day, Derek had taken to covering up the wall while I was over so I hadn't seen it since before Christmas.

"I did," Derek agreed, a smile overtaking his face as he watched me appraise his work. I kind of just stared in amazement. The way Derek had captured the grass stalks and the sparse vegetation made it seem as if the wind was blowing through the scene, making it appear as if the whole wall were in motion. I was surprised that I couldn't feel the sun shining down on me, feel the warmth of the heat, the wind on my arms, hear the rustling of the animals, or smell the dry grassland, it seemed that sensory. Most of the painting was calm, all the animals going about their everyday lives, but you could almost feel a very slight tension in the air. I searched the scene trying to figure out why. Spread out on the savannah, there was both a pack of gazelles and a pride of lions sunning, neither of which seemed very interested in the other. But off to the side stood one lone gazelle, legs bent slightly, ready. Her head was half raised from the meal she was eating, her gaze toward a spot in the distance where a lioness radiated with coiled energy.

It was a minute before I could gather myself enough to speak. "This is... phenomenal, Derek," I gasped.

He gave a maverick-like grin. "Save your praise, woman, you haven' seen tha best part yet! Close your eyes. Humor me," he said at my look. Once again I closed my eyes. "Okay, now take about ten steps forward."

"Big steps or small ones?"

"Your choice." I stepped forward, taking five big and five small steps, just for good measure. "Okay, now open your eyes!" he directed with a laugh. Once again I opened them, and my jaw actually dropped open this time. The entire mural had changed. Instead of seeing the scene of the savannah, I was looking at several different disconnected images. The whole wall was divided into squares, and in each square there was a different scene. The one directly in front of me was a distorted image of two lion cubs playing with each other. The one right next to it was of a crane splashing in the water. I took a few steps back and I was once again looking at the image of the savannah. When I got close, the crane returned. "*How'd* you do that?" I questioned, my voice filled with genuine awe.

"Magic," he whispered, mystically, laughing as he did so. "I kind uh stole tha idea from this famous paintin', and altered it uh little, but it's tha same basic concept. Your eyes register things differently closuh up than they do lookin' at somethin' from uh distance. So from uh distance you see tha bigguh picture, but tha closuh you get, tha more details your eyes can pick out."

"Kind of like life," I remarked, half-jokingly.

His arms encircled my waist. "I wouldn' know, you've nevuh let me get as close as I'd like to, to see."

I leaned back against them. "Oh, and how close would you like to get," I teased.

His hands claimed me possessively "This is uh good start," he remarked.

His mural reclaimed my eyes, and I pulled away from his arms, moving closer to the wall. "So how did you see the smaller picture in the bigger picture? How could you still see the bigger picture when you were doing each little square?" I realized that I was making little sense. I tried again. "How did you know what to do…when you were doing each individual square, in order to make it end the way you wanted it to?"

Somehow, Derek seemed to understand what I was trying to say. "When you're writin' somethin', don' you have uh general idea of how you want it to end up?" I nodded. He continued, "You use paragraphs to coordinate wit' tha theme, you use sentences to make up tha paragraphs, and words to make up tha sentences, right? Well, each of these squares are my words."

He made it seem so basic. "This is…this is really, really, unbelievable Derek, I-I don't know what to say." He was truly a remarkable person. I don't care what my mom thought; she didn't know this man right here. If she did, she'd love him as much as I did.

His smile was infectious. "I had Hank in tha other day, and he was blown away wit' tha place," he informed me. It took me a second to remember that Hank was the name of Derek's dad's friend who owned the studio. "I think I made him speechless. He thinks that this place should sell pretty quickly."

His words caught me off guard. "Wait, what? You're selling the studio?"

His eyes trailed the room. "It's done, babe," he said with a small sigh.

"No!" I looked around, too, as if I had missed something. "When did you finish it?" I questioned. It was easy enough to forget the work that had been done, even being here for it. The place was hardly recognizable from the cold, industrial square it had been when he first showed me the place.

"You've been here," he reminded me. "You've watched me work, and you've helped out. We're done. All that's left is uh few maintenance stuff, but othuh than that, it's good to go."

"You can't lose your studio!" Despite that I was leaving, this place was ours. "So you're getting thrown out on the street?"

"I'm not gettin' thrown out on tha street. You know I's only fixin' tha place up for Hank." He seemed as if he were reminding himself of those words. He walked towards his wall. "I won' be homeless," he remarked, tracing the outline of whatever item was in the square in front of him, "but I sure will miss this place."

There was longing in his voice, reflecting how true those words were. I walked up to him, placing a hand on his back. He turned in to me, letting my arms be the one to hold him for the moment. "I'm proud of tha work I put in here," he told me, "and I'm glad that he loves what I've done, but I'm kind of sad that I have to say good-bye; especially when I'm sayin' it to my girl, and my first home, all at tha same time."

"You're not saying good-bye to your girl," I responded. "Firstly, I'm a woman," I declared, removing my arms so that I could point a finger in his chest, "and secondly, I'll always be here," I concluded. He was already grinning from the woman comment, but his smile expanded at my words.

He kissed my hand before holding it to his chest. "Okay, Miss Woman," he teased, his eyes connecting with mine in a way that sent chills down my back. His arms dropped to hold me around my waist. "But that don' mean I ain't goinna miss you like hell, though."

"It's only for a little while," I supplied.

"Too long," Derek declared. "Tha *world* can happen in uh little while." He leaned in to kiss me. "You might forget that you love me."

"That'd never happen," I assured him. "You're already engraved on my heart."

"When you say stuff like that, it only makes it harduh to say good-bye... and partin' is such sweet sorrow." His chest poked out at those words. "That's Shakespeare, you know."

I laughed at his gesture. "Yes, it is."

I brought my hand up to brush his lips, but feeling self-conscious about the gesture, at the last minute I paused, touching the side of his chin instead. When I kissed him, I could feel the bristles from the hairs that remained from his last shave. He returned my peck before giving me a real one. The kiss elongated, and we sort of danced around each other until we fell back onto the couch, giggling, still in each other's arms.

When I locked eyes with Derek, I was met with the same intensity I'd always seen in them. They burned almost as if they were little fires, and similarly I stared into them the way you'd stare at a fire, mesmerized. For a long moment I imagined falling into the feeling, the embrace; the entire world shrunken to just the two of us holding each other and searching. I wanted to tell him this, tell him what I saw, what I felt, and everything else, but if I started talking, I knew I'd never stop. So in the end all I said was, "I love you," so softly it may have been a whisper.

After a while, gently, so as not to disturb the mood, Derek questioned, "Why don' you spend tha night tonight? Our last night togethuh, our last night togethuh in tha studio?" I wasn't quick with an answer so he quickly added, "That's not uh sex invite or anythin', Trace; I just don' want to say good-bye just yet."

I didn't want to say no to the request, so I didn't. "Okay," I responded.

He sat up in surprise. "Really?"

"I trust you, Derek, just let me call my mom."

"But that means you'll have to get up," he pouted.

I combed some hairs back. "I'll be right back," I assured him. He refused to let me go. He stood up with me still in his arms, duck walking with me to the phone. He held on to me the entire time that I was on the phone with my mother, and kept kissing me on the back of my neck. I spent the whole very short call trying my best not to laugh. I could almost hear her grinding her teeth through the phone about me spending the night with Derek, but surprisingly she didn't say anything about it. I hung up with her and went back to the spot we had eked out on the beanbag.

Some hours later, when we were just curled around each other, Derek questioned, "Do you think we'll always," he paused, "always be like this? Friends?"

"You think we won't be?" I questioned.

"I mean if somethin' were to happen to us, between us," he struggled, trying to find the words. "I mean, what I mean is…, I want to always be your friend, Trace." He hugged me to him. "I want to always be this close to you." I found his hand and weaved my fingers through his, marveled at the contrast between the backs of our hands. Derek's fingers were longer and thicker, mine were thinner with less work to them.

"Me too," I answered.

Derek also looked at our interlocked hands. "Know what my daddy said to me aftuh we told him? Aftuh my mom had her say?" I could imagine what Derek's mom had said. She had been about as happy about the news of our impending nuptials as my mom had been.

"What?"

"He said that he'd liked you from tha day he met you," he shared, giving my hand a squeeze. "And to always follow your heart. Just that."

"Is your dad really okay with us?"

"My dad can see me. He knows what I'm feelin' is real. It's just uh bit of uh coincidence that he liked you from tha day he met you, though, cause I did, too."

"I don't believe you."

"I did!" He let out a laugh that I felt and heard, and sounded almost sad. "I've nevuh felt so intertwined wit' someone before, Trace. Sometimes I wonder if fate threw you in my path that first day. Like we were meant to spend our lives togethuh."

"If it did, then I have some thanking to do."

I was surprised by the sound of surprise in his voice. "You sound like you actually love me," he remarked.

"Maybe that's because I actually do. You weren't the only one waiting for someone to come around."

He played idly with the ring on my finger. "Membuh when I said that I'd tell you that I loved you every day? Well…I love you, Tracy. I love you for who you are, for your heart, and your spirit. I love you because you're kind, and gentle, and courageous. I love you because you inspire me. I love you cause you keep me in line, and because you're beautiful, and because I can' imagine a future without you. I love you because when I'm near you, my heart changes its rhythm to match yours, and because our feet are nevuh out of step. I love you in uh way that is timeless, outside uh time. I love you simply because you're you, and I … will… *always*… love… you."

Derek's voice trailed off. Neither of us said anything else, and I started to drift off to sleep. I'd thought Derek was already sleeping, so I was surprised when I gave him one last look and saw that he was still looking devoutly at me. His eyes were bright, and when his hand moved quickly to his eyes, I understood why.

"What's wrong?" I questioned.

"Just missin' you already," he said, softly.

My mom was already up and ready to go when Derek and I showed up early in the morning. "Morning, mama," I greeted, followed shortly by Derek's, "Mornin', Mrs. Burrows."

My mom's appraising eyes went from a critique of what we were wearing (Derek was dressed in fresh clothes, I wasn't), and her eyes stopped momentarily on our intertwined hands.

"Good morning," she declared, cordially, though with no more attempt at being friendly than was necessary. I knew it would be awhile before my mom warmed to the idea of Derek as my fiancé, and the man I intended to marry. The words sounded strange, even to my ears, and I couldn't really expect her to get used to it before I did. I gave Derek a sideways look, trying to make the words fit him. Derek King, soon to be Mr. Tracy Burrows. I laughed to myself. They both looked at me.

"I was just remembering something I saw on TV," I said, dismissively. Derek gave me a knowing look, like he knew what was on my mind. I gave him a smile that I hoped made me appear innocent.

"Have y'all eaten?" Mom questioned, forcing the courtesy. I hoped that by the time we did get married, she could find a warm spot in her heart for him, if for no other reason than because I loved him. Derek glanced at me, and I nodded.

"Err...no ma'am," Derek said, awkwardly, "we haven', but we wouldn' want to trouble you."

"If it were trouble," she snapped, "I wouldn't have brought it up. Have a seat, and I'll fix you something."

Derek obediently sat down. "Well, thank you, ma'am," he said.

"You shouldn't call her ma'am," I stage-whispered, "you should start calling her mom." I was oddly buoyant as I got identical looks of incredulity from the two of them.

"Actually, mom, if you're going to make something for breakfast, I'm going to go get ready, that way I'm not wasting time. Will you two be able to get along for a few minutes while I'm gone?"

In response she told me what time my train was supposed to leave. I practically skipped up the stairs to my room. I took a quick shower and dressed in the outfit I had sat out the day before. I paused to take in my room, and it occurred to me that I should feel a little less exuberant, a little more contained, but it was hard to. Even the thought of stepping back into the tension in the kitchen didn't temper my underlying excitement.

By the time I went back downstairs, my best friend had joined the party. She was alternately talking to Derek and my mom so skillfully that you almost couldn't tell that the two of them weren't talking to each other. Derek turned at the sound of my footsteps, and his eyes lit up instantly.

"Hey, Trace," he said, hopping up to pull me into his arms, and give me a quick kiss. My hand went up to caress his face, and I left my own mark against his lips. It took me a moment to remember that there were two other people in the room; or rather that I should *care* that there were two other people in the room. Derek remembered at the same time, and he pulled away just a little bit.

"Good morning, Patrice," I greeted, grinning in embarrassment at my friend. But after all the sucking face I watched her do, she could indulge me this. I turned, though, only to see her smiling. I shot a look at my mom whose emotions were carefully masked behind the blank look on her face. "Sorry," I remarked. "It smells good. You need my help, mom?"

"I can manage on my own," was her gruff response. I left the comfort of Derek's arms, smoothed down my mom's hair, and gave her a kiss on the cheek.

"I love you, mom," I declared. "Always and forever." It was a strange statement, coming from me, but I was feeling oddly sentimental, and maybe overly emotional, at the moment.

We all sat down to breakfast together, and then afterwards we headed to the station. Derek and I had mostly said our good-byes earlier at the house, not wishing to attract the attention and stares of those who didn't understand us, but when it was time to go, Derek just couldn't watch me leave without hugging me tightly one last time. And even after we released each other, we still lingered until there was nothing left but for me to get on the train, or get left behind. When I saw the three of them standing there, I had the slightest moment of homesickness and worry, but that anxiety quickly vanished as the train started in motion.

I sat back in the seat, ready for the ride.

— 39 —
"Just Getting Started"

It was easy enough to pick my Aunt Joanne out of the crowd when the train came to a stop. I rushed into her awaiting arms as soon as I got off the train. "Aunt Jo!" I called, happily.

She beamed, hugging me tightly to her. "Hello, Miss Lady! I'm so glad that you came to stay with me!" She took one of my bags from me. "How was your journey," she wondered philosophically.

"Not as exciting as the destination," I returned. "How've you been?"

Her eyebrows knitted together, as if she was giving it serious thought. "Like an insect that's worked its way into a dark corner, only to find that they've awoken to become a butterfly."

"So where do you plan on going once your wings dry?" I posed.

She spread her arms as if testing them for flight. "Now, why on Earth would I make plans when the wind will just place me where it thinks I need to go?" she returned. "But my question for you is this: now that you're here, butterfly, do you want to get home, rest, and get settled in, or do you want to try to fly?"

I didn't even have to think about that one. "Fly," I declared.

We quickly stowed my bags at her apartment, before we were off to see what we could get involved in. One of the biggest reasons why my Aunt Joanne was the favorite of my parents' siblings was because, for her, there was never anything that was off limits. Even when I was little, she, like my Grandpa, had never made me feel as if I were a child. I'd always seen myself more like her; striving towards the same sort of futures: single, but content. For that reason, I felt somewhat guilty about the recent change in my life, and it took me awhile to get around to telling her that I was now engaged.

We were cooking one evening, and I blurted out the news over raw cut chicken, corn, and potatoes. She looked at me over the meal we were making together, and declared, "Okay."

I squinted at her. "That's it, just okay?"

"Well I knew that already," she declared nonchalantly. "I *was* wondering when you would get around to telling me, though."

"How did you know?"

She nodded at my hand. "Besides the ring you have on? Your mother told me." I wondered what exactly it was my mom had chosen to say.

"Derek proposed," I said by way of an explanation.

She gave me a probing look before she sat her ladle down. "I'm not sure if you know this, honey, but you don't have to say yes *just* because he asks. I hope that wasn't your only reason."

"It wasn't just because of that," I assured her. "I like the idea of it." I didn't sound as confident saying that as I should have. Standing beside her, sudden doubts cropped up. "You don't think it's wrong do you? Do you think that it'd be too hard to be married to a man who's not black, or that I'm too young to get married? Do you think that you can have a marriage *and* a career...you never got married?"

She chuckled. "Whoa, sweetheart, you should breathe a little. It gives the person you're talking to time to process your questions."

"Sorry," I apologized. I didn't mean to just bombard her like that, but I knew that I could pour out all of my worries and concerns to my aunt, and she would give me real advice, not just feed me the answers that would shift my outcome to the way she wanted it.

Her head moved, kind of pushing the words aside. "To answer your question, though, no, I don't think you're too young to do anything. I think that age, sex, race, and all of these categories that we like to place ourselves, and each other in, are just convenient blockers to keep us from doing the things that we really want, or don't want, to do. I'm not anti-marriage; I just chose to never get married. I've actually given it some serious thought before, though."

Her words were incongruous to the aunt that I knew. I'd always figured that she had just decided early on that she'd rather have a career. "Really?"

She nodded. "I did. You probably don't remember this, you were really young, 3 or 4 maybe, that time I came down to visit with you in St. Louis with my boyfriend of the day-,"

"Prince," I supplied, readily.

She turned to look at me, a smile dominating her features. "How could you possibly remember that?" She was obviously pleased.

"Because his name was Prince," I stated obviously. "Prince Henry."

"That's right! Oh how he *hated* that name! He got teased about it his whole life so that by the time I met him he only went by his last name, Henry. He'd get angry if anyone called him Prince, but for some reason that's how he introduced himself to you when we picked you up. I think maybe it was because he liked you; grown men get weird around little girls.

"Anyway, that day the three of us went into St. Louis, and had a picnic by the river. We were eating on the bank when, without warning, you jumped up and went splashing into the water. Once we fished you out, I asked you why you did it, and you just said, all cute as you wanted to be: "Because I'm a water person, Aunt Jo"!"

I laughed along with her, trying to picture myself that carefree. "In that moment, I knew I'd found a kindred spirit!" She gave me a one armed hug, pulling me to her side. "You just dived in, didn't worry about nothing. You weren't scared of much as a kid, you know that? Sibby used to say that you made up your mind about who you were going to be the day you came into the world, and that nothing here was going to change that."

I think I frowned at that description. "So I've always been predictable?" I asked.

"No, you've always known who you were," she corrected. "Like you telling me that you're a water person, or knowing that you want to be a lawyer. You've always set your mind to something and figured out how to get it done, no matter what. That's what Sibby was saying. She's always admired that in you."

"She has?" I questioned, surprise ringing in every fiber of my voice.

"Oh, your mother is right proud of you," she informed me. "Sibby loves being a mom, and yours in particular! She's always been reserved with her feelings, though, and that's probably my fault. I wasn't a very good mom to her; hardly a good sister. Besides, it's not easy being a single mom, raising a kid by yourself, and Sibby never thought she'd have to do it alone. She expected to stay with Ben forever."

She shifted away from that statement. "Anyway, after we finished our picnic on the bank, and while we waited for your clothes to dry, you fell asleep, and in that one moment, with the sun shining brilliantly on the Mississippi in the background, and your little self all curled up between the two of us, just swimming in Prince's shirt, I suddenly *got* why people got married, why they settled down. I thought maybe it was time for me to, too."

"But you didn't," I noted.

She shook her head a little sadly. "No," she agreed. "I didn't." Her gaze fell to the pots in front of us, but I knew she wasn't looking at them. "Although Prince was a nice, good, reliable man, he wasn't the right man that lay across from me in that moment. The image might have worked better, too, if it hadn't been the Mississippi in the background; the Mississippi belonged to me and Crisps."

I wondered at the name, having never heard it before. She didn't leave me wondering for long. "We, Crisps and I," she explained, "used to say that we were going to explore every inch of the Mississippi, from start to finish. We'd gotten a pretty decent start, too. We'd hiked its coast from Lake Itasca, to Minneapolis. In fact, the first time he proposed, it was on the bank in St. Anthony Falls, with a ring he won out of a Cracker Jack box." I could almost picture Derek doing that very thing.

Wait…proposed? She gave a lonely smile, looking at something that I couldn't see. "You never mentioned that you'd been proposed to before," I remarked.

My aunt gave me a look that could have contained the world. "Oh, *honey*, I've been proposed to more times than I can count."

"But you never got married."

"No," she agreed. She gave an absent stir to the pot in front of her. "No, I didn't."

"Why not?"

"Because no one could ever put it to me in the right way to make it sound appealing enough."

"Did this…Crisps break up with you when you said no?"

"No. That proposal came when I was still young; I didn't take it too seriously. I told him I'd marry him when we reached the end of the Mississippi. He told me not to deal out a hand if I wasn't going to play it." She gave me a sideways look. "You've never heard this story, have you?" I started to respond, but she answered her own question, "Well, I guess you wouldn't have; it's not exactly the kind of story that Sibby'd share with you. I guess it's not the one that mother's want their daughters to hear."

"And why is that?" I wondered, curiously.

"Because Crisps…," she smiled wickedly as she said his name, and I imagined that it was the passion with which she said it that had a lot to do with why she didn't think my mom would want her to share this story, "was the *very* guy that your parents warned you about. He was the one that fathers didn't let their daughters talk to after church, the one mothers steered you away from at the market, or that the good girls didn't want to have to sit next to in school; the bad boy, the rebel, the guy that was just no *good*." Her lips curled, though, contrary to the words she spoke.

She had my attention. I waited, but she seemed somewhat hesitant. "Sibby'll probably kill me if I told you," she reflected. She seemed to be thinking the decision over. A glance at my expectant face made up her mind. She pulled out one of the chairs beneath her table, and sat down, nodding at the seat across from her, indicating that I should do the same. "I'm not like Papa when it comes to the telling," she warned, "I don't even know the best place to start this one, it's always hard to remember where a story starts. I guess you could say that Crisps and I began when mama died, in a way. You know that she passed when I was 12, right?"

I nodded. "Well, she never really regained her health after Bobby was born, so I was already used to responsibility, but when she died, it was like from that moment on, I was a wife and a mother. I made sure Papa still functioned and did what he was supposed to, and I took care of Sibby and Bobby, made sure that they were clothed, dressed, clean. I was the oldest, and a proper young woman; I took that responsibility seriously.

"But, if you can imagine it, when I was around your age, I was the bee's knees. I was something of a looker, and even when I was young, I had this sophisticated and motherly air about me that was missing from all of the other girls my age. I practically had a sign over me that said, 'marry me', and all of the fine young men of Hartford wanted to do just that. I knew for certain that if I stayed there, I'd get caught up by one of those decent young men, and since I'd already played the role of family woman, I wasn't anxious to do it again.

"So, as soon as I felt that Sibby was old enough to take over," she whipped her hand in front of her with a sense of flair, "I hopped a bus to Boston with no intention of ever looking back."

I tried to image doing that very same thing, and realized that, in a way, I had. Even though my aunt lived here, I'd still given up a lot to make this trip.

"Two months from the day I got off the bus, I met Crisps Thomas." Her eyes took on that same fierce light that burned in Patrice's eyes whenever she was talking about one of her flames; the same light I knew showed in my eyes whenever I was around Derek.

"Crisps was short for Crispus, as in Attucks. That name goes in and out of style around us here in Boston," she informed me. "Crisps just happened to be born when the name was in, and he was just as daring, dangerous, reckless, and as ready to do battle with the world as his predecessor had been. He *loved* adventure: craved it the way normal people craved food. If every single day of his life was different than the day before, then that was as close to heaven as he ever thought he'd get.

"It was raining the day I met him, but it'd just stopped. I was coming out of the library, of all places, and there he was, like he had been waiting for me. He was straddling his Ducati, his white t-shirt soaked clean through, a cigarette playing between his lips."

I thought back to the first time I'd ever seen Derek, tried to imagine him approaching me after getting off a motorcycle. Derek wasn't that reckless boy, and I wasn't the kind of girl to go chasing after him, yet what she described seemed so familiar, as if maybe, in a different setting, we might have been.

"His eyes locked on me as he put out his smoke, hopped off his bike, and asked me, as smooth as you please, if he could bum a fag, because the one he had 'just didn't have the right *taste*'." She paused, remembering, "But boy did he!"

She laughed softly, giving me a sideways glance to see if I was scandalized by the looseness of her tongue. She smiled at the look I gave her. "Yes, I was *that* girl," she stated, openly. "And I fell for *that* boy. Crisps was everything that Papa wasn't. I *loved* that about him. Papa was short, solid, dark; Crisps was tall, wiry, and light. Papa was so dependable you could set your watch by him; the only thing you could count on Crisps for was a good time. He could out drink a drunk, spend money like he was the mint, make any lie seem like the gospel, and got philosophical when he was stoned. He said he used to see God when he looked at rainbows…"

Love permeated from every word of her description, and I tried to reconcile my mind to the image of my aunt in love.

"He used to say to me often: *'Baby, if you enjoy the ride, what's it matter how we get there?'* Most of the time we had no idea where we were going, but go we did. In the five years that we were together, we went all around the world. Crisp was one of those people who could pass for anything, and he wasn't afraid or ashamed to pass for everything. He never hesitated to take on a new role, no matter how ridiculous it seemed. We were poets in France, teachers in England, Blues Player's in Italy. We were diplomats to the Hague, American commie ambassadors in Russia and Korea, missionaries in Nairobi…you name it, we played it.

"I probably *should* say that I'm ashamed of half the things we did," she reflected, "but I can't honestly say that I am. We didn't fault people for their prejudice or ignorance, we used it to our advantage. If a stereotype helped us get to where we were going, then we'd let people low rate us to the bank. By the time they realized their mistake, we were already gone…"

She paused in her memories. "He used to ask me to marry him," she said, almost disconnectedly, as if she had forgotten what she was saying. "Even though we ran around together, we were never really *together*; we were always free to do whatever we wanted… but every now and then he'd say something like, *'Joanie why don't we go on and make it right?'* I never took him seriously because it was so conventional, and Crisps shed convention, continuity. It was always at random moments, too: rafting down a river, racing down a back road, running for our lives..."

I cocked my head to the side.

"Honest to goodness, he did that very thing, once. We were in...San Juan, maybe. There was this guy who meant to cheat us out of the money that we'd earned, so we cheated him first, and while we were running for dear life, Crisps pulls me into this alcove," laughter went through her body, "and clutching his side and out of breath, he seriously says to me, 'Woman, when you goinna quit all this making me chase after you, and go on and let me catch you already'?" When she smiled at the memory, her eyes bright, faced flushed, she looked 20 years younger. I saw how she must have been then: scared of nothing and laughing at the world.

"He met Papa, once," she said now. "Sometime after we'd gotten back from Spain. Papa, predictably, didn't like him. He took one look at him and thought he was too flighty, but he was solid enough to say that he liked how happy I seemed to be when I was with him. If nothing else, Papa loved love. I think that it might have been Crisps meeting Papa that really changed him," she said, contemplatively. "He got married a few months later to this baker's daughter.

"The night he met Papa, though, he told me that he had tickets to Venice in his pocket, and that he wanted me to come with him, so of course I did. He'd booked us on a tour as Cat Daddy Crisp and Blue Angel," she chuckled, fondly. "Crisps could blow on the sax," she mimed playing the instrument, "and I could belt it out," she sang a few notes, "and if we weren't the real deal, you'd never know. After a gig, when we were feeling really good and high on life, he proposed for real, with a ring not pulled from a snack box. I turned him down, like I always did, thinking nothing of it. A week later he'd sold the ring and handed me a ticket back to the States. He was married a few days later."

Surprisingly, she didn't sound bitter or angry at the words, just contemplative. "Did you ever see him again?" I questioned, anxious to hear the rest of her story.

Her eyes flickered. "What?" she questioned distractedly, looking at me.

She didn't readily continue, and I wondered if it had ended there. "So you came home?" I prodded.

She blinked, life returning to her features. "Oh, no way!" she remarked. "Crisps might have dismissed me, but I wasn't done, yet, with Italy. I kept the money and tried to keep up the musician charade, but Blue Angel was nothing without Cat Daddy...so I ended up waitressing in a small little bistro in Padua. That's where I was a year later when he showed up again. He was without wife, and without ring, and he never said why he got his marriage annulled, but that was the end of *that* little episode." She waved her hand, dismissively.

She stood up, suddenly, walking back to the counter to where our uncooked dinner sat, temporarily forgotten.

"So what happened?" I questioned, moving to be beside her.

Her brow furrowed in a pronounced frown. "We never reached the end of the Mississippi."

I waited, but she didn't seem like she was going to say anything else about it. "To answer your other question," she began awkwardly, as if she wasn't quite sure where she was, "I don't think that marriage and family are the antithesis of a career. I didn't choose one over the other, because, if you notice, I don't have a career, either. I have a life, and I have a job. I try not to live any farther in the future than is absolutely necessary to survive. I have some savings, no debt, and I make plans to share time with people, but there's nothing in my life that can't be changed or reversed."

Her actions shrugged without her moving her shoulders. "Most people live as if they're never going to die. I live knowing that someday, hell maybe even today, I will. One thing mama's death taught me is that none of the things that you do to keep you tied to this earth will actually keep you here. Even those who made that lasting impact are no less dead when they die."

My aunt paused to check on her greens, still not quite back to the present. I wanted to know the rest of her and Crisps story, but I knew not to ask. "I haven't gotten married as of yet because I don't have the time or patience for it. I love being you and your cousins' aunt, but I'm content not being a mother. I've never been exactly kosher with some guy seeing me as his property, either. I'm not saying that all guys are like that," she allowed, "but plenty of them see women like that." She shivered. "It all puts a bad taste in my mouth." I laughed at my aunt's acting.

"I don't think Derek's one of those types of people," I declared. "I mean he's used the 'my' adjective, but it doesn't give me the willies or anything. I don't feel owned. Or I do, but not in a bad way. We balance each other out. He needs me to remind him about the future; I need him because he keeps me in the present."

My aunt sat her knife on the counter. "Your ma'll kill me for saying this, but if you want to get married, do it. As long as you're happy, to me that's all that ever matters. Life's about experiences; marriage is just another experience. It's not the first, and it doesn't have to be the last. It just wasn't one that I was very interested in trying, but the great thing about the people in this world is that no one else has to be me."

She began quartering the chicken. "Cut up some onions for me?" I got down the wooden cutting board. "You know, while you're at it, go head and start on the rice," she directed. I nodded. Her knife stilled. "You can handle the chicken, too, right?"

She'd left the kitchen before I had a chance to answer.

— 40 —

"Shadow of the Stars"

I'd arrived in Boston the week before the summer term started, and that was just enough time to get situated at my aunt's. The night before classes, I had my familiar first-day-of-school jitters, and it just seemed wrong that I wasn't spending the night at my best friend's, talking into the early morning hours about clothes and boys. I'd gotten pretty familiar with Harvard's campus during the scholar's program, but I still left for campus early, arriving at my classroom nearly a half an hour before my class started. I wasn't nervous, just ready.

While I waited, I quietly checked the faces of the people as they came in, noting their clothes, posture, varying emotions. I was so excited I found it hard to sit still, nervous about taking my first true college course; well my first true Harvard college course. I'd dressed for the occasion too: I'd worn a pleated black skirt, white blouse, and a crimson summer sweater that my aunt and I had picked out a few days ago.

At the top of the hour, the teacher, a medium built, sandy-haired man, wearing clothes far more casual than I expected a teacher to show up wearing, walked into the room, shutting it without ceremony behind him. He paused only a moment to write his name, Mr. Jonah Michaels, on the board, before he started handing out a syllabus that was the size of a small book.

"Welcome to Comp," he remarked, his voice sounding somewhat pinched. He halved the rest of the stack and gave them to two students to finish passing out. "By the time you finish with this course you will know how to write a perfectly structured academic paper, on any subject material, in every format, or you will learn that this, perhaps, is not the correct school for you. Let's get started," he said, breathlessly.

Michaels' class didn't seem any more challenging than any of the courses during the scholar's program had been, and the pace was pretty much the same. On our first team assignment for Michaels, I met Monica Fairstaff, a short, buoyant, raven-haired journalist major, who had intense gray eyes that cut through you as if she were x-raying you. "Where're you from?" she wondered, her voice so old, and proper, and New England, that it excited me. It was thrilling to hear a voice that was so obviously not from the South.

Since she was unlikely to have heard of Bakersfield, I simply told her Alabama. "No bull," she replied. "Montgomery? Birmingham?" her words were like her eyes, eager, probing. By the way her fingers flickered about her, I could tell that she was a smoker, which may have contributed to the huskiness of her voice.

"No. I'm from Bakersfield. It's more north, close to Tennessee."

"Yea? Ever been to Birmingham? My father and I were there last year," she said breezily. "We were trying to get candid shots. He's a reporter. They broke his camera." I was amazed at how at ease she said the words. "How's the temperament in…you said Bakersfield?" she barely took a breath in-between words, and even that cadence was different from what I was used to.

I felt almost as if I was being interviewed, and I responded as if I were. "Technically the town is desegregated. Schools are slowly integrating. My high school was."

"You went to an integrated high school?" she remarked in delighted surprised. "In *Alabama*?"

"Bakersfield's a little bit more liberal," I explained. "It's because the Blackrock Arsenal, our military base, is getting so much publicity. Bakersfield's population was in the low teens a few decades ago, now it's over a 100,000. Most of those people are connected to the Arsenal, somehow, and come from other places in the country where segregation isn't as stringent. So you had all of these parents who were unhappy that they had to go out of their way to take the kids to different schools, demanding that something be done about it, and arsenal officials who just wanted to keep the peace. Integration was the end result."

"Meanwhile, the schools in Boston are going into a crisis over the issue, and white city officials keep quoting zoning issues for substandard inner city schools," Monica said wryly.

"You sound as if you are surprised," I noted.

"Only by their uninspired explanation," she responded. "You'd think by now they would have come up with something cleverer." The corners of her features turned up, almost in a smile. "You're all right," she informed me. "If you ever want to, I'd like to interview you for the Crimson. I'm mostly a photographer, but Father says that I should learn how to do interviews too, to round me out as a reporter."

"I don't know if I'm interesting enough to make it to the Crimson."

"How about you consider it?" she suggested. "And we'll see."

Even though my classes kept me busy, I didn't just bounce between them and the library, like I would have back home. I was intent on listening to the meaning of my own graduation speech, and not make the same mistakes that I'd made in high school. This was where I said I always wanted to be, and I was going to prove it. I wanted to participate in every club or organization that I could (once the fall semester rolled around), and there was so much going on, and to do, that I wasn't going to miss any of it.

Boston just seemed so much more *alive,* compared to Bakersfield. Being back in a city reminded me of how easy it was to simply get wrapped up in the pulse of it all. Bakersfield's population was inching past a hundred thousand, while Boston's population was that several times over. It made getting lost in a crowd that much easier, but it also made it more likely to find people that were more like yourself. I embraced my new city with a willingness that, I admit, I never embraced Bakersfield. But then again, I felt more of a connection with Boston than I ever had with Bakersfield.

And to my great surprise, school did not prove to be a problem. I took to heart every little bit of collegiate advice I'd been given; I sat in the front row, I read class material ahead of time, I utilized my teacher's office hours, I asked questions, I even read the auxiliary readings. I developed rapports with my teachers and got to know my classmates. Once you were able to get past her reporter stance, Monica was a real pleasure to be around. We discussed politics till both of us were blue in the face, and I occasioned trips off campus with her for photo-ops. Stephanie and I caught up within my first week of being back, and her controlling nature and relentless drive helped me stay ahead of my classes. One of the counselors from the scholars' program even got me a job in Langdell Hall, at the law library, so in my spare time I began to develop my background of legal knowledge.

I'd worried that I'd sat Cambridge on a pedestal, and that it would fall short of my expectations, but it was turning out to be everything that I'd been waiting for, and more. The only thing missing from my summer was Derek. I felt his absence in almost everything. Calling him, even once the polls changed, was just too expensive, and hearing his voice the times I did call, or he called me, filled me with too much longing. Writing letters was just as hard. Every time I tried to assemble a letter, I was hit with just how much I missed him, and how much I wished that he was here with me, discovering this new environment with me.

I'd take a walk around the square on campus, and think about me and him walking it hand and hand. I wondered where we would live when he moved here, wondered where he would get a job; wondered if we would have a dog. I even tried to mentally draw up pictures of what our children would look like, even though I'd never expressed the desire to have kids.

I thought about all this, but I couldn't put any of it in the correspondences I sent home. I'd write out page long letters, only to shorten them to three or four line notes, similar to the ones we passed back and forth the summer before. I even thought about sending him the pages that I had scribbled our names together on, as evidence of how much I thought about him. But instead, I simply sent him those short notes that did nothing to express how much I missed him, and wanted him here with me.

*

"Professor Nester must hate the world," Logan announced as we were heading across the Yard. "Shea Dwyer asked for a study guide for the final, so he gave us a thirty page study guide and told us to get started."

"I heard that no less than a 1/3rd of the students that sit his exam flunk it, and only a 1/3rd make higher than a C plus. It's a hundred questions, multiple choice, seven different answer choices, A-G," Asher shared.

"That's just a rumor," Stephanie remarked. "Grandfather went to school with Nester. He said that he copied and cheated his way through school, and wasn't able to make it in business, so he got his Ph.D. He enjoys taking out his mental ineptitude on those who dare to attend his class with any sense of optimism, purpose, or actual intelligence, but he's not intelligent enough to compose an exam that complicated."

"I hear Hambrick's exam's 25 questions, all essay."

"Hambrick?" Stephanie laughed. "My cousin Marty had her. All Hambrick's interested in seeing is whether or not you can argue a point with substantiation. Marty says she doesn't even really grade her tests based on actual knowledge of the subject, just the strength of the argument."

"Too bad *you're* not in Hambrick's class, huh, Tracy?" Asher questioned insultingly. Asher seemed to take my presence as some sort of personal assault. He was my reminder that there were Sam Williams' everywhere in the country. "There worthless drivel equates to an A."

"Yes, Ash, it's a shame that you won't have that to fall back on," I retorted. "I'm not a bit worried about *my* finals," I said with false bravado. I don't care if I *was* nervous; I wouldn't let a newt like Asher know it.

Beside me, something seemed to have caught Monica's eye. "Tracy, I think someone's trying to grab your attention," she remarked. She'd been talking to me, but we all looked across the Yard at the barely recognizable form moving in our general direction. I started to express my doubts about that, until I realized that some of the features seemed familiar…

In my haste, I dropped my books and ran across the grass to where Derek was waiting with his arms open. "What're you doing here?! How'd you get here? *When'd* you get here?" I didn't honestly care about his answers as much as I cared about how much I enjoyed having his arms around me. My lips strained from my smile, my heart racing in its excitement.

Derek laughed, giving my hand a quick squeeze. "Which one do you want me to answer first?" he teased. He gave me a brief kiss on the nose. "I wanted to see you so I took tha Greyhound."

"You know that I'm going to be home in a couple of weeks, right?"

"Course, I know that," he asserted, and I wondered if he'd felt the separation as acutely as I had. "I've been countin' down tha days, but I had some time off, and I wanted to see you before that, so here I am!"

"How long are you here for?" I questioned eagerly.

His eyes didn't leave my face. "Just 'til Sunday," he answered with regret. "Hey, where'd your stuff go…?"

I laughed, embarrassed by my behavior. We went back to where my friends and classmates were waiting with surprised looks on their faces. I guess I didn't give off the impression of someone who'd go dashing across the Yard into the arms of a boy. I grinned at them. "This is my boyfriend, Derek," I said, introducing him to them. When I said the word 'boyfriend', Monica looked like Christmas had come early. She shook Derek's hand vigorously, and I imagined I already knew the conversation that would follow her look.

We'd been heading off campus to grab lunch, so I dragged Derek along. As we walked along Mass Ave, searching out somewhere to eat, Derek mostly listened, while we continued to talk about teacher's exam styles, and the upcoming end of the semester. Both Monica and Stephanie posed a passing interest in Derek, if for somewhat different reasons. Monica seemed as if she was trying to put together an impromptu interview; Stephanie seemed to be vetting him. They threw the occasional question his way, which always seemed to throw him off guard.

When Derek answered their questions, his accent seemed to noticeably stand out, very much at odds with the quick pace and hustle of the city. Having been around it for years, I was used to the drawl, but they treated it like another language, and Asher, especially, kept asking Derek to repeat himself, or for clarification on a word, purposely mistaking the slowness of speech, elongating of sounds, and the dropping or adding of letters that was common in southern speech, as a sign of a lack of intelligence.

I could see Derek getting agitated, and it wasn't until we'd said good-bye to my classmates, and were finally alone, that Derek visibly relaxed into the Derek I knew. "Some friends you got there," he remarked at their absence.

"You just have to get used to them," I told him. "Except Asher; there's nothing to like about Asher."

Derek smiled broadly, and I grinned back at him. "So where's all *your* stuff?" I wondered.

"It's at your aunt's…*and*… I brought you uh surprise."

"What's the surprise?"

"Always impatient," Derek admonished. "If I tell you, you won' be surprised. You'll just have to wait'n see."

My aunt wasn't home when we made it back to her apartment, but Duke came rushing out when we opened the door, barking loudly and nearly tackling me to the ground. "Ssh…boy," I remarked. "Joanne forget to take you out?"

On cue, he gave a loud bark that echoed around the apartment. "He's sure some dog," Derek declared.

I rubbed his head in appreciation. "Yes, he is," I cooed.

I dropped my books off in the guest room, and gave a smile at Derek's suitcase neatly stacked in the corner. With only a look as a reminder, Derek went over to it and pulled out a cellophane wrapped package that he handed to me. "You didn't," I remarked, before I'd even unwrapped the item.

"Miz Hattie made it a'special, just for you. I thought you might like uh bit of home."

I unwrapped the piece of pecan pie for verification. "I can't believe you!" I remarked. I hugged him fiercely. "You're the greatest, Dare, you know that?" I questioned. He smiled in satisfaction.

Duke started to whine, so we got him leashed, and walked him to the park. I'd refused Derek's offer to take Duke's leash, so Duke towed me along while Derek walked beside me. We should definitely have a dog, I thought to myself. I could see us as dog people. "So, how's home?" I questioned.

"Lonesome without you," he responded. "I'm missin' you so much," he added.

"Me too," I breathed.

"Tell me everythin' I've missed since you got here."

I obliged and started talking about classes, about school and the new associations I was making. "Do you remember Monica," I questioned. "She was the dark haired one with glasses? She's a journalist. She's probably going to try to swing an interview with the two of us. Would you want to be interviewed?"

"For what?" he questioned.

"Because we're an interracial couple from Alabama, and she thinks that's news."

It seemed as if the thought had never occurred to him. He gave a kind of sideways smile, and a shrug. We talked about Stephanie, too, and about how much I disliked Asher. He seemed to be far more interested in Asher than Stephanie. "Now you don' 'dislike' Asher tha way you 'disliked' me, do you?" he questioned.

It was so absurd that I almost burst out laughing. "Not at all," I assured him. "So how's work? Denny, mom and dad?"

It was his turn to talk. I hadn't missed out too much on what was going on with him because his letters hadn't been in short supply, but he still found things to tell me about. "I can't believe you brought me a piece of pecan pie," I remarked, after something he said. It hadn't been long enough for me to have started really missing Bakersfield, but the gesture itself was so sweet. Derek really was one of the sweetest guys I knew. And he was mine.

Duke paused suddenly in his stride, stopping short of crashing into a woman on the path in front of us. She was pushing a stroller and trying to retain her grip on a stack of papers. Almost right as we pulled parallel, her stroller must have caught on a rock or something because she stumbled, and the papers went flying everywhere. Without hesitation, Derek and I both went scrambling to chase them down, and Duke helped by attempting to pull me in every direction but the one I wanted. It took a few minutes, but we gathered up all of the bits of paper, and handed them to the woman. She gave a grateful smile. "Thank you."

I smiled back at her in return. "You're welcome," I responded. Derek nodded in acknowledgment, and we waited a moment before our talk returned to Bakersfield.

My aunt had since made it home, by the time we got back to her apartment, and she'd dragged along company with her. Beer and chips lined the counters now, and the smells of cooking filled the apartment as two of her guests made themselves at home in the kitchen.

My aunt kissed me on the forehead when she saw me. "A package came for you while you were in class," she stated. "Did you get it?"

I grinned. "Yes, ma'am, I did, thank you, Aunt Joanne."

"Anytime," she responded. "Oh, and Erin Lane called," she let me know before getting swept away by one of her guests. Erin would be my roommate in the upcoming year. She lived out in California, but was currently spending her summer in Dublin. The message she left said that she was in town right now, on an unexpected stopover, so I was actually going to get the chance to meet her before the school year started. I called her at the number that was left, and we made arrangements to get together before she left the states again.

Once I hung up the phone, I took a seat in Derek's lap, and allowed myself to get swept up in the chatter of my aunt's guests. The TV was turned on, and the only thing showing was news of the Apollo mission. No one, the news anchors included, seemed too optimistic about this mission-so far ten other attempts had been made previously, all to no avail-and the general consensus when the Apollo 11 had taken off was that this mission would be like its predecessors. Yet, still we watched, anticipation mounting when it was reported that the Eagle had landed safely on the moon.

Several hours later, we were still crowded together in front of the TV, keeping an eye and ear to the set as the talk went from jobs, to life, to politics, and back again. I smiled down at Derek, liking the feel of him having to look up at me. "I'm glad you came," I told him.

"I'm glad I came, too," he responded.

The anticipation was starting to dwindle, Derek and I were starting to nod off, and one of my aunt's guests was making his preparations to leave, when Neil Armstrong exited the lunar module. With bated breath we watched as the scratchy image of his descent down the ladder was replayed back to us. After a delay, we saw the incredible transformation where the impossible passed through that incomprehensible realm of things that had somehow become possible: man had taken its first steps on the moon.

And with that one, small, gesture, President Kennedy had managed to fulfill one last promise to the American people: man had taken his place among the stars.

How in the world could anything seem impossible after that?

— 41 —
"Comings and Goings"

The night before Erin was supposed to arrive, I tossed in the bed, unable to sleep. My restlessness kept Derek awake, and he finally sat up in the bed. "What's wrong?" he wondered, reaching over me to switch on the lamp.

I stopped him, not wanting the light on, but I turned towards him in the darkness. "If I tell you, promise not to laugh?"

"Why would I laugh?" he questioned, sincerely.

"I'm worried about meeting Erin tomorrow," I admitted.

"Are you?" Derek sounded surprised. "Why're you worried 'bout that?"

"Just because," I said with a sigh.

Even in the dim light I could see him trying to figure out my motives. "You worried she won' like you?"

"Yes, but not exactly the way you think. We've written a few letters, and we seem to get along okay, but I'm worried that she won't like me...you know, once she finds out I'm black." From his silence I gathered that he wasn't expecting me to say that. "You'd think that I'd be used to people making decisions about me based on skin color," I mused, "but still, it's startling every time; it's not something you ever really get used to.

"Aria, my aunt's neighbor, says that she knew a girl who was treated so badly by her roommate that the girl dropped out of college entirely. I...I mean it's a big deal, meeting your roommate and everything."

Derek nodded, leaning in to kiss the top of my head before he secured his hold on me. "It is," he agreed. I could hear him considering his words before he spoke. "I wish I could say that she's goinna love you as much as I do, and I hate that I can'. If she don', though, you don' need her in your life no way. You're outta sight, baby, and if they don' get that, they're squares."

I laughed nervously at his words. Derek adjusted so we were facing each other, and I could just make out his outline in the light from the window. "I wish that everyone else saw what I see when I look at you."

"And what is it you see?" I wondered.

"Uh girl too beautiful for words. Someone whose inner is just as beautiful as her outsides. Tha smartest, strongest, woman I've evuh met, who takes whit from no one, includin' me."

"Especially you," I corrected, smoothing down a lock of his hair.

He kissed the inside of my hand. "I love you, Tracy," he said, fondly.

"I...too," I remarked, wondering why it was suddenly so hard to say the words. *I love you Derek,* I thought fiercely. "Dare?"

"Yeah?"

"When the dust settles?"

"I'll still be here."

He reached for my hand, and held it to his heart. Without realizing it, I synched our rhythms, breathing in and out, in tune with him. "Do you know, if everyone loved like this, there'd nevuh be any war?"

"Wouldn't that be something?" I wondered. Derek nodded. "What if you were to get drafted, Derek? That'd be...you couldn't go."

The thought troubled him. "I could and I would...but right now I'm in school, so let's hope that it's nevuh an issue. Would you write me?"

"Every day," I assured him.

"Would you wait for me?"

"Would you, for me?"

"I would wait for you as long as I had breath in my lungs, Tracy. You're it for me. You're all I evuh want."

"You're just saying that."

"Don' mean I don' mean it."

"Do you really love me?"

He hugged me close to him. "Are you kiddin' me, woman? Who else do I have in my arms right now?"

I smiled. "Why?" I questioned, just so I could hear the words that had become my own personal song. He said the words slowly, and I listened as if I had never heard them before. When he was finished, he pulled me close to him, placing a kiss on my lips. He brought my arms up to go around his neck. "If your aunt were to walk in and see us like this, what'd she say?"

"Nothing," I answered readily, "because she wouldn't walk in here in *case* we were doing something."

"I like her," Derek remarked.

"Most people do," I responded. I finished the kiss and for a long time neither of us spoke a word, our lips, hands, and bodies, engaged in other activities, moving in well-rehearsed harmony. My fingers found my way to his hair, and he pulled me closer to him. His weight on top of mine made me feel as if he were holding me to this earth, while his lips sent me out of the stratosphere. I wrapped my leg around his to try to stay grounded. We became like two orbiting bodies: our gravities drew us in and held us to each other, kept us in the same orbit. On this one night, with separating so close, I thought about losing my composure and letting nature take its course. What harm could one night really do? It wasn't as if I didn't want to be with Derek in that way. I wanted to be with him in every way possible, every minute of my life. Forever. Being with Derek seemed pretty close to perfection in this little moment in time.

"Marry me, Tracy," Derek said, pulling his lips from mine to speak the words. "Forget everythin' else. Let's do it now."

I kissed him deeper, rather than answer, my hands slipping beneath his shirt so I could feel the planes of his chest. I felt the muscles in his stomach constrict at the touch. His hands mirrored mine, and though it wasn't an entirely new sensation, I gasped, my body responding the way that it was designed to. I pressed myself tighter against him, realizing that there wasn't much closer we could get.

"We've got to meet Erin tomorrow," I murmured, adding just enough element of humor to the words so that Derek wouldn't feel dismissed. He kissed me harder, at the words, pulling my orbit closer into his.

I wore Derek's favorite dress to meet Erin, so he dressed to match me. We got to the café unnecessarily early. I sat facing the door, and my nerves caused my head to jump up every time the door opened. Derek sat on the bench beside me, watching me watch the door and the people around him. I knew he was cataloguing just by the way his eyes darted around, and I wondered which patron was going to be the subject of his next painting. "Is that her," he wondered, nodding at a girl who had come in behind a crowd.

The girl was thin and very slender, her long, brown, hair pulled into a very casual ponytail that hung down her back. Her clothes were just as casual. She didn't look like someone who went jetting across the world, but she was obviously looking to meet up with someone. I sighed in relief at the sight of her clothes, but then instantly tensed at the thought of the introduction. "Erin," I called gently, and held my breath. Maybe it wasn't her, but she turned, slowly. Her eyes searched the general direction of the sound of her name, looked over me, kept scanning, and then finally stopped again on us when we stood up.

"Are you Tracy Burrows?" she questioned, a slight apprehension ringing her voice.

I gave her the most courteous smile I could muster. "Yes, I am."

"Oh...you're black," she remarked, simply, like it was a comment on the weather. And then she must have realized what she said. "Sorry, I just," she shrugged, giving an uncomfortable smile. "I'm Erin," she offered, and she tentatively held out her hand. The way she did it made it seem as if it was only out of obligation, but I gave her hand a firm shake, not holding it longer than it needed to be held.

Behind me, Derek gave my shoulder a slight squeeze.

"I'm sorry, I- I wasn't expecting," she heaved a sigh that ended in a nervous chuckle. I smiled because I didn't really know what else to do. Erin's eyes took in Derek, and because I could see her curious look, I reached for his hand, which showed off the ring that rested against my finger. I saw her eyes take it in. "This is my fiancé, Derek," I remarked.

She seemed to take a moment, looking from me to him. Finally, something clicked. "You must think I'm a total spaz," Erin decided. She turned decidedly toward Derek, thrusting a hand out to him as well. "Nice to meet you, Derek," she said, cordially, her voice actually warming. "Tracy's told me some great things about you."

"Has she?" Derek questioned with genuine surprise. "What's she said," he asked, looking over at me in a way that made me want to blush. I smiled, giving a slight shrug.

Erin, too, smiled at the exchange. "Nothing but good things," she assured him. "She didn't lie about how handsome you were," she thought to add, and I really did blush.

Derek gave my shoulders a squeeze, and the look that he gave me was so loving that I blurted, "Well you are," without even thinking about it. Erin was almost forgotten, but I caught myself. "Will your uncle be joining us?" I asked.

"He's catching up with old acquaintances, and gave me free reign of the city," she told us after a slight hesitation. "The thought of touring a girl school didn't pose much interest to him," she added.

Over lunch things started to loosen up between the two of us. Whatever Erin's initial reaction, she didn't seem as if she would be screaming for a roommate change. We both talked about what little we knew about our third roommate, Olivia, and our speculations about the upcoming semester. After we'd eaten, we walked over to the campus, and I showed her the places I knew, where I was working, and the House that we'd be staying in once the fall semester started. Because they were occupied, we couldn't see our actual room, but they did show us the floor plan, and we spent some time discussing the logistics of our shared space.

I was surprised to find how much I liked Erin. After hearing about her exploits for the summer (she was heading off to Australia at the end of next week), I expected her to be some extremely rich, stuck up type of girl, but she wasn't that way at all. She seemed relaxed in a way that I associated with California, and unlike everyone else-myself included-didn't seem in any way preoccupied by the fact that she was attending Radcliffe.

The three of us spent the rest of the day together, and the next day Erin and I had breakfast together before she and her uncle left. After Erin was gone, Derek and I only had a few hours alone before I had to meet up with my classmates. As much as I enjoyed him being here, this week was really the worst time for him to come because with finals coming up, I just couldn't bail on my study group. So I dragged Derek along, and he mostly doodled while we tried to commit the class lectures, readings, and our notes to memory. I felt unprepared when we finally left, but it was starting to get late, we'd been at it for hours, and I realized that Derek was getting restless. So I said goodnight, and Derek and I headed back to my aunt's. "Sorry that took so long," I declared while we were waiting for the right bus.

Derek didn't look at me. "Yeah."

"You want to get something to eat before we head home?"

He sullenly kicked at the ground. "Why, you got someone *else* you want to meet up wit'?" he questioned, moodily.

"No," I said, slowly. "I thought maybe you were hungry." I'd pointedly ignored his jab.

"I didn' know you realized I's still here," he declared.

I turned towards him suddenly, aware of his sour mood. "What're you talking about, Dare?"

"Since I got here, you've barely spared uh minute to be wit' me," he griped.

"I can't just excuse myself from my classes. They have attendance policies, and if I don't go I'm going to fall behind."

"You're not in school all day, Tracy." Derek declared.

"I took off of work for the week," I reminded him. "We've spent time together. I made time for you."

"You made time for everyone but me! And don' give me that about it not bein' uh good time for me to be here cause you made time for Erin as soon as she said she was comin'."

"She's my roommate," I declared.

"Yeah, well I'm supposed to be your fiancé," Derek snapped.

I paused at his words. "What does that mean?"

"Just what I said: you introduced me to Erin as your fiancé, but you told your little snobby study buddies that I was your boyfriend."

"What does that have to do with anything? What does it matter what I call you?"

"It matters to me! There's uh huge difference between your boyfriend and your fiancé. Your boyfriend is someone you're just wastin' time wit'; your fiancé is someone that you intend to marry someday. Am I just someone that you're foolin' around wit, or do you really intend to marry me?"

"Why would you even ask that?" I wondered.

"It's uh valid question. You have my ring on your finguh. I think it deserves an answer."

"Of course I'm going to marry you," I responded. "I wouldn't have said that I would if I didn't mean it." I hugged him. "I love you, Derek. You know that."

"I should know that, yeah," he said, his voice as stiff in tone as he was in my arms.

"I do," I said again. "Don't doubt that."

He finally softened some, and put his arm around me. His pout didn't leave his face, though. "I know, but sometimes I do. I guess I'm just upset about havin' to say good-bye tomorrow," he declared. I worked my fingers around his.

"But it'll only be a couple of weeks, and then I'll be back home," I remarked. "The time's practically going to fly by."

"Yeah," he said unenthused. "Practically."

— 42 —
"Emblem of Wounded Pride"

T racy!" Patrice yelled loudly, waving. A couple of people turned to look at her, but she didn't care. "Ovuh here, girl!" I smiled and shook my head as I made my way over to my friend. "Girl!" she exclaimed, hugging me. "I missed you! It seems like you've been gone fo-eva! I hate that you're comin' back just as I'm leavin'."

"I know," I remarked, regretfully. "But at least I was able to make it back while you're still here!"

Patrice practically bounced on the balls of her feet. "You've no idea how excited I am! I can' *wait* 'til Friday! Chicago!" she said in amazement. "How many uh our classmates can boast that they're doin' somethin' so," she searched for the word and when nothing else came to mind she simply settled on, "Fabulous?"

"I know," I agreed. "Just don't get involved with the wrong kind of stuff," I cautioned.

She waved my words away. "Listen at you, soundin' just like mama. I ain't 'bout ta do somethin' stupid. I do have brains up here," she said, tapping her forehead.

"I know you do," I replied.

"And just cause I ain't 'bout ta be spendin' all my time in some library, don' mean that I'm goinna wind up back here inna few months, pregnant." she laughed. "I bet that's all you did while you was up in Boston," she remarked.

"If I was you, I would've just gone wild. Find some random fling..." She gave a suggestive smile.

"What do I need some random fling for when I've got Derek," I posed. "Besides: could you really imagine me going wild?"

She giggled. "No, but that's tha point! You've spent so much time in your sheltered little egg that you're bound to have some energy that needs releasin'! And if you wanted to, you could! You bein' on your own, no one ta be responsible to..." her voice trailed off. "I know I'm lookin' forward ta bein' 'round all those dangerous, non-southern men, myself."

"Listen to you!"

"Can you tell I'm excited?" she questioned. "I just hope that I on't get up there and they think that they made a mistake or somethin', or that I'm just some hick 'Bama."

"No chance, Pat, you're amazing-"

"I know!" she giggled. "Seriously, though, even though I'm makin' all this noise 'bout doin' everythan' while I'm up there, I know that I'm goin' to Chicago ta work and go to school. I'm not 'bout ta mess that up. Oh." Patrice sobered suddenly. "I forgot ta tell you that me'n Alex called it quits."

This was news. Last time I left them, Alex and Patrice were still heavily into each other. "Why?"

She gave a half-shrug. She was trying to be cavalier, but I knew she was more than a little hurt about it. "We both decided that we didn' want ta do tha whole long distance thing. He started talkin' 'bout how Gabe and his girl were tryin', and how difficult it was wit Gabe goin' away to Dix, and that he didn' want that, and that if we were really serious, I'd stick around."

"Oh, Pat, I'm sorry."

"Nah, it's okay," she decided. "It's alright. I'm goinna miss him," she allowed, "but I guess it wasn' meant to be. Not everyone ends up gettin' married."

I was a little surprised by her statement. "Did you want to marry him?" I wondered curiously.

"Right now? No! I'm too young ta be thinkin' like that!" She shot me a sideways glance, as if she'd said something wrong. "There's nothin' *wrong* with thinkin' 'bout marriage right now, it's just way too soon for me. And this way, I get to go to Chicago unattached. I can start ovuh, reinvent myself, or whatevuh. Be who I want to be."

"I've been saying that you should do that for years," I teased.

Patrice looked down at the stack of clothes in front of her. "So, how're you and Derek doin'?" she questioned. "Where is he? How come he's not here?"

Somehow her questions made me feel guilty. I picked at a thread that was coming undone in my shirt. "He's at work. I told him that I wanted to spend some time with you so that he didn't have to take off to come pick me up."

Patrice pointed at a stack of clothes, and I handed them to her. "How y'all two doin'?"

I thought about how we were doing. "We're good," I answered. "Well," I sighed. "We had an argument when he came up to Boston, but I think we're alright now."

"You think?" she repeated. "What was tha fight about?"

"Argument," I corrected. It hadn't been a fight. "He didn't seem to think I was spending enough time with him."

"And were you?" she posed.

"He just showed up! I spent time with him when I could, but of course I couldn't give him as much time as he would have liked. I just don't get why he's mad at me."

Patrice just kind of shook her head. "Don' be mad, Trace, but I can kind of see what he's mad about." I gave her a look, and she held up a hand to hold me off. "Just listen," she directed. "You and I've been friends since elementary school. I may've nevuh been able ta understand your dreams, but I've always respected you for havin' them. A lot uh tha time our friendship didn' seem ta make much sense to anyone else, but it's ours, it works; I wouldn' trade it for nothin'."

"I wouldn't either," I interjected.

She held a hand up, "I'm not finished, Trace. Look, you're my best girl, but for four years, I had to listen to you tell me no when I wanted ta spend time togethuh. No, not all tha time, but a good deal uh it. No ta spendin' time out togethuh, no ta spendin' tha night, ta goin' ta dances, ta just bein' teens togethuh. Memories that you should've been there for, are filled wit Lina, and Sylvie-Ann, and Mildred, and everyone else but you.

"I respect what you're doin', but there've been times when I *just* wanted ta be able ta hang out wit my best girlfriend, you know? And if I feel this way, and we're *just* friends, how do you think Derek feels? That's why he's mad, girl, because he's thinking that he shouldn't still have to beg for your time. That you should *want* to spend time wit' him."

"I do, Triece," I said sincerely. "It was all I wanted to do, actually, but once I start thinking like that, I'm going to end up with six kids and no career. I loved that he came up to see me, but we're not going to see each other all that much over the next couple of years, and I miss him more when I'm around him, so it's hard being around him. He practically accused me of not wanting to marry him."

"Well do you *want* to marry him?"

"Of course I do," I declared.

Patrice gave me one of her looks. "Do you really, or are you just scared of losin' him?"

"I *want* to be with him," I insisted. "When I'm at school, I think about all of those stupid things. I'm excited about our futures together."

"But?"

"It's Harvard, Pat. No one gives up Harvard."

"I guess."

"You didn't go to Spellman for Alex," I noted.

She shrugged.

"And he ain't movin' to Chicago ta stay wit' me," she stated. "But Alex and I don' really love each othuh, certainly not tha way you and Derek do. And you really want to marry him?"

"I do."

"Only...maybe just not right now?" she guessed.

"Yes, well, no." But I was spending a lot of time thinking about it. "I'm going to try to graduate in 2 ½ or 3 years, which means that I won't be able to take all of those fluff type classes that people take when they're in college. Steph thinks that I could use a semester abroad because I've never been out of the States, and she thinks that I 'lack the proper culture' so she says. But I can't really do that if I'm trying to get out of school as quickly as possible, and I want to do those kinds of things; I just want him to be there for them."

"Have you told Derek any of this?"

I shook my head. "No; I don't know how to. It's like if I tell him how much I care, I'll never stop talking, and I don't see the point in doing it because it's going to be at least two years before we can even be together. I don't want things to get too intense between us right now because then all I'll want to do is be around him, and if I allow myself to feel like that, then I'll start thinking things like maybe Harvard isn't all that important; every now and then I think about getting married to him right now."

"You know your mama would nevuh come around to tha two of you if you were ta get married now."

I nodded, vigorously. "I know," I agreed, "and if I didn't get my degree from Radcliffe, I'd probably never forgive myself, or Derek, either. It's Radcliffe! Ivy League!"

"That it is, chica," Patrice agreed.

"I grew up dreaming about going to that school," I went on. "Already the experiences I'm getting just from being in that arena are incalculable. The academics I'm exposed to; the different cultures, experiences."

"And you definitely won' get that here," she supplied.

"No," I agreed, fervently. In a few days, Patrice would fully understand what I meant. Chicago was an even bigger city than Boston, it had a different temperament, a different pervading culture. It just wasn't the same.

Patrice stared in quiet contemplation of the clothes in front of her. "Trace, we both know that you're smart, gifted, talented. You've got tha whole world ahead of you, but it's *your* life. How do *you* want to live it?"

Even though I'd spent all summer in Boston, it was such a weird feeling on Friday when Patrice got into Marline's car, and I said good-bye to my best friend. Until that moment, it hadn't really hit me that things were really changing. My best friend was gone, gone, and the only things that could breach the distance between us now were phones and letters.

Derek's arms were there waiting, once we were alone, and in the car the little tracks of tears that started to flow weren't staunched once their car was gone. I wasn't exactly sure what the motivation was for the tears, but I knew that they weren't entirely because my best friend had just left. Maybe it was because it was finally starting to sink in that things really were changing.

Once Patrice was gone, and with Derek working, I didn't really have anyone to talk to, and I was sharply reminded of why I'd wanted to leave Bakersfield in the first place. Being back in town was like having writer's block. Boston had just been so vibrant, so in color, Bakersfield was black and white. It just moved too slowly. Even though I'd only been there for two months, I'd already claimed Boston as my own. The summer had only whetted my appetite; I was ready for fall.

Sitting at home all day while Derek was at work did little for my nerves, so I sought out things that I could do around the house. My mom mentioned her company wishing to transfer her to Arizona, so to make things easy on her if she did move, I broke down my room. I set aside the things that I was going to be taking with me to Boston, and everything else I either packed up, or we donated. When I was done with that little project, I found another one to get started on.

Neither my mom, nor I, had done much upkeep around the place over the years; we both had been too heavily involved in our own lives to spend too much time worrying about the house. Now, though, I had time, and I spent it fixing up the place so that it looked like it had been lived in by people who had actually been concerned with its upkeep.

I invested some of the money I earned during the summer into repairs, and once my mom saw what I was doing, she found some more money for me. I started on the backyard and worked my way out front. Around the house, I cleaned windows, changed lights, organized the garage, planted a garden in the front yard, repainted the shutters, anything I could do, really, and gradually the place started to look different, better. Loved.

"You know, you're racking up all sorts of points with my mom for helping me do this," I told Derek one evening.

He gave a theatric grunt as he worked his screwdriver underneath the window pane. "Am I?" he posed. "I was kind of under tha impression that no matter what, I'm persona non grata."

"Look at you trying to impress me with your Latin skills," I teased.

He gave me a sideways smile. "Did it work." In response, I gave him a kiss on his lips, combing his hair down with my fingers, letting them lightly touch his scalp as I did. He shivered slightly.

"Very much," I whispered in his ear.

"Don' do that!" he hissed. I raised my hand to do it again, but he reached for it before I could, holding it firmly in his grasp. His lips smiled, but for a moment there was something off in his eyes. It was only there for a moment before he pulled me into the space between him and the window. We kissed, enjoying the complete emptiness of the house.

"I love you," I remarked. Derek took a step back, an unreadable look spreading across his features. "What?" I questioned.

He just shook his head, and this time I didn't imagine the distance in his gaze. Before I could question it, we were interrupted by the sound of the door opening. We quickly pulled apart, trying to put some distance between us before my mom could walk through.

"Hi, mama," I remarked at the same time that Derek said, "Hello, Mrs. Burrows."

She nodded at both of us, before she disappeared upstairs. "Yep, I can feel it: her heart's slowly warmin'," Derek commented, wryly. Derek went back to work. "I'mma go aftuh I fix this, alright?"

"You're not staying for dinner?"

"Can'," he said stiffly, "I got things I have to take care of." I was thrown off by his hasty exit; I'd been expecting to spend the whole evening with him. Actually, I kind of expected to spend every moment that he wasn't working, together, but I was seeing a lot less of my fiancé than I'd planned. Derek had seemed kind of vacant at our reunion, and I hadn't thought much about it before, but I was starting to wonder if maybe he was still upset with me. If he was trying to prove a point about time, he was succeeding, but these were the last few days we'd get to see each other until Thanksgiving. What point did it make for him to waste the little time that we had?

Since I couldn't fix the feelings between the two of us, I poured my efforts into fixing the house. As it slowly began to look better, I couldn't help but feel a little guilty at the way me and my mom had treated the place. The two of us had only lived here; we'd never made the place a home. And now we both were leaving it. The whole thing made me think of Derek and my relationship. I didn't want to leave him. Despite how much I disliked being back in Bakersfield, as summer got closer to its end, I realized that I wasn't entirely ready to go back to Boston, either.

As much as I tried to tell myself that it would only be a few months before I saw him again, and it'd only be this way for a couple of years, it didn't help. Writing wouldn't be easy, and calling would be just as hard. It wouldn't be impossible, but it would seem that way, and I can't say that I wasn't slightly worried about some other woman scooping him up in my absence; Derek was good looking and a hard worker, which made him something to desire. Even if he said that he didn't want anyone but me, how could I know for sure that in a moment of weakness…?

More and more, the words that Derek had spoken to me, back in a time when he was trying to convince me to stay, kept coming to mind. I *could* still attend Harvard for law school, and he *had* given up the school that he wanted to go to, to stay here with me. Was I really unwilling to make even the slightest sacrifice? But it was Harvard! Was a relationship worth giving that up? Did I really have to?

Early one afternoon, my plans for the day took me to Earl's. I hadn't spent more than a few minutes inside the store before I noticed a familiar form stalking the aisles. My excitement at seeing him was tempered by the realization that he was supposed to be at a construction site in Madison. The only thing that stopped me from saying hi, and/or confronting him, was the fact that he wasn't alone. I didn't know who she was, but the two of them were on the same height, and they didn't seem as if they were unfamiliar with each other. He was showing her some tool, and apparently it was fairly funny, because she kept smiling and laughing at him. I wasn't close enough to hear the conversation, just to watch their body language. She was taking every opportunity to touch him, and he didn't seem entirely bothered by it.

I stood rooted to the spot, not sure if I should make my presence known, or to just turn away without saying anything. Derek made the decision for me. He looked away for a moment, and his eyes fell on me. A look of pleased surprise crossed his features, and if it was faked, I couldn't tell.

"Hey, babe!" he greeted. "Fancy runnin' into you here."

The girl looked over at me at his words, and an extremely distasteful look laid claim to her facial features.

"Hi," I remarked stiffly.

The smile didn't stray from his face. He took in my features. "What's tha matter?" he wondered. My eyes trailed to the girl at his shoulder, and he looked over at her, too. "Oh hey, this is Lydia. Lydia, this is Tracy." I wondered if he'd deliberately not said the word fiancée.

Her eyes narrowed as she stood there, appraising me. But she only gave me a moment's worth of time, looking through me as if I weren't there. "So you were saying, Dare?" she questioned of him.

He touched her lightly on the back. "Just that it's simply uh matter of timin' and tha right amount of force. Let me go find Duck, he'll get you set right."

Her look turned scathingly hostile once he was gone, but she didn't say anything to me. Actually, she seemed determined to pretend that I didn't exist. I felt awkward standing there with whoever this girl was to Derek. Not liking the feeling, I decided to just go about the business that I'd come here for in the first place, and turned off the aisle, leaving Lydia standing there alone.

I was blindly walking down a random aisle when I felt a hand slip around my waist, alerting me to Derek's return. It didn't stay there long, we didn't touch much, or often, in public, but he snuck in a kiss that I received stiffly. "Why'd you run off? I said I'd be right back."

"Just thought I'd finish my errands while you were gone."

"What're we workin' on today?"

"The garden," I said brusquely, offering nothing else, not even an invitation for him to come over to help. He stepped in front of me, blocking my path. "What's wrong?" he questioned.

I angled away from him. "Nothing," I said, softly.

"Trace?" Derek stared at me, making me look at him. "You upset about Lydia?"

I shifted, uncomfortably. "Who *is* she?"

Derek pulled lightly on my braid, tucking a strand of hair back in place. "Absolutely no one," Derek assured.

I thought about how casually the two of them interacted with each other. "She didn't look like no one."

"Well she is." He made his lips form a pout. "Please don' waste time worryin' about inconsequential things."

I didn't want to give it up that easily. "What're *you* doing here?" I demanded, rather than accept his statement. "You're supposed to be in Madison."

He gave a chuckle. "I had to put in an orduh for some 2x4s."

"For Bill?"

"No. For Dick Scruggs. I don' think you met him, but I'm doin' some renovations for him. Some big renovations, actually." His excitement took over and a smile grew on his face. "Babe, you have to see what he's got me doin'," he said, enthusiastically. "Do you have some time to come out and see tha house?"

I dithered, wanting to still be mad at him. "Yes," I finally said.

He gave a grin. "Great!"

We went off to see to our own tasks and met up about 20 minutes later. Derek drove us out to Clinton, this little town just to the west of Madison. We drove down a short private road, to a fairly large southern style house that, despite its run down appearance, still came off as being impressive. The rooms were still grand beneath their layers of dust and ill-repair, still spacious.

"Ain' she pretty," Derek chirped. "Friend of Bill's saw tha work I did at tha studio and offered me uh renovation job just like that." He took my hand, leading me through the rooms. "Tha place used to belong to an old family. Last generation was two sistuhs who didn' give uh good crap about tha place; they inherited it when their parents died, but they hated it somethin' awful, you know? When tha youngest sistuh died, they auctioned tha house off and Dick bought it."

He stood in the middle of the grand room, letting the feel of the place surround us. I knew that in his mind he was seeing the place with sunlight beaming in through spotless windows, gleaming against polished hardwood floors. In his head he'd already stripped the place to the bones and reconstructed it, while all I could see was the same thing I'd seen when I saw the studio for the first time. "I won' get to be as creative wit' tha space as I got to be wit' tha studio, but still-" he grinned broadly, holding open his arms. "What d'ya think?"

I was still thinking about the girl from the hardware store. "It's nice, Derek." I remarked.

He looked around him. "Nice?" he questioned. "This place is gorgeous! I haven' even told you how much I'm goinna be gettin' for tha project neithuh. Guess, you'll nevuh guess!" He didn't seem to expect an answer. "Wit' what I made from tha studio, and what I'm goinna make wit' this job, and who knows, maybe I'll get somethin' like this aftuh that…I figure we'll be set to put uh down payment on uh house for ourselves in maybe tha next two or three years." He shrugged. "Nothin' as grand as this, though," he said, a little regretfully, "but you know, somethin' that's passable. We can save some money by gettin' one uh those fixer-upper numbers, and I can do tha repair work myself."

He shrugged again, looking around him. "Anyway, it's just an idea."

I realized he was waiting for me to say something. "I think it's a good idea," I responded, distractedly. At the least it'd give him something to do to make time pass when we weren't together. "So how long do you think this is going to take?" I questioned, trying to sound interested. "Are you going to be able to fit all this in?"

"If I stick to my time table, yeah."

"You sure it's not too much?"

"I'm sure, Trace. I'm young and strong," he joked.

I gave a smile. "Yes, you are, and you are really, really good at what you do, but you were tired all the time last semester, and you didn't really have the time that you needed to study. I thought you said that you wanted to make better grades this time around."

"It'll be fine," he said dismissively. "Bill did me uh huge favuh and cut me back to uh six hour uh day, five day uh week workweek 'stead of tha eight I'd been workin', and I can put in six-five on tha house. Well eight hours on Saturday, six on Sunday, and afternoons durin' tha week." he shrugged. "Besides, I need *somethin'* to distract me from tha fact that you're not here wit' me."

I paused in what I was about to say, realizing that there was something missing from his time table. "What about school?" I asked.

Derek bit down on his lower lip, as if he had revealed more than he'd wished. "'Bout that," he mumbled. "I'm not goinna be takin' any classes this semester."

"You're-,"

He held up his hands to hold me off. "Just hear me out, Trace, before you say anythin'," he said quickly. "In orduh for me to make tha time frame that I gave Dick, I had to drop somethin'."

I tried for patient understanding. "So you withdrew from school?" I questioned.

"For uh semester," he stressed, "I'm not quittin', I just took uh detour. It's only uh semester. I can' afford to lose my spot on Bill's crew, or turn down this offuh, and I would've if I stayed in school. And last semester I barely got through my classes, and I studied, babe, you know I studied my ass off. I understand that havin' that degree is important, but right now I'm makin' good money, and it's uh certainty. School…I'm still tryin' to work out if it's good for me."

"So you dropped out?"

"I withdrew," he corrected.

"You withdrew," I repeated.

"Only for uh semestuh, but it's uh good thin'! I didn' tell you how much we made on tha studio…and I'm goinna make more than that on this gig."

I heard what he said, but it was hard t to take in his words. "You didn't tell me that you were even considering withdrawing."

"I's goinna, I just didn' have tha time yet. I mean it was kinda just handed to me."

At least it halfway explained why I hadn't been seeing much of him since I'd been home, but he seemed to have found plenty of time to get to know this Lydia.

"Yet it's been long enough that you've already started on it," I stated. The look on his face was answer enough. "I can't believe you, Derek! How could you *not* tell me?"

I saw the enthusiasm drain from him at the same time that his eyes hardened. "Damn it, 'cause I didn' want that reaction from you, right there, Trace! Why can' you just be proud of me? I'm tryin' to get somethin' togethuh for tha two of us."

"Then why weren't 'we' involved in the decision."

"Don' be upset, Trace," he pleaded, holding his hands out. "It's only uh semestuh."

"You didn't even talk to me about this!" I admonished. "I have every right to be upset. I'm doing all that I can to get through school as quickly as possible, and you withdraw without even telling me? You don't see why that would bother me?"

"It's only for uh *semester*!" he repeated. "I didn' think you'd approve-"

"But that didn't stop you from going ahead and taking the job-,"

"Because it was my choice!" he asserted. "I lost my scholarships when I moved back here, so I have to pay for school tha best way I know how to do, all while havin' to worry 'bout our future. All you've done since you've left for school is talk about how great your Ivy League friends are, how y'all're goinna change tha world, and I'm back here workin' construction? I'm tryin' to get somethin' togethuh so you won' look down on me."

"I don't look down on you! As long as it makes you happy, I don't care what you do. I just want to be on the same page! How would you feel if I decided to go to Spain for a semester, and I didn't tell you until I was on the plane?"

"That ain' tha same, Trace."

"Why isn't it?" I wondered. "Because *I'm* the one who made that decision? What are we even doing together if we're just going to go about our own lives?"

His eyes flashed at my words, hardening. "That's uh good question, but I guess that's why you have so much trouble includin' me in your time."

So, he *had* been trying to prove a point, is that what that was? "What are you talking about Derek? Are you still upset about when you came up to Boston? You showed up without notice-"

"So did Erin,"

"And I made time for you!" I insisted.

"You *made time* for me?" he choked out. "I'm tha person you're supposed to *want* to spend tha rest of your life wit', not just someone that you have to make time for!"

"And you're supposed to share your decisions with me!" I reminded him. He was the one who'd asked to be thought of in my future; the least he could do is keep me current on his.

"Well I guess we both need to do some reevaluatin', then, don' we, Trace,"

Derek remarked. "Why don' you go analyze it, and if you have some time for me latuh, well then I guess we'll talk. I gotta get back to work."

He headed back towards his car without another word. I followed silently behind. We drove back to the hardware store in that same silence. I attempted to start a conversation several times, but in the end I said nothing. When I got out of the car, Derek drove off with scarcely a good-bye between us.

Alone, at home, the garden was forgotten as I replayed our conversation in my head. How could he drop out of school? I considered calling him when he got off of work, but I was still pretty angry, so I didn't. Derek was the one at fault; he should be the one to call. But the days passed, it got closer to me having to return to Boston, and still we hadn't talked.

— 43 —
"Afternoon by the River"

Would you believe that out of all of my years of working at MIT, I never saw this side of the beginning of the year process," my aunt commented idly as we elbowed our way down the narrow hallway of my House. Despite the windows on either end of the hall, and the light that streamed in liberally through each open room that we passed, it seemed not quite bright enough. The smell of aged wood reminded me very much like I was in the middle of a library. It wasn't unpleasant, just unfamiliar, and I grimaced.

I paused suddenly, beside one of the open doors. "I think this is my room," I realized. I checked the numbers against the paper before adjusting the boxes so that I had one hand free to push open the door. My aunt sidled up beside me, and for a second we just stood there looking. "Hmm…" she remarked, the first to speak. "It's sort of depressing, isn't it?"

She downed the box she was carrying while I took in the small, cramped space. I agreed with her assessment. It had that drafty feel of an older building, and even though it was bigger than my room back home, I hadn't had to share that with two other people.

"Little boxes," my aunt hummed idly. "So which bed is going to be yours?"

"I guess whichever one I want. Erin and I didn't really talk about that, and neither of us got the chance to really speak with Olivia over the summer."

I surveyed the room again, hoping that it would get bigger as my eyes took in the space. No chance. There wasn't much room no matter how you looked at it.

I'd never had to share a room before.

My aunt patted me on my back, reading my thoughts. "Don't worry, kid, the guest bedroom's still made up for you whenever you need it …if your roommates are too aggravating… you need some extra space…you want a boy over…" she said, leadingly.

"Joanne!" Willis, my aunt's friend scolded, though I couldn't tell if his outrage was real or fictional. "You're not supposed to encourage her!"

My aunt only smiled demurely. "You should go for the little alcove, thingy," she directed. "It has the most room."

There was movement behind us. "Actually, that's my bed," said a stiff voice. "It's already taken."

The three of us turned in unison to take in a face so unfriendly that she may as well have been shipped in from back home.

"You must be Olivia," I said, making an attempt at courtesy, though her attitude screamed, 'Don't bother'.

She gave me a snide look, flipping her dirty-blonde hair to the side. "Well how astute of you. Don't tell me that *you're* my roommate?" she questioned, taking me in. Under her scrutiny I felt somewhat dingy. A few strands of my hair had escaped from the sloppy pony tail that I had placed it in, and I was wearing only a pair of jeans and a cotton blouse. Although my clothes had been freshly laundered and ironed the night before, they didn't look so fresh now.

She, of course, looked remarkable. She wasn't entirely pretty, but she carried herself as if she was a model just off the runway, and I kind of believed it. I wondered if she'd had a pole tied to her back for posture the way Aria said Gloria Vanderbilt had when she was younger. She looked like she could be a cousin to the Vanderbilts, or some other such family. I felt less than glamorous beside her.

"I am," I responded, forcing enthusiasm into my words.

"Great," she said, not so softly. "I get to be the testing grounds for this *new* frontier."

My aunt got her back up. "You should consider yourself so lucky," she declared. "We didn't know that someone else had already laid claim to that spot."

"Well, someone has," she responded. My aunt looked as if she wanted to respond to that, but then we were joined by the rest of Olivia's entourage. They overlooked us, but saw the items that we'd sat down.

"So one of your roommates is here?" A woman who could only be her mother questioned eagerly. "Excellent! Have they been up already? I'd love to meet her, meet her family."

Olivia jabbed a finger at me. "Mummy, *this* apparently is my new roommate," she remarked, full pout.

Her mother actually looked at me this time. "Oh? Oh...," she looked horrified. Her nose went up in the air as if she'd smelled something unpleasant. "You're not serious! I wasn't aware that Radcliffe had lowered their standards so much. It certainly has changed a lot since I've been here..."

"Now, you wait just one minute," Willis started, even though he didn't know me from Adam. "Look here, you can't just go talking 'bout us any kind of way you feel. I won't stand to have someone talk down to me, or any of mine, to my face."

The man stepped in front of his wife. "Don't you dare raise your voice at my wife, you-,"

But what he was exactly was interrupted by someone exclaiming loudly from the doorway, "Oh, look Kimmy, I think we found the party!"

Everyone turned to look at the interloper, and instantly I felt better about myself. The newcomer was scantily clad in very short, bright red shorts that fabulously showed off her tan and her long legs. Her tie dye t-shirt came down almost as far as her shorts, and to top it off she had her long, brown hair tied sloppily beneath a bandana that perfectly matched her shirt. Beside her, her sister looked like a younger, more decently attired version of Erin. My lips very nearly pulled into a smile at the sight of my other roommate.

She assessed the tension in the room. "What'd we missed?" she questioned in obvious amusement.

Olivia's mother turned to take in this new development. "Oh, no," she said in a clipped voice, shaking her head, "this won't do. Don't worry, sweets, I'll go have a talk with the hall monitor to see about getting your room assignment changed."

Erin snickered as Mumsy, Daddy, Junior, and Olivia turned with near military precision. Erin clapped her hands together at their exit. "Oh, *wait* till

I tell the girls back home that I actually met the von Trapp Family Singers!" she said to their backs. "Amazing! One day on the East Coast and I'm rubbing elbows with celebrities! Who says movie stars are only in California?"

This time I did smile. Erin seemed to give the same glancing look of the room as I did, but it didn't seem to depress her as much as it had me. Her shoulders took on a determined set as she took everything in. Two new sets of footsteps paused in the doorway. "Honey, I think we may've passed your roommate in the hall," an older male voice said as he entered the room. He, and a thin, blonde-haired boy around our age, were both loaded down with boxes.

"She won't be my roommate for long," Erin remarked. "So daddy, this is my real roommate, Tracy, her aunt, Miss Montague, and-," she gave a searching look at Willis.

"Willis-," he remarked.

After the slightest hesitation, Mr. Lane motioned to shake hands, realized he still had the box in his, and sat it down. "Nice to meet yous," went all around. Erin's sister had yet to stop staring at me, so I made fish eyes at her. Erin caught me at it, but all she did was snicker, pulling playfully on one of her sister's thick pigtails.

"How much did I miss?" she wondered.

"Not much," I returned. "We only just arrived not even half an hour before you got here."

"Groovy! So, how was the rest of the summer?"

Before I had to answer, my aunt cleared her throat, and Erin's father sort of shifted his feet, so Erin and I cut the reunion short. We'd finished moving in all of my boxes, and my aunt and I were making up my bed, when Olivia's entourage came tripping back into the room. From the look on their faces, I correctly assumed that Olivia was stuck with us.

"I cannot believe how low Radcliffe has sunk," Mumsy made sure to declare, as she stood by and supervised Olivia's things being moved in by their black movers.

In a stage whisper, Erin remarked, "*She* thinks that she got the short end of the straw, but she's not the one that has to live with *her.*"

— 435 —

I tried my best not to laugh at that, while her dad looked at her like maybe he should say something, but wasn't quite sure what.

We let Olivia's family supervise their move-in, in peace, and since I was all unloaded, there was no real reason to put off good-byes. Logically, for my aunt and me it should have been more of a 'see you later' kind of thing, since she lived in the city, and I'd be visiting her often. I thought back to me and my mom's sterile good-bye earlier in the week. *That* should have been an emotional scene. At the very least it would be months before I saw her again, and if I couldn't make it home for the holidays, then I wouldn't see her before the summer; maybe not even then since I had no real reason to go home. I'd never been away from her for so long before. Yet when it'd been time to say good-bye, all we'd done was hug stiffly.

Willis feigned interest in a statue that stood in the doorway, making himself scarce so that we could say good-bye in private. My aunt fixed me with a look, and I squirmed under her gaze, but I didn't look away, wanting to get this over with as quickly as possible. Normally my aunt wasn't the one to pry, but today seemed like it was going to be the exception to the rule.

"You already know that if you need anything, *anything*, I'm only a phone call away," she declared. "Like I said, your bed's always made up for you." She made eye contact, and I knew what she was going to say next. "And if you want to talk about it, just come by. I can be a really good listener sometimes," she said, sincerely.

I did look away, then, biting down on my lip because I didn't want to think about the days between Derek and my fight, and my arrival back in the city, much less talk about it.

"I'm fine," I mumbled. The only thing I wanted to think about was the upcoming semester, and the challenges that the next few months would bring. Anything outside of that wasn't really up for discussion. She chucked me under the chin. "Still, I'm here," she reiterated. "Come by early on Saturday. We should do something crazy for your birthday; put all of this in the past."

"You don't have to make a big to-do for me," I said quickly, not really in the mood to celebrate.

"Like hell I don't! You only turn 18 once! What kind of aunt would I be if

— 436 —

we didn't do something big?" She gave me a big smile, which I half-heartedly returned.

We hugged good-bye, and since I didn't really feel like going back upstairs at the moment, I decided to sit out on the quad and watch the other girls, and their families, move into their respective Houses. As I took in the unfamiliar faces in varying degrees of excitement, trepidation, it was hard not to put into words what I was feeling, and what I should feel. I guess it was too soon for the reality to have set in, but I *was* glad to be in Boston, to be in the midst of all of the action and excitement currently taking place, not only in this country, but around the world. And, as long as I didn't think too hard, I could focus my emotions on the excitement of it all, and on nothing else. I made myself get excited about what lay before me, despite what I'd left behind.

On Saturday, I arrived at my aunt's bright and early, freshly starched, clean, and looking smart. I was used to my mom's birthday tradition, and completely forgot that my aunt was of a completely different breed of person. When she opened the door, she was wearing jeans, a heavy button down shirt, and some serious looking boots. She took one look at my clothing selection and smiled. "Oh, you're definitely Sibby's daughter, alright," she said with amusement. I was equally as amused as I took in her outfit. "We going logging, Aunt Jo?" I questioned, teasing, surprised that I could.

Her eyes wrinkled with her smile. "Not quite." She handed me a change of clothes. "I thought that maybe you and I could start our own traditions today. Hurry up and change. Adventure awaits!"

While we drove, I tried to guess our destination. Obviously I could rule out any place that required you to get dressed up, but considering what kind of person my aunt was, that should have been a given anyway. "We're going hiking," she informed me, amused by the look of concentration on my face. A few minutes later we parked, and she pulled two packs from the trunk. She donned the heavier of the two, and set off toward the closest path at a pace that had me scrambling to keep up. Despite her age, she moved deftly along the trail, and every now and then I'd had to take a couple of extra steps just to keep up with her. After maybe an hour or two, my aunt stopped in the middle of a clearing, relieving herself of her pack, indicating for me to do the same.

"Are we stopping here?" I asked, happy for the respite from the workout. I gratefully removed my pack, letting it fall to the ground unceremoniously.

"No," she breathed out heavily, showing the first sign of fatigue since we'd started. "The packs just get heavy after a while; I thought you could use the break." She pulled out two bags of Chex mix, handing one to me. After we ate, we left our packs behind, and continued on the trail. The more our path began to weave and climb upwards, the gladder I was that we had shed the heavy backpacks. Sometime after noon, we broke out of the line of trees and onto a rock ledge that had a surprising, and astonishing, view of a river. It looked like a scene from one of Derek's paintings; I was momentarily at a loss as I took everything in.

"So...?" she wondered, gesticulating grandly. "What do you think?" I nodded appreciatively as I gazed out at the river. "I know you've been feeling down since you've been back, so I thought I'd bring you here. This is where I always like to come when I'm feeling that particular hurt that you're feeling right now," my aunt shared. "The hike gives me time to myself, and this view," she paused in appreciation of her surroundings, "reminds me of the rest of the world. I commune with nature, and then I come here and commune with God." I was caught off guard by her words; I think it might have been the first time in my life that I'd heard her mention a god of any kind.

She walked over to the edge of the ledge, and sat down easily. I followed suit, sitting beside her, trying not to glance at the 30 foot, near-sheer drop. As we sat there, the events of the last couple of days came rushing back to me. My gaze fell to my hands...and to the piece of jewelry that was missing from my left one. Derek and I'd finally broken our silence on the day that I was supposed to leave for school. He'd shown up to help me make the drive, like he'd promised. Somewhere along the way, though, between awkward conversations and even more awkward silences, it was decided that maybe we *had* rushed into things, and we should use the time apart to explore the idea of other people.

I swallowed hard, trying to fight feelings that I didn't want to feel at the moment. I looked to my aunt, but she was merely watching the landscape, and I remembered that water always made her think of Crisps. She'd never finished their story. "So what happened with you and him?" I questioned.

Her eyes flickered. She didn't need to ask me who I was talking about because she was probably already there. "The same thing that happens to all young men who have no regard for the rules of the world that they're born into," she said, stiffly. "He died."

I wondered why I hadn't guessed that. "I'm sorry, Aunt Jo," I said, quickly. "I...I didn't know."

She gave the thinnest of smiles. "Of course you didn't," she said, dismissing my apology. "I guess I'd never finished our story. I told you, I'm bad when it comes to the telling..." She seemed to be trying to pull up the memory. "I left us in Italy, didn't I?" I nodded, but I don't think she saw the gesture. "I guess it's because I loved us most there," she mused. "We were good in Italy." She nodded to herself, assuring. "We stayed there for a couple more months before we returned to the States, never to leave them, together, again."

It took her a long moment to find her place. "It was just after we bought a new car. We met this fellow from Tennessee, Luke. He'd recently moved up to Boston, but was going home for Christmas to see his family. Crisps grandly offered to give him a ride home, wanting another adventure, I guess, because although he had been all over the world, he'd never once been down south. Before he left, he told me that we were going to finally finish that trip down the Mississippi, once and for all, and start our family in the back of that car along the way. "'This time', he'd said, 'I ain't goinna take no for no answer'. Those were the last words he ever said to me." She chuckled without any humor.

It was awhile before she spoke, and when she did her voice was much more controlled as she finished out their story in metered pieces. "The friend brought me back what was left of his car, but they buried him down in Tennessee. Apparently, while they were stopped at a fill-up station, some white man had nicked his car. Crisps must have said something to him about it. I can only imagine what happened from there...I didn't quite listen after a while, and I'll spare you the details that I did hear."

Her eyes flickered, remembering. "It's, life, is ironic. Crisps had never lived by any set rules but the ones that he created. He stole, he lied, he cheated; he'd done everything short of killing someone. He'd been in his share of fights, gotten his share of ass beatings. We risked our lives so many times, did so many crazy, even downright stupid things that we could have gotten killed for, or over, or while doing. But Crisps didn't die while doing stunts on his motorcycle, or going over Niagara Falls, or while mountain climbing; he didn't die playing chicken with his car, or in a bar fight, or gored by a bull, mauled by a bear." At those words I wondered just how much my aunt had managed to do in those years. "He didn't die overseas by a firing squad for impersonating a soldier, or by an unstable government regime. Out of all of the things he did, the one thing that he ended up losing his life over was a scratch in his car door. Because some man in Tennessee thought that mentioning a scratch was coming out of his *place*."

She wrung her hands together. "For a very long time I was so mad at Crisps, mad because he was always so cocksure, because he was someone who knew how to get things, and get things done, how to survive, yet he had never learned humility. I was mad because he'd left *me*, because he wasn't still here with me. It was the first time I'd ever truly felt real ownership of him, and I hated him more after he died than I did when he left me in Italy. I was hurt, and I was sad. For a long time I was sooo very sad."

I didn't realize that she had started crying until I saw her wipe away a tear. "I know the way that I lost Crisps, isn't the same as you and Derek, but I do know what it feels like, trying to heal after a loss. I know it doesn't seem like it right now, but time does heal most wounds, and from what I've learned so far, the narrative just keeps getting better and better."

I considered her words. "But you never got married to anyone," I observed.

"Not for lack of loving anyone else," she posed. "And I've loved a *lot* of people after him, just no one I wanted to take that journey with." Her face scrunched up in thought. "I think, and mind I'm no authority on this, but for me, life has never been one long narrative, just a series of moments wound together. I think that for every start, we're given our moments: these series of short, remarkable, life-altering moments, that manage to define us in every way possible. We don't realize it at the time, but while we're living them, they're changing us, and even though we want them to last forever, sometimes all we get *is* that moment. Sometimes, a lot of the times, I think that's all we need.

"So I've learned to take my moments as they come. To celebrate them when they start, live them while I'm in it, and appreciate it once they're over. I've never had any trouble with endings. The difference between Crisps and all of the other guys in my life, though, is that Crisps and I never got to end; to realize that we'd reached our moment. Crisps has the benefit of holding this unique spot in my memory. He gets to be my perfect man. He's forever suspended in a moment of time where I never had to make that choice between one thing and the other; where I can stay 21, young, dangerously in love, and able to imagine that it would have went either way.

"On bad days, I tell myself that I'm unmarried because Crisps had been killed, that if he had only come back to me, he would have been the one I'd married; that we would have been together forever. If I'm being honest with myself, though, I know that I probably wouldn't have; that Crisps and I would have never finished that trip down the Mississippi, because neither of us were ever really those people, and that life would have never made us happy.

"I mean, sure, one day maybe, the sun might have hit us right, the view might have been heart-shattering enough, death might have seemed eminent enough, or loneliness might have grabbed hold hard enough, to make me surrender. And that's exactly what it would have felt like, too: surrender. Even if I'd gotten married to him, and even if he was everything that I needed in that moment, it would have always felt like I was settling for what someone else wanted." There wasn't even a pause in her words. "Have you returned any of your young man's calls?"

I was caught off guard by her sudden asking. I tried to imagine what more there could possibly be to say between us. "No, ma'am," I said. I was sure that the only reason Derek called was to let me know that he'd gotten back to Bakersfield okay, and if it wasn't, whatever feeling I got at the thought of him calling, of us talking, was always ruined by the idea of him walking away.

"I think mom's right...," I said slowly. "Right now, the only thing I need to be concentrating on is school. I spent my whole life trying to make it to Harvard. I don't need my mind back in Bakersfield, constantly thinking about him." I felt my resolve build the more I talked. "The future is what's important. What Derek and I had, it was good. But it's traveled as far as it's going to go." I didn't want to believe that, didn't want things to be over between us because Derek felt like my Crisps, the one love of my life. But I also knew what my aunt meant, about trying to continue after the narrative was over. Maybe, maybe in a few months, once I truly got settled in in school, once I had a chance to work things out, once it stopped hurting so much, maybe I'd call him back.

My aunt only listened to my musings, and eventually I fell into silent contemplation of the space around us. An unsolicited image of Derek popped up. "Do you ever regret it? Not playing that hand?"

"It depends on the day," she admitted. "Sometimes, I see those old gray-haired couples who're still in love, and I know I've no one to grow old with. Every now and then I worry that I'll wake up to find that I was terribly wrong not to take one of those guys up on their offer, and that I missed out on something remarkable by choosing not to settle down...but, just maybe, one day I'll wake up to finally realize that while some of us take root and are content, others were born to just blow in the wind, spreading the most important parts of us as far as we can."

She closed her eyes, and spread her arms wide in supplication. In that moment, the wind picked up for just a second, whipping her hair around her face as if in agreement. With eyes still closed, she threw her head towards the sun, soaking up the light, and beaming brilliantly. She looked entirely angelic. "Time will only tell which one of the two it will be."

The silence that followed her statement was interrupted when one of our stomachs growled. My aunt looked up at the position of the sun in the sky. "It is late, isn't it? You hungry, kid?"

"Starving," I answered.

She shifted, suddenly, getting to her feet. She kicked off her shoes, and I watched her curiously as she carefully tied the shoestrings of her boots together.

"What're you doing?" I wondered.

"It's about a two hour's hike back down from this cliff, but it's only a few minutes jump from where we're standing. Way I see it, you've got two options: you can climb back down, if you want to, and find your way back-,"

I glanced knowingly toward the edge. "Or," I wondered, weakly, feeling sick just at the thought of it.

She put a hand on my belly. "Or you can reach down deep inside of you to that spot that challenges your deepest fears...and find the courage to jump."

"Are you serious?"

My aunt gestured to the space before her. "This is your life in front of you. You are standing at the precipice of your future, *right now*, and you can either run away from what's in front of you, or you can stare it down and let it know that you're not afraid of what comes next, even though you don't know what's going to happen."

The edge drew my gaze. "We're talking metaphorically, right?" I wondered hopefully.

Without taking the moment to answer, she took a running leap and disappeared over the edge. I was on my feet in time to see her sink gracefully beneath the water, a little dot that barely caused a ripple. Seconds later her head poked up from beneath the plane and she looked up at me. She seemed so small.

"Well," she shouted up at me. "Are you coming?"

I got closer to the edge of the cliff, looked down on her, tried to imagine jumping. I applauded her for the visual effect. It wasn't *that* long of a hike, and it *would* be downhill...

With a decision so sudden it seemed impossible that I had actually made it, I kicked off my shoes, and without giving myself too much time to think about it, I started running and propelled myself over the edge, drawing my arms and legs in, in the last moment. It seemed as if I hung suspended in the air for a long time, before gravity grabbed me and I fell. My stomach rose up to meet me, but before I knew it, I was sinking beneath the water, perfectly whole, and still very much alive.

My aunt was grinning widely at me when I surfaced only a few feet away. "I can't believe I just did that," I crowed, paddling to keep my head above the water.

She splashed me. "That's what I hear people say all the time," she told me, "when they do something they once thought was impossible..."

We swam to shore, and my aunt left me on the bank to go retrieve our packs from the spot on the trail that we'd left them. She wasn't gone for more than a minute or two. When she got back, we shed our wet clothes, wrapped ourselves in blankets, and after spreading the clothes out on the ground to dry, we had lunch.

While we ate, she sat with her legs in the water, kicking her feet freely. I watched the circles that they created as they rippled out and away from her. I was strongly reminded of why I felt so close to her: she didn't compromise. She made minor concessions, yes, but she stayed true to her character. My aunt had the life that she wanted, or, at the least, she had the life she could live with. It might not work for anyone else, but it worked for her, and what was it she had said…? The great thing about the people in this world is that no one else had to be her.

As I watched her movements, her eyes latched on to an eagle casually floating on a thermal of air. She pointed it out to me, and we watched it glide lazily. "That was always the one thing I never understood about Crisps," she murmured, surprising me with her voice. "He hated just about all convention, but even he wanted to turn me into a mother and settle me down. He would have been a good match, for me," she reflected. "A good mate. Crisps could make you feel as if you were flying without ever leaving the ground. He was perfect in almost every way…except I finally realized that I didn't want to settle…all I ever wanted to do was learn how to fly."

We both watched the bird until it was out of sight. "Thanks, Aunt Jo," I said, after a while.

She gave me a sideways look, and nodded. She knew exactly what I was saying. Later tonight, we'd go out to eat, catch a movie, get a drink, maybe even sneak into a bar, and we'd have a great time…but nothing would compare to the gift she was giving me right now. She knew that I understood that she wasn't telling me that I should, or shouldn't, be with Derek, only that I knew who I was, so I was the only one who could figure out the answers to my life.

"In the end, the thing that truly got me past Crisps death was that one day I realized that I could either move on from that point, or I could stay there. I could either just stop where I was, give up, or I could choose to go on." That I could accept the things that I'd learned from being with him, mourn the end of our relationship when I needed to, but ultimately continue on with my life. Derek didn't die, so he doesn't get the distinction of being my perfect man, or my one great love, just a complicated, and completely unforgettable moment, that was now over.

Somewhere down the line, there would be other guys who promised their own kinds of adventures, who would smile at me, and draw out my smile... though maybe not quite the same one that Derek forever gets to keep as his. For now, though, there was school, and really wasn't that what this had always been about: Harvard, law school, becoming a lawyer? Why change that dialogue now? There was still the world to change, after all.

"Sometimes, it really is that simple," she concluded.

I thought about the words that I'd sat in my aunt's guest bedroom scrawling out in my notebook a few nights before the start of the term. "I am kinetic energy," I half-joked.

My aunt hugged me to her side. "Exactly!" she exclaimed with gusto. "That's it *exactly*! Be."

Epilogue – The Wedding Song

I reached for the phone, and took it into the bathroom with me. The cord of the phone protested, at its limit, as I sat it down on the edge of the tub. I picked up the receiver, meaning to dial one set of numbers, and ended up dialing a completely different set instead. The phone rang twice, three times. Again. I was about to hang up when a groggy voice questioned, "Hello?" with uncertainty. "Hello?" he repeated, and for a moment I just listened to the voice I hadn't heard in years.

"Derek." It would have been a whisper; that one word all I could manage, and instantly he'd know who it is.

"Tracy?" He'd question, only he wouldn't say, "Tracy," but "Trace," the way he used to say it, as if he were drawing me to life. His masterpiece. Or as if I had taken his breath away, just that long, grateful, sigh.

"It's me," I'd say, not because I had to, but because I didn't want a chance for silence to creep in.

"What's…is everythin' okay, it's," he'd pause to check his watch. I didn't check the clock before I called, but I knew it wasn't decent phoning hours.

"Late," I supplied, reminded of that fact by the soft snoring that was coming from the room just beyond the bathroom walls. "I know. I'm…sorry I called. I'll let you get back to sleep."

"No, wait!" He'd say. "Don't hang up, Trace. I'm glad to hear your voice. I miss you, Tracy. I," his voice would falter, unsure of what he should say because he didn't trust himself.

"I just wanted to let you know," I would begin, but it would take me awhile, partly because of my doubts, but mostly because I knew that he knew what was coming. You really only called someone at this time of the morning, after years of not talking, for one thing. "I just wanted to let you know that I'm getting married tomorrow morning."

He wouldn't say anything, unable to figure out what to say. I wouldn't finish the statement, except in my head: I just called to let you know that I haven't stopped thinking about you since you walked away. That I loved you more than I was able to show you. I just want to know that I'm doing the right thing, that I'm with the right person; that everything's going to work out. I just wanted to call to let you know that someone else has taken your place. *"So congratulate me!" I'd say, attempting the fake nonchalance that he had never been able to perfect when he got jealous. And he would be jealous, I knew, because no matter what'd been said on the day we said good-bye, it hadn't been the truth. We both were still in love.*

Derek would think that he was half asleep, which would prompt him to say what he wouldn't when he was fully awake. "You can' get married because I'm still in love wit' you." There'd be a scuffle on the other end, as he moved around hastily. "Wait for me…I'm leavin' tha house now, wait for me, I'll be there in uh few days. But don' marry him, Trace; I…love you more."

"Who *is* this?" The real life voice questioned. There was something about the way it was said, the hope that was unmistakable in his voice even through the phone, that made me know that he knew who it was…and that it wasn't over. "T-,"

"Sorry, wrong number," I said thickly, slamming the receiver down before he could say my name. I put the phone back where it belonged, went back into my room, and lay there in the bed until I finally fell asleep.

Acknowledgments

Stories are never written, they are discovered, sometimes pulled unwillingly from the depths that they've tried to hide in, and polished until they shine. I wish to heartily thank the people in my life who have helped me bring this story to light. I wish to thank Laurena Casey for her early encouragement, and the Alabama School of Fine Arts for first giving me a platform to share my voice. I thank Lakendra Hogg and Katye Gilliland, who never failed to provide an ear for me to discuss Tracy's character. Vinnet Bradshaw, who has been my motivator and support. My sisters, Rachael Tabor and Renee Doherty, who have constantly pushed me forward, and of course my mother, Veronica White, who I originally had to win over, but who has since become Tracy's strongest champion and supporter. Lastly, I wish to thank the keepers of the histories: my coworkers, classmates, friends, and family, for if it weren't for the ladies and gentlemen who tolerated my endless questions about their childhoods, friendships, and memories, I would have been lost.

Don't miss what happens next...

For more information visit www.prose-playhouse.com

CPSIA information can be obtained at www.ICGtesting.com
Printed in the USA
BVOW03*2355190713

326180BV00002B/145/P